Anita Bunkl mainstream n the Texas Institute of Letters and an NAACP Image Award nominee, she lives in Houston, Texas, with her husband, Crawford. An avid reader all of her life, she was inspired to begin her writing career while researching the lives of interesting African-American women whose stories had not been told. A strong romantic theme has always been at the centre of her novels and now she is enjoying writing true romance for her many fans.

Approaching fifty Mills & Boon titles, **Dianne Drake** is still as passionate about writing romance as ever. As a former intensive care nurse, it's no wonder medicine has found its way into her writing, and she's grateful to Mills & Boon Medicals for allowing her to write her stories. 'They return me to the days I loved being a nurse and combine that with my love of the romance novels I've been reading since I was a young teen.'

By the time **Trish Wylie** reached her late teens, she already loved writing and told all her friends one day she would be a writer for Mills & Boon. Almost two decades later, after revising one of those early stories, she achieved her dream with her first submission! Despite being head-over-heels in love with New York, Trish still has her roots in Ireland, residing on the border between Counties Fermanagh and Donegal with the numerous four-legged members of her family.

Foreign Affairs

Foreign Affairs: New York Secrets

ANITA BUNKLEY

DIANNA DRAKE

TRISH WYLIE

MILLS & BOON

First Published in Great Britain 2023
By Mills & Boon, an imprint of HarperCollins*Publishers*
1 London Bridge Street, London, SE1 9GF

www.harpercollins.co.uk

HarperCollins*Publishers*
Macken House, 39/40 Mayor Street Upper,
Dublin 1, D01 C9W8, Ireland

ISBN: 978-0-263-31850-0

MIX
Paper | Supporting
responsible forestry
FSC™ C007454

This book is produced from independently certified FSC™ paper to ensure responsible forest management.

For more information visit: www.harpercollins.co.uk/green

Printed and Bound in Spain using 100% Renewable electricity at CPI Black Print, Barcelona

BOARDROOM SEDUCTION

ANITA BUNKLEY

To my husband, Crawford, with love.

Chapter 1

"And finally, here's my showstopper. I call this one Sheer Double Dip," Kacey Parker announced with pride, moving to stand beside the final photo in her PowerPoint presentation. She clicked the remote control and sent the image of a leggy model in a hot pink monokini and a dazzling bronze tan onto the screen. When the sultry image emerged, gasps of approval erupted from the two people seated at the conference table at Leeman's Retailers, Inc.

"This is the only swimsuit in my SunKissed line that looks totally natural when dry, but becomes sexily opaque when wet," Kacey went on, sliding her gaze toward Steve Hadley, eager to catch her boss's reaction.

At least he isn't frowning, and that's good, Kacey decided, hopeful that she had impressed him enough to green-light her swimsuit designs for his chain of department stores.

"Hmm, see-through fabric?" Ariana Mendio, the vice president of merchandising for the upscale department store, murmured. "That'll make for some stunning surprises when the ladies get out of the water," she noted in her well-modulated Italian accent.

Kacey smiled in agreement, happy to have Ariana, who'd been with Leeman's for eighteen years, on her side. The woman was an absolute fixture at the company and her opinion carried weight.

"Surprises? Absolutely," Kacey agreed with a nod in Ariana's direction. "The fabric is a new synthetic that designers are calling Naughty Net. It's soft, durable and becomes extremely sheer when water hits it."

Kacey took a deep breath, pleased, so far, with her presentation. She'd joined Leeman's as a sales clerk eight years ago, and her warm personality and flair for design had helped her move into the position of director of special promotions. In that job, she'd gained valuable knowledge about what buyers wanted, expected and would pay dearly for. A competitive swimmer in college, Kacey especially loved working on promotional events in women's sportswear and swimwear, where she enjoyed pulling together dramatic displays of the functional yet attractive apparel that drew customers' attention.

However, as fulfilling and demanding as her current job was, once she left the store, she dedicated herself to her dream job—becoming a swimsuit designer. Over the past year she created her portfolio and when she showed it to Ariana, her coworker immediately took it directly to Steve Hadley, who was so impressed, he invited Kacey to show him more of what she could do.

"Is this fabric readily available?" Steve asked, jotting notes in the margins of Kacey's portfolio.

"Right now, only from China," she answered, wishing she had better news. "But it makes this one-piece the sexiest swimsuit any woman could ever want. Just look at the detail. The plunging neckline, low scooped back and high-cut legs."

"Specialty fabrics could add thousands to production costs," he mused as he flipped through Kacey's proposal, a slight frown bridging his thick black eyebrows.

Kacey paused, inhaled and swallowed her apprehension, aware that her specs related to costs and materials would require a significant financial commitment at a time when upscale stores like Leeman's were nervously watching the bottom line.

"I know," she agreed. "However, I'm hoping to find better rates per unit in Thailand," she acknowledged, setting aside her remote control. "I'm sourcing that now."

Finished with her presentation, Kacey walked to the far side of the room and turned up the lights, allowing the Manhattan skyline to loom dark and gray in the expanse of glass windows that made up one wall. Kacey squinted at the heavy April rain pounding the buildings and slicking the skyline, weary of the thunderstorm that had started during the night and continued to rage. She was definitely not looking forward to a crowded train ride home to Harlem later in the day.

After taking a seat at the conference table across from her boss, Kacey looked directly at Steve Hadley, prepared to expand her pitch. "I know the specialty fabric could run up production costs, but the expense would pay off in the end. Using Naughty Net on the Sheer Double Dip would make it an instant bestseller."

"I love it," Ariana cut in, cooing her words in her sexy Italian voice as she slipped her fingers through a mass of white-blond, shoulder-length hair. Even though she'd lived in America for thirty years and was a naturalized citizen, Ariana took care to maintain her accent, which she laid on thick to dramatic effect when she wanted to make a point. "I adore all eight styles. Great line, Kacey. Wonderful photos. Linette pulled off some very attractive shots."

"Right. Linette is the best," Kacey agreed, referring to Linette Grier, Kacey's best friend and an up-and-coming photographer specializing in sportswear photos. "She's been so busy lately, I was lucky to get her."

"Ah, well, I'm glad you did," Ariana said. "Very nice. Well, Kacey, all I can say is that your designs are spot-on," she continued. "I especially like Twisted Bliss, the black one-piece that shows off just the right amount of skin but still offers full bottom coverage. Excellent choice for, uh…mature women who still keep in shape, shall we say?" She chuckled, winking at Kacey before turning her attention to Steve Hadley. "Older women with disposable cash are our most important demographic, right?"

Hadley inclined his head in brief acknowledgment of Ariana's point. "Kacey, I think your designs show promise and the line is worth exploring," he stated, choosing his words very carefully, without conveying his decision. "However, because you're an employee at Leeman's, it makes for a bit of a sticky situation."

"Conflict of interest, and all that?" Kacey injected.

Steve nodded at Kacey before going on. "Right. You'd

have to leave Leeman's and become a contractor if we decide to proceed with this. But first, let's get some samples made and assess the project, okay?"

"Whatever will work, " Kacey rushed to say, willing to do anything necessary to move her career as a swimsuit designer forward. After all, her goal was much larger than to simply do custom work for one retail outlet. She wanted to have her own design firm, have control of her future, and launch a creative explosion that would make hers a household name.

"However," Steve was saying, "We must source that specialty fabric at a much better price to make the investment pay off." He licked his lower lip in thought, his eyes riveted on the scantily clad model whose image still filled the screen. "I'm thinking that a totally domestic production would be the best option. Save shipping costs and time."

"I agree," Kacey replied, encouraged by the fact that he was leaning toward carrying SunKissed by Kacey in his fourteen Leeman's stores. All he needed was reassurance that the product would turn a profit.

"What about manufacturing in Mexico?" Ariana offered.

With a shift, Kacey smoothed the skirt of her burgundy power suit, crossed her arms and placed them on the table. Leaning toward her coworker, she made a slight grimace of concern. "I checked out a few south-of-the-border plants, but didn't have much luck. However, there are two manufacturers I'm still looking into."

"Kacey," Steve started, clearing his throat. "I want to be clear. I agreed to take a look at your collection because I think you have a good eye for what women want. You also have a great sense of style and I like your swimsuits very much."

Kacey beamed her thanks, but said nothing, holding her breath as Hadley continued.

"But," he went on, "I have concerns about the timing. It's very late into the spring shopping season to introduce a new line of swimwear."

"But women buy swimsuits year-round," Kacey countered, pushing tendrils of highlighted bangs away from her face, now wishing she'd had her spiral curls trimmed during yesterday's visit to the salon. However, she'd been in a rush to get out of the beauty shop and home to put the finishing touches on today's presentation, which it seemed, so far, was going pretty well.

"Exactly," Ariana, stated, agreeing with Kacey about year-round swimsuit purchases. "Winter cruises to the tropics, heated pools in homes and hotels, hot tubs in private residences. That's what keeps women buying swimwear through all the seasons. I know we're getting a late start, Steve, but if we can source the Naughty Net and include the Sheer Double Dip style, I think SunKissed by Kacey could be flying out of our stores in six weeks."

"Hmm," Steve murmured, fingers laced and tented in thought. "Only if we could get fast turnaround on production." He shifted his body to focus on Ariana. "What about Archer Industries? We've worked with them before and always had good results," he remarked. "What do you think?"

"Good possibility," Ariana agreed. "The Archer factory has a reputation for fast turnarounds, high-quality production and cost-effective shipping. They handle quite a few private labels."

"Old man Archer came through with that rare Hawaiian print we needed for the menswear line last year," Steve added.

"Yeah, and saved us a ton of money, too," Ariana agreed.

With a lift of her finger, Kacey joined in. "You're referring to Archer Industries in Texas, right?"

"Yes," Hadley replied. "Rockport. On the Gulf Coast. Not much else is there but the Archer factory. That family has been in business for years. The founder, Leon Archer, is getting on in years, but he runs that shop like a well-oiled machine. He's a dying breed...a good old-fashioned businessman who takes pride in doing a first class job, no matter how large or small."

"I phoned and sent an email to Archer," Kacey said, eager to let her boss know that she'd already considered the family-owned firm that had done quite a bit of business with Leeman's over the years. "I just received an email this morning to contact Nona James, the quality control manager. I'm going to call her as soon as we finish here." Kacey began to gather the papers she'd strewn over the conference table, anxious to return to her office, get on her computer and tie up all the loose ends related to her proposal.

"Don't bother with that," Steve stated. "Mr. Archer deserves a personal call from me. He's a throwback to the old days...likes to do business with the person in charge. In fact, I'll call him right now."

Kacey watched as Steve reached for his handheld, scrolled through his address book and punched in a number. Within seconds he was talking to Mr. Archer, giving the manufacturer an overview of Kacey's proposed swimsuit line.

"Sure, sure," Steve agreed in an expansive voice after several minutes of conversation. "The designer, Kacey Parker, can come down, meet with you and we'll go from there." He turned to Kacey, placing a hand over his phone as he whispered, "He thinks he can do it. And he would like to meet with you at the plant tomorrow afternoon. Go ahead and book a flight to Rockport," he said before returning his attention to his conversation.

"You'll have to fly into Corpus Christi…the closest big city," Ariana offered in a hushed tone. "Rent a car. The factory is on the outskirts of town. About half an hour from the airport."

Kacey nodded, grabbed a pen and began to jot down the instructions that Ariana was giving her while Steve ended his call.

Once he had finished and refocused on Kacey, he told her, "Take your portfolio, fabric samples and proposal to Texas and sell this line to Archer. He's the man we want."

Kacey grinned, drew in a gasp of surprise and then sighed. Had her boss actually given her the green light on her proposal? Was SunKissed by Kacey going to become a reality after so many months of dreaming and planning? She pushed back her chair and stood, papers clutched in one hand, her heartbeat increasing by the second.

"Then, you're saying, it's a go?" she prompted, needing to hear the words from Steve Hadley himself that her swimsuit line was headed into production.

"Yes, it's a tentative go. And if you manage a five percent reduction in overall manufacturing costs, there'll be a nice cash bonus in it for you," he offered, sounding strongly supportive of Kacey's project.

"Oh, I'm sure I can do that, Mr. Hadley. Five percent won't be a problem. Trust me. I'll work this out."

"I hope so. I'm impressed with your designs, Kacey, and if we can have product in stock by mid-June, I feel confident our customers will buy it."

Kacey struggled to appear calm, though she was desperate to scream with joy. She'd been dreaming about this day ever since she started her career in retail merchandising. Now, she had a real shot at shifting her focus toward designing for the masses instead of setting up displays and running in-store contests. She could hardly wait to start the journey.

While Kacey headed toward the conference room door, Steve remained seated, looking over his eyeglasses at her as he advised, "Pack well. You might be in Texas for a while."

"A while?" Kacey quipped, arching a shapely brown eyebrow in his direction. "Certainly Mr. Archer and I can accomplish all we need to do in a day. Two at the most."

"No, if all goes well, I want you to stick around there."

Kacey glanced suspiciously at her boss. "For how long?"

"For as long as it'll take to get SunKissed by Kacey into my stores. No need to rush back here, only to fly back and forth every few weeks," Hadley explained. "I know old man Archer will do his best to accommodate our time frame, but since this is such a rush job, and a risky midseason production as well, we can't afford any mistakes. He and I will iron out the contract details before you get there. I want you to stay close, oversee production and ensure an on-time delivery."

Kacey assessed Steve Hadley with dread in her heart, doubting he understood the enormity of what he was asking of her. Leaving New York City to spend God knows how long in rural Texas was not something she looked forward to. What in the world would she do for fun in a tiny Gulf Coast town with an old man as her business contact?

Suffer in silence, she guessed, prepared to sacrifice the lifestyle she loved to see her designs come to life.

Chapter 2

Back in her cubicle, Kacey immediately booked her flight to Corpus Christi, reserved a rental car and then phoned her friend Linette to share her good news. However, all Kacey got was the photographer's voice mail, so she left a message for Linette to call her back as soon as possible, adding that she had exciting news to share.

That ought to get her attention, Kacey thought as she ended the connection. It was always difficult to reach Linette, who was constantly on the move as she traveled from one location shoot to another. Sometimes it took a week for them to finally catch up with each other due to their busy, on-the-go lifestyles.

Taking a moment to reflect on the impact of her presentation, Kacey pondered the future, a ripple of excitement feathering her insides. She'd begun working on her designs last year, using computer-assisted design (CAD) software that turned her detailed sketches into actual computer drawings. Printed pattern pieces placed on swaths of bold-colored fabric quickly morphed into the samples that she had personally sewn and fitted on models for Linette to photograph. And now, at last, Hadley was giving her the opportunity to create sexy, stylish swimwear that she knew customers would be thrilled to wear.

Hadley was damn sure impressed and Ariana is totally behind me, Kacey mused in satisfaction, realizing how much support she had at Leeman's. If SunKissed by Kacey became the runaway hit she expected, her position with the chic retailer would open doors to all the exclusive shops on Rodeo Drive, as well as retailers like Bergdorf's, Saks, and Neiman's.

A competitive swimmer in college, Kacey loved challenges and loved to win. She knew her petite stature, flawless mocha skin and the thick brown hair that framed her face in curly tendrils made her look a lot younger and less savvy than she was. But at thirty-one, she had made plenty of hard decisions in her drive to become successful, and knew exactly where she wanted to go.

For more than a year, Kacey had labored over her drawing boards, studied the competition and focused on coming up with swimwear that would make such an impact on the marketplace that every retailer would clamor for her swimsuits. Even though the rights to her special label would belong to Leeman's, Kacey knew the professional credit and boost in her fledgling design career were more than she'd ever dreamed of.

Leaving her computer, she went to stand at the large

window behind her desk. Looking out, she swept her gaze over the towering buildings pressed together in midtown Manhattan. The steady rain continued to slick the traffic-clogged streets as dull gray clouds hovered above the tops of skyscrapers. She placed her palm against the glass and shivered. *Too damn cold,* she thought with a shudder, but that's the way it could be in early April in New York. There'd even been a snow flurry last week, but she prayed that warm weather was on the way.

In the foggy distance, Kacey could barely discern the outline of the building where she hoped to live one day. Four blocks from Leeman's, the newly renovated 780-square-foot apartment she dreamed about would be a vast improvement over the tiny closetlike studio in Harlem where she lived now. She'd been saving for two years to make the move, and now, if all went well, her SunKissed line would provide a much-needed boost in her income, allowing her to lease the new apartment in midtown.

But first, she had to go to Texas, get her designs into production, then into stores. And as much as she dreaded an extended stay in a small town like Rockport, she knew the trip would be a welcome break from the damp cold of the city.

"I've got to remain positive," she murmured, deciding to treat her trip like a mini-vacation, though seriously doubting she'd be able to do anything fun while she was there. After all, she was going to Texas to work, not play, and there'd be little time to fool around.

A tap at her door brought Kacey out of her thoughts. Swinging around, she waved Ariana into the room, noticing the bemused expression on her colleague's face.

"You really impressed Steve," Ariana informed Kacey, sliding into the chair near Kacey's desk.

"That's what I hoped to do," Kacey tossed back, returning to sit in front of her computer. "I've been working on this project for over a year, and I knew I'd only have one shot at getting him onboard."

"Oh, he's definitely behind you, honey. I've worked with Hadley for a long time and when he called Leon Archer personally from the conference room, I knew he was eager to move this project forward. He's sold. Don't think he's ever been as excited about a new line before."

"He's never seen swimsuits like mine before," Kacey countered with confidence.

"You're right about that," Ariana agreed, crossing her long legs and tilting back in her chair. She fluffed her bleached-white hair and puckered her full pink lips, a gesture that Kacey and her coworkers often mimicked when talking about Ariana. At fifty-six, Ariana Mendio was trim, shapely and still an alarmingly attractive woman. She'd been married three times; her current husband, Tony, was sixteen years her junior. He worked as a high-end menswear model for several fashion houses, a position that got Ariana and her boy-toy into exclusive society parties quite often. "SunKissed by Kacey is so sweet it could give a woman a toothache!" Ariana exclaimed with a giggle as she flicked her long fingers in the air toward Kacey.

Kacey laughed along with her coworker, shaking her head. "I don't plan to inflict any pain—only pleasure."

"I don't know. That black satin thong looked like it could put a hurting on some very tender spots."

"Please," Kacey shot back with a grin. "You know you're dying to wear it. In fact, I'm gonna send you the first manufacturer sample of that style as soon as it comes out of production. Size 8, right?" Kacey lifted a brow in question, her grin widening as she watched Ariana.

"Size 6, honey," Ariana corrected with a downward tilt of her head and a sweep of one hand over her flat stomach. "I've been hitting the gym with Tony."

"And it shows," Kacey finished, giving Ariana the compliment she'd been fishing for.

"Anyway, about SunKissed," Ariana went on. "I stopped by to tell you that Hadley wants me to get started on the marketing plan."

"Sounds good," Kacey replied.

"My thought is this. We position Leeman's as the first shopping stop that women must make before taking off on their next trip to the beach, to the pool or wherever the sun might take them. There's a swimsuit out there for every woman…"

"But finding the right one can take a whole lot of time," Kacey finished.

"Exactly. Shopping for swimwear can be a traumatic experience, but the eight styles offered through Sun-Kissed by Kacey make it a snap. I'm thinking our slogan could be 'Why Shop Anywhere Else?'"

"Why indeed?" Kacey agreed. "I love it! The bikinis, monokinis, full-coverage one-piece suits and two-piece styles offer multiple choices, especially since you can mix and match the bottoms and the tops."

A vigorous nod of assent from Ariana. "Your styles flatter all types of figures, and they're done in such luscious fabrics," she praised. "Archer Industries had better do a good job for us."

"For real. What do you know about the company?" Kacey asked, curious about where she was headed tomorrow and how she would get along with the owner.

"Only that it's a family-owned factory….employs most of the residents in Rockport. And in those parts… the Archer name has clout."

"Have you ever met Mr. Archer?"

Ariana shook her head. "No, but I've had more than a few conversations with him. He's a tough old bird who runs his factory with an iron fist. All about business. No warm fuzzies there."

"Gee, thanks for the warning," Kacey said, screwing up one side of her mouth. "Sounds like I'm in for a real test of wills—and skills."

"Well, don't worry too much," Ariana replied. "As long as you show up prepared to work long hours and take orders from a persnickety old man who really *can* run circles around his younger employees, you'll do fine."

"I'd better," Kacey murmured, beginning to feel the pressure of what she'd gotten herself into. Launching this line was a huge responsibility, and success depended on one thing: the perfect execution of her designs. Would Archer Industries deliver? Was she ready to place her future in the hands of a grumpy old man with no heart who couldn't possibly know what women want? *He may not know, but I do,* Kacey affirmed, determined to gain control of the process once she arrived in Rockport.

Chapter 3

Leon Archer Jr. drove his red Corvette convertible up the semicircular driveway that swept the front of his father's house and parked directly at the front door. Sitting back in his seat, he slid one hand over the smooth steering wheel and studied the black sedan already parked in the drive, the car that belonged to Gerald Ayers, his father's lawyer. What was going on? Why had his father summoned him to the house?

Leon had been a bit surprised when he arrived at the factory and had seen his father's parking spot empty. During all the years that Leon had worked at Archer Industries alongside his father, Leon Sr. had never failed to come to work by 6:00 a.m., making sure he arrived before his son or any of his employees reported for duty.

Now, curious about why his dad was still at home,

Leon turned his attention to the exterior of the hacienda-style mansion that his dad and mom had built nearly forty years ago. It had twenty rooms, seven bathrooms, an Olympic-size pool, a tennis court and a newly installed outdoor kitchen that rivaled anything shown on the home and garden shows that his mother loved to watch on television. The red tile roof sloped low over a center courtyard where exotic tropical flowers bloomed year-round. In fact, Leon Archer Sr.'s home had been featured in the prestigious *Southwest Homes* magazine, and continued to serve as the gathering spot for many Archer Industries company parties over the years. Since a good portion of Rockport residents either worked for Archer Industries or had a family member who did, most of the townsfolk had been hosted in the Archer home at one time or another.

Leon exited his car, slammed the door and strode up the flower-lined walkway. After letting himself in, Leon went directly to his father's study where the elder man was seated behind his walnut claw-foot desk, an unlit cigar stuck into the corner of his mouth. The sight made Leon smile…his mother had banned cigar smoking in the house long ago, but that didn't stop his old man from keeping up the appearance of enjoying a good smoke, especially when he was working at home.

"Hello, Dad. Hi, Gerald," Leon said as he greeted his father and the attorney who had handled Archer Industries' business for as long as Leon could remember. After a quick handshake with Gerald and a nod at his father, Leon sat down in the deep wingchair across from the huge, messy desk where Leon Sr. was busy signing papers that Gerald was handing to him.

"What's up? You doing okay?" Leon asked tentatively. Though his dad was seventy-four years old, and had never experienced any major health problems, Leon hoped his father's good luck had not taken an unexpected turn for the worse.

"Of course I'm okay," Leon Sr. shot back in a gruff voice, not looking up at his son. He placed another flourishing signature on a document and then muttered, "Why'd you ask something like that? Do I look sick to you?"

"No, no. Just wondering. When you didn't show up at the plant this morning, I got a little worried."

"No need," his father tossed out in a cavalier manner, now setting his pen aside. "I'm fine. In fact, I'm better than I've ever been, and God willing, I plan to stay that way for a long, long time."

"All right," Leon conceded, relieved by his father's bantering in his usually gruff voice. "So why are we here and not at work at the factory? There's a lot going on at the plant today. Three big orders came in last night and the Wilton shipment has to go out by noon."

"I know, I know," Leon Sr. acknowledged with a wave of one hand. "It'll all get done...don't worry. Nona's there, right?"

"Hey, you know she is. When I left yesterday, Nona was still on the phone arguing with FedEx over that package of samples from Seattle that got lost. I told her it could wait until today and for her to go home. She refused, so I left. Sometimes I think she takes her job way too seriously."

"Tell me about it," Leon Sr. agreed. He stopped what he was doing and pointed his cigar at his son. "She's a hard worker and great friend to all of us, but that woman needs a life. Other than her life at Archer, that is."

"Harrumph," Leon agreed with a shrug. "That's the truth."

"Well, you're the best person to handle her, I'm sure. She always does whatever you ask."

"Not always, but most of the time," Leon replied with a shake of his head, as if resigned to the fact that he had no choice but to tolerate the antics of his most trusted, but most temperamental, employee. "Okay… enough about Nona. What's really going on with you?" Leon wanted to know. He propped one foot on a knee and slipped back in his seat.

"Big changes," the elder Archer teased, raising his eyes from the final paper that the lawyer handed him to sign. He removed the unlit cigar from his mouth and set it aside. "This is what's up," he started, clasping his hands on his desk. "I'm retiring. As of this morning, I'm finished with the business."

Leon rolled his eyes in mock disbelief. "Oh? Really? And how many times have you said that?" he countered, knowing his father had made the same declaration several times before, only to renege on his decision and keep on working.

"I mean it this time," Leon Sr. said as he tapped his index finger on the stack of papers he'd signed and jerked his head toward his attorney. "Tell him, Gerald. It's done."

"That's right," the white-haired lawyer confirmed. "All the papers are in order. Your father has just made you the new owner of Archer Industries. It's all yours now."

Leon jerked forward, both hands steadied on his knees as he peered at his father in suspicion. "Is this for real?"

"Yes, for real. It's time for you to run the show, son, and I am more than ready to hand the whole thing over to you."

Leon sucked in a long breath and let the news settle in. He had known this day would come, but still, he was surprised. His father had made comments about retiring so many times that the running joke around the plant was that he'd leave when it snowed in Rockport, something that *had* happened, but nearly a century ago.

"Why now?" Leon wanted to know, wondering what had pushed his father to finally let go. He was an energetic man who walked four miles every day, ate only organic foods and never drank alcohol. And now that he'd given up cigars, his doctor had pronounced him healthier than ever.

"Because it's time."

"Are you telling me the truth?" Leon pressed. "You're not sick or anything, are you?"

"I'm in perfect health," his father replied with a snap. "In fact, that's the reason I'm doing this now. Your mother and I are leaving for a tour of Africa tomorrow. We're finally going on the trip we've put off for too many years. We decided last night that if we're going to go, we'd better go while I can still climb a mountain and stay up late enough to enjoy a sunset," Leon Sr. chuckled. "And we're taking our time, son. Probably be gone at least a month."

"A month, huh? Good for you!" But then Leon bit his bottom lip in concern. "Isn't this happening kinda fast?" He had thought he was prepared to take over the business, but now that Archer Industries had actually been turned over to him, the prospect of running things without his father nearby caught Leon off guard.

"Yes. That's right. No need to drag this out," Leon Sr. concurred. "It'll be an easy transition. I don't want any fancy retirement party or sappy farewells. I'm writing a personal letter to each employee, thanking them for their hard work and telling them they're in good hands. I know I can count on you to run the place the same way I have. So don't fuck things up, you hear?"

Leon had to laugh at his father's rare use of the F word.

"You practically grew up at the plant. You've been by my side since you were old enough to sit at my desk, so it won't take long for everyone to get used to taking orders from you instead of me."

"Orders?" Leon quipped. "I don't plan to run the place like a military operation."

His father laughed under his breath while brandishing his pen at his son. "Ha! That's what it takes to do business nowadays, son. The key is to act tough, keep everything under your control so no one gets the idea that they can operate outside the rules. If you're the man where the buck stops, then you're the man with the power…and you're gonna need power to succeed. You ready to be the boss?"

Leon hesitated, giving his mind a few seconds to wrap itself around the impact of his father's decision. The family company was now his to manage, and the responsibility was great. Was he prepared for the challenge and ready to step up to the plate?

"You bet I am," Leon confirmed with confidence, ready to make the difficult decisions that came with being in charge.

"I know you are, even though the old-timers will probably call you 'Junior,'" Leon's mother tossed out as she entered the room.

"Sara, that'll change now that he's the number one man," Mr. Archer told his wife, sending a scowl her way.

"I'll make sure of that," Leon agreed, warming to the idea that, at last, he'd be out from behind his father's shadow. Recently, he'd begun to feel confined, as if he were boxed into a place without an exit. Had his father sensed his restlessness? Was that what spurred his decision to retire? If so, the timing couldn't have been better.

Sara Archer, who stood a head shorter than her son, went over to him, patted him lightly on the cheek and reminded him in a sassy tone, "Well, you'll always be *Junior* to me."

Leon grimaced, and then broke into a smile, both annoyed and flattered by his mother's display of affection. As her only child, he had learned long ago that it did no good to protest her overprotective ways. As long as he lived, he would be her little boy and there was nothing he could do to change that.

"And I don't want you to worry about checking on the house while we're gone," Sara continued. "I gave Nona my keys so she can come in and water my plants and check on the aquarium. You'll have more important things on your mind than tending my African violets and feeding the fish."

"If that's what you and Nona arranged, it's fine with me," Leon conceded, aware of how much his mother liked and trusted Nona James, who was not only Archer

Industries' operations manager, but also a longtime family friend.

"I think that's it," Gerald Ayers stated as he snapped his briefcase closed and handed a packet of legal documents to the elder Archer, who put them into his safe.

Gerald leaned over to shake Leon's hand. "Congratulations, *Junior,*" the lawyer said, beaming his approval.

Leon pumped the attorney's hand, "Thanks, Gerald."

"No problem. You're going to do fine." Turning to Leon Sr., the lawyer said, "If that's all you need from me, I'll be going. I've got to leave for the airport in an hour."

"Please don't tell me you're leaving the country, too," Leon remarked, concerned.

"No, not at all. Going to visit my daughter in Baton Rouge. I'm only a phone call away if you need me, Leon. Call anytime, and I'll be here…. Just as I've been for your father over the years."

"Whew! That's a relief," Leon said, knowing how much he was going to need the seasoned attorney's advice.

After Gerald left, Leon and his father reviewed the transition process, and then conducted an in-depth examination of the current production schedule.

"Next up is a women's swimsuit line for Leeman's," Leon Sr. informed his son.

"A swimsuit line, huh? That ought to be a pretty simple run. Steve Hadley's company out of New York, right?" Leon said, remembering the previous orders Hadley had placed with Archer Industries.

"Right. But this one might be a bit tricky. The designer wants to use a fabric that's gonna take some serious negotiating to get down to the price Hadley wants to pay. Some kind of a specialty blend they sourced out of China."

"Could be pricey," Leon said.

"Exactly what I thought, so I put our man in New Delhi on it. Hopefully, he'll find a better price in India," his father offered.

"Sounds good. Where do we stand on the Leeman's contract?" Leon asked.

"All done. I finalized everything with Steve Hadley. Here's the name of the rep from his store who is due here this afternoon to consult on the project," he said, handing Leon a piece of paper on which he had written the name. "Make sure everything comes off without a hitch, you hear? We can't afford to lose this account. We're doing fine, but profits were down a point last quarter."

"I know," Leon agreed, reading over the note, which read: Mr. Kacey Parker, Leeman's. "Don't worry. Leave all the business problems to me," Leon advised. "You and Mom go have fun in Africa."

"We plan to," his father replied. "But don't *you* have too much fun while we're gone, okay?"

Leon rolled his eyes in exaggeration. *How much fun could I possibly have if I'm busy turning triangles of exotic fabric into swimsuits for curvy females?* he wondered with a smile.

Chapter 4

The two-lane highway leading to Rockport, Texas, was bordered by flat coastal plains on one side and the surging Gulf of Mexico on the other. The black ribbon of asphalt stretching out before Kacey pulled her along, bringing her ever closer to her destination. Few cars passed hers on the highway, and most of the buildings she encountered were either low-slung ranch houses surrounded by acres of green pasture or weather-worn beach cottages raised high on stilts. Kacey had to admit that the sudden sense of isolation that hit her was eerily disturbing, yet peaceful.

Continuing northward, she shifted her gaze from the road to the sky, where not a single white cloud marred the huge expanse of blue that seemed to go on forever. This kind of openness, emptiness and lack of population was a definite contrast to what Kacey was used to.

An Easterner born and bred, she considered herself a typical urban working woman who thrived on deadlines, pressure and competition in a fast-paced environment that included long hours at the office, lots of take-out dinners and hitting the live entertainment circuit with her friends to relax. Leaving all that behind to hole up in this small town was going to require a great deal of patience, flexibility and trust.

When Kacey's cell phone rang, she checked the screen and saw that Linette was calling her back. Kacey answered, intending to keep it brief.

"Hey. Where are you?" she asked, knowing Linette was never in the same place for very long.

"At the airport. LAX," Linette sputtered, sounding out of breath. "Just got here, and wouldn't you guess… one of my bags is missing. This sucks. I'm shooting stills for Roberto Rogales's new outerwear campaign tomorrow and I need my equipment!"

"Right," Kacey replied, recalling the assignment Linette had accepted with the former Ralph Lauren protégé. "Glad that job worked out for you. But don't worry. Your bag will show. Happens all the time."

"It had better," Linette tossed back. "The schedule Roberto sent looks pretty scary and I've got a lot to do. Anyway, I got your message. What's up with you?"

"Well, right now I'm driving down a two-lane highway along the Texas Gulf Coast, on my way to the factory that is going to manufacture SunKissed by Kacey." She paused to let Linette absorb her good news. "Can you believe it?"

"Get outta here! For real? Hadley accepted your swimsuit line for Leeman's?"

"He did," Kacey confirmed with a smile, eagerly

filling Linette in on the details of her meeting with her boss and her upcoming stay in Rockport.

"That's sooo exciting," Linette said, clearly happy for Kacey. "Your swimsuits are the bomb! They're gonna be a huge hit. I've never seen any like them."

"Your photos played a big part in winning Hadley over. And once the manufacturer's samples are finished, I want you to shoot those, too. My plan is to convince Hadley to send our models to Rockport for the fittings and the promotional photos. Think you can squeeze in a trip to Texas when I get to that point?"

"Of course. Count on it," Linette assured Kacey. "I should wrap up this job by the end of the week. Just give me a call and I'll be there."

"Great. By the time the samples are ready to be photographed, I'll be more than ready for some company. This temporary exile to Texas is not what I expected to be doing right now."

"Hey, I hear you. Just focus on your work and time will fly by," Linette advised in a rushed voice. "Hey, gotta go. My bag is here! We'll talk later, okay?"

"Right," Kacey agreed, ending the call and already missing her friend.

While Linette was rubbing shoulders with Hollywood types in Los Angeles, Kacey would be stuck with an old man in a factory in Texas. *But it'll be worth it,* she reminded herself, refocusing on the road, surprised to see that a herd of black and white cows had gathered along the barbed-wire fence running parallel to the highway, their large brown eyes trained on her. Shaking her head in disbelief, she turned up the volume on the CD player and let Whitney's new album fill the car.

Half an hour after leaving the Corpus Christi airport,

Kacey finally came to a billboard splashed with large red and blue letters that announced, *Welcome to Rockport. Home of Archer Industries.* Slowing down, she leaned over and scrutinized the huge sign, which showcased a two-story industrial building constructed of dark red brick, flanked by groves of leafy palm trees. A mature man was posed in front of the structure, chin raised high, a big smile on his face, his deep brown skin burnished like polished wood. In his dark business suit with his arms crossed at his chest he exuded the aura of a successful businessman.

"Old man Archer," Kacey decided, thinking the older man looked pleasant enough. Maybe working with him wouldn't be so bad after all.

Driving on, Kacey arrived at the center of town where a gas station, a convenience store, a beauty shop and a hardware outlet anchored the four corners of the old-fashioned square. Beyond the hub of the town, Kacey caught glimpses of lacey Victorian homes on broad green lawns, as well as modest bungalow-type homes facing each other across grassy esplanades. The quaint scene that greeted her was picturesque, charming and serene. Pretty to look at but not a place where she wanted to spend any more time than was absolutely necessary.

"I'd be bored out of my skull if I had to live here," Kacey murmured as she inched along the town's main street, where a scattering of people were busy running errands or chatting in clusters on the wide cement sidewalks.

At the far end of the main street, she saw Seaside Suites, the economy motel where she'd booked a room for the duration. The exterior of the nondescript building was in desperate need of a paint job and there were only three other cars in the parking lot, which adjoined a run-down apartment complex surrounded by a chain-link fence.

I'll check in after I meet with Mr. Archer, Kacey decided, glad she'd worn her Donna Karan navy suit and comfortable heels on the plane, so she could go straight to her meeting. She checked her makeup in the rearview mirror, pressed her shapely burgundy-tinted lips together and fluffed her honey-brown curls with one hand. Satisfied that all was fine, she nodded at her image. After all, she was representing Leeman's, one of the most exclusive retailers in the country. A good first impression was essential, and she planned to let Mr. Archer know from the get-go that she was not some underling who was there to take orders from him, but a designer whose swimsuit line was going to become the hottest fashion label in swimwear.

Slowly passing the motel, Kacey eyed the drab appearance of her future home and sighed. The thought of living there made her heart sink, but she refused to let it get her down.

"Oh, well, at least it's not raining," Kacey remarked, resigned to toughing it out for as long as it took to finish the job she'd come to do.

The woman who met Kacey in the lobby of the Archer Industries building greeted her with a vise grip of a handshake and a hearty hello.

"Welcome to Archer Industries. I'm Nona James. Operations manager," she said in a flat Texas accent that seemed to solidify her connection to the small-town plant.

"Hello, Nona. Kacey Parker. Good to meet you," Kacey said, eyeing the woman closely. She was at least a head taller than Kacey—big-boned, buxom and very statuesque. The makeup on her buff-hued face was flawless, but a bit heavy-handed, as were the intricate chandelier earrings dangling from her ears. An African-print headband held an explosion of natural hair off her face, creating a dark halo of frizz that translated into an inspired resemblance of a young Diana Ross.

"I'm so glad you're here," Nona said, her red lips widening into a full-blown grin. "Did you check into the motel? I assume you're staying at the Seaside. It's the best we have around here."

"I drove past on my way through town. It looks fine. I'll check in after I finish here," Kacey replied, taking care not to imply that the accommodations might not be up to snuff.

"Okay. If you need anything, let me know. The manager of the Seaside is my cousin, so I'll be on his case if you have any complaints."

"Sounds great. I'm anxious to get settled and started on production," Kacey replied, glancing around the sun-splashed lobby where large Lucite boxes showcased some of the clothes produced by Archer Industries. On display were activewear, all-weather jackets, chlorine-resistant swimsuits and water aerobic wear, which included pool shoes, sun hats and beach towels.

"Mr. Archer isn't here at the moment, but he's on his way in," Nona said. "He's eager to meet you. Come on back. You can wait in his office," Nona said, leading Kacey down a carpeted hallway toward a cluster of offices at the back of the building. "Can I get you something to drink?" she asked after escorting Kacey into a very spacious room where an oval conference table took up a good portion of the space. The table was crowded with papers, fabric samples, pattern books and cutting tools. Clearly, this was more of a workroom than an executive suite.

"Some cold water would be great," Kacey replied, before settling into a gray suede chair.

"No problem. Be right back," Nona said as she left the room.

Left alone, Kacey looked around, curious to learn what she could about Mr. Archer before he showed up. Groupings of framed certificates, awards and permits hung on the wall behind his desk. One family photo caught her attention. It was of a much younger Mr. Archer, seated on a sofa with an attractive woman whom Kacey guessed was his wife. On her lap sat a young boy holding a puppy, grinning into the camera.

He's a family man, Kacey mused, beginning to feel more comfortable about working with the man who had promised Steve Hadley that he could turn her dreams into reality.

"One bottle of cold water, right?"

The deep tenor voice forced Kacey's eyes from the photo. She turned toward the door and quickly saw that the person at the entryway was definitely not Nona James, but a drop-dead gorgeous man who was grinning at her as if pleasantly surprised to find her sitting in Mr. Archer's office. The man slanted his slender body against the doorframe and proceeded to trace a less than businesslike gaze over Kacey, emitting bold signals of more than a casual interest in her.

Since he seemed in no hurry to speak, Kacey countered by taking her time inspecting the guy. He had jet-black hair with a hint of waviness, cut close with a razor part. The angular planes of his face accented his vibrant pecan-brown skin and made his intriguing gray eyes impossible to ignore. His light blue oxford shirt was open at the collar. His crisply creased tan khaki pants were held in place by a beautiful leather belt that Kacey immediately recognized as one of Cole Haan's most popular designs, and the soft Italian leather shoes on his feet matched his ultraexpensive belt.

Not bad, Kacey decided, pleased to find such a put-together, preppy-looking brother in the middle of nowhere. He was attractive, in a sexy, clean-cut way, sending out signals of a conservative dresser who certainly had good taste.

"Oh. The water. Yes. Thanks," Kacey replied in a breathy voice that sounded as if it were coming from someone else. She stood, accepted the bottle of water and waited for him to speak, wondering what department this brother worked in at Archer and if she would be lucky enough to work with him.

The man stepped fully into the room. "So I can see that you're not *Mr.* Parker?"

Kacey laughed, watching as he analyzed her reaction. "Oh, yes, but it's *Ms.* Kacey Parker."

"Well, I have to admit, I wasn't expecting…" he stuttered, pulling out the piece of paper his father had handed him. "I guess…"

"You assumed I was a man?" Kacey finished with a hint of a challenge.

He gave her a sheepish smile and nodded. "Yeah. Guess we all did."

"Happens all the time," she concluded, shaking the

man's hand. "Hope you're not too disappointed," she finished.

"*Not at all,*" he replied with appreciative emphasis. "I'm Leon Archer. Good to meet you." Then he walked around the desk, keeping his eyes riveted on Kacey as he eased into the chair, clearly as if he belonged there.

Kacey slipped back into her seat, crossed her legs as well as her arms, and blinked, confused. "*You're* Mr. Archer?" she started, fishing for an explanation.

"Right. I'm Leon Archer." A beat, and then he added with a heart-pounding grin, "Junior."

"Ahh…then you must be Mr. Archer's…"

"Son," Leon finished. "As well as the new owner of Archer Industries," he clarified his statement with a downward tilt of his head. Looking up at Kacey, he said, "As of this morning, in fact."

"Oh, well…" she stammered. "Really? Then I guess congratulations are in order," she offered, sensing a definite increase in her pulse. So, the grumpy old man was out, and his superfine son was in? How'd she get so lucky? All of her worry about having to work with a crotchety old man had been wasted. Now, she had to worry about keeping her composure while his son's metal-gray eyes devoured her!

"Thanks," Leon said in a pride-filled manner. He propped his left elbow on the desk to rest his chin on curled fingers, which Kacey noted bore no rings.

"When did this change of leadership happen? I was prepared to meet with your father," Kacey stated, feeling her professional façade begin to melt under Leon Jr.'s disturbing stare. He certainly wasn't trying to hide his personal interest in her, and Kacey was definitely feeling flattered.

Breaking his gaze at last, Leon grinned. "Happened this morning. Dad unexpectedly decided to step down to enjoy his golden years traveling with my mom. They're leaving for Africa tomorrow."

"Oh, so soon?"

"Yeah. But don't worry about your swimsuits. You're in good hands."

"I'm sure I am," Kacey murmured, sensing a wave of heat surge through her stomach and ease down between her thighs, initiating a hint of dampness in her panties. *Get a grip, girl,* she silently admonished, forcing back a smile. "So *you'll* be working with me on production, then?" she had to clarify.

"Absolutely," Leon confirmed in a much bigger voice. "I'm totally familiar with the project, so you're stuck with me. Unless you'd prefer to work with Nona, my operations manager. She's been here almost as long as I have and can handle every stage of the process."

"No, that's all right," Kacey offered, a tad too quickly. Composing herself, she folded her hands together. "If you're on top of everything and can deliver what I want, that's all that counts."

"Trust me. I can deliver *whatever* you want. Just let me know what it is," he assured, using a voice that was so intentionally sexy that Kacey shivered, unable to think of a comeback.

This man is such a flirt, she decided, aware that he was no longer smiling. In fact, his hooded eyes were now slits of challenge, as if daring her to make him prove that he could deliver on more fronts than the production line.

"I'll definitely let you know," she tossed back with a lift of one shoulder, prepared to play his game of words.

"But I'm warning you, I can be very demanding, and particular."

"So can I," he replied with a hint of mockery.

"Fine. I'd love to see how we operate together."

"I was thinking the same thing. I have no doubt we're gonna get along just fine." The room fell quiet as Leon opened a folder and removed the photos that Hadley had emailed to the manufacturer. "I love your line. The designs are stunning. Utterly unique."

"Thanks," Kacey replied.

"You really know how to showcase a woman's best assets."

"That's what good design is all about," she replied, watching Leon as he held up one of the photos and tilted back in his chair.

"I especially love this one…your Sheer Double Dip," he commented, moving the picture aside to rake Kacey with a look that left no doubt in her mind that he was checking out more than her design credentials.

"It's the heart of my collection. All about the see-through fabric. Do you have a supplier for it, yet?"

"We're sourcing it now. Trust me, I'll get it at your price."

"Good. Then I guess we've got a lot to do," Kacey tossed out, clearly ready to get started.

"Sounds fine. I'm ready whenever you are," Leon said, leaning forward.

Kacey slowly unscrewed the cap on her bottle of water while assessing her new collaborator with interest. Though caught off guard by this shift in plans, the prospect of working with Leon Archer Jr. absolutely intrigued her. In the full five minutes since they'd met, she could already tell that collaborating with him was going to be a challenge. A challenge that she was more than ready to accept.

Chapter 5

Over the next hour, Kacey and Leon discussed each design in detail and shared thoughts on the execution of the various styles. They collaborated on pattern adjustments that would simplify production and keep costs down. However, it became clear right away that even though they shared the common goal of turning out a dynamite product at the best possible price, Leon was much more relaxed about the time frame than Kacey was.

"When will the first samples be ready?" she wanted to know.

"Depends," he casually replied.

"On what?"

"On how fast Bob Truett can get to your project."

"Bob Truett?" Kacey questioned.

"Our master patternmaker. He's the person who really

holds the power around here," Leon chuckled. "He's the best, though. Been with the company for years."

"You know I want to move this along as quickly as possible, don't you?" Kacey reminded Leon, not wanting to waste a second.

"We don't rush things around here. We move at the best pace to get the job done right, on schedule and to the customer's satisfaction."

"I'm sure you do, but I can't stick around Rockport forever."

"Don't be in such a rush. Relax. The workroom is pretty busy right now, but Truett knows your contract is a quick turnaround job," he assured Kacey, examining a page from the folder that contained the production schedule for SunKissed. "If all goes well, we should have your samples completed within a few days. However, I don't like to ask my employees to work overtime unless it's absolutely necessary."

Kacey simply watched Leon and held back from speaking while he scanned the document in silence. When he glanced up, he hooked Kacey with his magnetic gray eyes once again, creating an electric connection that made Kacey's heart turn over. Gulping back her unsettling reaction, she stilled, determined not to expose the stir of emotions cascading through her body.

"But you will ask for overtime if you have to, right?" she finally asked.

"Let's just see how things go," was all Leon offered.

"All right," Kacey conceded, hoping he would not be reluctant to push his employees hard to get the job done in record time. But that was his call to make, not hers, so she'd just have to trust him to do what he felt was best.

As he continued to explain the process, Kacey's eyes settled on Leon's full, well-formed lips, unable to keep from fantasizing about the warm, yummy taste she knew they would leave on her tongue. The idea of kissing Leon Archer made her nipples go hard in her bra and the core of her womanhood tense up. Such an intensely sexual arousal, prompted by a man she did not know, was like a lightning strike on a sunny day—completely out of the blue, but not impossible. In fact, getting excited over a man she did not know was exactly what she'd been yearning to feel for a very long time.

Kacey's personal life hummed along in an easy, uncomplicated way that she'd come to consider as normal. She didn't have a special man in her life, but she did have Jamal, the guy she turned to whenever she needed someone to rescue her from long spells of sexual abstinence. Kacey trusted and loved Jamal as a true friend, even though he wished she could love him like a man.

Jamal. Thinking of him made Kacey almost sigh. They'd known each other for eight years, and as much as she tried to shift her feelings for the devilishly handsome real estate investor into full romantic mode, it never quite happened. So, she'd settled on remaining good friends with occasional benefits, a perfect arrangement for Kacey, despite Jamal's desire for more.

When Leon cleared his throat with a fist to his mouth, as if aware of how distracted Kacey had become, she snapped to attention. Taking in his bemused expression, she tossed her crazy imaginings aside, placing fingertips to her chin to feel grounded in the moment.

"Ready to discuss the schedule?" Leon started, lifting one eyebrow while gracing her with a look as intimate as a kiss, which only served to rev her pulse a notch higher.

He's as caught up as I am, Kacey observed, exchanging a slow smile with him. "Sure," she replied, squeezing her legs together in an attempt to banish the itch that was definitely in need of scratching. Leaning forward in her chair, she focused her attention on the papers spread out on Leon's desk, avoiding his eyes completely.

"First, let's talk about your fabric," he stated.

"What do you think about the choices?" she asked Leon, her voice now crisply professional and efficient.

"Very nice. We have everything in stock except the imported Naughty Net, but we ought to find it soon."

"Perfect," Kacey commented. "And I'd like to come in at least five percent under budget," she told him, plunging back to earth with a definite crash, determined to make good on her promise to Hadley.

"Five percent? I dunno," Leon hedged. "You have eight different styles, and each one requires a lot of decorative detail. The cost of your raw materials eats up more than one-third of your budget," Leon warned with a tone of authority. "You might want to consider eliminating some of the expensive bling if you want to cut costs."

His candid assessment quickly dissolved Kacey's dreamy reaction to him. He sounded way too confident that she would be willing to go along with whatever he decided. Well, she had news for Leon Archer. His flirtatious overtures weren't going to distract her from holding firm on her designs. She knew her swimsuits contained the flashy touches that made them stand out from all the other swimwear currently available, and she had no plans to change that.

Certainly, this guy didn't expect her to drop the metallic gold rings on her bikini tops, did he? Or omit the polished Italian stone side clasps on the bottoms? Or trash the bronze beading on halter ties shot through with strands of gold and silver thread?

No, she could never eliminate her trademark sparkle or dull the shine that she adored.

"I have to disagree with your assessment," she told Leon firmly, after taking her time considering his point. "The accessory trim is what *makes* my styles, along with the custom cuts and imported fabrics. Unique accessorizing is key."

"I understand. But that's where the financial wiggle room is," Leon advised.

Kacey inclined her head in agreement, thinking about the financial bonus that Hadley had promised if she reduced production costs. Somehow, she had to prove to Hadley that she could get the job done, and done at his price.

"I understand where you're coming from, Leon," she finally agreed. "However, we'll have to cut costs someplace else."

Leon simply lifted his palms toward the ceiling as if at a loss to suggest an alternative.

"The estimates for labor per unit and packaging look good," Kacey said, searching for a way to make it all work.

"Oh, yes. Those are static costs that remain as is. No wiggle room there," Leon confirmed.

"Okaaay…so, if accessory trim is the wild card,"

Kacey restated, turning her thoughts to ways of saving money without sacrificing style, "I have an idea."

"Let's hear it," Leon prompted.

Kacey sank back in her chair, fingers tented at her lips, knowing she would have to adjust costs somewhere if she wanted that bonus money. Leaning forward, she launched her suggestion. "What if, instead of *eliminating* the more expensive trim, we simply reduce the quantity?"

"You know, that was going to be my next suggestion," Leon replied, appearing excited by her approach. He flipped through Kacey's portfolio and tapped a page with his finger. "Like the Lucite squares on this Retro Hipster style. The halter top has Lucite squares on the ends of the ties, and two smaller pieces at the bustline. Maybe if we use one larger piece, you'd get the same effect and spend less on trim."

Kacey made a subtle nod, knowing his solution made sense. Eliminating one piece of Lucite detail wouldn't detract from the overall look, and if this was what she had to do to make this line happen, she was willing to give it a try.

"Okay," she agreed with Leon, her earlier irritation beginning to ease. "I'll review each style and see where I can make similar adjustments."

"Great," Leon replied, pausing to review the last page of the production schedule before he spoke again. "Once you've done that, I'll revise the manufacturing estimate and email it to you so that you can send it over to Hadley for his approval."

"Fantastic," Kacey replied, ready to tackle the numbers, and pleased that Leon was onboard. The more energy he focused on her swimsuit line, the more quickly she'd be able to return to New York, even though her earlier determination to get out of Rockport as fast as she could didn't seem quite so pressing anymore.

"One thing I guess you've learned about me," Leon said after their revision session wound down. "I'm committed one hundred percent to making sure you *are* happy."

"What more could I ask for?" Kacey replied, buzzed by the sense of partnership that was rapidly developing between them. On this project, which was so special for Kacey, working with a talented African-American man who had the power, the insight and the creative drive to deliver on her vision was a drastic, and wonderful, development.

While doing promotional work for Leeman's, her vision and taste had been challenged many times. However, to stay on track and not become distracted by exaggerated promises from suppliers and vendors, she'd adopted a three-point approach that worked for her: Always be clear and upfront about her expectations, never sacrifice quality for quantity and steer clear of obvious over-the-top trends with limited appeal. Now she had to add one more point to her list: Never fantasize about making love with the manufacturer!

Finished with their meeting, Leon stood and motioned for Kacey to come with him. "I've set up a workspace for you to use while you're here. It's not very big, I'm afraid," he said, leading her down the hall to a small cubicle not far from his office. It was private, quiet and had a phone, a computer and a drafting table. All the equipment she needed to do her job.

Kacey followed him into the space, very aware of his

closeness, his scent and especially the silent electricity crackling in the air. His presence sucked her in, tingled her imagination and made her want to do things she hadn't thought of before. Like make the first move and kiss the hell out of this guy who was pushing her most intimate buttons.

"And you do have a window," Leon offered with a wave of one hand, moving to open the blinds and reveal a clear view of the parking lot.

Kacey moved toward the window, her shoulder brushing Leon's as she stepped past him, certain she'd felt him tense when their bodies touched. "That's the road that leads to the Coast, isn't it?" she asked, recognizing the highway that she'd taken on her way to Rockport.

"Right. If you hang a left out of the parking lot and go four miles, you'll hit Aransas Bay." He moved up behind her, so near that his breath warmed her neck and sent delightful shivers down Kacey's spine. "I live out that way, too. On the beach."

"You do?" she commented, turning around, her face stopping only inches from his, so near their lips could have easily met. And held. In a long, delicious kiss. The subtle sensuousness that shimmered between them was like an invisible thread, drawing them together. Neither took a backward step, yet a message of caution flashed into Kacey's brain, warning her to move—steer clear of temptation and concentrate on something other than his arresting grin, which was rattling her composure and provoking a ruffle of a smile on her lips. "Must be nice, living near the water," she said, her voice breathy and low. She enunciated her words slowly, as if carefully calibrating her reply to lead him into more personal revelations.

"It is nice," he agreed. "It's quiet out on the beach. Very private. I live alone, so it's a welcome escape from all the noise and hectic hours I put in here at the factory."

He lives alone, Kacey quickly registered, certain he'd deliberately dropped that nugget of private information to disarm any resistance she might have had about entering into a more intimate level of conversation. Deciding to play the game she knew he'd started, she lobbed the comeback she hoped he was expecting. "I hear you. My job at Leeman's can get pretty crazy, too, so going home to a quiet place…with no one around, is heaven."

"Do you live in Manhattan?" Leon quickly probed.

"No, in Harlem. But I'm planning on moving into the city when I return."

"I'll bet it's expensive, living in New York. Any roommates?"

"No, just me."

"So you like big-city life?"

"I love it. Born and raised in Harlem. Wouldn't give up New York for anything."

"Well, it's all about how you want to live your life," he replied laughingly, now stepping back to put more space between them. "Small town Texas is where I come from and Rockport has always been home. It's really a great place to live and work."

"Especially if you're an Archer, I'll bet," Kacey finished with a chuckle.

"Oh, yeah," he sheepishly acknowledged. "Guess you got me there."

With a duck of her head Kacey stepped even further away from Leon and put both of her hands on the back of the stool in front of her drafting table. Holding on to it, she watched Leon carefully, her heart racing in her chest. If he didn't leave soon, she knew she might embarrass herself by revealing more than she should, or asking too many questions. But she wasn't going to be in Rockport for long, and time would fly by. Would there be enough time to get to know Leon Archer better? And why did she feel so compelled to get answers to the questions that were crowding her mind?

"Think I'd better get busy on those revisions," she told him, slipping onto the stool. She picked up a pencil and pointed it at him. "I'll let you know when I'm finished."

"Good idea. Just push the red button on your phone and that'll buzz me in my office. When you're ready, I'd like to show you around the plant."

"Will do," Kacey replied. As she watched Leon leave her cubicle, she couldn't resist a shake of her head. Whew! That man was yanking all her chains and she didn't plan to stop him.

Chapter 6

Once Kacey had reviewed the revised production budget, she sent it to Steve Hadley, proud of herself, and Leon, for accomplishing their mission. Within fifteen minutes, Hadley replied to her email, congratulating her on reducing overall costs by seven percent and assuring her that he'd work out a contractor's agreement for her and that she would receive a nice bonus once the product had been received. Pleased with her achievement, as well as her boss's reply, she buzzed Leon, who quickly returned to her cubicle.

"Now that money matters are settled, let's take a tour of the factory," Leon suggested, lingering in the entry.

Kacey smiled, allowing herself to relax and savor the importance of the moment. Everything was falling into place. The tension that had been building inside her since launching her proposal for Hadley in New York began to dissipate. Partnering with Leon was going to be a definite change from anything she'd ever done, and she hoped there'd be no bumps in the road. But with his steel-gray eyes all over her and the hint of his cologne filling her head, it was going to be awfully damn hard to concentrate on work.

But I have to, she reminded herself, biting her lip as she powered down her computer. She shouldn't even be conjuring up romantic notions about a man she hardly knew. It was time to get serious about the work she'd come here to do.

"You guys about finished?"

Glancing up, Kacey saw that Nona had come up behind Leon and placed a ring-laden hand on his shoulder. When Nona's fingers grazed her boss's neck, Kacey squinted in surprise, thinking that was a pretty intimate gesture for an operations manager to make with the man who owned the place. However, Leon didn't seem bothered at all.

"Yeah. I'm about to give Kacey a tour of the plant," Leon replied, shifting more fully into Kacey's cubicle and away from Nona's touch.

Nona, who was holding a thick black binder in her other hand, followed him into the room. "Leon, I know you have a ton of things to take care of…with Mr. Archer leaving so sudden and all. Want me to show Kacey around, introduce her to the key people who'll be involved in the production?"

Leon tapped a finger on the corner of Kacey's desk as if considering Nona's suggestion. "No, that's okay. I'll show Kacey around."

"All right," Nona replied, sounding a tad disappointed. She smiled at Kacey and shrugged. "Guess I'll see you later." Then she left the room in a swish of African print fabric.

Turning to Kacey, Leon said, "Come on. Let's go out on the floor and get acquainted with everyone. We've got a lot to cover today."

Seated at her desk, Nona tossed back her head, jutted out her bottom lip and glared at the ceiling. With her eyes squinted into long-lashed slits, she pressed her tongue to the roof of her mouth. The swimsuit designer was much too attractive for Nona's liking. A slick, sexy professional woman from New York City could become a real distraction.

If Kacey Parker thinks Leon is gonna spend all his time fawning over her, she's sadly mistaken. But at least she won't be here that long, Nona decided, feeling a sweep of relief as she picked up a folder and got into her work for the day.

Kacey and Leon entered the corridor leading to the heart of the plant, walking side by side while making small talk about the factory.

"We pride ourselves on turning out high-quality items at competitive pricing levels," Leon told Kacey as he touted his company's track record with pride. "Our design capability and fabric quality is competitive with any name brand. Our motto, 'We Suit Every Body' is more than a catchy slogan. We mean it!"

"How long has your family been in business?" Kacey wanted to know.

"Fifty-two years."

"And you've been working here since…?"

"Since forever, it seems. My dad made me start out

at the bottom to learn the business from the ground up. My first real job was on the packing line…part-time while I was in high school," Leon replied, in a voice laden with pride. "Worked right alongside Nona, who started here the same day."

"Oh, really? She's been here that long?"

"Oh, yeah. Most of my classmates worked here at one time or another. Especially during summer vacations. We worked hard, but goofed off a lot, too. As soon as we'd get off work, we used to head straight to the beach and go skinny dipping. We'd stay out on the beach all night sometimes."

"You all swam in the nude?" Kacey had to comment, imagining how fine Leon must have looked when he was younger, and buck naked. Not that he wasn't fine now, because it was clear he took good care of himself.

The smothered laughter that bubbled up from Leon's throat was the only answer Kacey needed. "Sure. Why not?" he said. "We were young…friends just having fun. Nobody bothered us." A beat. "Our favorite place to swim was Barker's Bend. Wow, it's been a long time since I've thought about that." Shaking his head, Leon turned into another hallway and escorted Kacey through a set of metal double doors.

Kacey increased her pace to keep up with Leon, whose long strides were moving them along quickly. Anxious to keep him talking, she threw out the question she was burning to have answered. "So you and Nona have been friends a long time, huh?"

"Yeah. I've known her about all my life."

"So you two are…close?" she prompted, unable to shake the image of Nona's hand placed so possessively on Leon's shoulder and his apparent lack of displeasure.

One question was burning in her mind: *Did you two have a romantic relationship? What does she mean to you now?* But of course she couldn't ask that.

"Close? Oh, sure," Leon blithely confirmed with a flick of his hand. "My mom was her mother's best friend. When Nona's mother died, my mom kinda adopted Nona, so she's like a member of my family, really."

"I see," Kacey murmured. But that didn't explain the obvious possessiveness that Kacey had detected in Nona's attitude. Something told Kacey that she'd better watch Nona James closely and try not to get on her bad side.

Inside the noisy heart of the factory, Leon paused to let Kacey take in the buzz of activity swirling around them. Here industrial sewing machines and power-cutting tools were actively turning fabric into a variety of products. As they toured the plant, Leon pointed out the various stages of production as articles of clothing passed from cutting tables to sewing machines, pressing equipment and the final staging area for inventory storage and shipping.

"This is where everything happens," he explained. "Workers in that section on the left complete the manual steps needed to prepare the product before the tools and machines take over. Each employee has a specific job to do, and timing is critical…not only to maintain a steady production flow, but also to ensure a safe environment. If one person drops the ball, it can affect the entire run, so team effort is vitally important."

"That kind of interdependence probably helps create the family-type vibe that I can definitely feel around here," Kacey commented as she slid her gaze over the massive machinery where men and women were busy with their work.

Leon beamed his pleasure at Kacey's spot-on observation. "Absolutely right. We work hard together, we live close to each other and we depend on one another to get the job done right."

"That must be a good feeling...knowing your coworkers so well."

"Yes, it's a definite benefit of living in a small town where no one is a stranger."

"No one?" Kacey repeated, beginning to feel less like an intruder.

He turned back to Kacey, his face soft and somber. "No one," he repeated in a husky voice that delivered the seriousness of his message. "Not even you." He placed a hand on her arm, his fingers lingering on the sleeve of her navy jacket. "I mean that, Kacey. While you're here, I plan to do all I can to make you feel like a part of the Archer family."

The raw sensuousness in his voice sent involuntary shivers of arousal through Kacey, who lifted her face to Leon's. He'd said "the Archer family," hadn't he? Not the "Archer Industries family," making Kacey wonder if Leon was aware of the slip of the tongue he'd made.

"Thanks. I'd like that," she murmured, impressed by his genuine effort to put her at ease.

The tender expression that suffused his features told her that she'd interpreted his comment exactly as he'd hoped. "I want your experience here to be well worth your time," he went on, leading her deeper into the workroom.

He stopped at a metal rail that separated the walkway

from the work area, removed his hand from her arm and dipped his head. "I know Rockport is nothing like New York, but I think my hometown is a pretty special place. We have a lot to offer." The clacking cacophony of sounds that reverberated through the factory forced Leon to step closer to Kacey so that she could hear what he had to say. Continuing in a much stronger voice, he told her, "Since you're going to be around for a while, I hope you'll take the time to get to know the city...and me...a lot better."

"I hope so, too," Kacey confessed, aware of the vibrations from the massive machinery that suddenly engulfed them. Or was it the hum of her fast-racing heart that was causing the steady pulsations rocketing through her body?

Kacey gave Leon an affirmative nod, turned around and started down the walkway. He riveted his eyes on her exquisite backside, swallowing the lump of appreciation that crowded his throat. With her head held high, she sashayed to the end of the catwalk, and into a section that was walled off by a large section of glass. Leon followed close behind.

"I want you to meet Bob Truett, the head patternmaker I told you about," Leon said to Kacey as he guided her over to the man behind the glass wall who was busy moving pattern pieces around on his computer screen. "Bob Truett," Leon started, "this is Kacey Parker. The designer for the SunKissed line."

Bob, a short stocky man with a receding hairline who resembled Danny DeVito, shifted in his seat, looked up and beamed a toothy smile at Kacey. "Welcome to Archer," he said. "I was just uploading some of your specs."

"Great to meet you," Kacey replied, moving closer to his computer screen to study the images floating there, relieved to see that he was using the same CAD software that she used in New York. By storing her design styles and color choices on disks, they were easily accessed and managed. "Looks good," she commented perusing his work.

"Bob's a real whiz at pulling off computerized replicas of the most complicated clothing constructions," Leon agreed.

"Mind if I watch for a while?" Kacey asked.

"No, not at all," Bob replied, waving her into the empty chair beside his. "In fact, I need your input. Oh, and we'll receive the Naughty Net from India day after tomorrow."

"Fantastic," Kacey said, relieved to know that Archer had come through.

"Something I need to know now," Truett started. "Do you want the shirring on this tie-side bottom to run all the way around the hipline or just across the front?"

Scooting closer to the screen, Kacey studied the image and launched into her vision of the style, while Bob made the necessary adjustments in the pattern.

Leon retreated to the back of Bob's workstation to observe. *Damn, that woman is pretty!* he thought, pulling in a long, silent breath. *And talented, too,* he acknowledged. Kacey, the fashion designer, was the artistic force behind the line, and he was proud to act as the vehicle to channel her finished products into the heart of the apparel industry. Together, they could make a heck of a pair.

Was that why he was drawn to her like a magnet picking up pins from the cutting-room floor? Why the attraction he'd felt when he first saw her sitting in his office had hit him like a jolt of fresh air? He was still reeling from the encounter. When he'd discussed the Leeman's contract with his father, he had assumed he'd be working with some flighty male artistic type from New York, never expecting to be paired with a sexy woman who had so much going on. What a lucky break! And she'd told him that she lived alone, so she must be single. No roommates. No rings. No mention of a kid or a significant other she'd left behind in New York. He sure hoped Kacey Parker was as special, and available, as she appeared to be because he was going to do all he could to keep her in Rockport as long as possible.

As he listened to Kacey and Bob discussing the various stages that her samples would go through, Leon was impressed anew by the unusual creative flair of her swimwear. She certainly knew how to capitalize on a woman's best features while softening the appearance of those ever-present flaws. He'd never seen any female on the beach in a suit close to what SunKissed by Kacey had to offer, and he could hardly wait to see the finished products.

"What size do you want the samples made in?" Truett asked, busily re-creating the extra-wide straps of a white halter top on his computerized patternmaker.

"I think it might be best…" Kacey began, but was cut off when Leon's voice drifted from behind her and interrupted her reply.

"Bob, I think you should make the samples in Ms. Parker's size. Whatever that is," he finished, deliberately inserting a hint of a taunt in his comment.

Kacey's head whipped around and she glared at Leon, who simply let a sly smile curve his lips.

"For your information I wear a size 4...petite," she informed him without hesitation, clearly ready to accept his challenge.

So, she's game, Leon thought, his heart thudding at the thought of her wearing the sexy swimsuits now floating across Bob's computer monitor.

"If I were in New York," Kacey continued, "I'd have the in-house models at Leeman's fit them. I even considered having the models come to Rockport for the shoot, but I've changed my mind completely. Since I'm on a tight deadline and don't have time to ship the samples back to New York, I may as well fit them myself."

"Good point," Bob acknowledged, punching in more numbers. "That way I can make the adjustments on the spot and save a lot of time."

"Great," Kacey stated. "I can't wait until the samples are ready."

Neither can I, Leon silently admitted, realizing his suggestion hadn't thrown Kacey at all.

"If you're going to test-model the swimsuits, then Nona can help you with the fittings," Truett told Kacey.

Sorry, Bob, Leon quietly mused. *That'll be one job that belongs to the boss, even though Kacey doesn't know it...yet.*

Leon crossed the space between himself and Kacey to add a comment on one of her designs. "I like this black one-piece style. It's the definition of classic! It's sexy, and yet it's not like those teeny-weeny string silhouettes that show off a lot of skin. Your suits have glamour and class. Like old-time Hollywood pizzazz done up for women of today."

Kacey's head snapped up, her mouth open in surprise. "You hit the essence of my design concept right on the mark! Thanks for the compliment. You have a good eye for style," she told him. "I think I'm gonna like having you around."

Not as much as I'm gonna enjoy having you here, Leon thought, boldly raking Kacey with renewed appreciation. The afterbuzz of her remark fueled his sense that she was eager to explore whatever was developing between them. In her navy business attire, carefully coifed hair, shiny manicured nails and subtle, but stylish jewelry, she fit perfectly into the corporate image of a successful businesswoman. However, Leon could easily imagine what she would look like in the erotic red thong bikini that Truett was now dissecting on his computer-imaging machine. Even though she came off as the epitome of style, grace, good taste and high fashion, Leon suspected that underneath that crisp façade lurked a totally different woman, one who wore tight tank tops without a bra, stone-washed jeans without panties and was dying to break loose when she wasn't on the clock.

It sure would be fun to kick it with her while she's here, he mused as a rush of excitement swept through his body. The sudden surge of that heat settled low in his stomach, initiating the beginnings of an erection that took Leon by surprise. Quickly, he swiveled toward a desk and moved up close to shield himself from embarrassment.

What the hell was that about? He squared his shoulders, straightened his back and took a deep breath, knowing what was bothering him. His interest in Kacey Parker was quickly morphing into something more than professional, even though he knew better than to entertain such thoughts. He had to remember that she was still a city girl. Even her well-modulated voice screamed "East Coast Class," reminding Leon of how different they were. Though tempted, he worried about acting on the impulses that were hammering at his better judgment and creating a bulge in his pants. Getting personal with Kacey Parker might mess up his first big contract as the new owner of Archer Industries, disappointing his father—and himself.

Life in Rockport was slow, uncomplicated and casual, not at all like Kacey's, he imagined. But if she'd let him, he'd show her the upside of his hometown, as well as another side of himself—a side that he hadn't thought about sharing with anyone for a long, long time.

Chapter 7

The interior of the Seaside Suites was even drabber than Kacey had imagined it might be. A dark lobby filled with cheap furniture and a listless clerk who smelled of tobacco greeted her when she checked in.

After entering her room, Kacey tossed her suitcase onto the faded coverlet on the queen-size bed and then flopped into a pale green armchair by the window. She swept the room with a critical eye, appalled by the gaudy seashell motif that was plastered on every surface. Huge conch shells danced across blue wallpaper while flat white sand dollars dotted the deep red carpet. The clear glass bases of the bedside lamps were filled with a variety of tiny seashells, and the mirror over the dresser was framed with plastic replicas of various crustaceans, spray-painted bright golden yellow. Even the metal drawer pulls on the desk had been carved to resemble oyster husks.

Shaking her head in disbelief, Kacey turned her thoughts away from her dismal environment and back to the long, but rewarding day she'd had at Archer Industries. After working with Bob Truett to download all her patterns, she'd returned to her cubicle to make a few phone calls and finish some revisions. Leon had been very solicitous, almost too eager to make sure she was satisfied with the nips and tucks that Bob planned to make on the sample patterns. Before Leon left the building for a meeting in town he'd stopped by to give her his cell phone number in case she needed to talk to him.

Kacey had been both relieved and disappointed when Leon pulled out of the Archer parking lot with a squeal of tires and a flare of dust. She'd lingered at the window in her cubicle, watching the road long after his red Corvette had disappeared. The young Mr. Archer made her nervous as hell, but still, she liked the way he could put her at ease with only a smile. He made her heart race and her mouth go dry, yet she looked forward to being in the same room with him again tomorrow.

She had to admit it: Leon, the local playboy, had a lot going on. He drove a fiery red sports car, owned a house on the beach and clearly spared no expense to buy only the best of whatever he wanted. *Apparently, his family connections, good looks and magnetic personality must make him the most eligible bachelor in Rockport,* Kacey decided, imagining that Leon had probably romanced most of the available local women, and then some. Women who were only too happy to fawn over him, increasing his sense of self-importance. Women like Nona James.

The thought of Leon making love to Nona made Kacey flinch, though she knew she shouldn't give a hot damn about what he did or with whom. She had to settle her emotions, view Leon Archer Jr. as a professional colleague—nothing more. She had to concentrate on fabric choices and sample units, not the adorable way Leon tilted his head to the side when he looked at her or how seductively his torso tapered into his tight waist, creating perfect symmetry with his broad, muscular shoulders. Placing a hand to her stomach, Kacey sighed, trying to steady her nerves.

Tomorrow, the real work would begin as patterns hit the cutting boards and preparations for the first set of sample designs rolled forward. *That should keep my mind off Leon Archer's eyes, lips and his too fine butt.* At least for a while, she hoped, suddenly exhausted by the events of the day. All she wanted to do was take a hot shower, fall into bed and dream about ladies snatching her swimsuits off the racks inside Leeman's department stores.

When the thump-thump of a ball hitting the ground outside erupted, Kacey reached up, pulled the cord to open the mini blinds and peered into the courtyard of the apartment complex next door. She saw four young men racing around the well-worn asphalt lot, launching into a game of basketball. Their noisy play struck every nerve in Kacey's body, zapping her like jolts of electricity. The loud jeers and cheers as the boys called back and forth shattered the peace she had hoped to enjoy on her first night in Rockport.

"Oh, my God," Kacey groaned, quickly closing the

blinds. Was this a regular thing? Did the boys play there every evening? Annoyed, she grabbed the remote control off the desk and zapped the TV on, turning the volume up very loud in an attempt to drown out the ballplayers outside. However, her camouflage attempt prompted the person in the next room to pound on the wall and yell for her to turn the TV down. Clamping her teeth together, she bit back the urge to answer the knock with a pounding of her own, but lowered the volume, resigned to getting used to the noise coming from outside.

Why am I so edgy? she wondered. Living in the city, she was accustomed to the ever-present traffic noise and city sounds that rose up from the street and filtered into her third-floor apartment in Harlem. Why did it seem that, in Texas, everything was magnified and in her face—not as distant and impersonal as it was back home? Was it simply because she was in unfamiliar territory or because she was paying too much attention to her surroundings?

Either way, I don't think I'll ever get used to this place, she decided, reluctantly hanging her designer suits with matching blouses on wire hangers and placing her trendy pumps and sandals on the shabby carpet floor. Not knowing how long she'd be in Texas, she'd brought a good supply of clothing and shoes in order to be prepared for whatever might come up. She had several pairs of slacks and denim jeans. Capris matched with both dressy and casual tops. Sneakers. Her two favorite swimsuits and, of course, a generous supply of underwear and delicate lingerie.

As a teenager, Kacey had developed a passion for feminine, sexy underclothing and suspected that her love of these delicate items was what fostered her desire to create a swimwear line.

After arranging her toiletries and cosmetics on the ledge in the tiny bathroom, she stuck her empty suitcase on the top shelf of the closet and turned her thoughts to her next big decision: where to go for dinner.

She'd passed a pizza place and a cafeteria on her way to the motel, but neither choice struck her as particularly appealing, and she wasn't up for driving around hunting for a place to eat. In fact, she had no appetite at all.

Digging into her black patent Kate Spade tote, Kacey pulled out a plastic zipper bag containing tea bags, crackers, sweetener and packets of instant soup—the trusty emergency travel kit she never left home without. At least the Seaside Suites furnished a microwave oven and plastic cups. For tonight, that would have to do.

Leon parked his Corvette under the carport beside his house, turned off the engine and got out. As he walked along the sandy path leading to his back door, he admired the magnificent orange and gray sunset hovering just above the dark waters of the Gulf. The reflection of the sinking sun glimmering on the water turned the flat dusky expanse into a magical mirror weighted to the land. He climbed the steps leading up to his back deck and then paused, drinking in the sight that always greeted him. The only sounds that broke into his quiet cocoon were the gentle swish-swish of waves lapping at the shore and the occasional squawk of a seagull passing overhead.

Leon tossed his briefcase onto a canvas deck chair and leaned against the deck's polished wood rail, gazing out over the water. Though he'd grown up in his parents' huge traditional home and admired the old place with a passion, once he returned to Rockport after college and began to work for his father, he'd purchased and restored the dramatic one-story beach house that he now called home. It was the perfect place for him: he could be near the coastal waters that he loved so much, yet far enough away from the prying eyes of townsfolk and employees—who often took their familiarity with the Archer family too much to heart.

Born and raised in Rockport, Leon thought of himself as a country guy, content with small-town life—where everyone knew him and he fit right in. However, living in a place like Rockport, and being the only child of Mr. and Mrs. Archer, meant he belonged to the most influential and wealthy family in the city, a family that was respected and trusted by all.

The dramatic view from the wraparound deck that surrounded his house never failed to impress Leon, who had renovated the place with walls of glass on two sides, bringing the Gulf of Mexico right into his home. His nearest neighbor was one mile away and his location, far from the center of the city, was as close to perfect as could be appreciated. He could get to his mom and dad quickly in case of an emergency, yet he was far enough away to discourage impromptu visits.

After all, he *was* a bachelor, free to come and go as he pleased, and had no one to answer to but himself. Didn't he deserve to live in a luxurious seaside home that reflected his good taste and offered the privacy he craved? Leon took great pains to make his life as stress-free, and relationship-free, as possible, and at thirty-three he believed he had plenty of time before settling down to bring anyone else into his life. Until the urge to permanently bond with one particular woman hit him, he had no qualms about having as much fun as possible, while working as hard as he could.

The buzz of Leon's handheld interrupted his sunset watch. He checked the screen and grinned. It was Freddy, his longtime friend who lived in nearby Smithville, twenty miles inland from the coast.

"Hey, man. What's going on?" Leon answered, shoving his briefcase to the floor as he sat down in the deck chair.

"Everything," Freddy replied in his deeply melodious voice.

"Like?" Leon prompted, knowing Freddy well enough not to try to guess what he might be into at the moment. Freddy was a trust-fund baby with lots of cash, very little responsibility and a penchant for partying hard at the ranch he'd inherited from his parents.

"Got a call from Paul Grant…you remember him?" Freddy was saying.

"The rodeo dude who won all those medals—and cash—at the Houston Livestock show last year?"

"Yeah, that's the guy," Freddy confirmed.

"What about him?" Leon asked.

"He's bringing his crew and they're gonna put on a show here at the ranch weekend after next. Saturday *and* Sunday. It'll be the biggest roundup ever, man. Party time for real. I'm telling you, man. It's gonna be a blast. I've got folks coming in from as far away as Vegas to join in the fun. Booked a band. Top shelf liquor. Food for days. Girls galore. You've gotta come out for this one, bro. No kidding."

Leon hesitated, his mind spinning. When the close-knit atmosphere of life in Rockport became too claustrophobic and he needed to get away, Leon usually headed to Freddy's ranch, where he could drink beer, ride horses and hang out with his party buddies, who were ever-present at the ranch. At Freddy's ultramodern lodge in the semi-desert setting, the bar never closed, the stream of beautiful women never ended and the party never stopped. A weekend at Freddy's could chase away small-town blues and recharge Leon's batteries, increasing his appreciation of the quiet calm of Rockport when he returned.

"Sorry, wish I could, but I don't think I can make it," Leon told Freddy, adding the news that his father had just retired and turned the company over to him.

"All the more reason to celebrate, man. You don't wanna pass this one up."

The temptation to pack a bag and head to the ranch for a freewheeling good time challenged Leon's resistance. It would be a weekend trip. No need to worry about work. However, he knew he couldn't leave.

With a reluctant grimace, Leon told Freddy, "Sorry. Really. I'd better stick around here right now." Leon could sense his best friend's disappointment in the silence that hummed on the line. Rarely did Leon turn down one of Freddy's coveted invites, but this time it had to be done. "I've got a ton of work facing me, due to my dad's sudden retirement and all. Plus, I've got this designer in town...we have a contract to manufacture her swimsuit line. That's gonna take all my concentration."

"Can't Nona handle her?" Freddy quipped. "She knows as much about your dad's....uh, I mean, *your* company's operation as anybody."

"Naw, I promised Pop I'd handle this one personally,

and it's too important to leave with Nona, even though I know she could handle it."

"Okay, man. I hear you. Don't decide now. You've got time. Think about it."

"Okay," Leon agreed.

"Later," Freddy said, clicking off.

As the sunset gradually lost its luster, Leon remained on his deck, his thoughts centered on Kacey Parker. Suddenly, Freddy's invitation didn't strike him as very appealing. A wild rodeo weekend of drinking beer and partying wasn't what he wanted to do and he knew why. What he wanted to do was to stick around Rockport, get close enough to Kacey to see what made her tick. He had to find out if she was just a tease or if she was as stirred up as he was—if this crazy attraction he was feeling for her was on a two-way street.

Pushing up from his chair, Leon went inside and turned up the lights, illuminating the soft beige and gray décor of the interior of his house. The luster of chrome and glass contracted sharply with the warm tan walls and sectional that wrapped around a huge fireplace constructed of rough natural stone. Entering his golden granite kitchen, he went to the refrigerator and looked inside, suddenly very hungry. He grinned when he saw the large dish of lasagna, tossed salad and garlic bread that had been placed on the center shelf.

"Thank you, Mom," he murmured, knowing his mother, who loved to cook, must have dropped off the food while he was at work. Whenever she was about to leave town she always cooked up whatever was in her fridge and graciously donated her culinary creations to her son. *And it sure comes in on time tonight*, Leon thought, definitely too wired from his first day as owner of Archer Industries to begin to think about food.

Leon removed the casserole dish, set it on his kitchen counter and studied the oversized meal. *More than I can eat by myself,* he thought, as an idea began to form. Pulling out his cell phone he quickly dialed the number at the Seaside Suites Motel, his heart thumping crazily under his shirt.

Sitting with her back against the headboard of her too-soft bed, Kacey dunked a limp tea bag up and down in a cup of tepid water, and eyed the packet of crackers on her bedside table, resigned to eating her dreary meal alone. She settled in, took a sip from her cup and was just about to open the crackers when the room phone rang.

Startled, she nearly dropped the concoction that she was not looking forward to drinking. Reaching over, she picked up the receiver and answered, stunned, yet pleased to hear Leon's voice.

"Well, hello," she replied, determined to sound as if receiving a call from him was a perfectly natural thing.

"How's your room? Everything okay?" Leon asked.

"Oh, yes. It's fine," Kacey replied, thinking how nice it was of him to care about her comfort.

"Good. I was wondering if you'd had dinner," he asked right off.

Kacey laughed aloud, giving up a soft giggle that let him know he'd struck a chord. "Uh…if you can call a cup of lukewarm herbal tea and slightly stale crackers dinner, then yes."

Leon groaned in disgust. "How does homemade lasagna with hot garlic bread sound?"

"Heavenly." A beat. "So you cook, too, huh?"

"Naw. Compliments of my mom. She loves to feed me."

"All right. Sooo…are you inviting me to dinner?"

"Absolutely."

"I accept."

"I'll pick you up in fifteen minutes."

Chapter 8

From the road, Leon's home resembled an ordinary ranch house, with a low-slung profile, sleek horizontal windows and a tall brick chimney rising high above the roofline in the middle of the structure. However, as Kacey soon discovered, behind the building's rather nondescript façade was a fabulous home with a beach view that blew her mind.

After parking his Corvette under the carport, Leon walked with Kacey along the sandy path that led to the back entrance of the house. Her mouth dropped open in shock at the sight that greeted her. The entire rear of Leon's home was wrapped with a true mahogany deck that offered a spectacular view of the Gulf of Mexico. The tropical landscape leading down to the water resembled a cushy mat of lush green foliage punctuated by succulent blooming cacti and prickly heat-hardy plants. Nestled within the unusual, and intriguing, garden were bubbling fountains with cascades of silvery water where solar lights twinkled among the exotic flowering shrubs. The scent of salt water, mingled with jasmine, perfumed the air and pulled Kacey deeper into her fascination with Leon, as well as his private escape.

"What a fantastic place," she commented, mounting the steps to the deck, where a patio table had been draped with a white cloth and set with plates for dinner for two.

"Thanks. I like it, too," Leon replied as he lifted the glass hurricane shade in the center of the table and lit the thick white candle beneath it, shielding the flame from the brisk coastal winds with a cup of his hand. The light quickly shed a shimmer of gold over the gilt-rimmed wineglasses waiting to be filled and created a twinkle of amber light on plates that reflected the starry sky overhead.

"It's not too cool for you out here, is it?" he asked.

"Not at all. This is heaven, after all the cold rain in New York." Moving to stand at the deck's rail, Kacey stared out over the dark, wave-crested water, taking in the surreal scene. In the distance, a slow-moving private yacht drifted past, looking like a holiday sparkler with its tiny windows all ablaze. Beyond the pleasure boat, she spied a much larger vessel that broke the line of the horizon in a hulking oblong shadow.

"That's a cruise ship bound for Mexico," Leon told her before she had a chance to ask. "They pass by on a regular schedule. I could set my watch by the Kings Cruise ships. Very punctual line."

"How serene," Kacey remarked, parting her lips to

suck in a breath of sea air, loving the feel of the gentle breeze that caressed her face and ruffled the white linen tablecloth.

"Yes, it is peaceful," Leon agreed, reaching for the bottle of wine on the table. "Is red okay?" he asked, lifting up the bottle. "Produced in a local winery."

Kacey turned to face Leon, struck silent by a catch in her throat that held her words in check. Was it only this morning that she'd been grumbling about going to Rockport, feeling resentful about being stuck in Texas? Now, all she wanted to do was linger on this fantastic deck and drink wine with this handsome man until the sun came up. Why was her mind stuck on how damn handsome Leon Archer was and how quickly he was moving into her heart? It all seemed so fast...so surreal, yet so right. Was she complaining? Not at all. In fact, Kacey knew she wanted nothing more than for Leon Archer to make the first move. And after that, well, she wasn't sure *what* might happen, but she damn sure wanted to find out.

Kacey gave Leon a quick nod and smiled as he removed the cork from the wine bottle, poured two glasses and then moved next to her. She accepted the drink, cupping her fingers around the bowl of the glass as she tasted the wine. "Very nice."

"Good. I think so, too."

"And you said this is local?" she asked, impressed by the smooth, silky taste of the wine.

"Yep. The winery is not far from here." He placed a hand on her shoulder and pointed toward the east. "Just over that ridge. Where the land rises up at that jagged tree line. That's the vineyard. A beautiful piece of land."

"I've never drunk Texas wine," she admitted. Then she added, "In fact, I'd never thought about Texas as a place where wine was produced."

Leon chuckled. "You're not alone. But the word is getting out. More local growers are planting grapes instead of cotton. Something to tell your city friends about when you return home," Leon stated.

"For sure. I'm impressed with your hometown. What else should I know?"

"That we have real rodeo competitions around here."

"Rodeo? You mean roping steers and riding cows?" Kacey asked.

Leon sputtered in laughter. "Steers, horses and bulls get ridden, but not cows," he clarified. "Yes. It's true. There's a very active rodeo circuit in these parts," he told Kacey. "A friend of mine owns a ranch in Smithville— about twenty miles from here. His grandparents founded the oldest black rodeo in the state. In fact, he's hosting a pretty well-known rodeo crew weekend after next."

"Hmm…fascinating. I've never seen a rodeo," Kacey admitted.

"Really? I think you'd like it. I could take you if…"

"If I'm still here," Kacey finished with a lift of an eyebrow. "We might be finished with my line by then."

"You'll be here," Leon stated with such assurance that it sent a shiver of anticipation curling tightly around Kacey's heart.

"You love this part of the country, don't you?" Kacey said, her voice soft and sincere.

"Yeah, I do. I know this is not a very lively town, but Rockport's not bad at all. It's small, but a good place to live. Don't think I'd want to live anywhere else," Leon added.

After a short pause and another sip of wine, Kacey set her glass on the deck rail and leaned into the fragrant breeze. "I see why. You're a very lucky man."

"Lucky?" he repeated, questioning her remark. "I don't know if I'd use that word to describe me."

"Really, it's true," Kacey insisted. "Sounds like you have a very solid life here. You have a secure family business, you have a wonderful home and your parents are close by, too."

"Are yours?" he asked, voice low.

Kacey grew quiet, swallowed and then told Leon, "No. I'm an only child, like you, but my mom and dad divorced when I was ten. Now, she lives in Florida and my dad is in Seattle. I talk to them on holidays and birthdays, but we're not all that close."

"Sorry," Leon said. "I guess that's tough."

Kacey shrugged. "It's just the way things are. You have your own slice of paradise right here, and I have a tiny apartment in Harlem," she stated, tracing the angles of Leon's face, which glowed like hammered bronze in the candlelight. "This place is so beautiful and different from the rest of Rockport, especially the motel, which leaves a lot to be desired," she remarked, slowly twirling her wineglass, her attention on the water.

"Yeah, I guess the Seaside Suites is definitely not the best representative of Rockport."

"Amen to that," Kacey concurred. "After I checked into my room, I have to admit that I was beginning to regret coming here. It is so drab and depressing. And a bunch of rowdy boys use the parking lot next door to play basketball. The people in the room next to mine

pound on the walls if I turn up the volume on my TV."
She chuckled, and then added, "I wasn't feeling very
impressed with your city earlier tonight."

Leon grimaced. "I hate to think of you being unhappy
or depressed."

"Don't worry about me. I came here to work. I'll
manage just fine."

"I'm sure you will," Leon countered. "But I hope
you'll let me help make things a bit more comfortable
for you."

"You already have," Kacey admitted, as casually as
she could, tensing her fingers around the stem of her
glass and silently counting to ten. "Your invitation to
dinner came right on time. Got me out of the motel so
I could enjoy this wonderful view of the Gulf, and I'm
especially looking forward to the fabulous dinner you
promised."

Leon's eyes widened. "Yes, dinner! It's in the oven
heating up. Won't be long, I promise. In the meantime,
tell me more about yourself and your work. You strike
me as someone who has big plans and does not give up
very easily."

"Really? What do you base that on?" Kacey pressed,
surprised by Leon's comment and wanting to hear why
he'd said that.

"Oh, just the fact that you're launching your own line
of swimsuits is impressive enough. Not everyone can
do that."

"Well, it's something I've wanted to do for a long
time, and it feels great to finally be on the verge of
pulling it off."

Leon lifted his wineglass. "How about a toast to
SunKissed by Kacey?" he offered.

Kacey beamed her appreciation at Leon, grateful for his obvious desire to make sure her dream came off without a hitch. "I'll drink to that…and to a successful stay in Rockport," she added, finding the idea of working with Leon, and spending more personal time with him, very appealing.

"Definitely," Leon remarked as they clinked glasses, sipped and then locked eyes. "Kacey, I want you to know that I plan to do all I can to make sure your time here is well worth it. I know leaving New York to oversee the production of your swimsuit line was probably not something you wanted to do. But it will pay off, I promise. My first responsibility to you, and Leeman's, is to manufacture a product that meets your expectations, and I take that very seriously. However, I also feel responsible for your experience while you're in Rockport."

Kacey watched Leon closely, keenly aware of the double meaning in his words, feeling challenged by his admission that he planned to commit personal time to her outside of their working relationship.

"I want to make sure you leave my hometown with good memories," he added.

"Starting with tonight, I assume?" Kacey murmured, her voice drifting off into the wind.

"Absolutely," he replied, moving a step closer. "It started as soon as you accepted my invitation."

"Because I was desperate to be rescued from a pitiful excuse of a meal alone in my room."

"Exactly! I came to your rescue, so…I guess you have to call me your hero?" he taunted with a grin.

"My hero?" she quipped, letting Leon know that she

was happy to banter with him as they got to know each other.

"Absolutely," Leon countered. "As long as you're in Rockport, I plan to make sure you're never bored...or lonely again. That is, if you'll let me," he finished, his words thick with hope.

Kacey tensed to hear the tenderness in his promise, and knew he was tempting her to make a decision. Should she allow this personal connection to deepen? Had she already gone too far by coming to his home? Should she step back, clear her head and resolve to keep everything between them strictly business? Knowing that the prospect of having a romantic relationship with Leon was actually not that far-fetched, Kacey hesitated to speak. The guy was handsome. Smart. Obviously attracted to her. And she was definitely melting under his intense steel-gray gaze.

Why not go for it? she thought, her eyes tracing over his features as he waited for her to say something. So far, he had not offered to take her inside his house—which was fine with her. A friendly dinner outside on his patio and a quick ride back to the motel was the best way to handle their first encounter away from the office. Wasn't it?

However...I'll only be in town a short time. I might as well have an experience worth sharing with Linette, who always has exciting, outrageous things happen to her when she's working a photo shoot. This time, Kacey would have a juicy story of her own to dish when they went for drinks on a Friday happy hour.

"I just might take you up on that. I'd be happy to call you my hero," she jokingly confessed, looking forward to finding out what Leon had in mind. However, the pensive glimmer in his eyes told Kacey that he was dead serious about lavishing his hospitality on her and extending their relationship beyond its business borders. Fine, because she was more than ready for the grand Texas adventure he was offering.

And it's already started, she recognized, deciding that jumping all the way in was the best way to find out just how strong her attraction to Leon Archer was, and how dangerously close he'd come to capturing her heart.

When Leon leaned over and brushed his lips over Kacey's, the gesture did not surprise her, offend her or make her want to run away. When her tongue sprang to life and twined lazily with his, he opened his mouth wider to intensify the connection. Kacey felt her limbs go weak when his arms came up and encircled her. She sank against him, relaxing as if she'd been in his embrace many times before. When he snaked his hands down and clasped them together in the hollow of her back, she let him guide her to a deck post and brace her back against it. Sealed together, their lips and arms were so tightly locked that Kacey could hardly breathe. However, letting Leon go did not cross her mind as she held him in place and accepted the flurry of kisses that he placed on her cheeks, her neck, the hollow of her throat.

When they finally came up for air, Leon groaned, shifted to place his hip against the deck rail and sat sideways as he gazed at Kacey. "You're so beautiful, standing here with the candlelight behind you. I couldn't resist."

Kacey gave him a languid blink, recovering from their kiss, feeling buoyant, yet grounded in her decision to explore the explosive chemistry that was rapidly building between them.

"I could hold you, kiss you, forever," he murmured, reaching up to touch her chin with a finger.

"Not forever, I hope. And let me starve to death?" Kacey joked, desperate to defuse the awkward aftermath of that too serious, too soon, too damn delicious kiss!

With a jolt, Leon stood and gaped at the house. "Damn! The food! It's on its way. Wait. You sit down. I'll be right back." He dashed into the kitchen, which Kacey could see was right off the deck, leaving her laughing as he fled to the oven.

Within moments, Leon returned carrying a steaming casserole dish, the smell of pungent lasagna drifting out before him.

Seated at the table on the deck, they chatted easily over a dinner of the best lasagna Kacey had ever eaten, paired with a tangy Italian salad, cheesy garlic bread and the local red wine that rivaled any produced in California.

After the meal, Leon stood up and picked up his plate. Kacey quickly assisted in clearing the table.

"Come on inside," he invited, starting toward the house. "I can use your help cleaning up."

"Oh, yeah?" Kacey quipped. "So that's the only reason you're inviting me inside?"

Turning to face her, he grinned. "No, of course not. I'd love to show you the rest of the house. You don't have to leave right away, do you?"

As Kacey stared at Leon, her mind was flooded with all the reasons she should tell him, *I really can't stay long. I need to get back to the motel and far away from temptation*. However, her legs paid no attention to such rational thinking as she followed him inside.

Leon's once-modest ranch house had been renovated into a surprisingly open floor plan with few walls to obscure its dramatic views of the Gulf. Sleek modern furnishings, contemporary art and walls painted in subdued shades of tan and gray welcomed Kacey, who saw that Leon's sophisticated décor compared favorably with any cushy Manhattan penthouse. Brushed nickel and glass tables, sleek black and white marble statues on mirrored pedestals and oversized rugs in geometric patterns completed the updated interior that felt open and airy, yet comfortably intimate. His spacious bedroom was done in an African safari theme, with gorgeous prints of exotic animals on the walls and luxurious bedding that added to the wildly exotic theme.

After the tour of the house, they did the dishes and then settled at the kitchen bar, more glasses of wine in hand. At Leon's urging, Kacey gave him a quick overview of what growing up in the bustling community of Harlem had been like, and then he described his small town upbringing in Rockport, where his family's roots went back four generations.

They communicated in an easy, friendly way that made all of Kacey's earlier apprehension vanish. All she wanted at that moment was to stay there with Leon and delve deeper into the life of this man who was pushing all her buttons with such grace and ease.

Chapter 9

For five minutes straight, Nona focused on the clock above her kitchen sink, wondering what Leon was doing. Certainly, he was at home by now, alone, and hopefully enjoying the lasagna she'd baked and delivered to his house—just as his mother would have done.

After rinsing the single plate, glass and fork Nona had used for her own dinner of spaghetti and meatballs, she placed the dishes in the drying rack and hung her towel on its bar, her thoughts locked on Leon in a particularly insistent way.

She was proud of herself for accepting his mother's request to look after the plants and her fish—things Mrs. Archer cared deeply about. And that certainly included her son, didn't it? The trust Mrs. Archer placed in Nona made her heart swell with satisfaction.

Knowing that Leon loved his mom's lasagna, Nona

had taken great pains to hone the family recipe, just as she worked on honing her relationship with Mrs. Archer, who treated Nona like a daughter.

"And one day, *daughter-in-law*," she murmured, a wave of desire sweeping through her body. She had known Leon almost all her life. She'd lost her virginity to him at Barker's Bend when she was sixteen years old, and was convinced that she and Leon were destined to be together. However, their ultimate union was taking longer than Nona had ever expected it would and she was growing impatient. For so many years she had stood on the sidelines, watching while Leon raced from one disastrous romantic relationship to another. His frantic desire to play the local playboy was starting to wear on her nerves. How much longer could she remain in the shadows, steadfastly supportive of him, offering an ear primed to listen to his troubles as each of his misguided relationships fell by the wayside?

Leon's getting older every day. I am, too. He needs to get his act together and stop playing the field. Those days are about to be over for him. It's time he settled down, got married and started his family, she reassured herself. And since he was at that point in his life, wasn't she the woman he ought to turn to? Didn't she understand him better than anyone? Didn't she have his parents' blessing as the hometown girl who'd grown up with him and knew what made him tick? Though they hadn't had sex since they were in high school, she knew what pleased Leon sexually, and was more than ready to prove it.

It's just a matter of time, Nona told herself, her ever-recurring fantasy of living with Leon in his fantastic house on the beach rising up to swamp her mind. Her favorite part of the fantasy was imagining how beautiful their children would be, with her smooth, light brown skin and his startling gray eyes. The image made her shiver with anticipation and delight.

Overwhelmed by a need to hear his voice, Nona dried her hands on a towel and reached for the green plastic phone on her wall. Feeling smugly possessive, she punched in Leon's number, roused by the delicious quiver of longing that contracted the walls of her dormant womanhood.

"Hello?" Leon answered, irritated to be interrupted just when things between Kacey and him were beginning to warm up. He'd made the right move, inviting her to dinner, and he'd been on target about her interest in getting together with him outside the office, too.

I damn sure know how to read a woman, he thought smugly, smothering a smile and looking forward to spending as much time as he could with Kacey. However, the prospect of her leaving Rockport hung like a dark shadow in the back of Leon's mind. He'd have to deal with that eventually, but for now, he planned to show her a good time and enjoy her company, proving to her that his hometown could be as good a place, or better, than New York City. Oh, yes, and he planned to produce a swimsuit line that would bring her rave reviews.

"How was it?" Nona asked Leon, pressing her voice through the line and forcing his attention back to the phone call.

"What are you calling about?" Leon asked, adopting a cool, businesslike tone to let Nona know that he was not up for one of her rambling treks back into ancient history. When she was lonely, depressed or had drunk too much brandy, she called—mumbling on and on about their high school days until she ran out of steam. Though he had been involved with her when he was a teenager, he now thought of her more like a sister, one on whom he could never turn his back. But all that stuff she liked to talk about was just a bunch of dusty memories, better off forgotten. They'd both moved on since then. At least he had. He wasn't so sure about Nona. However, one thing was clear: he had to stop accommodating her pity parties, even though he hated to cut her off. She always made him feel obligated to listen, and was quick to remind him that his mom and hers had been best friends forever.

"Duh! How was the lasagna that I made for you?" Nona shot back. "Was it as good as your mom's?"

Leon stilled, his mind processing what Nona was telling him, and not liking what he'd heard. "Could you clarify that?" he asked, shrugging at Kacey while mouthing the words, *Nona—something about an order,* wanting to keep her out of this mess. As much as he genuinely liked and trusted his longtime friend, at times Nona could be a pain in the ass. The last thing he needed was a dose of her overprotective mothering to spoil the romantic mood he was attempting to create with Kacey.

"Oh, it was your mom's suggestion," Nona was saying. "She gave me her keys and asked me to kinda keep an eye on her plants and feed her fish while she and Mr. Archer were away."

"Oh, now I understand," Leon stated, forcing a calm vibe into his carefully chosen words. *And you thought that included feeding me?* he silently fumed, irritated as hell that Nona would assume she had the right to use the key he had given to his mother to do what she did.

"There's no need for that," he said, desperate to sound as if he and Nona were talking about work.

"Oh, I know. But it would make your mom happy to know that I'm making sure you eat well. So I made the lasagna and brought it over this afternoon while you were at your meeting."

"I wish you had said something to me about this at the office," Leon quipped. Damn! He loved his mother but he didn't like the way she doted on Nona. His mom might want Nona James for a daughter-in-law, but Leon sure as hell had no intention of ever making good on that far-fetched wish.

"No need. I just hope it was good," Nona replied in a whispery voice.

"It was," he said, his mind fishing for the perfect way to end Nona's interruption. A long pause, and then Leon tossed out the zinger that he knew would bring silence to the other end of the line. "You know, I'm sitting here talking to *Kacey* about that right now," he launched, eager to send Nona the message that he was not alone and he did not have time to talk.

"Oh? Kacey Parker is there?" Nona snapped, sounding disappointed.

"Right," Leon answered.

"Uh, then I guess you can't talk, huh?"

"Right again."

"Okay, then. I'll see you at the office tomorrow," Nona finished in a dispirited murmur.

"Yes. We'll finish discussing this at the office," Leon said, quickly ending the call.

"Is everything okay?" Kacey asked, once Leon had clicked off.

Composing his expression, he erased the frown

creasing his brow and took a deep breath, giving Kacey a look that let her know nothing urgent was going on. He certainly didn't want Kacey to know that Nona was calling about some stupid prank she'd pulled. A prank that did not please him at all.

"Oh, nothing important. Nona had a question about a work order." He hated to lie about something as inconsequential as a dish of lasagna, but Nona's call left him worried. She was treading too close to his personal life, and it had to stop. But how could he push back without offending her? How could he convince Nona that she'd overstepped her boundaries, when his parents were always treating her as if she were a permanent fixture in the family? He'd told his mom and dad time and time again that he had no intention of ever marrying Nona, but they paid no attention, stuck on the fact that Nona James was the hometown girl he was destined to settle down with—the woman who would stand by him and help him run the family business, just as his mother had done with his father.

They just don't understand, Leon silently complained, wondering what they would think and how they would react if he brought a sophisticated woman like Kacey Parker home to meet them.

Nona slung herself into the frayed red recliner that faced her ash-filled fireplace, stretched out her legs and squeezed back tears. *Why is Leon wasting his time with that citified designer?* she silently asked herself, her teeth clamped together tightly in despair. *She might be pretty, but she's an outsider who will never fit in here. Leon needs me. I need him. We understand each other.*

Chapter 10

Kacey's second day in Rockport started with an early morning phone call. The ringing sound brought a smile to her lips as she reached across her bed to answer. *Leon,* was her first thought, prompting vivid images of their evening together. Their romantic dinner on the deck. The quiet way they had talked about their careers and their lives over wine in his kitchen. The ride back to the motel with the convertible top down and soft jazz playing in the car. And then, the good-night kiss that had created a connection that left her sizzling with desire and her nipples as hard as tiny pebbles on the beach.

Grabbing the phone, Kacey whispered a sexy hello, only to have her fantasy shattered when she heard Ariana Mendio's voice barking a too-loud greeting over the line.

"Oh, hi, Ariana," Kacey said, sitting up to brace her

back against the headboard and push visions of Leon's lean hard body tangled among animal print sheets on his king-size bed from her mind. Hoping to sound alert and very much on top of things, she strengthened her voice when she commented, "You're on the job early, huh?"

"Early?" Ariana threw out. "It's seven-thirty in New York."

Kacey looked at the clock. "And six-thirty here."

"Ah, so it is," Arian admitted, as if it really didn't matter. "I need an update on everything. Hadley wants daily reports. I'll be calling every day…early. Before you get into your day."

"Well, you've certainly done that," Kacey commented, a tad irritated to learn how closely Hadley planned to track her activity. He'd never done that before. But she shouldn't be surprised. He was taking a great risk in green-lighting her line and she knew he expected nothing less than perfect results.

"What do you want to know first?" Kacey inquired, deciding it would be best to let Ariana ask for what she wanted rather than try to relate every detail of her time at Archer Industries so far.

"Well, how did your first encounter with Archer go? You and the old man getting along?"

A wry chuckle flew from Kacey's lips, erasing her annoyance with Ariana's early-morning phone call. "I haven't even met Mr. Archer," Kacey informed her coworker.

"What? Why not?" Ariana's voice rose one octave below a screech.

"Because he's in Africa," Kacey coolly teased.

"Africa? What's going on?"

"Calm down," Kacey advised, proceeding to tell Ariana about the sudden change in ownership at Archer and that Leon Archer Jr. was now in charge.

"Really? I'm surprised that Leon Sr. stepped down. He didn't seem like the type who would ever let go."

"Well, there comes a time for change in every situation," Kacey commented, thinking about how quickly her feelings for Leon had morphed into something she was still trying to figure out. "Guess it was my lucky day to arrive when change came to this place."

"So, what's young Mr. Archer like?" Ariana asked.

Sexy. Magnetic. Intriguing, Kacey wanted to say, still basking in the afterglow of their evening together. *A tall, brown tower of a man who is creeping under my skin and into my heart.*

However, instead of confessing her fast-growing attraction to Leon, she hastily composed a more acceptable response. "He's very helpful. Dedicated to making our line a smashing success, and completely confident that we'll bring SunKissed in on time and on budget."

"That's all we care about," Ariana blithely agreed. "Hadley gave me your revised projections. Everything looks good. However, there's not a second to waste. I'm starting the promotional campaign today. I have to line up models for the test photo shoot and book the photographer. When will the samples arrive?"

"Oh, about that," Kacey stammered, biting her bottom lip as she studied the seashells in the base of her bedside lamp, concerned. She had not informed Hadley about her decision to make the samples in her size, and it was too late to revise her plan. Truett had already adjusted the patterns and they planned to start cutting today.

"I decided to change things a bit," Kacey began. "I'm

going to shoot the samples here in Rockport. I called Linette…she can fly in from LA to do it."

"Kacey," Ariana responded in a throaty growl that conveyed her obvious displeasure. "That's not going to work. No, no, no. Hadley will never agree to fly all the models to Texas just for the test-shoot. What are you thinking? You know how closely he's monitoring the money. We can't blow a bundle on airfare and all the expense to do that, please. Just FedEx the samples to me when they're ready."

"Don't worry, Ariana. I don't want the models to come to Texas. My plan won't increase the budget. In fact, it'll reduce it."

"How? Explain, please."

"I'm having the samples made to fit *me*…and I'll be the model that Linette can shoot. Okay?" The silence that stretched between Texas and New York let Kacey know she'd dropped a bombshell that was about to explode.

"Crazy!"

"No, it's not. I can save the company time and money," she defended, eager to defuse the situation and keep Ariana on her side. "This would only be for the manufacturer's samples, just to see how the colors and styles photograph. When we get to the final takes for the website and the brochures, we'll use the models, and we can shoot the catalog pics in the studio in New York. Just as we always do, okay?"

"Well, maybe," Ariana hedged, not sounding fully convinced. "You know, I really don't care if you want to model your swimsuits. What I want is for you to stay on target as far as final delivery is concerned."

Mentally clicking through her tightly arranged

schedule, Kacey reviewed her time frame with Ariana. "The patterns have been adjusted. All the fabric is in, even the Naughty Net should arrive tomorrow."

"I hope so, since the see-through-when-wet piece is a featured style."

"If all goes well, I think we can have everything finalized and start full production sooner than I'd hoped."

"All right," Ariana agreed. "I'll be checking in every day. I'm counting on you to deliver, Kacey. Don't let me down."

"I won't," Kacey promised, sensing the weight of her responsibilities more than ever.

Flinging back the bed sheet, she went into the bathroom to take a shower and get ready for the day. Standing under the stream of warm water, she rotated her head from side to side, loosening the tension that had gathered in her neck during her exchange with Ariana, whose phone call had put Kacey on notice: there was a lot to accomplish in a very short time frame, and she didn't dare stray off course. Kacey had come to Rockport with only one desire—to see her swimsuit line to completion. But could she deny that Leon Archer was quickly rearranging her list of priorities and it didn't bother Kacey in the least?

Dressed in black raw linen slacks, a deep-cuffed white silk shirt and gladiator sandals with just enough heel to increase her height without making her look overdressed for the office, Kacey sat down at her desk. However, immediately after settling into her cubicle at Archer Industries, everything went dark, plunging the factory into silence. The chatter of employees immediately dropped off. The buzz of ringing telephones died and the hum of machinery ground to a halt. Though startled by the blackout, Kacey didn't panic. She'd experienced blackouts, brownouts and unexpected electrical blips many times in the city, and knew that, usually, the problem was resolved very quickly. However, the prospect of any delay in the work she planned to accomplish today made her nervously tap her fingers on the arm of her chair as she waited for the lights to come back on. The last thing she needed was a power failure to throw her off schedule, searing her pledge to Ariana more deeply into her mind.

From out in the corridor, Kacey heard Leon reassuring his staff that everything was under control. "The power company is here," he was saying. "They'll get everything up and running as soon as possible. No need to panic. Just stay where you are."

Kacey smiled to herself. He sounded very calm, in control and steady, creating a sense of safety that was comforting. No wonder his employees were so loyal to him.

Leon stuck his head into Kacey's workspace and handed her a flashlight. Looking up at him she felt her heart lurch when his seductive gray eyes locked on hers, sending her whirling back in time—to the night before as they stood together on the candlelit deck, testing each other's will to deny the attraction that was clearly binding them together.

The ring of Leon's cell phone shattered her reminiscence, but she kept her eyes trained on him as he answered.

"Any idea how long we'll be down?" he asked his caller.

Kacey raised a brow and waited until he'd finished before asking him the same thing.

"Longer than I'd hoped," Leon told her, scowling with regret. He squinted into the light that Kacey leveled on his face. "That was the power company. The transmitter behind the plant exploded. Has to be replaced."

"How long will that take?"

"Most of the day," Leon replied, clearly unhappy about the situation. "Which means I have to shut down the plant and send everybody home."

"What about backup generators?" Lacey inquired, searching for a way to keep going. In New York, many private residences and companies maintained a second source of power for situations like this.

"We do have several I could fire up, however, they'd only keep the ceiling lights and air conditioners going. Not strong enough to run industrial machinery for very long."

Kacey glumly nodded her understanding, swallowing the unease that swept through her at this unexpected delay.

"Don't look so anxious," Leon reassured her, stepping deeper into her cubicle. "I know you're worried about the schedule, but we can make up for today and still meet your deadline—I promise."

Within the circle of light coming from her flashlight, Kacey watched as Leon extended his hand toward her, as if trying to touch her arm in reassurance. She surprised herself by stepping closer, eager for his overture of comfort, yet feeling somewhat ashamed of herself for allowing him to see how much she wanted to feel his hands on her once again.

In the dim room, their bodies swayed together, as if

drawn like magnets toward wills of steel. Leon touched Kacey on the shoulder, and then moved his hand up to her cheek, where he slid his thumb along her chin. "If we were anyplace other than here at the plant, I'd switch off this flashlight and kiss the hell out of you."

His remark sent a flare of arousal straight into Kacey's core, heating her up and making her want to feel more than his hands on her body. Surrounded by darkness, his sensuous remark slid into her heart and created a quirky mix of danger and desire that she had never felt before. Knowing his bold declaration required a bold comeback, she jumped right in to deliver.

"If we were anyplace other than here at the plant, I just might let you," she stated, fully aware of what might happen and totally at ease with the hardness of his manhood when it suddenly pressed against her leg.

Leon slowly eased his hand down the side of her neck and onto her shoulder, which he squeezed in reassurance before inching closer. "Then maybe we need to go someplace else?" he huskily suggested.

"Like where?" she teased, excited by the idea of tumbling totally into this blinding flash of desire that threatened to consume her.

"Several places come to mind, but let me think this over."

"Go on…. I'm game."

"Okay, since we can't work today, how does a tour of my hometown sound?"

"Might be nice," she confessed, truly interested in seeing more of the area.

"Okay. Stay put. I'll be right back," he said, beaming his flashlight out into the hallway. "I have to release everyone for the rest of the day and secure the plant. Is your cell phone on?" he inquired, breaking the tension that wired the room like an unseen electrical grid.

Shining her flashlight onto her purse, Kacey located her cell phone and pressed it on. "It is now," she said.

"Good, what's your number?" he asked, punching it into his phone as she rattled it off. "All set. I'll call you from outside as soon as I get everything under control. Keep your phone handy." Then he disappeared into the dark corridor, his footsteps echoing through the building, leaving Kacey staring after him.

"I am crazy as hell," she admonished herself, swallowing the spurt of longing that had risen in her throat and engulfed her during their brief encounter. *I'll be right here when you come back, and hopefully, after my hometown tour, we can pick up where we left off, and in a more private location, too.*

Standing alone in the dark, Kacey prayed she was not making a huge mistake by allowing Leon to get so personal with her. But she couldn't help herself. She was mesmerized by his sensual personality, entranced by his gentleness, already addicted to his kisses and far too eager to explore the sexual tension that jumped to life the moment their eyes met.

However, as much as she wanted Leon Archer as a man, she still had business to take care of. With the production of her line at stake, any delay was unacceptable. But all she really *could* do was trust Leon and work with him to make up for lost time.

Placing the flashlight on her desk, Kacey sank into her chair, her heart thudding in question. As irritated as she was about the blackout, she had to admit that she wanted to be alone with Leon, to let him touch her in places that yearned to feel his fingertips, his lips, his hands. What she longed for was a chance to relive the shivers of delight that had swept through her when he'd held her close last night.

"What's wrong with me?" she fretted, unnerved by the conflicting emotions assaulting her in the dark. Desperate for a reality check, she impulsively pressed Linette's phone number into her cell, eager to spill all to her girlfriend and get her take on what had transpired since her arrival in Rockport. However, after punching in the number, Kacey disconnected the call after the first ring. It was early morning on the West Coast. Linette, who was always groggy in the morning, would be furious with her for calling at the crack of dawn.

Setting her phone aside, Kacey tried to relax, though she felt as if she were about to explode. What she needed was a way to release all this pent-up energy and unfulfilled desire. What she needed was for Leon Archer to come back and finish what he'd started.

Chapter 11

Nona moved quietly down the corridor toward Kacey's cubicle, shining her flashlight along the carpeted floor. Having decided that sticking close to the woman whom Leon had obviously targeted as his next romantic conquest would be the best way to stay on top of whatever was going on, Nona was on a mission. She'd play the cooperative coworker, gain the designer's trust and, hopefully, get Kacey to open up about whatever was going on between her and Leon. Having been through too many of Leon's casual flirtations to count, Nona had no doubt that this lopsided romance would be short-lived because those two had absolutely nothing in common.

"You okay in there?" Nona asked, stepping into Kacey's cubicle and shining her light all around.

"Oh! Yes. Hello, Nona," Kacey replied, blinking into the sudden beam that illuminated the room.

"Just thought I'd check," Nona offered, settling against the doorframe, her eyes focused on Kacey. "I was worried about you, being unfamiliar with the plant and all."

"Thanks for your concern. It is kinda creepy sitting here in the dark," Kacey replied in a voice that let Nona know she was glad to have some company.

"I just spoke to Leon. He told me to tell you it'll be empty around here real soon. Want me to walk out with you?"

"No, but thanks. Leon asked me to wait here for him," Kacey replied. "But I appreciate your offer. I just hope this power outage will be resolved by tomorrow."

"Oh, probably so," Nona replied casually. Not about to be dismissed so easily, Nona sat down across from Kacey, ready for business. She was still seething over the fact that this woman had shared the meal she'd prepared especially for Leon. No need to play hide-and-seek with her. "How'd things go last night?" Nona inquired, tilting her head to one side and allowing an explosion of natural curls to cover one eye.

"Last night? Uh…okay, I guess. The motel was kind of noisy and that apartment complex next door is…"

"I wasn't referring to the Seaside Suites," Nona interrupted coolly. "I mean with you and Leon…at his house." Nona bit back the smile that threatened to erupt at the stunned expression that claimed Kacey's features. Clearly, she was rattling the designer, and that was exactly what she'd hoped to do.

"Oh, right. Leon and I had a very nice time," Kacey replied. "I was glad that he rescued me from a meal of weak tea and crackers at the motel. We were outside on the deck and enjoyed the night breeze off the water. I loved his house. He has a very beautiful home."

"I know," Nona deadpanned. "I've been there hundreds of times." A short pause before she said, "And how was the lasagna?" Nona let the slightest wrinkle of a self-satisfied grin tug her upper lip when Kacey's jaw went slack in surprise. *You might be a fancy designer, and think you know so much but you don't know anything at all,* she mused, crossing her arms as she took in Kacey's reaction.

"He told you what we had to eat, too?" Kacey remarked, shifting to one side, clearly uneasy over Nona's knowledge of such details. "The lasagna was delicious. The best I've ever had, I think."

"Thanks. I appreciate that. Guess I've finally perfected Mrs. Archer's recipe. Been working at it for a while."

"What? You mean, *you* made the lasagna?" Kacey snapped forward, squinting at Nona in the beam of light trained on her face.

"I sure did. Didn't Leon tell you I made dinner for him?"

"No, he didn't." Kacey's words were tinged with ice.

"Must have slipped his mind," Nona commented coolly. Slumping back in her chair, she focused on a far wall, allowing memories to surge forward and fill her mind. "When Leon and I were younger, his mother used to invite me over to his house on Friday nights to give me cooking lessons. You see, my mom died when I was twelve years old and I was left with the job of cooking for my sister and my dad. Mrs. Archer taught me how to cook and loved giving me tips on what Leon liked best. Now, I guess he can't tell the difference between my food and his mom's. Isn't that just like a man?"

Kacey narrowed her eyes at Nona and silently counted to ten, unsure about how she ought to react to this rather odd revelation. Obviously, Nona was taking great pleasure in flaunting her longstanding friendship with Leon. But why? What was this woman after?

"Uh, yeah. I guess most men are like that," Kacey finally managed, curious to know more about Nona James. She hesitated, drew in a silent breath and then boldly plunged ahead. If Nona wanted to shift the conversation into overshare mode, Kacey certainly wasn't going to stop her. Why not pump this obvious resource on Leon Archer and get all the information she could? Since Nona and Leon shared a history that had deep roots, Kacey planned to dig for gold.

"So, you and Leon used to be *together?* Romantically?" she queried venturing as politely as possible into the subject she had avoided so far.

"Together?" Nona shot back with a knowing chuckle. "Absolutely. We were inseparable all through high school and even for a while after he went off to college in Dallas. That's the only time we've ever actually been apart. He spent four long years at SMU," Nona said, her voice drifting out on a sigh, as if recalling a happier time. "But I stayed right here in Rockport. I was here when he came home," she stated, jutting out her chin. "I'll never leave Rockport. I love this town, and everybody in it," she added, with a determined clench of her jaw.

Kacey stared at Nona, both intrigued and concerned. The woman seemed transfixed, as if she'd entered a world of her own and had no idea that Kacey was even in the room. The transformation was unsettling, making Kacey wonder about Nona James's emotional state. Was she as loopy as she appeared to be or was she putting on an act to impress Kacey? Obviously, Nona wanted Kacey to know that she was close to Leon, but how close was she? Kacey wondered.

The lights flickered, dimmed and then suddenly went out again, signaling the continuation of the blackout. Nona shook her head as if to clear away the fog and gave Kacey a crooked half smile. "Time to get out of here. See you tomorrow…I hope," she said with wry humor. Then she stood and left the room.

Kacey swiveled back and forth in her chair, shaking her head in amazement. Why hadn't Leon told her that Nona had prepared their dinner? What exactly was their relationship all about, she wondered, glancing up when Leon arrived.

"Everything okay?" he asked as he set his flashlight on the edge of Kacey's desk and moved toward her.

"I'm fine," she replied, pushing Nona out of her mind. The last thing she wanted to do right then was start a conversation about his operations manager, who was obviously stuck in the past. What she craved was to pick up where they'd left off, to be cocooned once again in Leon's arms. Having lost her battle of romantic restraint, she was clearly ready to surrender.

"All right, then. Nothing more we can do here," Leon stated. "The power company is on the job. So let's go see what Rockport is all about."

"I'm more than ready," Kacey said, relieved to get out of the dark and eager to spend the day with Leon.

Circling her desk, she approached him, easing into the hazy beam of yellow light that cut the room in half.

"However, the building *is* empty," he informed her in a hushed voice, as if reading her mind.

"And?" she prompted, anticipating the move she so desperately craved and hoped he'd make.

"So that means nobody is around to interrupt."

"Interrupt what?" she taunted, watching him through hooded eyes, her heart thumping crazily in her chest, her body sizzling with unmet needs that he'd awakened the night before.

"This," he whispered, opening his arms to Kacey, who slipped into them and let him hold her in a loose embrace. She marveled at how easily she'd tossed aside her reservations about exploring a blazing-hot romance with a man she would probably never see again once her mission here was completed. However, this might be just what she needed to put some spice in her life and pass the time while she was stuck in Rockport.

Anyway, she had never felt anything like this with Jamal. *And I never will,* she realized, the clarity of her uncomplicated, routine love life blazing white and bright in her mind. For too long, she'd been willing to settle for predictable sex with a predictable man who did not stir her soul, ignite her heart or slick her tunnel of love like an oil well on fire. She'd submerged her true needs to accommodate a situation that had been convenient, but that had definitely run its course. Now it was time for her to explore the hidden side of her heart.

"Where were we before I left you all alone in the dark?" he asked, placing two fingers under Kacey's chin.

"Right about here," Kacey replied, pressing her body

to his, not about to erect any barriers that would interfere with this raw, sexual awakening that he'd stirred inside her. Though shocked by the intensity of her need to be near him, she loved the sensation of isolation and privacy that descended on her as she stood in his arms.

The shower of slow kisses that he traced from her forehead to her temple and over her cheeks, left her silently panting and choked with desire. When he moved his sweet assault down the side of her neck, she responded to his feather-light touches with a low, pleasure-filled groan that let him know he was on the right track. Between a series of soft, sexy pecks that he placed on all her exposed skin, his hands crept downward—moving along her spine until they clasped her buttocks in a firm caress and crushed her soft womanhood into his rigid sex, fusing them together like two pattern pieces perfectly joined at the seam.

Succumbing to his tantalizing move, Kacey opened her mouth and took his tongue deep into her throat, letting his languid thrusts satisfy a thirst for Leon that she felt might never be quenched. As the dizzying current of attraction raced through her veins, Kacey knew Leon Archer had awakened a flame of desire that would not be easily extinguished, a white-hot heat that would have to burn itself out. As his hands roamed her body and her love tunnel pulsed to the beat of her heart, she silently questioned what was happening to her.

Am I head over hells in lust with this man, or head over heels in love?

Chapter 12

"I can see for miles!" Kacey exclaimed, her splayed fingers shading her eyes against the sun. Leaning forward, she peered through the open lighthouse window high above the water and filled her lungs with salty Gulf Coast air, slowly exhaling as she savored the exhilarating sense of floating high in the blue Texas sky.

"That's an old coastal fort over there," Leon said, coming up behind her to point toward a rugged stone building farther down the coastline that had gaping holes in its walls. "According to old-timers who've lived here for generations, the pirate Jean Lafitte and his band of thieves used to hide out in that fort between raids on ships entering the Gulf."

"Really?" Kacey remarked, assessing the mysterious structure more closely. "It looks so small," she added, turning her head ever so slightly, enjoying the slight brush of Leon's breath on her temple.

"Yes, it does look small from here. But if you get closer, you'll see that it's pretty spacious," Leon informed her.

"Big enough to hold all the pirates and their loot," Kacey joked, savoring the spectacular coastal view from atop the restored lighthouse.

"Exactly. We'll go over next time we have a day when we can goof off," Leon decided, linking his arm through hers to guide her to the other side of the tower to check out a different view of the landscape.

"Another day to goof off?" Kacey repeated, giving Leon a skeptical look. "We can't afford to lose any more time. Today…okay, I'll give you this one because of the unexpected power failure. But from now on, I don't plan to do any more sightseeing. I came here to work, not play tourist on vacation."

"Relax," Leon told her. He clucked his tongue, as if admonishing Kacey for taking her assignment too seriously. "You're way too tense. Forget about your job for today. We'll get everything done, and on schedule, too. Trust me. You have nothing to worry about."

His offhand remark made Kacey's temper flare. What was it with Leon and his cool, relaxed attitude? Maybe that's the way folks operated in Rockport, Texas, but in New York, staying on top of—or even ahead of— schedules was vital. However, she had to trust Leon to be good for his word, and so far, he'd kept his promise to show Kacey a side of Rockport that would impress and intrigue her.

After leaving Archer Industries, their first stop had been the historic Fulton Mansion, a beautifully restored

Victorian house located in the resort area of Rockport-Fulton. With its mansard roof and ornate trim, interior gas lighting, flush toilets and other refinements it was one of the most progressive and luxurious homes built in 1877. As Kacey walked through the restored home and its exquisite gardens, she got a glimpse into the lifestyle of an affluent family in early Texas, giving her a new appreciation for the small coastal town and the early settlers who'd chosen to live there.

After leaving the mansion, they ate homemade doughnuts and drank strong coffee at a quaint café built to resemble a true Texas log cabin. The display case at the café offered more information of coastal life in years past.

Next, they drove to Texas's smallest state park: the Port Isabel Lighthouse Historical Park, where they climbed to the top of the beacon-lit tower, which had been destroyed during the Civil War and fully restored in 2000. As the only lighthouse in Texas open to the public, they took on the challenge and climbed all eighty-two feet of the interior spiral staircase to enjoy panoramic views of Laguna Madre and South Padre Island. The trip had been well worth the minor exertion required to reach the top, where fifteen huge lamps and twenty-one reflectors remained mounted and ready for use.

"Now, how about lunch?" Leon ventured as they headed down the spiral staircase that would take them back down to earth.

"Sounds good. I'm starving. What do you suggest?" Kacey asked, content to leave all the decisions up to Leon, who seemed to be enjoying their excursion even more than she was. With each stop they'd made, Kacey had been impressed by the facts and stories that Leon tossed out about his hometown's past, both entertaining and educating her. He told her about his grandfather's decision to come to Texas from Mississippi and how he'd built a small textile factory from bricks made by hand. He had encouraged many of his friends and relatives to move west and work for him, and that among those who came were Nona James's ancestors, who had been friends with the Archers back in Mississippi.

Hanging out with Leon was fun and relaxing. It had been a long time since she'd felt so alive and fully engaged in something so different. Soaking up the past of Leon's hometown filled Kacey with an intense admiration for him and his family. But who was Leon Archer Jr., really? And why was he so obviously romancing her? Simply to prove that he could, or because he truly had growing feelings for her?

Kacey pondered these questions as she descended the stairs, one hand on Leon's shoulder to steady herself. He felt solid and secure, as if he were a man she could trust to be honest with her. So far, she had not brought up the subject of Nona's strange conversation. But if she did, could she trust Leon to tell her the truth? She was still puzzled about the woman who seemed so deeply embedded in his life.

"Only one choice," Leon was saying, bringing Kacey out of her mental musings. "You have to have Buddy Boy's Barbecue for lunch. No one comes to Rockport without eating at Buddy's."

"I'm game," Kacey agreed, looking forward to some real Texas barbecue and all the trimmings.

Leon chose a booth at the back of the restaurant, where it was quiet, secluded and far from the noisy lunch crowd hanging around the bar. As soon as they were served, he laughed at Kacey's reaction to the oversized platter of ribs, chicken and sausage that the waiter placed on the table, accompanied by separate bowls of fries, coleslaw and beans.

"My God! This is enough for a family of four!" she exclaimed, staring at the oval plate mounded with meat.

Leon laughed in understanding. "Yep. Buddy believes in giving his customers their money's worth."

"You were right," Kacey agreed. "Thankfully, we decided to split one order of meat."

"Hey, there are plenty of folks in here who could polish off that platter and then ask for seconds."

"Well, I doubt I'll make a dent in my half."

"Speak for yourself," Leon tossed back, picking up a rib.

Shaking her head in wonder, Kacey simply watched as Leon cleaned a bone with one bite and then wiped his fingers on a paper napkin and grinned.

"That's how we eat ribs in these parts," he said with a wink, picking up another rib, which he held up to Kacey's lips. "Go ahead. Your turn. You gotta clean the bone in one bite," he challenged, a smirk on his face,

Kacey hesitated, gave him a challenging wink and then leaned over. Quickly, she ran her tongue over one side of the rib bone, allowing her tongue to graze Leon's fingers in the process. A flash of heat shot into Leon's stomach and hit him in the groin when she slid her lips over his fingers and clamped them down in a hard pucker that held his hand in place. Without hesitation, Kacey drew his fingers fully into her mouth, using her tongue to tease his hold on the spicy bone as she removed every shred of meat. He froze, eyes riveted on her as she sucked the bone, sucked his index finger hard, and then licked his thumb, stirring the pot of simmering need that was rapidly building in his groin.

Giggling in satisfaction, Kacey finally opened her mouth and released Leon's fingers, as well as the bone, which was totally cleaned of meat.

"That was absolutely delicious!" she exclaimed, rolling her eyes in satisfaction. "How'd I do?"

"Girl, you are too much," Leon laughed, settling back in his seat. With deliberate calmness, he let his eyes linger on Kacey's face, as if trying to memorize her features.

"I'll let you call yourself an adopted Texan, now."

"Gee, thanks. This sure is good."

"My fingers or the 'cue?"

"Both," she replied, giving him a sassy smile.

"Glad you liked them," Leon responded, picking up his fork to dig into his bowl of beans.

Kacey tasted her beans and groaned. "Damn, these are good. You sure called it right," she said, dabbing a French fry into a pool of ketchup.

"I try," Leon replied, knowing he'd called it right with Kacey Parker, too. *If she can suck my fingers like that, just think what she could do to other parts of my body* he mused, knowing just where he planned to take her after lunch.

Chapter 13

"How about a walk on the beach to burn off those ribs?" Leon suggested after they were back in his Corvette, cruising down Main Street with the top down. The warm April sun hit Kacey's face and added to her sense of contentment. After such a heavy meal in the middle of the day, a walk on the beach sounded like a plan.

"I'd love to...but not dressed like this," she remarked, touching the collar of her silk shirt.

"No problem, I can swing by the Seaside so you can change, okay?"

"Okay," Kacey replied, not wanting this free time with Leon to end, because tomorrow it was back to business. There'd be no more days like this, so she might as well take advantage of the situation and enjoy what was left of her rare chance to goof off.

After Leon parked in front of the motel, Kacey got

out and headed inside to change, leaving him sitting in his car as he watched her walk away. His eyes ran the length of her back and lingered on her round tight booty. He could just imagine how she would look naked, in his bed, her brown curls spread out on a pillow, her legs spread open wide and begging him to enter, her generous breasts plump and round, ready to be fondled. His runaway thoughts brought on an arousal that almost made him gasp. At that moment he had only one desire, to make love to Kacey Parker. But would their relationship ever evolve to that point? Was he just teasing himself with the idea of possessing her completely? Or was he inching his way into her heart?

There's only one way to find out. Test her, he decided, fantasizing about holding Kacey naked in his arms, her lips clamped tightly over his as they began the passion-filled journey he'd been searching for so long.

Kacey raced into her room, stripped off her good slacks, her silk blouse and her midheel sandals. She laid out a pair of capris and a T-shirt on the bed—perfect for her walk on the beach. Moving past the mirror, she paused, taking in her semi-nude reflection. In her thong and bra, she was wearing little more than one of her swimsuits. Turning to the left, then the right, she checked out her profile, the thought of modeling swimsuit samples for Leon rushing to mind. He would be looking at her with even more skin exposed, and the thought of his eyes sliding up and down her figure sparked a prickly sensation that brought on a spasm of delight.

She swept trembling fingers over her abdomen, imagining Leon's palms roaming the flat of her stomach, the curve of her waist, inching ever closer to the Brazilian waxed V that bridged her thighs. She drew in a long breath and sighed, imagining how it would feel to be caressed by his hand as he probed parts of her anatomy that had been long untouched. She wanted his large, but tender hands, unhooking her bra and cupping her breasts. She yearned for his full sensuous lips sucking on nipples that were already jumping to attention. She wanted to taste his maleness on her tongue.

At that moment, her only one desire was for Leon Archer to possess her completely and turn her fantasies into reality. But would that ever happen?

There's only one way to find out, she decided. *Test him.*

They walked along the shoreline that bordered Leon's property, where the waves on his private beach lapped at their bare feet and tickled their toes. Kacey collected a pocket full of pretty shells and twisted pieces of smooth driftwood, while Leon collected mental images of Kacey in the sunlight. He marveled at the way the sun created highlights of gold in her thick brown curls. How the wind pressed her T-shirt into the valley between her lovely molded breasts. How the sprinkling of sand on her arms and legs left a sparkly sheen that made her glow in the sunlight.

Without a doubt, she was the most beautiful woman he had ever known and he had no plans of ever letting her escape the paradise he'd been hoping to share with the right woman one day. It had to be Kacey, he was sure of it. Of all the women he'd spent time with, she was the only one who possessed the qualities he was searching for. She was smart, creative, hungry for suc-

cess and not ashamed to admit it. She was fun to be
with, eager to try new things and made his heart go
into a crazy dance whenever she hooked him with her
sultry brown eyes. She was interested in the process of
textile manufacturing, and understood the demands of
his profession. And even though they came from very
different worlds, they meshed emotionally like grains
of sand on the beach.

Today, he'd noticed how impressed she'd been with
the history of his hometown, and suspected that she
respected small town life much more now than when
she'd first arrived. Getting away from the big city had
been a good thing for her and a coup for him. Now, all
he had to do was find a way to make her stay.

"We'd better turn around and head back to the house,"
Leon told Kacey when they came to a deep curve in the
beach where the sand gave way to a rocky shoreline.

"Right. It is getting late," Kacey remarked turning
around to start back. They walked in silence, holding
hands while splashing through the shallow water that
lazily caressed their ankles. When they arrived at Leon's
house, they mounted the steps leading up to the deck.

"Want something to drink?" he asked Kacey, who
had moved to the rail and was looking out over the
water.

"Sure. Anything cold," she told Leon, who went
inside and returned with a glass of cool lemonade.

"This has been so much fun, Leon. Really. Thanks
for everything. I'm beginning to feel more at home in
Rockport now." A murmured chuckle slipped out, adding lightness to the sincerity of her remark. "But I think
it's time to call an end to our day of playing hooky, don't
you?"

Leon tilted his head to one side. He detected a reluctant tone in Kacey's words, and was sure she really didn't want to go back to the motel. What was she going to do for the rest of the evening, anyway? Sit in her room and stare at a TV screen? He doubted that she wanted to do that, and he sure didn't want her to leave.

"Our day together doesn't have to end right now," Leon ventured, taking her hand in his. "This has been a much-needed break for me, too. I forgot about work altogether for the first time in months. Kacey, I loved showing you around. Thanks for letting me spend the day with you." He eased along the deck rail, stopping when his thigh touched hers.

"No, thank *you*," she murmured. "You didn't have to do this. With the power failure and the plant shut down, I know you have other things that are more important on your mind than playing tourist guide for me."

"Not true," he told her in a voice that was raw and sincere. "The power company didn't want anyone on the premises while they were working, and my employees got a day off with pay. Win-win for them, and for us, too…right?"

With an incline of her head, Kacey silently agreed.

"I'm not sure if you're feeling the same vibes that are hitting me," Leon stammered, "but, well… Dammit, Kacey. I…I'm *very* attracted to you."

Kacey watched him closely, aware of how difficult it had been for him to utter those words. Her heart was thudding hard and fast. He'd just told her what she wanted to hear, and now that he had, she was frozen with indecision, knowing he was waiting for her reply. Their time together today had created an amazing sense of closeness. He wanted her. He had feelings for her. But was he being honest with her? Did she dare confess what was really in her heart?

"Leon," she started. "I hear you...I do. And I don't know what's going on, either. But one thing is certain— you sure are making me nervous."

He shook his head and gave her a quick brush of a kiss on her cheek. "Don't be nervous," he comforted, tracing his thumb along her jaw. "We're adults. We can talk about our feelings in a rational way, can't we?"

"I guess so, but I'm still nervous about how fast things are moving. I can't deny that I'm attracted to you, too, but my gut tells me to slow down. After all, I won't be here that long."

"All the more reason to take advantage of me now," he joked. "That way you won't return to New York, wondering...what if?"

Kacey slapped playfully at Leon's arm, knowing he was telling the truth. She would forever regret not exploring her attraction to Leon if she let this opportunity pass. "I can't help worrying," Kacey confessed. "This has been a perfect day. A wonderful afternoon. All that history I've learned. Touring the area. A fantastic lunch. Our walk on the beach. It's all so surreal. I don't usually do things like this at home. And never on a weekday. I hate to see it end."

"I told you, it doesn't have to end." *Ever, if you want it that way,* he wished he could add. Leaning over, he kissed her firmly on the lips, pressing home his point as he pressed his mouth to hers.

With a silent moan of relief, Kacey opened her mouth and accepted his tongue, loving the way he flicked it gently back and forth, teasing her entire body with his feathery touch. "I know," Kacey confessed, when the kiss ended. Licking her glossy lips, she toyed with a wind-tangled curl hanging over one eye, keenly aware of what he wanted…to go inside and explore their attraction more deeply, to shift their attraction to a more intimate level. She knew how impulsive and dangerous it would be to go that far with Leon, but it was exactly what she wanted, too.

When he tugged on her hand, she hesitated, eyeing him with caution as a whirl of thoughts tumbled through her mind: *It's time for me to stop fooling myself. Sex with Jamal is not all that I need. A friend with benefits can't satisfy me forever. I want to feel excited, to fall completely into the experience and lose myself in this gorgeous man.*

Kacey was tired of the empty feeling that came over her after she and Jamal got off and then got dressed. She wanted more. She needed to put her whole heart and soul into a sexual encounter that would allow her to let go and explore the unknown side of her pent-up desires.

"If you want me to take you back to the motel, I will," Leon offered.

Kacey's insides were churning like choppy waves in a storm, but she wasn't in the least bit worried about drowning. Her soul ached for Leon's touch, which she knew would keep her afloat and steady the ride.

It's now or never, girl, she told herself, teetering on the edge of the most important personal decision she had been forced to make in years, knowing she was prepared to take the plunge.

"I can stay," she whispered, smoldering eyes now leveled on Leon. "I think I can stay a while longer."

"Good," he replied, slipping an arm around her waist as they headed into the house.

Heart pounding, legs weak with anticipation, Kacey followed Leon through the open patio doors, across his gleaming kitchen and into the dim haven of his seductively themed bedroom. While the paper tigers and lions and giraffes watched in silence from the walls, Kacey and Leon embraced. Their lips locked and held as soon as they reached the foot of his king-size bed. Their arms remained entwined in a natural grip that held them together like two lost hunters who'd finally found each other in the jungle of love. Tumbling onto the wildly colorful animal print spread, Kacey sank into the heat of the moment, determined to quench her thirst for Leon, which had been growing steadily stronger all day.

Letting Leon slowly undress her felt extraordinarily good, and she had no problem helping him shed his clothes in record time. When their naked bodies touched for the first time, Kacey flinched, electrified by the contact. However, she welcomed the flash of the charge that raced through her body and set her heart afire.

Involuntary shivers of need, fueled by arousal, undulated in the pit of her stomach and wound their way into her throat. She gulped back the surge of sexual exclamations that claimed her tongue and crowded her voice. The fragile shell of forced satisfaction, on which she'd relied during sex with Jamal, evaporated, leaving Kacey raw and vulnerable. Floating on a golden wave of passion that carried her sweetly into Leon's arms, she snuggled up against him.

The hint of stubble on his chin contrasted with the soft feel of his hands as he held her in place and brushed his face along her bare shoulder, nibbling his way onto her right breast. The fire he created as he licked and tugged on her nipple spread hotly through her veins. Kacey curved back her shoulders, giving him complete access to pleasure her intensely, which he did, until she could no longer remain silent and cried out in joy. Revved from the thrill of how her body was responding to Leon's delicious assault, she spread her legs and accepted the two fingers that he slid inside her tunnel of love, which was dripping wet with love juices as never before.

Riding his probing touch, she rotated her hips and let him plunge deeper, eagerly preparing for his stiff tool, which had risen up between them. Sleek and tall, it begged for her attention, making Kacey reach down and surround his throbbing erection with a soft caress. Using her thumb, she made tiny circles on the tip, and was pleased to hear Leon's groans of satisfaction, letting her know she was giving him what he wanted. Increasing her pace, she moved her index finger alongside her thumb, rubbing faster and faster, while devouring him with kisses. Too emotion-filled to think of anything other than the indescribable pleasure of being in Leon's arms, she sank into him, releasing all the dormant sexuality that she'd harbored for too long. Her desire to experience all that Leon had to give overrode any inhibitions she may have had about surrendering to his advances.

Leon eased his fingers from her love-slick center and slid them over her pulsing bud, twirling it with a rhythmic touch that took Kacey to the edge. When he stopped and reached into the bedside table for a condom, she tensed, terrified that she was going to lose the sharp edge of desire that he'd created. However, once his protection was in place and he resumed his tender ministrations, she knew he hadn't spoiled the moment she was searching for.

With a swift move, Kacey guided Leon's shaft down between her legs and into her core, struck by the heat of his body as it coursed through her and the size of his member as it filled her up. His hardness jolted her with satisfaction. Clamping her thighs together she savored the feeling of being totally and firmly connected to Leon. With both hands anchored to his broad brown shoulders, she buried her face in his neck and inhaled the sensuous smell of his skin, surrendering totally to fiery sensations that melted her world.

At first, his languid strokes were easy and tender, as if he were entering a narrow passage leading straight to her heart. Then his pace increased to searing thrusts that flooded her body with a white fire that raged hotter with each move. As he rocked her back and forth, she let her sweetness drain over him, slicking them both as they rose higher and higher toward the mutual climax they both sought. She wished she could ride this wave forever, but knew it had to crash down soon. Hanging onto Leon's shoulders, Kacey bucked along with him until a strong gust of need shook her like a stray leaf in the wind that was quickly drawn out to sea. The shuddering surrender that claimed Kacey, hit Leon at the same time, leaving Kacey gasping for air and Leon quivering in relief. Both thoroughly satisfied, yet not quite ready to let go.

Holding on to Kacey filled Leon with the most contented feeling he had ever known. With her head resting on his chest and her arm flung across his stomach, he melted under the weight of her closeness, as well as her trust in him. Tonight, she had trusted him with her heart and her body, leaving him reeling from her decision. He was tempted to pinch himself to prove that he was not dreaming. She'd made love to him with such fiery intensity that he knew he must be doing something right.

Outside, Leon could hear the waves washing gently onto the beach and the quiet wind as it rushed through the palm trees surrounding his house. The serene setting lulled him into a realization of what he had been missing. For too long, his love life had been a series of romantic misadventures with women he met while traveling for business. Hooking up with beautiful women in faraway cities had been exciting, sexually fulfilling, yet devoid of any real substance.

One of the drawbacks of living and working in a small town like Rockport was that he knew everyone, so he had to leave home to find romance, often forming relationships that were short-lived, with little chance of maturing. He could count on one hand the number of women he'd brought home to his beach house in hopes of creating a more lasting bond. None had ever worked out. After a few visits, they usually drifted away, not interested in settling down in his hometown and knowing he would never move away. His family's business, his future, his parents and his ties to the community held him in place, scaring off women he'd thought he cared about enough to broach the subject of marriage. None had loved him enough to stick with him, so his romances had never worked out. As he shifted his eyes to study Kacey's beautiful profile, he wondered why he was fantasizing about this city girl, Kacey Parker, being any different.

Somehow, he had find a way to convince this lovely, sophisticated, creative professional to leave New York and come live with him in his private slice of paradise on the water. He didn't have much time to make his case, but he was damn sure going to give it his best shot.

Chapter 14

Kacey bit her lip in thought as she headed down the corridor toward Bob Truett's workstation, thankful that the power blip was over and the plant was running smoothly again. Yesterday's outing with Leon had been a wonderful, unplanned escape, capped off by the most satisfying sex she had ever experienced, but that was all behind her and would never happen again. Or would it? Her mind kept turning back to their second go-round in bed. That one had been even better than the first. More tender, less urgent, but just as deliciously electrifying. Now Kacey contracted the muscles of her vagina as she walked down the hallway, aware that her bud was still throbbing in the aftermath of her gutsy tryst with Leon.

It had been nearly two o'clock in the morning when he drove her back to her motel, making for an early rise that began with the expected progress call from Ariana. Groggy and impatient to get up and into the shower, Kacey had opted not to tell Ariana about the power failure or the fact that absolutely no progress had been made on the SunKissed production. She didn't want to get Ariana in a tizzy when there was nothing anyone could do. Today, they'd get back on schedule.

"Good morning!"

Kacey stopped in her tracks when Nona rounded a corner at the end of the corridor, stopped and lifted her hand in greeting.

"Oh, hi, Nona," Kacey called back, but when she started to walk past the operations manager, Nona blocked Kacey's path.

"Enjoy your day off with Leon?" Nona asked, giving Kacey a tight smile.

Kacey narrowed her eyes, not surprised that Nona knew about their outing. In a place like Rockport, it was clear that nothing was kept private very long. "Yes, we had a wonderful time," she answered, adding a hint of smugness to her reply.

"Hmm," Nona murmured. "Leon really deserved some time off. I've been telling him for months that he works too hard. Glad he finally took my advice and got away from the factory for a day."

"I'm just happy that he chose to spend his free day showing me around," Kacey boldly countered.

"I heard you had quite a lunch at Buddy's," Nona continued, arching a brow as she squinted at Kacey.

"You did?"

"Oh, yeah. Nothing new escapes people around here. Talking about strangers is actually one of our favorite pastimes. Gives everyone something to do, I guess,"

Nona went on. "Buddy's Barbecue is the place to be seen if you want to make your presence known around Rockport. Everyone knows what you and Leon ate, drank and probably what you talked about, too."

But do they know how we ended our day? Kacey wondered, lifting her chin as she tried to decipher Nona's motivation. The woman was hard to figure out—was she going to be helpful or hurtful to Kacey in the long run? Were her feelings for Leon just overprotective friendship or something else? Kacey wasn't sure what was going on, but she did know that Nona James was far too interested in Leon's private life and Kacey didn't plan to let this woman get under her skin.

"Leon and I really had a ball," Kacey went on in a deliberately cool tone. "He's the best. A great tour guide. He gave me a history lesson, showed me around, treated me to lunch, and our walk on his beach last night was the perfect ending to our day. I stayed at his house so late that I didn't get back to the motel until nearly two o'clock. I'm a bit sleep-deprived...but I'm here!" *You want something to talk about? Well, take that bit of info to your gossipy friends,* Kacey thought, hoping she hadn't made a huge mistake by telling Nona too much.

With a fast roll of her eyes, Nona dismissed Kacey's remark, as if her comment meant nothing.

"Whatever," Nona said, lifting a finger. "What I stopped to ask you was...do you have the backup disk with the adjusted pattern files on it?"

Kacey frowned, sensing trouble. "No, I left everything with Mr. Truett when we finished. Why?" she asked.

"Seems the adjustments you two made on his computer got wiped out during the power failure. His hard drive, including the CAD software, were fried."

"What? You've got to be kidding!"

"Wish I were."

"You can't mean…we've lost *everything?*" Kacey stuttered, as a sinking feeling swept into her stomach.

"Seems so," Nona stated in a tone that seemed awfully casual as far as Kacey was concerned.

"Are you sure Truett didn't save our changes on a backup?" she pressed.

"I don't know why, but he didn't," Nona confirmed.

"This is a real problem," Kacey sighed, incredulous that she now faced another day's delay. "I'd better talk to Leon about this. Where is he?"

"In his office, I suppose," Nona offered coolly.

Turning around, Kacey headed to Leon's office, entering just as he was hanging up the phone.

"Hey. Good morning. You look lovely," Leon greeted Kacey in a devilishly sexy voice. His heart raced at the sight of Kacey looking so professional and sleek in her business attire. Last night, she'd been a completely different person. Loose and wild and totally free. She'd ridden him like a tiger quenching its thirst after a difficult hunt, and he had given her everything he had—and more. He had never pushed himself so hard to fulfill a woman's needs, but he had gone the distance with her and knew he was a goner. He was totally lost in loving her, but he didn't care. This fabulous woman was exactly who he'd been looking for and he planned to hold on to her forever.

"I was just about to come down to see you," he said, looking her up and down in appreciation. "Baby, last night was…"

"Leon...not now, please. We have more important things to discuss," Kacey advised, making sure she closed his door. The last thing she wanted was for Nona, or any employee, to overhear a discussion about her and Leon's sexual tryst.

Leon shrugged, looking contrite, but nodded in understanding.

"So, what's up?" he asked.

"Nona just told me that the alterations Mr. Truett and I completed were wiped out in the power failure."

"Really?" Leon stood, concerned by the worried expression on Kacey's face. "How could that happen? Truett always safeguards designs with a backup."

"Obviously, this time, he failed."

Leon grabbed his phone, punched in a number and asked Truett to come into his office.

Within seconds the head patternmaker arrived, looking wary and nervous as he stood in front of Leon.

"What happened to the SunKissed file?" Leon asked.

"I don't know, Leon. Somehow, it got corrupted. Must have been the power blip that did it."

Kacey groaned in dismay, but held her tongue.

Truett let out a dispirited sigh. "I know, I know I dropped the ball. I never dreamed something like this would happen," he sputtered, sounding contrite.

"So, we've...lost all that work," Kacey verified, her frustration rising. She turned to Leon, hoping he had an answer. "What do we do now?" she asked, holding in her disappointment.

"Start over, I guess," Leon offered.

"But I'm on such a tight deadline. This is awful!"

she said, hoping Steve Hadley hadn't made a mistake by deciding to use Archer Industries.

Silence reigned while everyone pondered the next move.

"I understand your frustration," Leon finally offered. "I wish this hadn't happened, but it did, and now all we can do is move fast to fix the problem and push forward." He focused on Truett. "Pull up the master file and get started on re-creating everything you and Ms. Parker did!"

"Right away," Truett replied, scurrying from the room.

As Kacey watched Truett leave, her heart thudded in her chest. "Is he reliable?" she asked, worried that this might be just the beginning of a series of setbacks.

"Oh, yes, of course," Leon defended. "The power failure wasn't his fault."

"I understand that, but his lack of security is very disappointing," she countered, biting her lip. But as soon as she saw the look of disappointment on Leon's face, she was sorry for making such a comment. The words had just flown out of her mouth before she'd had a chance to think. If Mr. Truett had been working in the garment district in New York, he might be on his way out the door for making such a mistake. But she wasn't in New York. She was in Rockport, Texas, and she trusted Leon's belief in his employee.

"Truett has been with Archer for twenty-seven years," Leon went on. "This is the first time he's ever messed up. He's always been a loyal employee."

A moment of silence slipped past before Kacey dared speak again. If the circumstances had been different, she might have been inclined to walk away from Archer

Industries without looking back, taking the Leeman's contract elsewhere. But redoing the pattern adjustments would only take a few hours, while sourcing a new manufacturer might take days, even weeks. And besides, she was definitely not about to walk away from Leon Archer, especially not after last night.

"All right. Let's get busy, then," Kacey conceded, determined to put the setback behind her. "However," she began, "I'd like to become a bit more involved in all stages of production. Would that be a problem?" She didn't want to sound bossy, but Hadley trusted her to get the job done right, and on time. She was the one who would be held accountable for how every seam was sewn and she planned to make sure there'd be no more delays.

"Absolutely, I agree," Leon replied. "Feel free to observe, and if you have any problems, bring them to me."

"Thank you," Kacey murmured, letting her shoulders sag, realizing how tense she'd become during their exchange.

"We'll work all day…all night if we have to, to get this back on track. All my other clients' projects will be put on hold until SunKissed is finished. We'll make your deadline," Leon vowed.

"I know we will," Kacey agreed, buoyed by Leon's optimistic attitude and the sense that they were a true team, in this together to the end. He understood her position and did not resent her need to take a keener interest in the production. She would focus entirely on the business she'd come to Rockport to do.

But that doesn't mean I plan to stop playing around with Leon Archer, she decided. No way was that possible, because her entire body flushed hot whenever she thought about the way his sleek sex tool had driven her over the edge and into a chasm of longing from which she hoped never to escape.

The next three days flew by in a flurry of activity as all the Archer employees devoted themselves to the SunKissed by Kacey line. Leon watched as Kacey roamed the factory floor and listened with interest when his employees explained each step of the process. He was proud of the way she put them at ease without trying to interfere.

Kacey worked hard to move the SunKissed project along, rushing the new patterns to the cutters as soon as they were finished, and then standing by as they turned swaths of vibrantly colored fabric into the first pieces of the swimsuit line. Whenever a unit did not meet Leon's exacting standards, he asked the operator restitch it until it was perfect. He'd promised to give Kacey his full cooperation and he did not renege on that.

After four days of full-speed-ahead work, the first units came off the production line. They were perfect examples of Kacey's vision and when Leon suggested that the two of them celebrate at his house on the beach, Kacey quickly agreed.

As they drank champagne and discussed the project, the first glass of bubbly heightened Kacey's awareness of how much she loved designing. The second glass reminded her of how much she loved working with Leon. And by the third glass, she was snuggled against him on one of his comfy chaise longues, with her back spooned against his chest, with his arms holding her close. She felt relaxed and happy that they'd come so far so quickly—both at work and in their rapidly evolving relationship.

"We're almost there," Kacey murmured as she snuggled deeper into Leon's arms.

"Yes, we are," he replied, his breath warm against her neck. "You know, I've got the best employees in the world."

"And why not? After all, they have a wonderful boss," Kacey added, turning her head to place a quick kiss on Leon's chin. "And the most handsome." She kissed the tip of his nose. "And the sexiest." Another peck, this time on the cheek. "And the most..."

But she didn't have a chance to finish her next compliment because Leon eased her fully around, captured her lips in a hungry clench and swept his tongue over hers while pressing his rock-hard sex into the softness of her stomach. She melted under his touch when he slipped his hands beneath her blouse to thumb her nipples until she nearly screamed.

"Kacey..." he whispered.

"Um-hmm," she murmured, not really wanting to talk, only wanting to feel and remember every stroke of his fingertips.

"I have something to tell you."

"Um...what?"

"I... I'm sure I'm falling in love with you," he admitted in a voice raw with desire. "Do you...feel the same way?"

"Yes," she whispered without hesitation, sinking into the beauty of the moment as she gazed up into his eyes. "I can't deny it, Leon. I know I'm falling fast for you," she confessed with a sigh that released all the breath from her body. While the weight of his body pressed down on her, Kacey wiggled out of her jeans and then slipped down on her back. Primed to receive him and eager for his touch, she opened herself to him, knowing their troubles were behind them and an exciting future lay ahead. She also knew that, somehow she would fit into Leon's world and bring him into hers.

Chapter 15

The first-run samples, having been created to fit Kacey's perfect size 4 body, were ready for fitting by her second week in Rockport. As the employees closed down their machines and prepared to head home for the day, Kacey made it a point to walk through the workroom and thank each one for doing such a good job under pressure. No one was upset with Kacey. In fact, their responses let Kacey know that they were proud to have pulled off the task assigned to them, and that their Herculean effort had solved Kacey's problem.

"They're perfect!" Kacey exclaimed when Leon presented her with the final units. She turned each piece of swimwear inside out, examining every seam and tuck. "They've done a good job. Carefully crafted and well made."

"Exactly what I expect from my staff."

"Then the next step is the fitting," Kacey said.

"If you want, there's a dressing room on the second floor that used to be the boardroom. We can use it for the fittings. Need any help?" Leon prompted.

Kacey grinned knowingly. "Sure, why not?"

"My pleasure," he replied voice rough with understanding. "But first, I have a few calls to make. Maybe we can do the fittings a bit later?" he asked.

"Sounds good. Let me know when you're ready," she added, giving Leon a quick wave before leaving his office.

Back in her cubicle, she admired the samples again, realizing how wrong she'd been about Archer Industries, and Leon, too. Steve Hadley had been right. This factory turned out fantastic work. It was precisely the right place to produce the SunKissed line, and Leon Archer was the perfect man for her project...and for her.

It was very late in the day when Kacey and Leon finally got together in the boardroom that had been converted into a dressing room. Everyone had gone home and the factory was quiet. Kacey excitedly modeled each swimsuit for Leon, emerging from the changing cubicle to stand half-naked in front of him while he studied, tugged and pinched the small squares of fabric covering her most private, and sensitive, parts. His smug suggestions and unnecessary ministrations did not fool her at all, and his nonstop touches swept her deeper into her attraction for him. Kacey's desire to make love to him grew more intense as each minute ticked by.

Though Leon was supposed to be helping her create the perfect fit for her sexy bathing suits, he was definitely more interested in examining the curves of her body than the straightness of the seams. When Kacey put on the final suit—a sea-green number with a beaded top and a side tie hipster bottom, his fingers strayed from adjusting the line of the top to touch the rise of her breast.

"I'd tighten this here," Leon said, running a finger across the sprinkling of beads on the bandeau bikini top.

"Uh-uh," Kacey mocked her protest with a frown. "That would hide the beads. That little bit of sparkle has to show...very important for the woman who likes glamour."

"You know best," he smilingly gave in. "You're right. It looks too damn good on you to change. And besides, I'd never want to make you unhappy."

"Never?"

"Never," Leon murmured with conviction, easing his hand beneath the stretchy fabric to capture and stroke a nipple.

Kacey shook her head and rolled her eyes. "You're not paying attention, Mr. Archer," she cautioned in a tease.

"Not true. I'm totally engrossed in what I'm doing," he countered swiftly, slipping her strapless top down and onto the waistband of her hipster bottom.

"Engrossed in what? My body or the fit of the swimsuit?"

"Hey, I'm a pretty clever guy. I can tend to both and do a good job, too, don't you think?"

Kacey giggled and dipped her head. "I guess so."

Leon bent to whisper in her ear, "Let me prove it."

Kacey's entire body went on alert as a spiral of

longing tensed her core. "Here?" she questioned in a rough whisper.

"Why not? We're alone. No one else is in the building," Leon assured her as he leaned in and kissed the space between Kacey's perky breasts. "I'd love to fit something other than a bathing suit on you."

"But that's not what we're supposed to be doing," she huskily replied, groaning as his exploration slipped lower.

"But seeing as how we're finished with the swimwear, all that is left is this." He took her hand and guided it to the bulge in his pants.

Kacey smiled, eased her hand down and wrapped her fingers about his hard rod. She tilted her face up to his to accept the kiss that he pressed to her lips while her hand began a steady up and down motion along his shaft.

Intensifying without breaking their kiss, Leon maneuvered Kacey to the worktable at the back of the room. With a sweep of his hand, he cleared the surface of fabric, clothing, scissors and measuring tapes, and then lifted Kacey up onto it. When she spread her legs, he moved to stand between them, pressing himself into the V-shaped opening as his tongue and hands continued their hungry exploration. The urgency of their passion rushed through Kacey and clouded her brain, blocking out all rational thoughts. Teased by his kisses and inflamed by his touch, she wanted nothing more than to abandon herself to the raw surge of longing that radiated inside her. As bursting gusts of desire orchestrated their tangled limbs, Kacey luxuriated in the anticipation of making love to Leon. He had proven that he knew what she wanted and knew how to deliver, and she was primed for more. As she yielded once again to his embrace, she was shocked by the magnitude of her own desire, but hypnotized by his awesome ability to flood her with uncontrollable joy.

Changing his approach, Leon went from feathering his tongue over her chest to licking a line from her belly button to the top of her swimsuit bottom. Using his teeth, he undid the knot on one side tie and jiggled the fabric until it fell to the floor. Fully exposed, Kacey leaned back and groaned when Leon's lips claimed her vibrating kernel of seduction, which he sucked so hard she let out a gasp. Flooded with uncontrollable sensations of a fast-approaching climax, she braced herself on her elbows, held his head in place and urged Leon to take her where she had never gone before, a place from which she hoped never to return.

How could anything be more perfect, she thought as the climactic wave of release struck, sending her shuddering and laughing and crying and quivering over the edge and deeper into Leon s heart.

Chapter 16

After Kacey slipped into his car, Leon shut the passenger side door and walked around to the driver's side. Pausing, he glanced up at the dark Archer Industries sign above his building and blinked. A sigh of contentment slipped out into the night air. He knew he must look like a love-struck teenager: He couldn't stop smiling. His heartbeat raced like a power sewing machine. And his groin remained aflame with need, though he didn't regret holding back from taking Kacey completely. He hadn't come to the office prepared to make love to her, but he sure hadn't wanted to pass up the opportunity to give her what she obviously wanted and enjoyed.

When she'd told him about her relationship with Jamal, Leon had wished he could thank the guy for priming Kacey to appreciate the kind of loving he knew he could deliver—the kind that Kacey deserved. He appreciated her bold moves, her openness about her sexual needs and the fact that she never made him feel uneasy. Loving a woman like Kacey forever was his only desire, and he planned to put all his energy into solidifying their relationship.

I'm gonna do this one right, Leon decided as he got into his car and started the engine.

While at the office, he struggled to maintain a professional distance from Kacey. In a place like Rockport, it didn't take much to start rumors, and he'd already taken a huge risk by staying alone with her in the building after hours. The last thing he wanted was for Kacey to become the butt of jokes or rumors around the plant. He'd never had sex with a woman in his building and the realization of what he'd just done was titillating, but as he drove into the Seaside Suites Motel parking lot and stopped at the entrance, he decided that it couldn't happen again.

He leaned across to open Kacey's door, and was pleasantly surprised when she captured his lips with hers.

"Guess I'll see you tomorrow," she whispered when the kiss ended.

"Right. Tomorrow," he replied, pulling away. He had to put some space between them because if he didn't, he knew anything might happen.

"Now that the fittings are finished, I'll get Linette onboard," Kacey advised, stepping out of the car. She bent down to look in at Leon, resting her arms in the open window.

"Good idea," Leon said, taking Kacey's hand in his.

He kissed her fingertips, gave her a long look and then let her go. "Call me later…if you want."

"Maybe I will," she tossed back before turning around to enter the motel.

Leon sped out of the parking lot and took the long way home, needing time to process everything that was happening, and happening so fast.

Was she using him to satisfy needs that had been bottled up too long? Was she just out for a fling with a country guy so she'd have something to talk about when she returned to New York? Or was she really, truly in love? As hard as it was to think it could happen, Leon felt in his heart that he had finally found the woman of his dreams.

Kacey called Linette right away and filled her in on everything that was going on between her and Leon. "Girl, this assignment is turning out to be a lot more than I bargained for," she said. "The personal stuff is getting real personal, if you know what I mean."

"Trust me, I do," Linette tossed out.

"Everything's all tangled up. We have to work together, you know. It's absolutely crazy! I need to talk to you because things are moving way too fast."

"Says who?"

"Says me! I know I shouldn't be all cozy with Leon, but damn, he's hard to resist. And a really good guy, too."

"And from what you've told me, he has a secret admirer who may not be so pleased with you and him hooking up?"

"Yeah, Nona. The operations manager. I can't get

a fix on her. She seems friendly enough, but there's something about her I don't trust."

"Leave me alone with her for fifteen minutes and I'll get all the answers you want."

"Girl, I don't doubt that," Kacey chuckled, aware of her friend's blunt, inquisitive nature. "So how soon can you come?"

"I can be there late on Friday…the day after tomorrow. Is that okay?"

"Sure. We can do the shoot on Saturday. Hopefully, at the beach because the weather is expected to be very warm."

"Good. Text me directions to the factory."

"Will do. I can't wait for you to meet Leon. He's easy to work with. And he even might have some photo work for you. I was kinda wary about using Archer Industries, but now I'm glad Leon is doing my line."

Linette laughed into the phone. "Hmm. Sounds like he's more interested in doing *you* than a line of swimsuits," she remarked.

"Hey, you may be right. But as long as he produces on both fronts, I'm happy."

"Sounds serious… I'm really looking forward to meeting your new friend. Later," Linette said, ending the call.

"Later," Kacey murmured into the silent phone, anxious to have Linette around to talk to, if only for a day or two.

While she and Leon had been turning her designs into real swimsuits, Kacey had been turning her heart over to the man whose sensual touch was far more dangerous than his power cutters and industrial sewing machines. This feeling of blissful happiness was so strong, and so foreign, it frightened Kacey. *Can it last?* she wondered, sliding down onto the bed to stare at the ceiling and replay every moment of her dressing room love session with Leon.

Chapter 17

The following day went even better than Kacey had hoped and by the close of business on Friday all the adjustments had been made, the first-run samples were complete and she was ready for the photo shoot. When Leon suggested that Linette use the shoreline along his property to photograph the line, Kacey agreed that it would be the perfect background to show off her swimsuits.

Friday afternoon, Linette arrived at Archer Industries with her load of cameras and supplies. She met Kacey with a hard hug, wrapping her well-toned arms around her friend. An avid runner, Linette kept herself in great shape, taking time between jobs to train for marathons, and wore her reddish brown hair in a short sassy style— easy to manage on the road, she said. Her standard dress was cargo pants with lots of pockets to hold her rolls of film, and tight T-shirts that showed off her fabulously fit body.

"Ready to get to work?" Kacey asked as she walked with Linette toward Leon's office.

"Absolutely," Linette replied, following her friend. "I've been pumped about this shoot ever since you told me that it was finally going to happen. Can't wait to see what you've done."

"I think you're gonna like SunKissed by Kacey. As a matter of fact there is one suit in the line that is perfect for you. A two-piece number in cinnamon that'll look great on your hourglass figure."

After a handshake with Leon when Kacey introduced them, Linette cut her eyes at Kacey, indicating her approval.

Now she sees what I've been talkin' about, Kacey thought, giving Linette an imperceptible nod of understanding as they sat down to discuss their schedule for the next day's shoot.

Once all was set, Kacey drove Linette to the Seaside, where she checked into a room across from Kacey's.

While Linette unpacked, the two friends got busy catching up on personal matters.

"He is too damn fine," Linette commented about Leon as she placed an oversized striped shirt on a hanger.

"Isn't he?" Kacey giggled in agreement. "And sexy as hell, too. At the office he tries to be all businesslike and impersonal, but I know how to wear him down," Kacey confessed, going on to add a few more details about her rapidly evolving romance with Leon.

"I'm happy that you've finally found a serious man to date, after wasting so much time with Jamal."

"Yeah, I know. I've been fooling myself. Trying to act like I was happy with Jamal, but now... Whew! I didn't know what I was missing."

"You sure jumped in all the way. I'm proud of you, girlfriend."

"It is moving kinda fast, huh?" Kacey admitted. "But I...you know what? I think we make a good team. In business and other things, too. Maybe, I'm actually in love?"

"That's pretty damn obvious, Kacey. Anyone can see that," Linette dryly observed. "And I can see that Leon is, too."

"Uh...think so?"

"Yeah. But that's a good thing. You need to stop stressin' so much. What's wrong with great sex with a man you have feelings for? Let it all play out, Kacey. Relax and see where things go. Don't overanalyze the situation and wind up blowing it. You two might have a shot at a real future together."

"I wish...but how could that happen? With me in New York and him in Texas? I told you how he feels about this place. Deep, deep, roots. No way he'd ever leave Rockport."

"It'll work itself out if it's meant to be. For now, just enjoy the journey."

Kacey held back from voicing another round of self-doubts, deciding to take Linette's words to heart. If she and Leon were destined to be together, somehow they'd bridge the differences between where they lived and how they loved. It could be done, couldn't it?

Saturday morning dawned clear and warm, offering the perfect day to photograph SunKissed by Kacey at

Leon's beach house. Linette set up her equipment while Kacey put on the first swimsuit of the shoot—a red satin bikini that showed off her curves with a high-waisted thong and a full-coverage triangle top. The gauzy matching cover-up hit her at midthigh, adding a little extra drama to the ensemble.

Leon watched the action from his deck as Kacey took direction from her friend. He was as impressed with Linette's ability to get just the right poses out of Kacey as he was with the way Kacey's swimwear hugged her body in a perfect fit.

Kacey knows what she's doing, all right, he thought, convinced that any woman would look good in that ensemble, no matter what her figure.

As the shoot continued, Leon began to better understand what Kacey had meant when she'd assured him with confidence that SunKissed would fly out of stores. She was right. Once her line hit the retail market, there'd be no stopping her.

Sitting back, Leon watched the action with pride, admiring the swimsuits that his company had produced. There were low, sexy peekaboo cuts. Retro one-piece units that were ultrachic, and bikinis that featured the tiniest of bottoms as well as skirted styles. He ogled plunging necklines and backless suits that showed off Kacey's soft, mounded breasts and her perfect rear end. He gaped in admiration at a monokini in a passion-purple tone that paid homage to Kacey's smooth Brazilian wax.

A leopard print two-piece with a bandeau top and a boy-cut bottom was his favorite. Created out of the imported Naughty Net, it was electrifying on her. When Leon saw her emerge from the water, her nipples and smooth pubic area peeking through the transparent fabric, the sight made him suddenly go hard. Though he tried to keep his attention focused on the swimsuit, it was difficult to concentrate on anything but the woman who was wearing it. With his eyes riveted on Kacey's seductive brown body as it whirled in front of him, he clenched his teeth, remaining perpetually aroused and primed for action.

He liked what he saw for another reason, too. Kacey and Linette worked well together, and the shoot was progressing without a hitch. No drama, arguing, prodding or delays. Linette impressed him as a talented professional with whom he'd love to work again.

After all the swimsuits had been photographed and Kacey was once again dressed in her jeans and a tie-dyed cotton shirt, they left the beach and drove into town for dinner at Buddy's.

"Where are you off to next?" Leon asked Linette, after they'd been seated and placed their orders.

"I'm heading to Chicago. Don't know if I'll leave tomorrow or Monday morning."

"What kind of a job this time?" Kacey asked.

"A catalog for a parents' magazine. Lots of nursery furniture, toys and strollers."

"And crying babies all over the place?" Kacey prompted.

"Yeah, that, too," Linette agreed with a smirk.

"But it ought to be interesting," Leon commented with a laugh. "Guess your work lets you see the inner workings of a lot of different companies."

Linette nodded. "Absolutely. And it's one of the things that keeps me in love with my profession."

"Ever photographed a Texas rodeo?" he asked, hunching over his glass of soda as he pursed his lips.

"No," Linette replied. "No rodeo—Texan or otherwise."

"Well, if you can stick around tomorrow, I'd love to take you…and Kacey to a rodeo. My friend, Freddy Mathews, has a ranch in Smithville and this rodeo will be a big deal. Townsfolk come out in droves, and out-of-towners, too. A lot of the people who work at Archer will be there, and it ought to be a lot of fun."

"Oh? Sounds like something I don't dare pass up," Linette remarked, shifting her attention to Kacey.

With a shrug, Kacey eyed her friend. "Leon mentioned it a few days ago, but I hadn't thought much about it. You wanna go?"

"Of course," Linette quickly replied. Turning to Leon, she asked, "And it's okay to take photos?"

"Absolutely."

"Then I definitely want to see your rodeo."

"Me, too," Kacey decided, looking forward to meeting people outside of Archer Industries who knew Leon. She could learn a lot about a man by getting to know his friends, and right then, Kacey wanted to know everything about Leon Archer's past. How else could she envision a future with him?

Chapter 18

"This started as an all-black rodeo," Freddy told Kacey and Linette as he guided them toward a huge arena where a crowd of rowdy, yelling rodeo fans were screaming at a man who was trying to stay on a bull that definitely didn't want him to succeed. "However, most people don't think of how important that was for blacks in Texas long ago."

"I know that's the truth," Linette commented. "But Bill Pickett invented bulldogging and was a huge rodeo star, right?"

"Correct," Freddy replied, as he motioned for Leon—who'd lagged behind to say hello to one of his mother's neighbors—to hurry and catch up.

"Pickett was one of the most colorful characters in the history of Wild West shows and rodeo circuits," Kacey added to the conversation.

"I see you two young ladies know your black history," Freddy commented with a chuckle, guiding Linette, Kacey and, finally, Leon into front-row seats. As they settled down, they were greeted by warm hellos and expressions of welcome from many of Leon's friends. Clearly, Leon Archer and his parents knew people from all over the area and were well respected, too.

From her up close and personal location, Kacey watched the action in the rodeo arena with her mouth gaping, impressed by the bravery, skill and awesome strength of the riders who struggled to keep their balance on bucking bulls while holding on to a rigging strap with only one hand. From the expressions on their faces, Kacey could tell that the thrill of the ride overshadowed the pain of the fall when they crashed to the ground or were thrown against a barrier by a testy bull.

"Amazing," Linette commented.

"Here's where you see the true test of a cowboy," Freddy replied.

"It must take a lot of work to put this rodeo on," Linette said.

"Yeah, but it's fun. It all started when my granddad decided to host a bull-roping contest on his farm so his friends could have some fun," said Freddy. "Now, we draw close to a thousand people over the weekend, and contestants travel from as far away as California and Oklahoma to join in."

When a Caucasian cowgirl in a flamboyant black-fringed outfit entered the area on a beautiful bay, the crowd erupted in a volley of loud cheers. "Mary Clayton. Very popular," Freddy explained. "She's a town girl. A newcomer to our rodeo, but she's a favorite to win the barrel race."

"What's that?" Kacey asked.

"In the barrel race, cowgirls ride their horses against the clock, making a cloverleaf pattern as they pass by a series of three barrels."

"So it's not just a black folks' rodeo, huh?" Linette commented.

"Nope. Any cowboy or cowgirl who wants to participate is invited to ride here. No exclusions because of race or culture. Everyone is welcome," said Freddy.

"I've gotta get her on film," Linette decided. She stood, lifted her camera to her face and began to snap away as she moved to the edge of the barrier.

Kacey focused on the lively barrel race, her attitude about Texas beginning to soften as she got into the heart-stopping excitement of the rowdy competition. She'd arrived in Rockport determined to hate her foray into small town America, but here she was, having more fun than she'd had in years. In fact, she had not been bored or homesick since her arrival.

Thanks to Leon, she thought. He'd opened her eyes to the pleasant side of life in his hometown, with their peaceful walks along the beach, their explorations of local history and meals in a barbecue joint where she was now greeted by first name. In Rockport, it seemed that folks either knew you, or went out of their way to befriend you. She had not missed the big city hustle—and hassle—at all, and was finding this slower-paced life to be rather sensual, and definitely worth exploring further...especially with Leon.

Kacey pressed her shoulder against Leon's and tilted her head toward him, suddenly wanting to feel him next to her. He gave her a squeeze and kissed her quickly on the forehead. "Having fun?" he whispered in her ear.

"Yes. It's very exciting, but it sure is dusty," she added fanning away a cloud of dust that suddenly surged up into her face when a cowgirl raced past on a beautiful white horse.

"Yeah, but that's part of the experience. Want a soda?" Leon asked.

"Sure. That would be great. Orange, if they have it."

"They do," Leon assured her, easing out of their embrace. "Be right back."

Kacey had just begun to concentrate on the next rider in the arena when Nona slipped into the space that Leon had just vacated.

"Hi," she said to Kacey, who was waving at Linette on the far side of the arena.

Kacey shifted to the side to check out Nona's outfit. She was wearing a red-and-blue-plaid shirt embedded with gold threads, tight black jeans that hugged her sturdy frame and heavily tooled cowgirl boots with metal clips on the toes. A red felt cowboy hat topped off her Western ensemble.

"You look like you ought to be out there on a horse," Kacey remarked, taking in Nona's flashy Western attire.

"Not me. I do ride pretty well, but I have no desire to compete in a rodeo." She paused, lifted her face to the sunshine and grinned. "Leon and I used to ride all the time. We spent hours roaming these parts."

"That's nice," Kacey muttered through tight lips, inwardly groaning. She was sick and tired of Nona's irritating trips down memory lane. Didn't this woman have anything on her mind other than faded, youthful memories of her and Leon's past? Determined not to show her distaste for Nona's remark, Kacey decided to rub in the fact that *she'd* been invited to come to the rodeo with Leon, not Nona. "I'm having such a good time. Leon insisted that Linette and I come out here today. He's been so good about making sure I enjoy myself while I'm here."

"Leon is a very thoughtful man."

"Yes, he is," Kacey agreed.

"But he's not *perfect,* you know?" Nona abruptly countered.

Kacey leveled a puzzled look on Nona, and then shrugged, returning her attention to a petite Hispanic girl on a huge sable-brown horse who was revving up the crowd as she raced around the barrels.

"No one is," Kacey commented, almost to herself.

"That's true, and Leon's had his share of troubles," Nona continued, measuring her words, as if trying to gauge Kacey's reaction.

"Really? Well, I wouldn't know, or care, about his problems from the past," Kacey snapped, irritated that Nona would dare bring up Leon's personal life with her.

"Well, most people around here know all about what happened. In Rockport, nothing is secret for long," Nona said, adopting a cool tone. "I've known Leon forever, and there's nothing I don't know about him."

"Nothing?" Kacey's head whipped around in disgust, exhausted by Nona's obvious prodding. "I doubt that. There are a lot of things I could tell you about your boss that I'm sure you don't know." She was tempted to ask Nona if she knew that Leon had made love to Kacey in the fitting room at Archer. If she knew that he and Kacey had lain, naked, on his private beach while cool water swept over them. That she'd sucked his cock like a hungry person devouring a lollipop. No….she couldn't, but she wasn't going to tiptoe around Nona any longer, either. It was time for Kacey to show Nona her Harlem-street-tough side and set this woman straight.

"Is there a point to this conversation?" Kacey snapped, letting her frustration fly. "I don't have time for your stupid little games, Nona. If there's something you want me to know, spill it or shut up."

A beat. "You don't have to get snippy."

"I'm not being snippy, just real. If you're so tight with Leon, why aren't you here with him, and not me? As you can see, we're together and you're intruding!"

"Well," Nona began as she sidled up to Kacey. "I only came over because I wanted to warn you."

"About what?" Kacey shot back.

"It's Leon. You seem to be getting pretty close to him, but he's much more complicated than you think."

"Most men are," Kacey deadpanned with a roll of her eyes.

"Did he tell you he has a criminal record?"

Kacey did not reply.

"Leon did time in prison."

Kacey squinted in disgust. "If he did time, then I guess he paid for his mistake, whatever it was."

"Ask him about it," Nona urged.

"If he wants me to know, he'll tell me."

"Bet he didn't tell you he's been engaged four times."

Kacey tensed, but pressed her lips together, not wanting to get into a discussion about Leon's love life with Nona.

"He's the local playboy," Nona continued. "Everybody

knows he can't stick with one woman for more than a few weeks. I'll bet he's told you all kinds of things to make you think he cares for you, but, trust me, he's not really interested. Not romantically, that is."

"And how would you know?"

"Because I know him too well. You're not his type."

"And I guess you are?" Kacey sneered, outraged by this woman's impertinent, know-it-all attitude.

"As a matter of fact, yes, I am. He's only spending time with you because you're the new girl in town. He's curious, but your novelty will wear off soon enough. He'll dump you, just as he's dumped all his women when he's through with them. So why don't you back off before you get hurt? My friendship with Leon is a whole lot stronger than anything he'll ever feel for you."

Kacey looked at Nona as if the woman had lost her mind. "Ha! And you call yourself his friend? Does he know that you go behind his back to spread gossip to hurt him?"

"I'm not hurting him. I'm helping him."

"Obviously you don't care *that* much about his feelings. If you did, you'd respect him, and his privacy, don't you think?" Kacey inclined her head toward the end of the bleachers as Leon approached. "Here he comes now. Why don't you tell him to his face what you just told me?"

"I'll leave that for you to do," Nona challenged in a taunt.

"I plan to," Kacey promised, shocked by the odd conversation she'd just had with Nona. But then, most of her conversations with Nona had been rather odd, now that she thought about it.

"Hey, Nona. How's it going?" Leon asked as he stepped onto the riser. "You're looking real Western. I like your boots," he remarked, reaching past her as he handed Kacey a frosty orange bottle.

Nona smiled cattily at Leon and scooted past him, deliberately brushing her mountainous breast against his arm. "It's all good, Leon. Talk to you later." She wiggled her fingers at Kacey. "See you at work. Have fun you guys."

"What were you two talking about?" Leon asked.

"Nothing important," Kacey replied, turning her attention back to the camera.

Though it was hard to do, Kacey held back from discussing Nona's revelations with Leon, deciding not to ruin their outing. Shoving aside the questions that roamed her mind, Kacey concentrated on the stream of rodeo clowns spilling out of a tiny wreck of a car, determined to have a good time.

When the last event wound down, Leon nudged Kacey and cocked his head toward the exit. They both agreed it was time to leave, but Linette wanted to hang around and take more photos of the rodeo riders. When Freddy volunteered to drive her back to Rockport, Kacey was relieved that she and Leon would be alone in the car, where she planned to grill him until she got to the truth about his and Nona's relationship, and a few other troubling matters.

Thankfully, bidding Linette good-bye helped Kacey disguise her rising anxiety. She hugged her friend hard, wishing Linette could stick around a while longer.

"Sure you don't want to meet for breakfast?" Kacey asked her friend.

"No way," Linette answered with a smile. "I'll be long

gone before you even wake up. Got an early flight out of Corpus in the morning. The next assignment calls."

"Well, good luck in Chicago. And don't let all those crying babies get to you."

"I won't," Linette promised with a laugh.

"Gee, I'm so glad you were able to come and help me out," Kacey added as she gave Linette a final hug. "We'll talk...*soon*."

Once Kacey and Leon were on the road back to Rockport, Leon turned to her. "So what do you think about rodeos now?" he asked.

"It was great. Very entertaining. However, I can't say the same about Nona's performance," Kacey quipped.

Leon grimaced, cut his eyes at Kacey and cocked his head to one side. "Performance? What'd she do?"

"It's not what she did, it's what she said," Kacey tossed out, ending her sentence with a loud huff of disgust that told Leon something was definitely wrong.

He tightened his grip on the steering wheel and listened while Kacey recounted everything that Nona had said, his temper rising to the boiling point as she registered her complaints. "I don't know Nona well enough to gauge her motivation, but you do. What's going on with her? "

Leon stared out the windshield, furious with Nona, yet somewhat relieved that she'd provided the opening he needed to talk about a painful period in his past, of which he was very ashamed. Sooner or later he would have had to tell Kacey about the youthful mistake that had been a source of town gossip for years. It had also been a turning point in his life, forcing him to make big changes and grow up.

"First," he began, "don't believe any of Nona's stupid talk. I wasn't engaged four times only once. And it ended when my fiancée left me for another man. Sure, I've dated around and had some fun. But I'm not a serial heartbreaker."

"What about Nona? Why does she act like you two have something going on?"

"Me and Nona?" He sputtered in laughter. "Absolutely nothing. Other than a longtime friendship. She has a way of exaggerating things. Always has. Yes, it's true that Nona and I dated in high school, but I already told you that."

"She must be stuck in high school then, because she seems determined to try to make me believe that nothing has changed since then."

"Doesn't surprise me that she'd tell you I have romantic feelings for her, which I certainly do not."

"Why is she doing that?"

"Jealous, I guess. You see, she's never really had a serious relationship or dated anyone special. She's a loner. Guess I've always felt kinda sorry for her, and I know I go out of my way to pay attention to her."

"Like how?"

"Oh, sometimes I'll ask her to go to a movie or out to eat, just to cheer her up. Kind of like a big brother would do, you know?"

"But don't you realize how seriously she takes your brotherly acts of kindness? She's in love with you!"

"I dunno about that. She's just lonely," Leon defended.

"No, she's just crazy!" Kacey decided. "And dangerous, too. She told me you did time in prison. Did you?"

"Oh, well, about that. Yeah, but it was county jail, not prison. See how she exaggerates?"

"Why were you arrested?" Kacey wanted to know.

Leon quickly struck back with the truth. "I was young. Running with the wrong crowd. I went to the police to turn my friends in when they held up a store, but I got rounded up with the other guys who were involved in the robbery and spent six weeks in county jail." He paused. "That was so long ago. I can't believe Nona would drag that mess out of the closet. I'm gonna have a serious talk with her."

"A talk? I think you ought to fire her!" Kacey threw out. "I don't understand why you put up with her nonsense, let alone keep her on your payroll."

Leon sighed, feeling Kacey's frustration. He was used to Nona and her quirky ways, but not everyone could tolerate her, as he'd learned to do. "It's not that easy to fire her, or any employee at Archer. Nona has worked for my family's company forever. Only job she's ever had. Where would she go if I fired her? How would she support herself? She'd have to leave Rockport to find a new job."

"And maybe find a new life," Kacey mumbled.

"I can't do that to her. She'll be okay."

"Think so?"

"Yeah, I do."

"Then you're dreaming, Leon. You're way too trusting of her."

"Maybe you're too suspicious. Living in a crime-filled city's made you too paranoid. You're always looking for the worst in a person, instead of the best."

"I'm simply being realistic. You're too damn laid-back."

"You're too tense!" Leon threw back, raising one hand from the steering wheel to slap it back down for emphasis.

"That woman is dead set on causing trouble. And when everything blows apart, I don't plan to be around," Kacey vowed.

Leon bit his lip in concern. Kacey was putting him in a difficult spot. How could he choose between alienating a longtime friend and keeping the woman he had grown to love? How had his life gotten so damn complicated, so quickly?

Kacey sat in silence during the remainder of the drive back to the motel. The tension in the car was depressing. Their argument over Nona had spoiled what had been a perfect outing at the rodeo, and Kacey silently fumed. The fact that Leon seemed to accept Nona's rude behavior was disturbing. What was it going to take for him to see how dangerous she was?

When they arrived at the Seaside Suites, Kacey turned and looked at Leon, knowing her feelings for him had been put to the test. Should she disregard the unsettling tales that Nona was determined to tell? Close her eyes to Nona's attempts to live in the past? Trust Leon to handle things? Or should she get out of Rockport and return to New York, leaving this mess behind?

As much as she wanted to untangle herself from this small town muddle, she knew she had to stay until Archer completed the full production of SunKissed by Kacey. Tomorrow, and during the days that followed, she would work with Leon and finish the job she'd come to Rockport to do because she had plans that depended on successfully bringing her designs to market. She couldn't afford to stumble. What about the apartment in midtown Manhattan that she wanted to lease? Her financial freedom? The sense of professional accomplishment she craved? She'd stick it out with Leon because they made a good team and she needed a successful launch of her designs.

Kacey bit her lip. In business, and in bed, they certainly clicked. The sexual chemistry between them was hotter than any Kacey had never known, but was that enough to counter Nona's dogged interference? Would Leon's odd determination to maintain his friendship with her eventually take its toll on his relationship with Kacey? Did Kacey even want to stick with him long enough to find out? After all, she had a swimwear line to produce. A career to protect. Even though she may have found the man of her dreams, she might have to let him go.

After dropping Kacey at the Seaside, Leon drove along the beach road, his spirits sagging as low as the palm fronds swaying on the dark horizon. He knew he was head over heels in love with Kacey, but worried about what she must think of him now. Maybe he shouldn't have gotten so emotionally involved with this city girl. Nona was right about one thing: Kacey would only be around for a few more days. By next week she might be gone. Falling for a sophisticated woman like Kacey could only lead to a broken heart, anyway. Could Nona be right? Was he fooling himself to think that a woman like Kacey could ever fully understand him or his loyalty to his longtime friends, many of whom were his employees? How much would he have to give up if he wanted to keep Kacey Parker in his life?

Chapter 19

On Monday morning, Kacey went straight into her cubicle without stopping by Leon's office to say good morning. She got busy on her computer, desperate to forget about her testy exchange with Nona and the pain of her argument with Leon. Her impulsive affair with Leon had evolved much too quickly, and she'd allowed herself to tumble into an intimate relationship without considering the consequences. There could be no more daydreams about making love with Leon. No more fantasies about escaping the city to live with him in his paradise on the beach. Instead of allowing herself to be consumed by romantic plans that had no future, she was going to focus on the present. And that required a total break with Leon.

Gulping back her disappointment at the way things had turned out on the personal side of her Rockport adventure, Kacey began to read her emails. The first was a message from Steve Hadley. He'd reviewed the photos that Linette shot on the beach and had approved the samples, giving Kacey the go-ahead she needed to finalize production. He'd copied Leon as well, advising him to institute overtime at the plant if he had to, but to proceed quickly with the SunKissed line. Hadley expected to have finished products shipped by the end of the following week.

That means I don't have much time left in Rockport, she calculated, relieved that Hadley's time frame would help her accept the fact that her stay in Rockport was rapidly coming to an end. Kacey had to make sure that nothing interfered with the scheduled delivery of her swimsuits to Leeman's warehouse in New York.

The remainder of the morning was consumed by a phone conversation with Adriana as Kacey went over their marketing plan. And when Leon buzzed Kacey to invite her to lunch so they could talk, she turned him down, desperate for space and time to cool things down between them.

Leon pulled out of the Archer parking lot and headed to Buddy's for lunch. He'd hoped Kacey might join him so they could begin to patch up whatever had gone wrong. Dammit! He'd instituted mandatory overtime for all his key staff members to push the swimsuit project into its final stage. However, instead of feeling elated, Leon was depressed. At least his father would be pleased to know that the plant was running full tilt and smoothly...even though his attempt to woo Kacey Parker had gone terribly off track.

Kacey was barely speaking to him. Nona was acting

very agitated and remote. And even Bob Truett was unhappy with Leon's push to get the SunKissed line finished ahead of all their other projects. Leon was worried about Bob, who had been acting very nervous and edgy lately. When he stormed into Leon's office to complain about his decision to fast-track Kacey's project over other pending jobs, Leon had been surprised by how upset Truett had been. He'd told Leon that Mr. Archer had never called for mandatory overtime for the entire staff, and that he didn't like pushing those who worked under him so hard. Besides, the decision to let pending contracts languish was going to upset valuable longtime clients and hurt business. He told Leon that by creating such an intense atmosphere in the plant that morale would surely fall and accidents were likely to happen. "Leon Sr. would never have treated his employees this way," Truett boldly admonished.

"Well, Truett, you'll just have to get used to my way of doing things," Leon grumbled to himself as he pulled into the parking lot at the busy barbecue joint.

Sitting in his car, he watched people he'd known all his life come and go, his thoughts centered on the first time he'd brought Kacey to the restaurant. It had been a clear, sunny day like this. They'd had an unforgettable time together. But then, they'd had many unforgettable times, hadn't they? He smiled to recall the night at Archer when they were fitting samples in the dressing room and he wound up pleasuring her on the worktable. He could still feel the rush of desire that gripped him during her erotic photo shoot on the beach. And how could he forget the excitement on Kacey's face as she'd watched her first rodeo? During those moments, he had been absolutely certain that his happiness was grounded in a future with Kacey. But now, he wasn't so sure.

With a shake of his head, Leon got out of his car and entered Buddy's barbecue joint. After picking up a chopped beef sandwich and a soda at the counter, he was headed to a table at the back of the dining room when he heard Nona calling out to him.

"Over here," she invited, motioning for him to join her at the table they'd often shared at the front of the eatery. Through reluctant to do so, he knew it would look awfully strange for him to sit alone in the back of Buddy's when, for so many years, he and Nona and Truett had lunched together at their favorite table near the windows facing the street. Though not pleased to have been trapped into sitting with Nona, Leon decided that doing so might give him the perfect opportunity to talk to her about what she'd told Kacey at the rodeo.

"What's going on?" Nona asked casually, as soon as Leon was seated across from her.

What was going on? Leon wondered, thinking back over the past week, recalling how close he'd gotten to Kacey and how much he didn't want to hurt her. Where had he messed up? All he had done was tell her the truth about his past and defend his friendship with Nona. Was that so bad?

Leon cocked an eyebrow at Nona, then took a bite of his sandwich, and followed it with a long sip of his soda. When he finished, he zeroed in on Nona, ready to hash everything out. "What happened yesterday?"

"Yesterday?" Nona replied, sounding confused. She slid back in her seat, eyes beamed at half mast on Leon.

"Why did you tell Kacey all that mess about my past?" Leon demanded.

With a shrug, Nona frowned, hooked her fingers together in her lap and puckered her plum-colored lips. "I just wanted her to know you better. So I decided to tell her about our old times together, kinda fill her in on you and me."

"You and me?" Leon growled in a tightly controlled voice, no longer struggling to hide his anger. He remained stone-cold still for a long moment before he managed to speak again. "What do you mean by that?"

Silence thickened the tension hanging between them as his question settled in. He watched Nona nervously clench her fingernails into her palms, clearly upset by his angry tone. Perhaps he had been too protective of Nona over the years. By befriending her and allowing her to creep so deeply into his and his parent's lives, he'd made her believe that she belonged to him, that he belonged to her, that their lives would forever be emotionally entwined.

Now, Leon knew he had made a big mistake and it was time for a reality check, even if it destroyed their friendship.

Too bad, he decided. *She's gonna answer to me for getting Kacey so upset, and we're going to settle this right now.*

"I wanted Kacey to know that you and I shared a lot in the past, and we're still close."

"Get this straight, Nona. There is no you and me. No *us*, okay?" Leon paced his words for emphasis.

"I…I only wanted Kacey to know how tight we are. How much I care about you," Nona whined, her voice growing smaller with each word, in definite contrast to her outsize presence.

"I do care about you Nona, you know that. But don't talk about our friendship as if it were romantic!"

"I didn't do that," Nona shot back, suddenly jerking forward. "I never said I was your girlfriend or anything like that. I only told her we used to date."

"Yes, we did. But that's ancient history. Stop living in the past, Nona. You've been my good friend for a long time, but don't try to make it sound like you're more than that. Kacey doesn't need to hear about our past... which is *past*. Understand? There's no need go there, okay?"

"So, are you in love with her?" Nona's question was barely a whisper.

Slowly, Leon nodded. "Yes, I am," he admitted. "And I've told her so." He was tired of playing the field, and knew that he wanted to get married and start a family, but only with Kacey Parker.

"So, it's like that, huh?" Nona huffed her disdain, as if mocking Leon's confession.

Leon flinched to see Nona's face suddenly crumple into a contorted frown, her raw disappointment very clear.

With a sniff, Nona went on. "Kacey's nothin' but another notch to add to your belt of broken hearts."

"Not true. I don't plan to break Kacey's heart," Leon vowed.

"Ha! She'll break *yours* first," Nona snapped. "What do you think is gonna happen when she's finished here? She'll leave you and go back to New York where she belongs. A woman like Kacey Parker would never live in Rockport, and even if she did, she'd never love it like you...and I do. Face it, Leon, it'll never work out for you and her."

"That's not for you to say, Nona. I plan to do whatever I can to make it work with her, and I expect you to respect her. Leave her…and me…alone. Got that?"

"That's kinda hard to do, since your mother and father are like parents to me…and your mom expects me to take care of you."

Leon shook his head in frustration. Nona was determined to cling to him via his mother's emotional ties to Nona's family, but that was not going to work. "My mother didn't ask you to do anything for me! Stop twisting her words. I can take care of myself, so please butt out of my life!"

Leon was not surprised to see tears well up in Nona's eyes, run down her face and streak her makeup. He hated to see her cry. Wished he didn't have to be so harsh with her, but she'd crossed the line and he had no choice but to put her in her place.

Nona sent Leon a cutting look, threw her napkin over her unfinished lunch and stood. Leaning low over Leon, with both hands gripping the table's edge, she told him, "I belong here. Kacey doesn't. You're gonna regret putting all your trust in her." Then she turned, swishing her large hips from side to side as she sashayed out of the dining room, leaving Leon exasperated, yet certain he'd done the right thing. His one and only desire was to keep Kacey in his life, and if he had to push Nona under the bus to make that happen, he didn't care.

Chapter 20

Sleep eluded Kacey. In her bed at the Seaside Suites, she tumbled from side to side, twisting her sheets into knots as visions of her time in Rockport swept through her mind. A miserable week had passed since her rodeo outing and the awful argument with Leon, but so much had changed between them. First, for the worse, and then for the better. And now, everything seemed to be moving ahead smoothly.

The fragrant red roses on her nightstand symbolized how far she and Leon had come in repairing their relationship, and with each breath she took, the scent brought him deeper into her heart. She loved Leon and believed him when he told her that he loved her, too. But would it last? Would the things that made them so uniquely suited for each other overshadow the differences that lurked below the surface? Kacey certainly hoped so, because she yearned for the kind of steadfast love that would last a lifetime, bonding her to Leon for eternity.

With a sigh, Kacey let her thoughts slip back to review the hectic, emotion-filled week, still thrilled, but cautious about all that had transpired. Monday had been the hardest day to get through, and she had only managed to do so by remaining in her office all day, and then leaving the factory very early. On Tuesday, Leon flew to Dallas for a meeting with a potential client, so she'd had a full day without worry over how to avoid him. On Wednesday, they'd been forced to dispense with the mutual silent treatment to discuss a glitch in the production of SunKissed, during which they both agreed that the swimsuits looked fine, but the unit packaging had to be revised. By Thursday, Kacey was so miserable she felt ill, and finally relented when Leon invited her to lunch where they apologized to each other for the harsh words they'd flung at one another in the car. And when Friday arrived, and Leon invited Kacey to attend a Texas beachwear trade show in Houston, where they would have to spend the night, she agreed, prepared to put their troubles behind them and get their relationship back on track.

While trapped in Leon's sports car during the four-hour trip from Rockport to Houston, he and Kacey melted all barriers. They discussed their childhoods, how Kacey had launched her career in retail, their hopes, dreams and visions of the future. And neither mentioned Nona James or her erratic personality.

No longer trying to skirt their emotions, they were able to share personal feelings about love, happiness and even marriage. The ease with which they were able to converse about such deeply private subjects cracked the wall of silence and misguided resentment that had hung uneasily between them all week.

When they arrived at the convention hall in Houston, they playfully explored the exhibits and took in all the excitement of discovering new products and sampling new wares. It was as if the tension and silence of the past had never occurred. They left their private troubles behind and enjoyed the trade show—going with the flow as this new stage in their relationship unfolded.

Now, Kacey turned onto her side and pushed her cheek into her near-flat pillow, reliving the delicious make-up sex they'd experienced while in Houston. Even though they'd been all about business while at the trade show, afterward, when he brought her back to the Hyatt Regency Houston, where they were staying, she'd cratered emotionally and invited him to her room.

Discarding their clothes as soon as the door was shut, they succumbed to a sizzling, skyrocketing sexual joining that fed Kacey's seemingly insatiable hunger for Leon. His sensual tongue had entered every orifice of her body and slicked every inch of her skin. His probing fingers set her spirit aflame and melted all resistance to loving him completely. Lying with him as his hands grazed her body with a possessive, yet tender touch, she eagerly returned his kisses, drinking in his presence with soul-drenching gulps.

By welcoming Leon back into her heart, and her body, Kacey had created a new path to the future, where fiery mutual climaxes, gentle returns to earth and a lifetime of love awaited.

Now, Kacey could still feel the shock of their commitment and shivered in its aftermath. Loving Leon left her tingling with satisfaction and ready to admit that she never wanted to let him go. However, neither of them wanted a long-distance love affair. What they wanted was to be together in one place, and to build a life together. But how?

He was such a loving man. He treated her as if she were a precious gift, which he unwrapped slowly and cherished deeply. Even when they had not been on speaking terms, he had continued to treat her with respect, without pressing or prodding her to change her mind about him, but only to understand. He had been right to leave her alone to make her own decisions about whether or not they had a future together. Now, as they went around town, Kacey no longer felt like a stranger, there to do business and move on. She was Leon Archer's woman and he made no effort to hide the fact that he was totally and hopelessly in love with her.

Despite the pressures of her career in retail and their contrasting lifestyles, Kacey was determined to remain optimistic about sharing a future with Leon. With a smothered groan, she closed her eyes and forced back the lump that was growing in her throat. Too soon, she'd have to go back to New York to work with Steve Hadley as Leeman's launched her swimsuit line. But once the product was in stores and selling well, she planned to come back to Rockport, and back into Leon's waiting arms. As hard as it might be, she had to face facts. Sacrificing her city-bound lifestyle to be with the man she loved might be the only solution.

As her mind weighed her options, she realized that the energy-packed streets of New York and the prospect of moving into a new apartment were not so appealing.

She didn't look forward to getting on a plane headed east, leaving Leon behind—with Nona standing in the shadows, gloating. Even though it was hard to admit, Kacey knew Leon would never be happy in New York. He was a country guy at heart, and trying to change him would only court disaster.

Luckily, Nona had kept her distance since their flap at the rodeo, and that was fine with Kacey. As far as she was concerned, the woman was a pathetic figure trapped in a past that kept her company at night because she didn't have a man of her own. Kacey believed Leon when he said that Nona was only a dear friend, but she still worried that his refusal to acknowledge how dangerous Nona's jealous nature could become might be a big mistake.

"I pity Nona, but she'd have to keep her distance from me and Leon if I moved to Rockport," Kacey murmured, knowing it would be hell to live there as Leon Archer's wife as long as Nona James was hanging around. *But she'll never leave Rockport and he'll never fire her. Something had to give. But what?* Kacey wondered as she drifted off to sleep.

Kacey bolted awake to the shrieking sounds of sirens. She sat up in bed and squinted around the room, confused by the blur of flashing red lights that illuminated the windows. Gasping in alarm, she jumped out of bed, yanked up the blinds and quickly saw that the frightening sounds were coming from two fire trucks that had raced past the motel and were speeding down the road. Troubled by the sight, Kacey's heart pounded in agitation as she watched the vehicles disappear into the night.

Rattled by the disturbance, she went to her minifridge and got a bottle of water. After taking a long swig, she slid back into bed, hoping she'd be able to get back to sleep. However, the phone on her nightstand rang before she could lie down. Panicked, she snatched the receiver while checking the clock. At 2:45 in the morning, who could it be?

"Hello?" she ventured, feeling totally disoriented from the sudden jolt that had awakened her in the middle of the night.

"Kacey. It's Leon. There's a fire at the plant. I'm on my way over there now."

"Oh, no! Not a fire!" Kacey shouted in alarm. "I ll meet you there!" she yelled, slamming down the phone as she hurried to get dressed.

Chapter 21

The sight that greeted Leon when he arrived on the scene made his stomach turn over in despair. Three fire trucks were already pouring water onto the crackling inferno when he stepped out of his car and surveyed the scene from across the road, feeling the heat on his face.

Within minutes, local residents, Archer employees and curious passersby began to gather, pulling their cars to a stop on the road across from Archer.

When Leon saw Roger Evans, the county fire chief, actively directing his men as they struggled to get the fire under control, he raced forward, wishing he could dash inside and rescue Kacey's swimwear, which was boxed and stacked on the loading dock, prepared to be shipped. It was all going up in smoke before his eyes. The sight sent tears streaming down his face.

"Stay back," Roger warned, frowning at Leon, who knew the firefighters were doing everything possible to get the upper hand on the blaze, which seemed to grow hotter by the second. When a burst of flames shot high in the air, Leon screamed, "Oh, no! Roger! Any hope of saving the building?" Then he raced as close to the fire as he dared.

"We're trying!" the fire chief yelled back, waving his arm toward Leon. "Don't go any closer, Leon. This is a pretty aggressive blaze we've got here. Stay back. I know you have solvents inside that can really rev this up and make it blow." Then he turned away from Leon and hurried over to help a fireman who was setting up a fourth hose to attack the raging flames.

Leon sagged against the side of his car and watched in stunned silence as the company his family had built slowly turned into a pile of ashes. The only thing that was not engulfed in flames was the Archer Industries sign, rising high in the dark sky atop the two-story building.

When Kacey arrived and slid her arm around his waist, he pulled her to his side and used the back of his hand to wipe away tears that filled his smoke-stung eyes.

"This is awful," he moaned, voice raw with pain.

"A tragedy," Kacey agreed. "Thank God, no one was hurt."

"For real. I'm gonna find out how this happened—count on it," Leon said through gritted teeth while Kacey stroked his back.

It was midmorning when the last fire truck pulled away from the charred shell that had once been Archer

Industries. Chief Evans stayed behind with the arson crew that arrived to determine the cause of the fire. As Kacey and Leon surveyed the damage, they held onto each other—as if afraid that the fire might consume them, too.

Nona, who'd arrived on the scene shortly after Kacey, remained in her car, looking so stone-faced and angry that Kacey wondered if the jealous woman might know something about what happened. However, Kacey held her tongue. All Leon would do is defend his longtime friend, anyway.

Knots of employees who worked at the plant were standing around, shaking their heads and wondering what had caused the fire that had taken their livelihoods away.

"Leon. I need to talk to you!" Roger Evans called out as he emerged from the ruins and approached Leon, who hurried forward to consult with the fire chief.

Kacey hung back by the edge of the road while the two men engaged in what appeared to be a very serious conversation. As she watched them walk around the still-smoking site, her heart raced and her mind whirled with the implications of this disaster.

Everything was gone. All her hard work had gone up in smoke. Though she knew her thoughts were selfish, all she could think about at that moment was finding another manufacturer to start over, so she could get her swimwear into Leeman's by the end of the month. This disaster could not signal the end for her long-held dream. Surely, Steve Hadley would want to go forward, wouldn't he? But what if he didn't? She began to feel physically ill.

* * *

"The fire chief suspects it might have been arson," Leon told Kacey when he returned to where she waited.

"Arson!" Kacey repeated in shock. "Really? Who would do something so terrible?'

"I dunno," Leon replied, shaking his head.

"I hate to say this…but I wouldn't put it past Nona," Kacey now boldly accused. "She'd do anything to see my swimwear line fail."

Leon jerked back a few steps and peered angrily at Kacey. "Don't you dare accuse Nona of setting this fire! She loves this place as much as I do."

"Just thinking out loud," Kacey defended.

"Don't! That's a terrible thing to say! You don't know Nona the way I do."

"I know that Nona James is not a stable woman and it wouldn't surprise me if she'd do something like this, just to hurt me…and for the attention. All…"

"Stop it, Kacey," Leon interrupted, his voice getting louder and angrier by the moment. "You're way off base. Why would she destroy the company where she makes her living?"

"People under pressure have done stranger things," Kacey threw back.

"Maybe in New York, but not in Rockport. Folks in these parts don't do crazy stuff like that."

"Harrumph," Kacey grunted, jerking her head toward Nona's car. "Believe that if you want to, Leon, but if I were you, I'd be over there asking *her* a whole lot of questions."

Leon shook his head in denial, glowering at Kacey. "I can't have this discussion now." He walked a few steps away and then stopped. "I've gotta go over to the sheriff's headquarters to fill out a bunch of papers. He's the one who asks the questions, not me." Leon hesitated, as if steadying his emotions. "I've gotta do all I can to help the fire department figure this out as soon as possible because the insurance company won't come through until every question is resolved."

"Sure, I know. I'm sorry," Kacey relented, realizing that he was under a lot of pressure and she shouldn't have brought his friendship with Nona into the mix. Maybe Leon was right. Maybe Kacey was jumping to the wrong conclusion and ought to trust his judgment. After all, he knew his employees better than she did and it was his problem to solve. "Yeah, you go ahead," she told him, stepping closer, letting him know she was sorry. "I'm going back to the motel to call Hadley. Gotta let him know what happened."

Leon opened his arms and Kacey moved into them as he held her tight. "Forgive me for yelling. I'm sorry," he murmured against her hair.

"Forget it. This is not your fault," she comforted.

"But I feel responsible. Your dream went up in ashes on my watch."

"Yours did, too," Kacey comforted, feeling the rapid beat of Leon's heart against her breast. She knew he was devastated, as he should be. All she could do was be there for him, encourage him to remain positive. At least no one had been hurt. Archer's insurance would kick in so the family could rebuild and go on.

But can I? Kacey worried, dreading the phone call to Hadley that she knew she had to make.

"I'll catch up with you later," Leon told Kacey, giving her a firm kiss on the lips before letting her go.

"Stay strong," she told him, returning his kiss, one hand caressing his cheek.

As Kacey headed across the road, she looked over at Nona, who had been watching her and Leon. "I hope you saw whatever you were looking for," Kacey said in a voice loud enough for Nona to hear. As she passed by Nona's car, Kacey gave the woman a withering look, then got in her car, made a U-turn and headed back toward town.

Chapter 22

The days following the fire passed in a blur of activity, during which Kacey rarely saw Leon, who was swamped with complaints from upset clients, interrogations with the sheriff's office, and calls from his insurance company. He helped his employees file for unemployment—which everyone took except Nona. Leon decided to keep her on the payroll to help him piece together company records that he'd salvaged from the fire. At least many contracts had been safeguarded in the fireproof safe.

When Leon wasn't comforting anxious employees or meeting with the Archer family lawyer, he was relaying messages to his parents through their travel agent because his mom and dad were in the middle of the desert on safari. His dad had given him three directives to follow: First, do not cancel any contracts; let the clients do the canceling. Second, contact American Textile in Houston and arrange for them to finish any pending projects. And finally, Leon was to use the family house as Archer Industries headquarters until everything was resolved.

With his company in ashes, Leon did as his father asked. He successfully arranged for American Textile Manufacturing to take over clients who did not want to cancel their contracts, and set up a temporary office in his father's study. As he and Nona worked through the paperwork nightmare, he quickly saw that the financial loss for Archer was going to be substantial. Even though Archer's insurance would eventually cover most of his losses, getting cash in hand was going to take some time. However, taking care of his clients was his first priority because once Archer was back in business, he hoped they would return.

Under great strain, Leon stayed closeted in his makeshift office with either Nona or Gerald Ayers day and night as they feverishly worked to sort everything out.

While Leon dealt with Archer Industries' problems, Kacey made progress of her own. She asked Hadley not to cancel their agreement with Archer, but to allow Leon to shift the production to American Textile in order to complete her swimsuit line. He agreed to think about it, but ordered Kacey back to New York until the decision was made.

Hopeful that SunKissed could be saved, Kacey packed her bags and prepared to head home, relieved to have Hadley's fragile support. Leon, who wasn't happy to see Kacey go, was at least grateful that the Leeman's contract remained under his control.

On the night before her departure, she went to see Leon at his beach house for a final evening together.

During the drive there, she thought back over all that had happened since her arrival, which seemed like ages ago. She'd never guessed when she arrived in Rockport that leaving would be so difficult, but then she had never thought she'd fall in love, either. Leon was trying hard to be brave about the separation, but she knew he was hurting as much as she was. Hopefully, they'd find their way back to each other before too long. At least, that was what she kept telling herself as the coastal landscape slipped by.

Leon welcomed Kacey with a deep kiss that totally aroused her need for him and made her moan in satisfaction. As his tongue explored hers, she cupped her hands around his tight, hard butt and squeezed, ready to surrender. However, their goodbye session was quickly interrupted when Leon's cell phone rang. Answering it, he scowled, let go of Kacey and went to sit down on one of the canvas lounge chairs on the deck.

"What did you say?" he snapped, voice sharp and hard. "You've got to be kidding!" He covered the mouthpiece and whispered "Chief Evans" at Kacey, who sat down beside Leon on the chaise.

"What's going on?" she hissed into Leon's ear.

He placed a hand on her thigh and answered with a slow shake of his head, as if whatever the fire chief was saying was too incredible to interrupt. "Impossible. I'm shocked," Leon finally stated, sinking back into his chair to stare glumly at the blue-black sky. "Yeah, I can do that, chief. I'll be there first thing in the morning." And then he clicked off.

Running his thumb over the screen of his cell phone, he focused on the floor of the deck while shaking his head in amazement. "That was Rodney Evans, the fire chief."

"Yeah…I know. So what'd he want?"

"The mystery of the fire has been solved."

"Damn! Does he know who did it?"

Leon swung his head back and forth while a stream of air escaped his lips. "Yeah. It was Bob Truett."

"Bob Truett! You've gotta be kidding."

"Wish I were."

"Why? How'd they find out it was him?"

"He confessed." Leon tilted his body forward, gulping back his shock. "The chief said Truett walked into the sheriff's office tonight and turned himself in. He confessed to setting the fire, and he was responsible for sabotaging the electrical grid and the backup pattern disk, too."

"What? But why?" Kacey pressed.

"Evans said Truett was rambling on about how much he missed working for my father. That he didn't like the way I was running the plant. That I was overworking him and he couldn't take the stress. "

"What did Truett do? How'd he start the fire?"

"He placed open containers of cleaning solvents next to the fabric cutting machines and left them running all night. They overheated and started the fire." A pause while Leon sat in stunned silence. "I can't believe he'd rather see the place destroyed than work for me. He could have quit. He was old enough to retire," Leon said, sounding depressed.

Kacey touched Leon on the arm. "Well, at least, the sheriff can close the case, and now you know what happened."

Leon simply nodded.

Kacey bit her lip, took a deep breath and then plunged ahead with what she knew she had to say. "Leon, I was wrong about Nona. I never should have accused her. I'm sorry, Leon."

Leon took her hand and squeezed it. "That's okay. I understand."

"Thanks, because I didn't. She's your friend, and I shouldn't have doubted your trust in her. I'm sorry, really, I am."

"I appreciate your saying that, Kacey. I know this hasn't been easy for you, either. I'm just happy that Leeman's might still go forward with your line with American taking it over."

"Another good thing that will come out of this," Kacey started, "is that Truett's confession means the insurance company can settle your claim."

"Yeah, so I can start to rebuild."

Kacey nodded. "Right. So why don't we focus on the positive side of the chief's news and not dwell on anything sad tonight."

Leon stood, took Kacey by the hand and tugged her to her feet. "Good idea. I'm not about to let a phone call ruin my last night with you. Now, can we pick up where we left off before my cell phone rang?"

"Absolutely. Let's go inside," Kacey agreed in a voice that drifted into a whisper.

After entering Leon's wild–animal themed bedroom, they came together in a tender embrace, gently and deliberately, as if creating memories to last until they could reunite. Not knowing when that would happen added tension to the experience, creating an invisible thread of caution that heightened their anxiety, as well as their drive to seal their commitment.

Fueled by the tormenting prospect of a long separation, Leon used his lips to nibble a path along Kacey's neck, over her chest and onto each breast, fondling her nipples with his slippery tongue. His hands swept her torso and seared her thighs, massaging her silken skin. When he reached the pleasure point between Kacey's legs, she bucked upward, accommodating his fingers, which he slid deep inside to slick her pulsing core. With his other hand he reached over to grab protection, which Kacey helped him open and slide on.

Impatient to have him completely, Kacey gripped his rock-hard manhood and guided it inside, replacing his fingers with what she craved most—the sensation of his rigid rod filling her up, taking her completely and burning itself into her flesh. As she groaned, writhed and moved under the weight of his naked body, Leon transported her to a place where none of their troubles existed. All that mattered was the connection that bound them, the love that they shared and the promise of tomorrow.

Afterward, they lay side by side in his huge bed, wrapped in each other's arms as they struggled to define the shape of their future.

"I don't want you to go," Leon told Kacey, stroking her hair as he kissed her on the forehead.

"I don't want to leave, either, but I have to," she replied, reaching up to cup her fingers around Leon's chin.

He kissed her fingertips, dragging his tongue over her skin in a sensuous sweep. "You don't *have* to go. Not really. Didn't you say that Hadley has already talked with American?"

"Yes," she whispered.

"So why do you need to go to New York?"

"Because I have work to do. I do have a job, remember?" Kacey responded, shifting in Leon's arms to look at him, trembling with longing as his gray eyes penetrated hers.

"Stay here with me for a few more days," Leon begged. "I need you, Kacey. Hadley can manage the production. You don't need to go."

"Yes, I do," Kacey replied, hating to sound so cold, but knowing it was time to return to reality. The dream escape was over, for now, and she had to face the truth. "I can't throw away my career. I worked hard to get where I am, Leeman's has invested a lot in me and Hadley expects results. As much as I'd like to stay, I can't. I have to leave tomorrow."

Leon shook his head and ran a finger along the side of her face, studying her as if trying to memorize her face. "Kacey, I don't know how I'll stand it, being so far from you. I understand why you have to go, but I still don't like it. I wish you would leave New York completely. Live here with me. We'll get married. Rebuild the plant. Start over together. Leeman's can sell your swimsuits and send you a fat check for your designs. Cut ties with them—and the city—and stay."

"I can't do that," Kacey told Leon, edging out of his arms. She got out of bed and started to dress. Looking out his bedroom window, she saw that the full moon had made a silvery path on the surface of the pitch-black Gulf, leaving a shimmering road that seemed to have no end. As her eyes traced the moonlit water, she thought that the pathway resembled the long road ahead that she and Leon faced. Where would it end? How long would the journey last until they reunited? What awaited them on the other side?

"If you loved me, you'd stay," Leon suddenly challenged.

With her back to Leon, Kacey frowned, troubled by his remark, as well as his attitude. Didn't he see how torn she was over her complicated dilemma? No way could she simply walk away from her career. Why didn't he understand?

Whirling around, she faced Leon, irritated that he expected so much from her while giving up so little of himself.

"Why are you making this so difficult for me? Aren't you being a bit selfish?" she pushed back, confused by his inability, or refusal, to realize that she wouldn't dream of bailing on Steve Hadley, who'd gone to great lengths to advance her career as a designer.

"No, I'm not being selfish," Leon countered. "I love you. I want you with me."

"Leon, I love you, too, but I can't be with you now."

"You could...you could stay. You don't have to live or work in New York to be a swimsuit designer."

"Don't you understand what returning to New York means? That's where I earn a living. The city is my home. Where I belong. At least for now."

"You belong wherever you can be happy, and you can't tell me that you're going to be happy if we're apart."

Kacey sucked in a long breath, allowing his words to roam her mind, knowing what he said was true. "You're right...I won't be happy, but under these circumstances

I'm willing to sacrifice my personal happiness to achieve something just as important."

"What?"

"Success in my career."

"Ah...now I see where you're coming from. You choose career over love. Okay, go for it, Kacey. Thanks for letting me know exactly where I stand."

Kacey stared at Leon, shocked by the hurt in his voice. Was she finally seeing Leon for who he really was? A self-centered man with no feelings for things that meant so much to her? With the future of her swimsuit line in jeopardy and Leon's crazy attitude filling her head with doubts, maybe the best thing Kacey could do was return to New York. She wasn't that keen on small town life, anyway.

"I've got to go," Kacey told Leon, now dressed. She reached for her purse. At least she'd didn't have to ask him to drive her to the motel.

Still naked, Leon got out of bed and walked toward Kacey, appearing disappointed and upset. "Not yet," he murmured, reaching out to her. "I hate that I snapped. It's just so damn hard to let you go. Forgive me?"

Kacey nodded, feeling his misery, and knowing how hard it was going to be for them both. "I'd better leave now. Let's use this time apart to think about what we want and how we can keep our lives together."

"I know what I want," he whispered, inching closer to Kacey, his manhood at attention. "I have only one desire, to live happily ever after with you. To love you forever. If I have to leave Rockport and move to New York, I will. I'd sacrifice all I have here to be with you. You know that, don't you, Kacey?"

Kacey swallowed the pain that stabbed her heart to

hear him say those words. "Yes…and everything *will* work out for us, Leon…but we need time to sort this out. Will you give it to us?"

He pulled her hard to his chest and crushed his mouth to hers. "Yes, you know I will. But let's not take too long," he murmured against her neck.

Without a reply, Kacey pulled away, raced out of his bedroom and across the deck, as the sound of waves hitting the shore pounded in her ears and tears of longing filled her eyes.

Chapter 23

Leon spent his days working out plans to rebuild the factory and his nights reflecting on his and Kacey's dilemma. They spoke on the phone every night, but nothing was the same. The strain of their separation was taking a toll. He missed her like crazy but refused to press her about the fate of their relationship, willing to bide his time until her swimwear was in Leeman's stores and selling well, until she had completed the most important step in her new career. Then, they'd make a decision about what they ought to do.

One thing Leon knew: remaining stuck in limbo as precious time slipped away made him feel like a prisoner awaiting his sentence—hoping for the best, but dreading the worse. The situation grew more unbearable every day.

Two weeks after he and Kacey parted, Nona showed

up at Leon's beach house, holding a bottle of brandy and wearing a too-tight tank top that made her nipples stand out like two silver dollars. When she swept inside and started gloating over the fact that now that Kacey was out of Rockport, everything was back to normal between them, Leon's patience snapped.

"You know I care about you…like a sister, Nona," he told her while pacing his kitchen floor. "But I don't want to ever hear you mention Kacey's name again."

"Oh, don't be so sensitive," Nona poo-poohed. "Face it, Leon. She took my advice. She finally realized that you and I shared a past that was too strong to ignore."

"Stop it! Your gossipy tongue and possessive attitude almost ruined my relationship with her. Leave it alone, okay?"

"*Almost ruined your relationship?* She's *gone* isn't she?" Nona mocked in delight.

"A temporary separation," Leon clarified in a snap.

"Harrumph." Nona braced one hand on her generous hip and cocked her head at Leon. "Temporary my ass. She won't be back. If she loved you, she never would have left."

"That's enough, Nona. I don't need your take on my love life. Whether or not Kacey comes back is not important. We'll be together somehow, even if we have to fly back and forth. We'll get married, I'll rebuild the factory. We could even work together at Archer and create a good life here in Rockport, if that is what she wants."

"You're dreamin', honey." Nona laughed aloud. "That city gal would never work at the factory with you. Not like I did. She wouldn't fit in."

"And I guess you'd make sure of that, huh?" Leon challenged.

"Yeah, I'd do my best to open her eyes to the way things ought to be."

"How?" Leon prodded, wanting to see just how far Nona would go to get between him and Kacey.

"Like this," Nona said, sidling up to Leon to ease her arms around his waist. When she snuggled her head beneath his chin, Leon froze, determined to let Nona hang herself. Feeling her press herself up against his sex sent a spiral of disgust into his stomach and he knew he'd had enough.

"Kacey was right," he told Nona, untangling himself from her tight embrace. He shoved her away. "You'll never see things the way they really are. You're living in the past and you're pathetic. You know what, Nona? I want you to go away and leave me alone."

"You know you need me here. We've still got a lot of records to process, a ton of work to do."

"I don't think so. As a matter of fact, you're fired," he stated, announcing his decision in a calm voice. Saying those words filled him with a sense of satisfaction he had not expected.

"You can't fire me! Your father would never…"

"My father no longer calls the shots, remember? I own Archer Industries, and there's no place for you in the business."

"You've gotta be kidding. What will I do?" Nona whined.

"I have no idea, but I do know Kacey was right. You think you belong to my family, but you don't. You need to get a life, and get out of mine. Go anywhere. I don't care. Just get the hell outta here right now and leave my mother's key on the counter."

When Nona's face crumbled and tears fell from her eyes, Leon grasped for a way to smooth over his decision. He knew his parents' doting affection over the years had played a huge part in Nona's misplaced affection, and he was at fault, too. He had let things slide too long. "Listen, Nona. Archer Industries is gonna be closed for months. Maybe for a year or more. I'll make sure you draw unemployment and I'll give you a hefty severance payment. You could go to Cleveland, live with your sister."

Nona squinted in question at Leon, but let her shoulders drop in resignation. A tremble of a smile began to tease her lips. "How hefty?" she inquired slyly.

Without missing a beat, Leon told her, "Hefty enough to take care of you, *and* your sister for a long time."

"Well…it's your money," Nona quipped as she dug into her purse and pulled out his key. She slammed it down on Leon's kitchen counter. "All right. I'll go, but you'll be sorry," she told Leon, and then she flounced out the door.

I doubt that, Leon thought, feeling a great sense of freedom. He had severed a troublesome link to his past and he didn't feel the least bit guilty about it. His parents were no longer hovering in the shadows, judging his every move. He was in charge and had no one to answer to but himself. Suddenly, leaving Rockport seemed possible, even plausible. He could join Kacey in New York. But if he showed up on her turf, would he fit into her hectic, sophisticated world? And did he really want to live in New York City?

* * *

Kacey stared at Ariana, stunned. "What do you mean, Steve Hadley is out?"

"Yes, darling. Replaced by his younger brother, Paul. You know. The one who used to run the store in Los Angeles."

"Why?"

"I don't know why or how, but Paul Hadley managed to push Steve out and take his place as head of the company," Ariana finished, fluffing her blond hair with one hand.

"Damn, what does that mean for us?" Kacey wanted to know.

"I don't know, but we'll find out soon. Staff meeting at ten," Ariana told Kacey, smiling secretively as she left Kacey's office.

Kacey nervously watched the clock until it was time for the gathering in Leeman's conference room. Sitting there, she recalled her pitch for the SunKissed line and how excited she'd been when Steve had green-lighted her project. Now she sat in the same room waiting for Paul Hadley to decide her fate.

It did not take long for her new boss to confirm Kacey's worst fears. He was canceling all of Steve's pending projects, including SunKissed by Kacey, and was reassigning the staff to new departments.

"Kacey, you'll oversee promotions for the winter collection," Paul Hadley informed her as he went down the list of changes he'd initiated at the company. "Here's your portfolio. Look it over and we'll get together to discuss the trade show schedule and the target audience for the High Mountain ski collection tomorrow." He handed Kacey a thick binder and then turned his attention to Ariana.

Kacey did not hear anything Paul said to her colleagues. Her heart was pounding, her mouth was dry and her insides boiled in resentment. How did this happen? she thought, mad as hell that her beautiful swimsuits would never make it to market. Leeman's still owned the rights to her designs. She was left with nothing! Everything was gone because Steve Hadley's brother had decided to pull the plug on Kacey's future.

Kacey was tempted to throw the winterwear catalog at Paul Hadley and walk out. But she couldn't. She needed her job and had no choice but to let go of her dream just as she'd had to do with Leon Archer.

Chapter 24

Kacey tried to be a team player, but her heart was not in her new assignment. Things did not go well between her and Paul; they did not see eye to eye on any of her concepts. Every meeting they had ended with her compromising her vision to please him, deepening her resentment and increasing the tension in the office.

When she presented him with ideas for a contest to be held at the winterwear trade show, he dismissed her idea as boring and made snide comments about her being out of touch. When she suggested a new retail floor layout, he picked it apart and eventually turned the project over to an intern who'd never designed a retail promotional booth before. And when she failed to turn in her weekly expense report by noon on a Friday, Paul erupted in a tirade, calling her irresponsible and reducing her to tears.

When she fired back with "You have no right to talk to me like that! I just need fifteen minutes to finish my report," he simply told her, "I don't give second chances."

"I'm not asking for one," Kacey boldly countered, sick and tired of Paul Hadley's imperious attitude.

"Good. Because I hate to watch people grovel," Paul snapped back.

"I'd never grovel to you!" Kacey spat out, glaring at him and wondering how far she dared to push her new boss.

"Fine. I hope you never do," he huffed.

"I certainly won't…because…I quit!" The words flew from Kacey's lips before she could stop herself, but once they were out, she wasn't sorry.

Paul's face turned dark red and his green eyes bulged as he stared at Kacey in disbelief. "Fine, then. Clean out your desk and turn in your keys."

Without a word, Kacey did as Paul ordered, and within ten minutes she was walking like a zombie through the lobby of the building, as miserable as she'd ever been in her life.

On the train headed home to Harlem, she tried to convince herself that quitting her job at Leeman's didn't matter. But she was worried. Finding a comparable job in retail was going to be nearly impossible in this depressed economy. Since she'd quit, there'd be no unemployment checks or severance pay to fall back on. All she had was the nest egg she'd accumulated to buy her new apartment, which was now completely out of the picture.

When Leon called Kacey that evening, she acted as if everything was fine, determined to keep the truth from him about her impulsive decision to quit, though she did tell him that Paul Hadley had canceled the Leeman's contract.

"Gee, I'm sorry, Kacey. I know how much you wanted to see your swimsuits in stores. Maybe you could approach another retailer?"

"No. It's not gonna happen."

When he asked how things were going with her new position, she dodged the question, not able to tell him that she'd quit her job. What would he think if he knew she'd folded under pressure, after all her talk about holding on to her job and how much she valued her career? She'd left Leon to protect her career and now everything was gone. She had no man, no job, no swimsuit line in stores—absolutely nothing to show for all she'd given up to fulfill her dreams.

"You don't sound very happy. I want to come to New York and see you," Leon told Kacey in an urgent tone. "I can fly in tomorrow. Take you out to dinner, to a movie and, afterwards, make passionate love to you."

"Oh, that sounds so good, but not now. I'm soooo busy, Leon. This is not a good time," she protested, using a tone that she hoped would indicate how rushed she was.

"But you're always busy. It's never a good time with you. I need to see you, Kacey. I'll only stay a day or two. If I fly in on…"

"Sorry, but I might be out of town. An assignment might come up, " she floundered, choosing her words very carefully, not wanting to flat-out lie.

"Oh, okay, if it's like that. Well," Leon stuttered, deflated. "Yeah, I understand. Call me when you've got some free time that you can spare, okay." Then without saying goodbye, he hung up.

Sitting in the dark, Leon felt his heart shatter into a million pieces. Kacey was pulling away from him, and he didn't know what to do. He couldn't force himself on her. Yet, he refused to let this separation destroy what they'd created together. He had to reach her, convince her that their love was worth fighting for. He had to hold it all together and get through this rough patch without giving up. Walking away was not an option.

"We'll work it out somehow," he told himself, determined not to let Kacey go.

Leon's parents' arrival back in Rockport was not as joyous as Leon had expected it to be. He was happy to see his mom and dad and anxious to hear all about their trip, but the destruction of the factory and the arrest of Bob Truett cast a sad shadow over the family reunion.

Once Leon finished bringing his father up-to-date on where things stood with company matters, he told his dad all about Kacey—even confessing his feelings for her.

"I knew you two were in love when I first saw you together," his father teased, laughing when Leon squinted at his dad in confusion.

"You saw us? How? When?"

Leon Sr. chuckled and tapped the screen of his handheld device. "This little thing kept me in touch with everything that was going on in Rockport while I was away. Do you really think you can hide anything as newsworthy as a love affair with a city girl in a town like Rockport?"

"You mean people here were spying on me? Sending you photos?"

"Yep, and I'm glad they did. Kacey Parker is a beauty, and she seems like a real smart woman, too. The kind of girl I've always hoped you'd settle down with. You can't imagine how many emails and photos of her I got. Almost every day someone made sure to post a tidbit about her…and my son's romantic adventure. Buddy was the worst. Every time you two entered his barbecue joint or walked down Main Street, he managed to snap a photo and email it to me."

"You mean you've known about us all along?" Leon asked, shocked, yet glad that his father liked Kacey. If he planned to marry her, and he definitely did, he wanted his parents' stamp of approval. "Then you must know about Nona. She left town," he added.

"Yes. Maybe it was time for her to go. She wasn't really happy here, and she was missing out on life. No use in hiding behind memories and sticking to the past. I think she'll be happy in Cleveland. I know your mom will miss Nona, but sometimes we have to put the past where it belongs and move on." Rising from his chair, he went to his safe and began to rotate the combination knob. "Now, about Kacey Parker's swimwear line. You said Leeman's *canceled* their plans to manufacture, and did not sign on at American Textile?"

"That's right. It's such a shame. And Kacey can't take the line to another manufacturer because Leeman's owns the rights," Leon added, feeling a punch of failure hit his gut at the thought of how devastated Kacey must be.

"Hmmm, that's not entirely true," his father remarked as he removed a packet of papers from his safe. He zapped his son with a knowing expression, one eye squinted closed. "Son, your girlfriend needs to know something very important. Here, I want you to read this."

"What is it?" Leon asked as he took the sealed envelope from his dad began to read.

"That's an addendum to the original contract for the SunKissed by Kacey swimwear line that I signed with Steve Hadley. Read it over carefully and you'll see what I mean."

Shrugging, as if the legal document were nothing out of the ordinary, Leon scanned it while his father watched. When he finished, a huge smile spread over Leon's face. "Dad. You shrewd old dog. You sneaked *that* into the contract?"

Leon Sr. beamed in amusement and nodded at his son. "I sure did. And aren't you glad I did?"

Leon let out a whistle of a breath, grabbed his car keys off his father's desk and stood. "I've gotta go," he mumbled, hurrying toward the door.

"To New York, I hope," his father called out, but Leon didn't answer. He was already in his car.

Chapter 25

The taxi ride from JFK to Kacey's apartment in Harlem seemed to take forever. As Leon watched the gritty urban landscape slide by, he knew he would never be happy living in a crowded high-rise building, and worried that he might be wasting his time by trying to get Kacey to leave the lifestyle she loved so much. He desperately wanted to see her, deliver his news and bridge the gap that was keeping them from forging a life together, but he was nervous as hell about her reaction.

After paying the taxi driver, Leon shifted his flight bag onto this shoulder and entered the outer lobby of her building. He scanned the address labels on the buzzers, found hers and pressed—his heart throbbing as he waited to hear her voice.

"Yes?" Kacey's sweet voice drifted through the intercom, sending a jolt of hope into Leon, who took a calming breath and then plunged ahead. "It's me. Leon. I have to talk to you."

A short silence before Kacey acknowledged her visitor. "Leon!" A long hush followed her remark. "Why are you here? I asked you not to come."

"I know, but please I have to see you. I have some very important news."

Without a reply, she buzzed him in.

Leon raced through the lobby, into the elevator, and stood with his shoulder pressed against the elevator wall as it ascended to her floor. Once there, he took long strides down the hall to her apartment, where he impatiently pressed her bell.

When Kacey opened the door, he stopped in his tracks and simply looked at her, wanting to drink in the sight of her and refresh his memories of her beautiful face. She was wearing tight stretch capri pants and a loose pink T-shirt, looking as if she'd just finished a yoga class. Leon tightened his lips as silence hung between them, giving Kacey time to adjust to his unexpected arrival. When she stepped aside, he entered, shutting the door with a backhand push. Without waiting for a word of hello, he took her in his arms, leaned in and teased her with a brush of his lips over hers, testing her resistance and measuring his chances of accomplishing his mission. When she melted under his touch and arched into him, Leon devoured her with a kiss that let her know how much he'd missed her.

As she sank more deeply into his embrace, Leon felt reassured. He had done the right thing, coming to New York unannounced. She did miss him. She desired his touch as much as he desired hers. Why had she buried her true feelings beneath a lot of words that meant nothing?

Kacey opened her mouth and accepted the sweep of Leon's tongue as it caressed hers. Pressing her breasts to his chest, her arms tightened around him until she was breathlessly fused to him, feeling as close as two people could get.

Kacey was stunned, but thrilled that Leon had disregarded her request to stay away. She'd missed him terribly, and having him back in her arms was exactly what she needed. With her world spinning out of control, having him at her side was all that mattered. She wasn't alone. She didn't have to face an uncertain future by herself. He'd proven that he would never abandon her or take their love for granted. At this critical time, he was giving her what she needed most: steadfast devotion and love that would last.

When their kiss broke off, Kacey guided Leon over to her black leather sofa. They sank down together, remaining entwined in each other's arms.

"Leon, I've been miserable without you," she started. "Things have gotten so complicated since I came back. There's a lot that I need to tell you."

Leon placed a finger to her lips and shushed her, shaking his head. "I've been crazy without you, Kacey. I know you didn't want me to come and that you're busy with your job, but I couldn't stay away any longer."

Kacey sucked in a long breath, knowing she had to tell him the truth. "I wish that were true."

"What?"

"I wish I were swamped with work, but the truth is, I'm not busy at all." She stopped, shifted more erect in her seat and looked at the floor. "Leon, I have more time on my hands than I know what to do with." She glanced up at him with soulful eyes. "I quit my job. I walked out on Leeman's, and my career."

With a jerk, Leon leaned to the side and eyed Kacey with suspicion. "You quit? Why?" he demanded, shifting to face her. He hooked his fingers together with hers and waited for her answer.

"I just couldn't work with Paul Hadley. He was so demeaning, so rigid. I tried to keep my temper when he yelled at me over a stupid expense report, but I lost it and walked out."

"Good for you," Leon assured her. "You don't have to take crap from a loser like that."

"Right," she agreed, her voice growing stronger as she described her confrontation with Paul and her impulsive decision to sever ties with her employer.

"I know you were devoted to that company. How could Paul disregard all that you had contributed to Leeman's? What a bastard. He could've tried harder to work things out with you."

"No. He wanted to fire me, but I refused to give him the satisfaction. Someone had to go, and it wasn't going to be Paul Hadley."

"I wish you'd told me about this when it happened. You didn't have to go through such hell all alone," Leon stated, his words tinged with irritation. "You should've called me right away."

"And say what?" Kacey questioned. "That you were right all along? That I shouldn't have allowed myself to put such trust in Leeman's? I shouldn't have believed that my career was rock solid?" Kacey swallowed, twisting her fingers together as she grasped for words to explain what she was feeling. "I didn't want you to know that I'd failed."

"You didn't fail," Leon murmured. "Paul Hadley failed you."

Kacey quickly reconnected with Leon, her lower lip trembling as she continued. "I was a bit naive, I guess. I'd convinced myself that a supportive boss, my own swimwear line in stores and my career were perfectly safe. I thought I had everything, but the truth is, I have nothing now."

Leon pulled Kacey to his side, kissed her on the top of her head, and then gently stroked her shoulder. "Not true. You have me," he murmured. "*And* you still have SunKissed by Kacey."

Kacey dipped her head and studied Leon's dark gray eyes. "If only that were true."

"It is," he insisted.

"No, it isn't. Don't you understand? Because I was working for Leeman's when I came up with my line, I assigned the company all rights to SunKissed," Kacey countered.

Easing out of Kacey's arms, Leon reached for his flight bag, which he'd dropped on the floor when he entered. He unzipped the outside pocket, pulled out the contract that his father had given him and unfolded the legal document.

"Listen to this," he began. "According to the terms of this contract between Steve Hadley (Leeman's , Inc.) and Leon Archer Sr. (Archer Industries), all protected rights to the SunKissed by Kacey swimwear designs will revert to Archer Industries if Leeman's cancels its manufacturing contract for any reason after full production has begun."

Kacey stilled, taking in Leon's revelation, chewing her bottom lip. "Even if there's been a fire? Which was ruled arson?"

Leon handed the contract to Kacey. "Yes. My father had Gerald, our attorney, read it over and he agrees. We were willing to subcontract with American Textile to complete jobs in progress to keep the original contract in force. But since Leeman's canceled...they forfeited their rights. There are no exceptions stated here, so your designs do belong to Archer."

"You mean, to you?" Kacey clarified.

"To *us*," Leon whispered, eyes shining in glee.

"I can't believe this," Kacey whispered, rereading the page that held the key to rebuilding her career. In silence, her eyes traced the densely written page, and then a frown came over her face. "Leon! If you knew about this all along, why didn't you tell me sooner?"

"I just found out."

"When?" Kacey probed, beginning to sound upset.

"This morning. Kacey, believe me, I didn't know."

"You sure?"

"Of course. It was all my father's doing. He and Mom returned from Africa yesterday, so I went to see him to discuss my plans to rebuild the plant. He took your contract out of his safe and handed it to me. I was as shocked as you are. He added that clause to the contract, never dreaming it would be so important. Even Gerald, the company lawyer, didn't know about it."

Stunned by this miraculous turn of events, Kacey slumped back on her spine and gazed at the ceiling. "Then this means that..." she started.

"That you can produce your swimsuits with any

manufacturer you choose," Leon finished. "All we need to do is find one and get started."

"This is…incredible," Kacey sighed. "And after you rebuild Archer Industries…"

"You mean after *we* rebuild Archer, don't you?" Leon stressed, sounding both confident and hopeful.

With a grin, Kacey agreed. "Absolutely. We have a lot to do, don't we?"

Settled on the sofa with Kacey at his side, Leon took her hand in his. "The new facility will be a state-of-the-art manufacturing plant," he said. "As soon as it is up and running, we'll gear up production and launch a lot more of your designs," Leon promised, "You know…I've been thinking…maybe your next project should be a collection of swim trunks for men."

As a hint of a smile teased her lips, Kacey considered his remark. "Oh, really? And I can just guess who'll be my model, huh?" she toyed.

Leon grinned. "Who else? I sure wouldn't want some strange, hunky dude parading around half-naked in front of my *wife* wearing a skimpy male thong bikini or skintight Speedo briefs."

Kacey swatted jokingly at Leon, and then rested her chin on her hand, appearing bemused. "Did I hear you right? You did say, your wife, didn't you?"

Leon studied Kacey with hungry eyes. "Absolutely. That is, if you're willing to leave New York and live with me in Rockport, Texas."

Kacey touched Leon's chiseled jaw, smiling to feel the hint of stubble on his chin, knowing how far and long he'd traveled to bring her such important news. Her heart swelling with joy, she told Leon, "I can't think of a better place to start over, with you." Her husky voice was taut with emotion. "You know…that's an intriguing idea… designing a swimwear line for men. But I'm gonna need some serious inspiration," she taunted, reaching for the top button of his shirt.

Leon edged up to Kacey and let her undo his buttons. "Then, we'd better get started," he urged, shedding his shirt to reveal a smooth brown chest and rippling six-pack abs.

"I'm already inspired," Kacey whispered, sweeping both hands over his torso. Closing her eyes, she smiled and rested her cheek on Leon's bare shoulder.

Leaving New York was going to be easy because Kacey knew the unshakable love that she and Leon shared would only sizzle more hotly under a bright Texas sun.

* * * * *

NEW YORK DOC, THAILAND PROPOSAL

DIANNE DRAKE

To Mike Cramer, one of the hardest-working and best doctors I ever knew.

The world is a little less bright without you, my friend. RIP.

CHAPTER ONE

"I KNOW WHAT we were, Mother. But two years deserves a better ending than what we had, and when this opportunity came…"

Dr. Oliver Benedict, Layla Morrison's boss, mentor and, yes, Arlo's grandfather, had three spots open for volunteers—specifically the three candidates he was looking at to be his new assistant chief of surgery.

"No, I don't know if Arlo knows I'm the one Ollie picked for this assignment. It's only been five days from the time he gave me the nod until now, and Ollie specifically said communication with Arlo wasn't always available. So, yes, I might be a surprise."

But the need was legitimate. According to Ollie, Arlo was alone right now. His medical assistant had gone home to India for a while and after living with Arlo for two years herself, and listening to him talk about the way he wanted to practice medicine here, in Thailand, Layla knew what she was getting herself into.

Jungle medicine. Nothing easy. Nothing convenient. It was hard work. Sometimes backbreaking. And it was so embedded in Arlo's heart it had caused their breakup. Two years into their relationship and the call of the jungle had beaten her.

"No, I don't know if this will give me a lock on a

promotion, but it will finally give me some closure. We didn't have that. It was too difficult at the end and we were both hurt. So, I'm hoping that this will help me, maybe even Arlo, finally move on."

Layla had had one disastrous attempt at a relationship after Arlo and had compared everything Brad did against the way Arlo had done it. Nothing *could* compare, though, and now it was time to fix that so she could finally move on with her personal life since the professional side was rolling along quite nicely.

Layla was one of the top general surgeons in Ollie's practice, highly regarded for her skills, in line for a promotion. That part was just what she wanted and, finally, she had time to look beyond that, to having a life outside medicine. Except there was Arlo. She hadn't been able to shake him off. Not in the physical sense, but in the emotional. All the what-ifs? They wouldn't let go, so now it was time to purge them and move on.

Layla sighed loudly enough for her mother to hear. "Look, it's only two months, then I'll be home and hopefully in a new position. Ollie hinted that I'm the forerunner. So, please, just wish me luck here because working in a jungle hospital scares me a little bit." But not as much as facing Arlo after all this time.

"Yes, Mother, I'll be careful. And tell Daddy thanks for the SUV. The way these roads are turning out to be, it's exactly what I needed." Her dad had made a couple of phone calls and, just like magic, it had been waiting for her at the airport. But he had connections here in Thailand. In fact, he had connections everywhere so what he'd done for Layla had been easy. Everything her parents had ever done for her had made her life easier. Which was one of the reasons Arlo had always called her spoiled. She'd taken advantage of that from time to time. Until Arlo had pointed that out.

Still, her parents always supported her in what she wanted to do. Sometimes the support was a little grudging, since their ideas of what they wanted for her were entirely different from what Layla wanted for herself. But there hadn't been a time since she was a little girl that she'd seen herself as anything other than a doctor, and now Layla was on her way to do some doctoring in the jungle with a man who'd been her partner for two years. Talk about an improbable situation.

"Two years," she said out loud, as she swerved to miss a rut in the dirt road. Arlo Benedict had been at her level during their medical residency, and the arrangement to share an apartment had been a practical one. For Arlo, it had been about money. His grandfather, Ollie, had been supporting him through school, but just barely, since his own surgery was quite costly to operate. And Arlo's parents—they were like Arlo was now. Jungle doctors, living on practically nothing.

When Layla had first met Arlo, he'd been struggling. Not complaining, though. But his life had been hard, and he hadn't had many extras. No going out with friends for pizza and beer. Working an extra job when he'd really needed to be studying. He had been so dedicated— dedicated in a way she'd never seen in anyone, and she admired that. Plus, he was easy on the eye, and maybe she'd had a little crush.

She didn't know for sure, but when she'd mentioned she had a bedroom to rent, he'd jumped at the chance. Layla had told herself that having someone there was simply a matter of practicality. But in the case of asking Arlo to be her roomie, it had possibly been something more. Certainly, she'd been open to suggestions at the time. He had been smart, drop-dead gorgeous and quite emphatic that he'd be gone once his residence was completed.

Arlo had come with everything she'd wanted, and something she hadn't wanted—a long-term relationship. She hadn't been about to tie herself up that way until she'd started climbing the ladder, and that had still been a long way off.

Well, she had been wrong about the relationship. Just being with Arlo had made her want to be with him all the more. No, he had not been a long-termer and, yes, he had been clear he wouldn't stay. But being with Arlo for two years had changed her. Made her want things she hadn't known she wanted. Made her want Arlo in ways she'd known he hadn't been available.

Had it been the challenge of him, or the allure? Probably some of both. But when her real feelings had started getting in the way, the allure had taken over in a big way. Not that it mattered because, in the end, he'd left her. It was always his plan, he'd told her. But she'd truly thought she could change his mind.

Unfortunately, Layla couldn't. And their ending had been bad. Arguments they'd never had before. Shouting. Crying. Naturally, she'd blamed Arlo for everything but, deep down, she'd always known she couldn't hang onto him. She'd just tried ignoring it.

Initially, Arlo's resistance at accepting her offer, and he did resist, had been quelled by her declaration that theirs would be a friends-only situation. Sure, she'd wanted more. Which, as it had turned out, had been the case with Arlo as well. And within two weeks a cozy night when two weary surgical residents had shared a bottle of wine and a bowl of popcorn on the couch had turned into…

Of course, there'd been early morning promises that what they'd done was a one-time thing. Except it wasn't. For two years. Now, nearly five years down the road, while Layla was perfectly on track with her career, Arlo was the loose end she needed to tie up because she didn't want to be alone for the rest of her life. Because she was a total washout when it came to relationships—just ask Brad, her only attempt at another relationship after Arlo. Then there was the whole ticking of the biological clock thing going on. Yet she couldn't take that step forward because—well, she was blaming it on their lack of closure, even though they'd both known, at the start, that Arlo would eventually go one way and she another.

It had seemed easy enough when they'd talked about it, but when the time had come, it wasn't. Had Layla loved Arlo then? Yes, in a lot of different ways. But had she loved him enough to give up her dreams to follow his? No. Absolutely not. And neither had he been prepared to give up his dreams for her.

So, why was she here? To be honest with herself, she'd jumped at the chance before she'd thought it through. And once she'd committed, she wasn't going to back down. Her plan—her only plan—to earn this promotion was do everything required to move her forward.

To back out of two months in a Thailand jungle hospital with her former lover would shove her back, not push her forward. So, here she was, feeling a lot of trepidation about Arlo's reaction if Ollie hadn't contacted him yet, and scared to death of a two-month commitment that, at one point in her life, might have turned into a lifetime commitment, had things worked out differently.

As her dad always said, *Whatever it takes to get you to the next level*. And while Layla didn't know if this assignment would do that, it would certainly allow her to experience a side of medicine she knew little about. That, if nothing else, was a good thing as it would help make her a better doctor. So in two months she could be a better doctor who'd finally shut the door on an old relationship. It was good. All good because she needed Ollie to see she was a team player. Sometimes she wasn't. Layla knew her reputation—she could be a little aloof, sometimes standing alone.

But growing up the way she had, with a photojournalist father who made documentaries all over the world, and her mother a film actress who, like her father, worked all over the world, she'd learned to be independent at a young age. Sometimes she could be too independent, which wasn't necessarily in her best interest all the time. Even she recognized that. Although Arlo had pointed that out as well. More times than she cared to remember.

Still, most memories Layla had of her parents were of one or both of them walking away from her, going off in pursuit of their careers, which, if nothing else, had been the impetus for her independence. Arlo walking away had simply shored up what was already there—the notion that she wasn't worth hanging around for. And for Layla, hiding behind the stone wall of independence she'd built around herself was easier than risking another rejection. She'd assumed that over time she'd learn to be happy there. Well, happy enough.

But sometimes the memories of a bottle of wine and a bowl of popcorn and what that had started did slip in. They hung on more tenaciously than almost any other memory of her life. And it was because of that memory Layla had been stalled in a place where there was no room for her. Where she wasn't wanted. A place she had to fix and move beyond.

While this trip to Thailand to work with Arlo had been

providential, it was also necessary. It was her chance to prove to herself that the feelings she'd had for Arlo were simply feelings meant only for that time and place, and had no bearing on anything else in her life. Then, and even now.

So, where was she anyway? Normally a quick check of an online map site was all Layla needed, but there was no cell reception out here, let alone a road that had been charted on a map. So she was only guessing she was headed in the right direction. A direction where she didn't expect modern facilities, let alone the basics like running water and electricity.

That's what Arlo had told her he'd come from, and that's what he'd always said would be the kind of place he would practice his medicine. He'd grown up in the jungle, traveled with his parents, who were both doctors. And it's what he'd said he wanted for his own life as he simply fit there better. Shortly, she would see if he did.

Layla looked ahead of her, saw a man riding atop an elephant and nearly ran herself off the road staring at him. It wasn't the elephant that got her, though, not even the crater she swerved to avoid hitting. It was the wavering turn out of the swerve that wobbled her back and forth across the road. Unfortunately, it resulted in her landing in a drainage ditch with a flat tire, the front end down, back end up. Royally stuck and—she checked her phone even though it was pointless, and the result was what she expected—there was no way to contact anyone, anywhere.

"Damn it," Layla huffed, throwing her phone back into the car as she stood alone on the road, trying to figure out what to do. "No bars. Not a single, lousy blip on the bar indicator." Her first test out here, and she was already failing it.

After walking around her car several times, assessing and reassessing the situation, Layla finally sat down in the dirt, hoping someone would come by to help her. Someone in a truck with a tow rope, she hoped. Maybe even Arlo? But the only person who did pass was a withered little old man with a pushcart filled with fruits and herbs. He smiled graciously at her, then began a long-winded discussion, none of which she understood. After he finished speaking, he tipped his straw hat to her, picked up the hand grips of his cart and meandered on down the road at a pace that would favor a snail in a race.

"Well, so much for that," Layla said, deciding to hike on down the road and hope that somewhere along the way she stumbled on someone who could help her. Or maybe even stumble on the village itself.

An hour later, making very little progress due to the road conditions, Layla stopped to rest, sitting down on a roadside rock and watching some kind of wild pig munching the droppings of a papaya tree. And this was why she and Arlo hadn't succeeded at their relationship. They'd talked about it *ad nauseam* for the last few months they'd been together. While she'd never been in the jungle, she could see it in detail through Arlo's description. There were good people here, leading extremely hard lives, in a place where nothing came easily. Transportation was limited, according to Arlo. As were communications. It was his passion, and she didn't condemn him for it. But it wasn't her passion. She wasn't the kind of person who could survive here. Even two months were beginning to seem like an eternity.

"You and your passion, Arlo," Layla grumbled, as she stood to resume her hike. Much to her surprise, the little man with the pushcart was coming back into view. Slowly.

Was he coming to rescue her? Her knight in shining armor? A man with a receding hairline, bushy gray eyebrows and some wispy chin fringe?

Naturally, when he arrived at her side, he was already chattering words she still didn't understand. His gestures were clear, though. She was to climb into the part-empty cart and be pushed wherever he wanted to take her. "Village by the big fig tree," she said, knowing he wouldn't understand the English interpretation of the village's name. But she couldn't pronounce it in Thai and any mispronounced attempt might land her someplace she didn't want to go, so she pointed to a small fig tree sapling off the side of the road, then attempted to gesture a much larger tree. Wouldn't Arlo just laugh at her now, standing in the middle of nowhere playing a game of charades?

"Big fig tree," Layla said a couple of times, even though the man had no idea what she was saying. He smiled, though, let her charade herself into more embarrassment before he gestured her to the cart again. Her taxi was waiting, and she couldn't have been happier to see it, despite the prickly straw in the bottom, and the caged chickens she had to share her ride with. Oh, and the dog. The little old man had picked up a scraggly, lap-sized brown and white mutt somewhere along the way.

So, forcing a gracious smile, Layla climbed in, found a spot among the other passengers and shut her eyes. All those years ago, when Arlo had walked away from her, calling her too damned ambitious, it had hurt, even though it was true. Today—right this moment—she was glad her ambitions had kept her in modern society, as this was simply too hard already, and she hadn't even started.

Maybe it was what Arlo wanted from his life, living here and practicing jungle medicine, and maybe he was one of the most benevolent, altruistic and humane people she'd ever known, but none of this was for her, and if she hadn't known it then, she surely did now.

"Of all the doctors in the world, he sent you?" Arlo shook his head, not in disbelief so much as amusement. "You working in the jungle is as improbable as me working in a modern hospital somewhere. But you've certainly got the skill I need, so…" He visibly bit back a laugh. "Welcome."

Layla opened her eyes, which she'd purposely kept shut so she could avoid the full picture of her impetuous volunteering, and there he was, taking away her breath the way he always had. Only maybe a little more since the jungle setting made him seem…better.

Tall, roguishly handsome as ever and a little weathered, which became him. His blond hair looked sun bleached, and it was long, still with its gentle curl. She'd always liked those curls and the way they had felt in her fingers. And the penetrating blue eyes that still penetrated. But the thing that had always attracted her most were his dimples. Honest-to-gosh sexy dimples when he smiled.

"I'd have made my grand entrance differently if I could have, but I suppose this works," she said as she picked straw from her hair. "Oh, and to answer your question, yes, he sent me."

"He didn't tell me it was you he was sending," Arlo said.

"Probably because he was as surprised as I was that it was my hand that went up first to volunteer. Also, because he couldn't get in touch with you."

"Ah, yes. It's all about the soon-to-be-open assistant chief position, isn't it? When he told me he was going to announce it, I assumed you'd be the one fighting to get to the front of the line. Didn't count on Ollie sending you out here as part of your climb up his ladder, though. Especially since we haven't spoken in five years."

"Three," she corrected. "We spoke that time you came to New York to visit him."

"One word, Layla. You said hello in passing."

"And you acknowledged it by bobbing your head and grunting."

"That's not exactly speaking."

"I was civil," she said, trying to right herself in the cart, wishing Arlo would help her out so she wouldn't look quite so undignified. But he was standing back, arms folded across his chest, the way he'd always done when they'd argued. So, was he expecting this to turn into an argument? "And in a hurry."

"You were always in a hurry, Layla. And I'm assuming it's paying off, taking on more and more just to prove yourself to him."

"Not denying it," she said.

"Nope, you never did. I think I saw that in you the first time we met."

Of course, Arlo could see what he wanted to see in her. That was part of their fundamental problem. What he wanted versus what she wanted. Or, in their case, needed. "Part of my basic make-up, I suppose. But I never heard you object," she said, stepping out of the cart, trying not to disturb the chickens while also trying to shoo the dog back in.

"Probably because I didn't object. I liked your ambition. I was raised by pacifist parents who took things as they came, which is pretty much my style. Someone with your kind of ambition—I don't recall ever seeing it in anyone before you. Not living in the jungle for as long as I did. It was an eye-opener for me, and also…well, sexy."

Layla turned to thank the old man for the ride by bowing to him, then tucked a few Thai coins into his hand which he pocketed eagerly as he returned her bow, then scurried away with his cart. "Right up until the day you walked out." She brushed the straw off her backside, then stood at the bottom of the rough-hewn wooden stairs and looked up at Arlo. "It's two months. You need the help, I'm available, and—"

"And in the bargain it makes you look good because you want that promotion. You haven't changed, Layla. I'll give you credit for that. Where you are now is where you were when we split. Still trying to climb that ladder."

"I'm not the only one in the running."

"No, but you're the only one who'd come to Thailand to impress him. That's huge, even if you don't want to admit it."

"I also came to see a side of medicine I've never seen." And try to make things right between them—things that seemed like they were already off to a shaky start.

"I offered you that. Remember?"

"For a lifetime, Arlo. You wanted a lifetime commitment and we weren't even…" Layla wanted to say *in love*, but that was implied. Their relationship had been about many things, but love had never been mentioned. In fact, because of their circumstances, she was sure that was the reason it never had been mentioned. It was too complicated. It got in the way. There were no compromises that would work for both of them. Even though her feelings for him might have been—well, that didn't matter now, did it?

"Anyway, Ollie's deal is for two months. I couldn't

have done a lifetime, Arlo. You knew that from the beginning. But I can do two months, and you do need that help. So this is good for both of us. You get an extra doctor for a while and I gain extra knowledge." And closure, because she really did need to move on, and the only way she could think to do it was ending things better with Arlo.

But for Arlo? She'd spent too much time wondering if he'd needed more at the end the way she had. Now she had two months to find out, and put things into proper perspective. Then, hopefully, close the book on that story once and for all.

"Do you really think that helping the boss's grandson will get you any special notice? Ollie's not like that, Layla. In fact, it could go against you, volunteering to come here, when he knows how badly we ended. He could look at it as being very manipulative. I mean, if I were in his place, I might."

"Or he could look at it as a way for me to improve my skills." And, keeping her fingers crossed, she was on the inside track because of her work. Nothing else. "So, in the meantime, I've got my medical bag with me, but my personal bags are in my car, which is stuck in a ditch somewhere between here and God only knows where. Do you know someone who can go get my car unstuck and bring it here?" She looked up at the sign over the door behind Arlo and smiled. "Seriously, you named this place Happy Hospital?"

They'd actually named this hospital together years ago. They were being silly one night, and maybe a little drunk, and the pillow talk had turned to the kind of hospital where each of them could see themselves in the future. Naturally, Layla had described something large and state-of-the art, whereas he'd simply said he wanted to work at a happy hospital. She hadn't remembered that until now. Apparently, he hadn't forgotten it. In a way, it made her feel flattered that he'd thought of her.

"Things are simple here, Layla. I know you're not used to that, but that's how we are. And the hospital name fits because when we don't have enough insulin to treat all our patients and don't have the means to go get it for another week or two, or when some other hospital like this one is ahead of us on the list, pushing us down the waiting list, we can either go all gloom and doom over our situation or try to make the best of it. Being happy with what we have helps."

"I didn't mean to imply it was a bad name, Arlo. But out here, in the middle of the jungle, it just seems—out of place."

"People are just as happy here as they are where you come from. It's all relative to their expectations."

"But are you happy here, Arlo? I know you always said this is what you wanted, but sometimes I've wondered what might have happened to you if you'd gone into your grandfather's surgery the way he'd wanted, or accepted any of the offers you had."

"I was happy here when I was a kid, traipsing around from village to village with my parents, and I still am. It was the choice I had to make because I wouldn't have been happy anyplace else, practicing any other kind of medicine."

He'd never doubted his decision either. He'd lived the traditional life for a while, and he'd lived this life. Ultimately, this was where he wanted to be. Where his heart was. And when he and Layla were together, that had always been the thing she couldn't, or had refused to understand. Accepting a position elsewhere might have been easier, but easier didn't mean better. At least, not for him.

"Anyway, I don't really have good sleeping accommodations for you. Tallaja, my assistant, usually sleeps in the ward when we have patients or the office when we don't. He's pretty flexible about that, but I'm guessing you won't be."

"As long as I have mosquito netting, it doesn't matter."

"Seriously? You've been doing your homework, haven't you?"

"I don't step into things blindly, Arlo. Except maybe our relationship."

"I never considered it being blind. Not one day of it." Arlo stepped aside as Layla marched up steps and pushed past him into Happy Hospital, brushing up against him just slightly, but enough to raise goosebumps on his arms. It was a familiar feeling—one he didn't want to have. But every time she'd ever touched him, even innocently like just now, she'd caused that reaction that would, inevitably, lead to another reaction, then another, until... Damn. Why these thoughts? Why now when he was just coming to terms with the fact that he would never have enough to offer anyone else a decent life?

Even when he had been with Layla, Arlo had always known she would come to her senses about who he was and what he'd never have to offer her. It hadn't stopped him from getting involved, but it had always held him back from getting too involved. Back at the beginning, he'd drawn his own line in the sand then taken good care never, ever to step over it, except for that one moment near the end when he'd asked her to come to Thailand with him.

Stupid mistake. He'd known that as the words had come out, and he'd still felt the sting of her rejection a week later when he'd walked away, even though he'd always known how she would answer if he'd asked. "So, look around. There's not much to see, but it could be a lot worse."

Layla stopped just inside the hospital door, looked around and turned back to face him. "How many people can you accommodate?" she asked.

"Ten on the worst day ever. We do a lot of our treatment in-home because people here prefer it that way. But for the most part we dispense our medicine and treatments any way we can. My goal isn't so much the 'where' as the 'what.'"

And it wasn't an easy goal. Already he could tell that Layla was chastising herself for volunteering. She liked her creature comforts too much. And to think there'd been a time when he'd imagined they could work shoulder to shoulder here, that she wouldn't be bothered by the overall difficulty of pretty much everything. Well, he'd been wrong about that. Stars in his eyes. That's what he told himself afterward. Or maybe it had been the first time in his life he'd connected to a woman the way he had Layla.

Unfortunately, his situation doomed a relationship. But, if he were to pack up and leave for the sake of love, chances were nobody would come to take his place. The thought of letting down the people in his care made Arlo queasy and with that came the unrelenting knowledge that letting himself down was his course to follow. Forever alone. So, this is where he was, however it had happened. His choice, of course. And in that he'd been as stubborn or independent as he'd accused Layla of being.

"Your other option is to share my hut. It has a little more privacy—not much—but it's someplace where you can get away when you need to. Unless there's an emergency, people here know not to bother me when I'm in there." Arlo hadn't intended to ask her but now that he had, he didn't regret it.

When they had been together, they'd had fun evenings. Sitting, talking. Laughing. So maybe that was a bit of nostalgia creeping in. But those had been nice times and he didn't mind the reminders. Because once he and Layla had been very good together. Unfortunately, that had ended, but maybe having her here could shut the book on the bad and leave him with only the good. He hoped so as he didn't want to carry the weight of the bad with him for the rest of his life and, if he planned to spend that life alone, he wanted the good memories to look back on.

"You don't have to stand there looking so stressed, Arlo. I can do this job. Even more, I want to do this job."

"Because it's just another rung higher on your climb."

"Yes. I won't lie about that. Ollie needs team players in his surgery, and that's what I've been for quite a while now."

"Is it a struggle? Because I've never seen you as a team player. And I don't say that to offend you. But you always prided yourself on standing alone."

Layla laughed. "Because when you knew me, that's all I'd ever done. Stood alone. So, it's always a struggle joining in, and I know that. So does Ollie. But this promotion means everything, so I've got a lot of work to do if I want to earn it. That demon of ambition is still there, Arlo, chipping away at me, and I thought something unexpected, like coming here, to the last place I thought I'd ever want to be, would help me learn what I need to know outside what I already know."

Arlo cocked his head and looked at her for a moment, then smiled. "I thought maybe he'd twisted your arm."

"You're the only one who ever tried to twist my arm and look how that turned out."

"I still can't believe you chose this, Layla. What were his other options?"

"Going to a sister hospital in Miami or working as assistant surgeon for a football team. Both short-term, fill-in positions like this. So, to be honest, I'm as surprised as you that I raised my hand for this. Especially since it scares me that I won't have what it takes to give your patients what they need. And you scare me, because—well, you fit here, and I don't." Layla bit down hard on her lip, and for a moment stared off into space.

"I—I don't want to fail, Arlo. I want to be the kind of person who can step into a situation—any situation—and do what needs to be done. I mean, you've always known I have a huge fear of failure. And look at me now—marching into the center ring, pretty much without a clue. For me, this is really pushing the envelope, as they say. And while the whole you and me relationship thing is off the table, I need to be able to depend on you to help me, or at least point me in the right direction so I can figure it out myself.

"Even though being here and doing what I'm about to do scares me, I don't want to take the easy way out." Like giving in and going with him when she'd always known the life he led would make her miserable. Oh, she'd weighed the decision, for months. Made the mental pros and cons list. But in the end one thing had always tilted out of proportion to everything else—to be the best doctor she could be meant she had to be satisfied with her lifestyle.

What Arlo offered would never satisfy her. And, sure, maybe that was the leaning of the materialistic girl in her, but it was something that couldn't be overlooked. Layla had lost sleep over it, paced a rut in the carpet, bitten her nails to the quick, trying to figure out how to change herself, but, in the end, even her feelings for Arlo hadn't been strong enough to bring that about. Sadly, that was the answer. If she'd loved him enough, she should have been able to make the necessary changes in herself. But she couldn't, which meant she hadn't.

"Nope. You never were easy, and you never took the easy way out."

Arlo was decked out in tan cargo shorts and a faded navy blue T-shirt with the Voltaire saying on it: *The art of medicine consists of amusing the patient while nature cures the disease.* He looked like he belonged here. Layla was glad for him because she'd never really found that yet—a place where she belonged.

Working with Ollie in his hospital was good, and she liked it. But did she love it? She wanted to, but because there seemed to be such a long distance between like and love, she wondered if love could really exist—for what she did, or for the person she might spend her life with. The bottom line was she didn't know. Wasn't even sure she knew what love was.

"Maybe not being easy was some of my charm?"

"You had many charms, Layla. Trust me, you had more charm than you ever gave yourself credit for."

"You're just saying that because I was…convenient."

"You were a lot of things, but convenient was never one of them." He chuckled. "Even if I hadn't been raised in the jungle where I really didn't have much of an opportunity to get to know women, I'd have never called you convenient. Not in anything."

"Should I take that as a compliment?"

"There were many, many times I took it as a frustration. But it's who you were. Maybe still are. And, yes, it is a compliment because I did like your independence. It made you different from the others."

"Ah, yes. All the girls chasing after jungle boy. You did have your fair share, didn't you?"

"None who could hold my attention the way you did."

"Do you have someone now, Arlo? Are you married, or otherwise committed? I mean, I think Ollie might have told me, but you know how he is, the way he keeps as much to himself as possible. And I think he's gone out of his way not to mention you because, well—you know. It was awkward."

"There's no one. I did see someone in Bangkok for a while after I got back, but it didn't work out. She wanted attention all the time, and I didn't often have time to get there to give it to her. And she wouldn't come here. Eventually, she got to be very clingy, then demanding, when I refused an offer in one of the hospitals there. She'd set it up, assuming I'd take it but, well—you know me. You can take the jungle doc out of the jungle, but you can't take the jungle out of the jungle doc. I didn't conform enough for her and I certainly didn't want her to assume she could control me with a good job offer."

Arlo shook his head. "We lasted six long, difficult months then she met someone who could—and eventually did—give her all the things she wanted that I couldn't."

"I'm sorry to hear that."

"I'm not. She did much better than me. Besides, it's the story of my life. I can't bring anything to a relationship but me. I've got no money. Where I live—well, you'll see that for yourself. I don't own things. I work ridiculous hours. It wouldn't be fair of me to expect anybody to live that life, and it wasn't fair of me back then to ask you to, then end it the way I did, when you told me all the reasons you couldn't. At the time I was so…angry. Eventually I realized that anger was disappointment, and not in you. But in myself for expecting that I could ever have any kind of real relationship in my life since I have nothing to offer."

"You have yourself. If someone loves you, that should be enough."

"But that's not enough, Layla. You know it and I know it. But I made this choice, it was a promise to my mother. Now a lot of people depend on me. And if not me… there's nobody."

Layla shook her head as well. "I almost got myself into something once, but it's a long, complicated story. Girl on rebound meets wrong boy, mistakes his overtures for true love, boy tries to change girl to fit his mold, girl's not the type to bend into anybody's mold. In the end not a heartbreaker so much as an eye-opener and a huge caution that I'm better sticking to something where my heart doesn't get involved." And the last sentence of it went something like: Besides, he didn't measure up to Arlo. But Arlo didn't need to know that.

"Sorry to hear that. Even sorrier that I had a part in it."

She forced a sad smile to her face. "The truth is, I don't know what love is, Arlo. I recognize the kind my parents gave me—more obligatory love than the genuine thing. And don't get me wrong. They've spent a lifetime trying hard, not always getting it right, but trying. Which, I suppose, is love in some variation. At least the only way they knew how to give it. Then there's what I felt for you, which came with a time limit. I thought if I ignored it, it would magically disappear. Then Brad… I don't get it right, or don't do something right. Not sure which."

"Your parents you can't help. With me—us—the boundaries were there before we…" He swallowed hard.

"Before we turned our friendship into something it wasn't meant to be. And with Brad, everybody makes that mistake sooner or later. The rebound affair. That's what I had with Gayle, I suppose. Someone to fill in the gaps."

"Then you were rebounding from me even though we weren't…"

"Readjusting," he said.

"I like that. And maybe that's what I was doing…readjusting." Readjusting to life after Arlo. Yet here she was, the one place she didn't belong given the feelings for him she'd had. But this time she was prepared. At least, she hoped she was. Because she needed to close this chapter. Even after all this time. "So, now that we know each other's biggest mistakes, how about showing me your hut?"

"Are you sure you'd actually stay with me after…"

"Just consider it like sleeping in on-call. Remember those days during our residency after long, hard hours where you barely had time to eat, let alone sleep, when any bed would do as long as the person occupying the bed next to you didn't snore?" She paused for a moment, and despite herself laughed. "You didn't start snoring, did you?"

"Haven't had any complaints. At least, on the nights when I sleep in the hospital, the patients I'm watching haven't said anything. Neither has Chauncy."

"Who's Chauncy?"

Arlo chuckled. "You'll meet him soon enough. And probably get to sleep with him as well."

She didn't know what this was about, but his eyes were sparkling with laughter the way she remembered. It was nice seeing that again. Nice being part of it.

"No door?" she asked, as he pulled back the mosquito netting on his hut to let her in.

"Not yet. It's on the list of things I want, but the hospital gets the little funding we raise, not me, so it's not a priority."

A quick look revealed a small area where he prepared food, a desk off in one corner, a couple of rough-hewn chairs and a thin curtain separating a small area at the back from the rest of what was, essentially, a one-room hut. It was clear, and as basic a space as she'd ever seen, and she could picture Arlo living here. He'd always been a man of simple needs—something she'd admired about him. "So…no facilities?"

"Over at the hospital. Once you get used to it, it's not so bad."

"Bad, as in…?"

"Adequate. A hose through a window that brings water from a tank outside and takes a while to prime and get running. Or you can heat a bucket of water on the stove over there if you prefer a warm bath." He smiled. "I've lived in much more primitive digs than this so, to me, this is all good."

"Primitive for me was that weekend you took me to a cabin in the Catskills. Remember that?"

"It had indoor plumbing," he said defensively, smiling.

"And I had to carry in wood to the fireplace. In my life, a fireplace is turned on with a little knob off to the side. One little flick, gas turns on and, *voilà*, a fire." That had been a nice holiday, though. A wonderful holiday. No trappings like her parents required. Just simplicity and—the two of them. Snow outside, safe and warm with Arlo inside. Feeling protected by him. Drinking hot chocolate. Playing chess for hours on end. Making love for even more hours. Watching, through the plate-glass window, the snow coming down outside and being glad she was in Arlo's arms, inside. Perfect.

He chuckled. "I always did say you were a wimp."

"So, where's the switch to turn on your lights?" she asked, looking around for it.

"I have a generator, but fuel to run it's pretty expensive and hard to come by out here, so most of the time I light the place with a kerosene lamp. And candles. One of the women here makes candles for me."

While Ollie had tried to prepare Layla for Arlo's lifestyle, he hadn't come close. Yet she was here anyway. But it was only for two months, which did concern her—not the lack of amenities but being so close to Arlo because, already, memories she didn't want coming back were flooding in. The Catskills. Going to farmers' markets on the weekends. Reading out loud to each other at night—she liked Charles Dickens, he liked Stephen King. The way he'd always shown up at the hospital to walk her home when it was dark. Or check the oil and battery in her car, then go fill it up to make sure she wouldn't get stranded somewhere on the road. The big things... the little things. The things she'd taken for granted. So many of them were coming back to her now.

She'd expected some of that, but not so much, which made her wonder if what she'd thought of as a nice romance, or even an intense one at times, had really been much more. She knew she'd fallen in love with Arlo, but suddenly some of their memories were tearing at her heart. Even so, she didn't regret her decision to come to Thailand as there was a possibility she needed closure much more than she'd thought she did.

"And this is how you get along on a daily basis?" she asked, wondering if she could as well. Because she didn't want to embarrass herself in front of Arlo. There'd been too many times when he'd teased her about being a spoiled little rich girl, which had bothered her more than she'd expected it to. What she wanted more than anything was to show him she could do this on her own. Live this way. Be a good doctor. Be someone he respected. Because that's the one thing she'd never been sure she'd had from him—his respect. And now, even after all this time, she wanted it. Why? She didn't know. But it mattered. Mattered much more than she'd have ever guessed it would.

CHAPTER TWO

"SERIOUSLY? YOU CAN'T get antibiotics?"

Layla was reacting to a definite lack of supplies in Arlo's medicine lock-up. She'd taken a peek while she was over there and had been totally shocked. In comparison to what she'd had available to her all the time this was crazy. Yet it was Arlo's crazy, and he seemed good with it.

"I can, but it's not as easy as you'd think. Medical care is free, but I have to wait for my allotment, then it's sent to the regional hospital for me to pick up. Getting there isn't always easy. I don't always have time. And I can't have someone do it who isn't medically qualified."

"But don't you have an assistant?"

"He's a student, Layla. A college graduate who's getting ready to go to med school. And he's a good medic in the field. Trained by me, though. So he's not licensed or certified in any medical capacity yet, which means he can't make that trip. I have a nurse who'll bring my supplies out when he can, but doctors and nurses are in critically short supply outside the big cities, so he's not always free to help me either. Meaning if I need something immediately, sometimes I can go get it, sometimes I must wait, depending on what else is going on.

"Bottom line—what I need is available, but the ability to go after it is often lacking. So we wait, and make do until we can rectify the situation."

"I guess I never realized how difficult some medical situations can get, even when supplies are available."

"Most people don't. It's not their fault, but who wants to hear about what I do here when what's happening with medicine in Bangkok's hospitals is a huge contributor to the medical world in general. That's just the way it is."

In *her* medical world, a quick call to the pharmacy or central supply got her what she needed within minutes. Layla couldn't even begin to imagine the frustration of knowing you had what you needed available, yet you couldn't get to it. Maybe that was something she could fix. Something where her admin skills would prove to him she was good at what she did. Certainly it was worth looking into.

"So, can you stock ahead? Keep a few things back in case of emergency?"

"I do, but I don't have a lot of storage capacity here. And sometimes no electricity for days, which means the drugs that require refrigeration go bad."

It kept getting worse. No easy access to drugs that were his. Sometimes no ability to store them properly. And Arlo had chosen this over his grandfather's surgery? "Can't say that I understand any of this, Arlo. When you used to talk about coming back here, what you have isn't what you described. I pictured a modern facility tucked away in the jungle. Not a rundown structure that lacked supplies, personnel and anything that could be construed as convenient or up to date."

"But that's who we are. And this is what I knew I'd be getting when I came back."

"Do you have a bed?"

"Sure do. And it will be yours if you want it. Also, it's not a bed so much as a cot."

"And with the facilities across the street…"

"Consider it a little bit of rustic camping."

"For two months, Arlo. I can do that. But this is the rest of your life and even though I can see it, and I do have a better understanding of the need here…"

"Let me guess. You still don't get it?"

"Oh, I get it. But this isn't who you were when we were together. You talked about this life, but you didn't live anything close to it."

"Consider that as me being on holiday."

"And I was part of that holiday?"

Arlo didn't answer the question. Instead, he pulled back a thin sheet separating the main part of the room from what looked to be a tiny space for a bedroom. "And you're in luck. Chauncy isn't here right now. So the cot is all yours if you want to rest until I can find someone to get your car."

Layla looked out the window above her cot and sighed. It was beginning to rain. Big fat drops. Hitting the dirt road and turning it into instant mud. And here she was, in a hut without a door, assigned to sleep with something or someone called Chauncy, and just now learning that what she'd thought might have been love in some form had been merely a holiday for Arlo. She'd been merely a holiday. Well, she was here. And she had to make the best of it while she was. But her spirits were as dreary as the gray sky outside. She'd hoped for something different, something more. And the truth hurt.

"I don't suppose this Chauncy happens to have an umbrella, does he? I'd like to go back across the road and get myself acquainted with the hospital."

"Actually, I have an umbrella. But you should be careful because some snakes love the rain and come out to play, while others are making a mad dash to get out of it."

Yep, that's all she needed to add to her mood. Snakes in the puddles. "Seriously?"

"Seriously, but the good news is we have a nice supply of antivenin always handy. That's the one thing that's delivered to my door because the pharmaceutical reps deem my snakebite findings useful to them. So, use the antivenin, fill out some paperwork, answer some questions and they keep the supply coming."

Snakes *and* snakebites. Somehow none of this was brightening her day. Not this holiday girl.

"You trying to get rid of me already, Arlo?" Layla asked, walking into a small room, one of only three with real doors in the hospital, then stopping halfway inside to look around. It was a basic exam room. One hard, flat, old-fashioned exam table, an open cabinet with supplies like gloves, bandages and tongue depressors. The medicine cabinet she'd already seen. It wasn't great, but it wasn't hopeless either. More like something new in her collection of medical experiences.

"So, do you have a usual time to order supplies?"

"On a PRN basis." As needed.

"And you get that order sent by…?"

"Going to an elephant rescue near here and getting on their internet." Arlo smiled. "It may seem difficult, but it works out."

But would she work out inside Arlo's system? That was the question that kept coming to mind. She wanted to help him, to do a good job, but practically speaking, could she? "And I'll fit into this how?"

"Any way you want to. I operate on the same system as

my orders are submitted. PRN. It works, as long as I don't get distracted. And that's when everything falls apart."

"What distracts you?" Layla was curious, as Arlo had never seemed the type to get distracted when they'd been together.

"A lot of things. Too much need, too little of me to go around. Medicines I can't get when I need them. The hole in the roof over my cot. Actually, now that you've displaced me that's one less distraction I'll have to deal with."

"Did you always feel that way about me, Arlo? That I distracted you?"

He gave her a questioning look. "How do you mean?"

"That I was a distraction you didn't want to have?"

"You were always a distraction, Layla. But I wanted that distraction. Wanted that time we had together. It meant—everything."

To her, it had. But she wasn't sure about Arlo. One thing was certain, though. He'd been her distraction. And he'd displaced her feelings in a way no one would ever do again. Before him, she'd been sure what she wanted. But after him there had been times when she hadn't been so sure.

"Well, however it worked out, I'm glad you have everything you wanted," she said, walking out into the short corridor leading to the single room holding ten beds. All empty now. And everything bare bones. Meager. Medicine on a level she'd never seen. "Do you think Ollie might have provided you with more, had he known how bare your hospital is?"

"He knows, Layla. He's been here. But he's so heavily invested in his surgical practice—putting me through med school was enough. It was a very generous thing to do, especially considering that if he hadn't done it, I might still be struggling to earn enough money to get through. Besides, my parents were able to manage under difficult circumstances and so am I."

"I hope so. For your sake, as well as your patients'."

"You think I don't do what's best for my patients? You're here all of an hour and you're already making judgments?"

"Not at all. I'm beginning to realize how difficult it must be to exist here." She was almost gaining a deeper insight into him now, seeing him differently than she had in those years they had been together. And this side of Arlo was...admirable. He was someone to be respected. And it was so frightening, knowing he was out here, practically on his own, trying to make a difference she still didn't understand. "Since I've come a long way to work with you, I have the right to wonder. And worry, if that's the way it turns out. If that bothers you, sorry. But there's nothing I can do about it. At least, not until I understand more."

As Layla passed by Arlo on her way to the tiny kitchen at the rear of the ward, she paused when they were almost chest to chest and looked up at him. "I never worked directly with you when we were residents because of our personal situation. Fraternization wasn't allowed. But now it's different. And what we had, or what we meant to each other, can't get in the way. OK? The past is the past. So, keep in mind, Arlo, that this can't turn into something that's only about us. Taking offense too quickly at things not intended to be offensive, overreacting—we can't do that. We can't wipe the slate clean either. But we've got to find a way to make this work for a while. If that's what you want for your hospital. If it's not..."

She shrugged, then ducked into the tiny kitchen to assess the two-burner stove, the small utility table, and the knee-high refrigerator that looked to be a decade past its prime. It was working off a small generator that ran only the kitchen. Well, for now she'd have to get used to it. For better or worse, she had to make a go of this. And of Arlo.

For the first time, Layla really wondered why she had raised her hand so quickly. But it was too late to worry over that, especially when she had so many other things to fret about now. Snakes, something called Chauncy, rain, difficult conditions, Arlo... It was almost too much. Still, she was here, trying to convince herself she could do this. She had to. Arlo might suffer a little if she backed out, but his patients were the ones who really counted. Because of them, Layla would fight her way through and hope she was good enough. No matter what Arlo or anybody else thought, she was about being a doctor. A good doctor. As good a doctor as Arlo.

"What happened to your back?" Layla asked, as they both went to greet a patient who'd wandered in the door. A little boy with a scratch on his arm. He couldn't have been more than five or six, and Layla escorted the child to the exam room and pointed to the table, indicating for the child to hop up.

"I strained it a little," Arlo said, surprised and even flattered that she was paying that much attention. But Layla had always been observant. Sometimes too observant, especially when she'd picked up on one of his moods—moods he'd tried hard never to show. Yet she'd always known, just like now. "I fell off a roof. Actually, the roof caved in a little under my weight. That accounts for the hole over your cot." He said something to the child, who giggled with delight then made hand gestures to indicate someone falling. "Which is tarped, by the way. So the leak is only a drip."

"Should I ask what you were doing on a roof?" Layla found the antiseptic and scrubbed the child's wound, then dressed it with a bandage.

"Not unless you want to hear all about Chauncy."

"Ah, yes, my mysterious bed partner. So, why were you up on the roof with this Chauncy?"

"He got stuck. I had to help him down." Arlo dug into his cargo pockets and pulled out a sweet for the child, said something to him again, then sent the boy on his way, holding onto his sweet like it was the best prize in the world.

"Do children often come here alone?" Layla asked.

"The children here mature at an early age. Chanchai, the little boy who was just here, scratched his arm bringing in fishing nets."

"But he's only—"

"I know. By your standards you see a very young child. But by the standards here, he's a contributing member of the village and he has an important job. The twenty or thirty bahts here might only be a dollar or less in your currency, but that money goes to help support his family, making Chanchai's contribution very important."

"He's very…resilient."

"All the people here are. They work hard for their families, and even the young ones know to come to me if they're hurt, or not feeling well. Of course, it's easy to persuade them when they know you carry sweets in your pockets." He smiled. "Which isn't so different from anywhere, is it? I remember you during your pediatric rotation always stocking up candy for the children, even though your attending physician frowned on it."

"Because my doctor did that when I was a child. It made the whole medical experience less frightening."

Arlo chuckled. "Remember that one little boy who'd

follow you up and down the hall in his wheelchair, never saying a word but always giving you that sad look when you gave a sweet to another child?"

"Geordie. I haven't thought of him in years. He did manage to finagle his fair share, didn't he?"

"Because you were a pushover when it came to children. It surprised me that you went into general surgery and not pediatrics. You were so good with the kids."

"Pediatrics broke my heart too often. I—um— To be an effective doctor I needed to be more detached."

For someone who tried so hard to be stone-hearted, he'd seen through the façade to a very soft, caring woman. It had shone in Layla's face every time she'd looked at one of her pediatric patients. She couldn't hide it—at least, not from him. "Well, you would have been good at it, and you will get your fair share of children to treat here."

"Hope I'm up to it better than you were up to your climb on the roof with Chauncy. Who is…?"

Arlo put the antiseptic and bandages back in the cabinet, looked out the window and spun around to face her.

"He's actually just come home. Want to come meet him?"

He waved at Samron, an aged widow who spent several hours each day in Happy Hospital, cleaning, doing laundry, serving meals and other jobs that gave her something to keep her busy. She was also the self-appointed receptionist who greeted patients when they came in.

"I'll be across the street if you need me," he said to her.

Yes," she answered, smiling. "With pretty lady doc. Your wife?"

Arlo chuckled, then explained to Layla. "They all want me to settle down, get married, start a family. I'm usually on the receiving end of a fix-up at least twice a month. Somebody's sister, or cousin, or daughter."

"Sounds like they care about you."

"Maybe a little too much." He smiled at Samron and shook his head. "Not wife. New lady doc. Doc Layla."

Samron nodded, but her smile told the story, and it was all about Arlo and Layla, together. "Doc Layla," she repeated, then pressed the palms of her hands together in a prayer-like fashion, bent her head ever so slightly and said, *"Wai,"* a customary Thai greeting.

Layla did the same, then followed Arlo into the road. "She seems very nice," she said.

"And very helpful. She also volunteers at the school. And on the weekends she spends time with new mothers in the village, helping them with their babies. She's a very respected person here."

"Respect is important," Layla said. "Too many people have forgotten what it is."

"Well, it's not like that here. If you earn respect, you're given respect." Arlo entered his hut and went straight to the curtain separating the room into two. Then pulled it back to reveal…

"What is that?" Layla asked, her eyes wide open.

"This is Chauncy, my civet cat. We co-habit."

"A civet cat is…?"

"Something like a cat, only a little larger with a face kind of like a big rat. They're nocturnal so they have really glowy eyes."

"And your civet cat got stuck up on the roof and when you went to get him you fell through? Couldn't he have come down himself? I'm assuming civet cats can climb. You know, the law of jungle survival and all that."

"They can, but Chauncy's not good at it. He had a broken leg when I found him, and it healed leaving him lame. So he can climb up pretty well, but getting down is the problem."

"And now he's your house cat?"

"Pretty much." Arlo smiled. "You'll get used to him."

Layla took a couple steps closer, then stared down at the creature who didn't resemble a cat, curled up on the cot she would use. "He's clean, I suppose," she said, bending down to pet him. "And he doesn't bite?"

"Very clean. He doesn't really wander out in the jungle anymore. He's pretty domesticated, and since the people here all know him, they feed him, which makes him too fat, which also makes him lazy. And, no, he doesn't bite. Also, his scent gland was removed since he had to be domesticated for his survival, so you're safe there as well."

She bent to pet Chauncy, who raised his head long enough to decide she was no threat, then immediately went back to sleep. "He's...beautiful," she said, speaking in a whisper so she didn't disturb him.

"I recall you liked cats." Arlo had been concerned that living with a wild animal might cause Layla problems since she was strictly big city but watching her relate to Chauncy gave him a whole new appreciation for her. In fact, he admired the way she simply accepted the fact that she'd be curling up with a jungle creature. That wasn't the Layla he remembered. She'd been...highly strung.

"Cats, dogs, civet cats. All God's creatures, Arlo. Just didn't expect to be sleeping with one. But when you're in the jungle I suppose you sleep with the civet cats when you must." She tiptoed away from Chauncy then moved to the opposite side of the cottage. "Just no snakes," she said. "They're free to roam around all they want outside the hut, but not inside, please."

Arlo laughed. He'd always liked her practicality. When other female med students had been trying to attract him by flirting or making offers that hadn't interested him, Layla had been the one who hadn't noticed him. Which had made him want her to.

And he'd worked hard to get her attention, finding out afterward, when they were together, that's what she'd wanted all along. But she'd been so inexperienced—not shy, though—as much as reserved. Like she had been testing the water and he had been the water. But it had been cute watching her find her way in their relationship. Even after that night with the popcorn, there had been so many things she hadn't known. Things he'd delighted in showing her. Simple things like hiking in the woods. Complicated things such as the profound pleasure an un-complicated massage could offer.

She'd led a sheltered life, though. Hadn't ever really had anyone there to guide her. She also hadn't had to con-tend with civet cats, snakes and elephants daily, the way he'd done, growing up. Talk about opposites... Honestly, he'd always been a little protective of that side of her. Now he wondered if it still existed, and if it did, would it bring that out in him again? "Snakes have their place. If you know which ones won't kill you."

"Good information to have handy," Layla said in the matter-of-fact tone Arlo remembered, oh, so well, as she sat cross-legged on the floor near the door and patted the floor next to her. It was a tone that meant she was try-ing to stay aloof, trying to avoid contact, commitment or whatever else frightened her. Understandably, she was probably more frightened of him right now than snakes. Yet here she was, trying to face it. That was a new side of her, one he liked a lot.

"So, since we don't have proper facilities in here, I suppose buying a luxurious spa tub with soothing jets and all kinds of bubble bath is out of the question? As well as a heated towel rack?"

Arlo laughed as he sat down "Afraid so, but we've got a stream about half a mile from here where the water's pretty warm this time of year. And if the temperature's hot enough, the rocks heat up so you can consider that your heated towel rack."

"You always kept me amused, Arlo. I remember some of those long nights of studying after a long day of working in the hospital, when I thought I wasn't cut out to be a doctor. Then there you'd be, cooking me some of the worst food I'd ever eaten, or strumming your guitar and making up songs that didn't make sense."

"They were in Thai," he defended.

"No, they were in gibberish. Even I recognized that. And if I hadn't, the look on your face would have given you away."

"There were good times, weren't there?" Arlo asked, twisting his back to find a comfortable position.

"And bad ones. I just wish we'd had the bad ones at the beginning so when we finally decided to call it quits we'd have had the good ones closest to us. It would have made the memories better, I think."

He had good memories of her and that was the problem. The memories were too good for a couple that was destined to break up. "And here we are, together again."

"But not for that reason," Layla warned. "I really do want to prove myself and working here should earn me some..."

"Some what?" he asked.

She shook her head. "Has your cooking gotten any better?" she asked, deliberately changing the subject.

"Actually, my brother Eric—you remember me talking about him, don't you?"

"The rich one."

"One and the same. Anyway, he sent me a yakitori grill. And while I'm not good at preparing a meal on it, I do make a mean cup of tea."

"A yakitori grill? Does that mean you've been to Japan?"

"No, my brother lives there. He sent it to me. But I haven't had time to visit him yet."

"So, you've got a civet cat *and* a yakitori." She reached out and squeezed Arlo's arm—an affectionate gesture from the past that came so naturally.

"That about sums it up."

"And that makes you a happy man?"

"Along with my practice. You know me. Simple needs."

"And mine weren't, were they?"

"Let's just say that you gravitated more toward the finer things in life. Probably still do, for all I know."

Layla sighed. "To be honest, I don't have time for all the finer things in life. Most of my time is spent working."

"Why am I not surprised?"

"Probably because you always knew I was ambitious. I think I probably slammed that in your face a thousand times in those two years, didn't I?"

He chuckled. "Let's just say that I was well aware of your preferences and leave it at that."

"Was I that bad, Arlo?"

"You were never bad, Layla. Neither was I. But as a couple…well, our destinies precluded everything else. Maybe that's what was bad. That, and those fifty pairs of shoes on the closet floor that left me no room for my two pairs."

He smiled, thinking about how he'd practically lived

out of a suitcase during those two years because her clothes had taken up every inch of hanging space in both bedrooms. But that had been part of her charm. At least, to him it had been, because he'd loved watching her make the decision of what to wear.

It would take hours sometimes, and she'd always asked his opinion. *Do you like me in this? Is this one better than the other one?* It always made him feel a part of something other than the jungle or his parents' life. Something he liked, even though it was temporary.

"Never more than forty, Arlo. Unless you count boots."

He laughed out loud. Couldn't help himself. Even though they weren't a couple, something about the old familiarity was sinking back in, making him feel like, well—what he hadn't felt like since they had been a couple. "Well, no worries about that here, since this hut doesn't have a closet."

"To think this is where you expected me to live. And that was back when I only had thirty pairs of shoes."

"Sixty," he teased.

"We'll compromise at twenty," she said, smiling.

"Well, for what it's worth, I never expected you to take me up on my offer. But in a few of my more stupid moments, I did hope."

"Not stupid, Arlo. Hope is never stupid."

"Except when it came to us."

Layla smiled, but it was tinged with sadness. "So, is a hose for a shower and no closets what you still want? I know you feel an obligation to stay here, but has anything changed?"

"No, not really. Because this is where I've always worked from the time I was five or six, just like little Chanchai. It's everything I knew I wanted, probably because this is the kind of medicine my parents practiced, and I respected what they did. I mean, I was raised in the jungle, Layla. Conceived here, born here. It's what I know. What I want. Taking care of people who wouldn't otherwise get medical help—I could have gone in with Ollie after I graduated, but it wouldn't have made me happy, not the way my practice here does."

"Then you're where you belong. Following your heart is always the best way."

"Have you ever done that, Layla? Followed your heart?"

She shook her head. "That's not who I am. I follow my choices, but you already knew that."

"I hope your choices have made you happy so far."

"They've made me what I want to be—successful."

And somehow Layla seemed almost as vulnerable as she had when they'd first been together. The girl who'd been afraid to approach him. The girl who'd never fully invested herself in life. Was it because of her money? Did she still rely on that the way she had when they'd been together? Trusting that rather than trusting people?

There'd been so many times when she'd found it easier to buy her way into a situation rather than rely on her intellect and amazing abilities to come up with a better way. Was that who she still was? Because that was a part of Layla he'd never understood. So independent, yet so willing to fall back into habits she'd said she wanted to be rid of. Even if they hadn't been going in separate directions, that's the thing that would have killed them.

"I suppose I thought that after you'd spent so much time back in the States during medical school, then residency, maybe this wouldn't have the same appeal you remembered."

"It has more, now that I'm an adult and can fully appreciate what I have here—like the freedom of doing what I want to do without a lot of interference from any-one. My patients are the best, which makes up for my less than spectacular accommodation. And it's nice caring for people who are grateful for my services and not ones who make unreasonable demands."

He laughed. "Remember the surgical patient who wanted me to do both a hernia repair and a nose reduction in the same surgery? The guy actually reported me to Administration because I refused, not that my attending would have allowed such a thing even if I'd wanted to. Which I didn't. But he made my life miserable for a couple of weeks, calling and complaining over and over."

"If I recall, he thought he'd get a discount that way. Two surgeries for the price of one anesthesia. Guess he didn't consider that general surgeons aren't plastic surgeons. Or maybe that didn't matter to him. You were pretty agitated at the time."

"And you made me chicken noodle soup—from a can."

"Because it was supposed to make you feel better."

"When you were ailing, Layla. I wasn't ailing. I was angry." He smiled. "But it was a nice gesture, having someone take care of me like that. Did I ever tell you how much I appreciated that?"

"No. You told me it wasn't hot enough, then told me to reheat it in the microwave. But you did leave me that flower the next day—the one you picked from the garden at our apartment building. I pressed it and kept it until, well—I probably still have it tucked in a book some-where. It was the first gift you ever gave me." Layla smiled, and leaned her head over on his shoulder, a natural thing she'd always done once upon a time. "I'm glad it's working for you, Arlo."

"I…um…" Arlo pulled away from her so quickly she

almost fell sideways to the ground. "We've got work to do," he said, his voice suddenly stiff.

"Did I do something?" she asked, trying to recover from his abruptness.

Arlo shook his head as he stood. "We did something a long time ago and I don't want to repeat it. You're not easy to resist, Layla. God knows, I was never able to. But not anymore. My work—my practice here won't allow me that kind of distraction."

"That's right. I was just your holiday girl, wasn't I? Well, don't worry. I'm nobody's holiday now, and I never will be again." Without another word, Layla marched out of the hut and across the road to the hospital, grabbed the schedule off the desk at the front and saw that the next three patients due in needed general care—a wound check, an antibiotic shot and a maternity appointment. They weren't there yet, but when they arrived they would find Dr. Layla Morrison waiting for them in the exam.

And Dr. Arlo Benedict standing outside in the road, in the rain, wondering how two people who'd gotten it so right could have also gotten it so wrong.

CHAPTER THREE

IT WAS GETTING ON in the day when Layla finally gathered up the courage to go back to the hut to face him. Overall, seven patients had come to the hospital and she'd managed to figure out what each one wanted. Luck had been with her on that one. That, plus some translation help from Samron, who seemed genuinely pleased to be useful.

"Have you eaten yet?" she asked Arlo, who was heading back to the hut at the same time she was.

"A couple of times. My house call patients always like to offer food." He handed her a wooden plate covered with a cloth napkin. "Khao pad. It's a fried rice with several different vegetables and pork in it. There's also some mixed fruit."

"I, um—I don't know what to say except thank you and I'm sorry. This is awkward and I know it, and I shouldn't have gotten so familiar. Leaning against you that way was inappropriate, but just for a few minutes we were almost—us. The way we started anyway. From now on I'll keep my distance."

"And I never meant to imply you were a holiday girl. You were my break from reality, and you knew that. But I never thought of you as someone who was there only for a good time, someone to use at my convenience, and I'm sorry that's how it sounded."

"I know who we were, Arlo. From the very first day until the last one, I always knew. I also know that's not what you thought of me but, like I said, it's awkward now." She peeked at the food under the cloth, and her mouth practically watered. "Mind if I heat this up on your yakitori?"

"Communal property while you're here, Layla. What's mine is yours."

"So, where do I put my fifty pairs of shoes?"

He laughed as they went inside together, she straight to the yakitori, to lay the fire beneath it, and he to his mat on the floor. But when he lowered himself to it, he winced.

"I really do need to have a look at that," she said, pulling a matchbox from a shelf and lighting the fire. "Even if I can't see anything, maybe I can feel which muscle is giving you problems and manipulate some of that soreness out of it. Strictly medical, of course." She turned around and studied him for a moment. It wasn't quite dark in the hut yet, but it wasn't quite light either. Yet somewhere in the ebbing of the day she saw traces of the man who'd shared her bed for nearly two years mingling with traces of a man she didn't know.

"You've changed," Layla said, not caring that he could see her assess him. His hands—yes, she was a handsy type. Always looked at the hands second. Neck first. Eyes. Mouth. But right now she was wondering if his hands would still be soft. They looked soft, and she wondered what they would feel like on her skin again. Caressing her. Causing her to tingle…

No, this wasn't allowed. No memories. No fond thoughts of what they'd had. Still, Arlo Benedict, for his un-trendy ways, was a rugged and well-proportioned man. A head-turner. Always had been, and she was pretty sure he'd never even been aware of it.

"How?" he asked. "And if it's in a bad way, please lie to me. I know the jungle can be harsh."

"Quite the contrary. You look…more mature. Not so much in the physical sense as what I can see in your eyes."

"I think that's called wisdom. Before I went to medical school I was here with my parents, working as their helper. They had everything under control and that's what I expected to come back to. But when I did come back, my mother was gone, and my dad wasn't the same. He stayed around long enough to help me find my way, then he went to live his own life, leaving me here with a lot of expectations that weren't mine to have. I expected what my parents had but my reality was that I had to build my own place here, gain trust that was mine and not my parents'. So I wised up pretty fast. Had to in order to survive."

"Well, it looks good on you." Layla turned back to the yakitori, pulled a metal pot off the shelf above it and dumped in her fried rice. While it heated, she ate large chunks of papaya and mango with her fingers.

"You've changed, too," Arlo said, still wrestling to find a comfortable position. "You used to be…reserved. Or at least not as sure of yourself. You grew out of that a little while we were together but now you're this dynamic ball of fire that plows through everything. Instead of talking about what you wanted to happen, you're making things happen in your life, and I'm glad it's working out for you."

She pulled the rice off the little stove then turned back to face him. "Care to share?" she asked, thinking of the many times they'd ordered one meal and shared it, both eating from the same plate. Sometimes feeding each other. Often with just fingers. So nice. Sensual. So much intimacy in such a simple gesture.

Patting his flat belly, Arlo shook his head. "When I make evening calls, I have to pace myself with what I eat because everybody wants to cook for me."

"And I usually grab something from the hospital before I leave for the evening." She wrinkled her nose. "Haven't learned to cook properly yet."

"Well, I didn't move in with you because you were a domestic goddess. And I did know that you sneaked in a maid to do the cleaning."

"Seriously?" And she'd thought she'd been so stealthy about it.

"Remember that vacuum we bought? You didn't even know how to turn it on. It was a flip switch. On and off. And you didn't know how. Yet the apartment was always spotless." He laughed so hard it caused a spasm in his back. "I let you keep your secret because you were trying so hard to be domestic that I didn't want you to know I was well aware of the *real* you."

"Only once a week," she said, taking her plate of rice across the room and sitting down across from Arlo. At a safe distance. So there was no way to lean, or touch, or even accidentally brush up against him. "And I really thought you didn't catch on."

"Oh, I caught on. But it was…cute, how you'd try to hide things. Like more shoes, when you bought them. I was always wise to you, Layla."

"But I was never wise to you. So, how did that happen?"

"I think we see what we want to see. Or we don't see what we don't want to see. I don't think you wanted to see the real me."

"Yet you wanted to see the real me."

"Because there was so much to see. So many facets." He smiled. "And secrets."

"Secrets? Besides the shoes and the maid, and the takeaway food. Oh, and the laundry…"

"You had someone do the laundry?"

She nodded, watching his face for a reaction. Which happened immediately in a broad smile and a loud laugh. "Are you kidding me? Because I never knew that."

"I didn't want you thinking I was too incompetent. But I didn't know how to sort laundry or even turn on a machine."

"So, who?"

"The woman who worked for my mother. She'd stop by a couple times a week, grab what needed to be cleaned and leave what she'd already done. So, is there a secret behind those sandals?" She referred to the well-worn pair sitting on the shelf outside the door. "Because I don't see another pair of shoes in here." Traditionally, shoes were left outside on a rack, and houses were entered either barefoot or in socks. It was interesting that Arlo respected tradition enough to do that in his own hut, where he wouldn't have to if he didn't want to. It was a nice quality, paying homage to a tradition that wasn't his. Yet he fit this place so well. Much better than any place she'd ever tried to fit. She envied him that as it was something she doubted she'd ever have.

"Until I can afford a new pair, it's them or nothing."

"And I'm betting that once you have enough money for a new pair, you put that money to what you would consider a better use." Arlo was like that. Always taking care of others before he took care of himself. Even when they'd been together and Layla had been struggling through a particularly difficult lesson in physiology or couldn't quite remember the function of every bone in the body, he'd stop his studying to help her through hers.

There were so many little details she'd taken for granted then, which were coming back to her now. To think she'd had so much yet couldn't hold onto it. And maybe, in some ways, she'd pushed it away, knowing she came in second to his dream—a dream that would never include her.

"I might," he confessed. "But the soles are still intact, the straps keep them on me, and with a little tape I'm good for now. Besides, I don't have a closet, so where would I put them since you've got, what? Ten pairs lined up against the wall?" He tossed her a sexy wink.

There was something to be said for a doctor who devoted everything he had to his practice. She did admire that. Much more now that she could see it than before, when it had been mere words. And while none of this was for her in the long term, she was anxious to see how it worked. To see how Arlo worked. For his sake, she hoped everything was good for him because, despite their rocky time at the end, she did want him to be happy with his choice, even though his choice didn't include her.

"You don't happen to still have some of those socks I bought you, do you? They'd look stunning with your sandals."

She smiled, thinking of all the outrageous socks and underpants she'd bought him over the course of their relationship, trying to loosen him up a bit. Not that he was stodgy. But he was a man of habit. Everything was the same—all his socks alike, the same with his underpants. So every now and then she'd thrown in something a little different and hidden one of his tried-and-trues.

At first, it had simply been colors. Red socks, plaid socks. Then figures—pickles, kittens. Santas for Christmas. Hearts for Valentine's Day. Eventually came the unicorn socks, underpants and T-shirts. And that was when he'd finally commented. Actually, his comment had been to balk at wearing them, but by the time the unicorns had arrived he'd had no choice but to wear what she'd bought as she'd hidden everything else.

"Ah, yes. The unicorns. Those got dumped in the trash shortly after I left."

"But you wore them."

"Did I have a choice? You took away everything else. And did I ever tell you how badly I was ridiculed in the locker room at the hospital when I changed into my scrubs?"

"You never said a word, but I heard."

"Everybody heard, and I was so…"

"Cute. Maybe even a little bit sexy."

"In unicorns? I was going to say I was so humiliated."

"Yeah, but remember the night you came home and paraded those unicorns around the—" This was going too far. The memories were of something she shouldn't be remembering. Yet being around Arlo seemed to knock down all her defenses—defenses she'd struggled to raise in the few days she'd had between knowing she was coming here until arriving. "You know what? Instead of tea, I think I'd like to go back over to the hospital to make sure I've replaced everything I used today."

"You can't run from it, Layla. We have history, and considering what we were together I'm not sure you should have come."

She pushed herself off the floor and took the plate over to the bucket that was used for washing dishes. "I'm not denying what we had, Arlo. And you're not the reason I'm here. I want that promotion and I thought that if

Ollie saw how well I could function under adversity, that would put me one step closer."

"Is the jungle the real adversity here, or am I?"

She didn't answer him, because she didn't know what to say. So maybe she'd deluded herself into believing that Arlo wouldn't be a factor in her goals. Or maybe she'd simply hoped he wouldn't. Whatever the case, he was an obstacle and she was going to have to be very careful. Because in the span of only one day a new truth about the way she'd felt about Arlo was trying to force itself in. And it was a truth she didn't want to admit was there.

It was interesting, getting to *again* know someone he'd shared a bed with for two years. In many ways she was still the same, yet in as many ways she was different. She'd never really asked questions about how he'd live his life here when they'd been together. Mostly, she'd assumed what it would be, and had let that play on the way she accepted things. Now, watching her face his reality, she wasn't overwhelmed the way she might have been years ago. Curious, yes. Even ready to be involved. But she was looking at things differently. Even seeing him differently. Of course, he was seeing her differently as well. Time and maturity, he supposed. And also a good dose of their own, personal realities.

"Tell me about Eric," she said, from the other side of the curtain.

It was late, but he wasn't ready to sleep. Neither was she, as he'd been listening to her over there for the past hour, settling in, making adjustments, arranging her belongings. Getting her cot well away from the drippy ceiling so she wouldn't feel the splash as the leaking water hit the bucket. As he recalled, she'd never been the first to go to sleep. She was more of a polyphasic sleeper—

sleeping in bursts, napping in between—while he was a hunker down and get to sleep as fast as he could kind of guy. He remembered the many nights when he'd waken briefly to find her simply staring at him. It was nice, knowing she watched him sleep.

"He's got a good life going. Married, has a son. Living in Japan."

"Did he ever get to see your mom before she—?"

"He did. It was difficult for both of them, especially with the way she left him when he was so young."

"And you didn't even know you had a brother until you were, what? Twenty?"

"Almost twenty-one."

"I never knew how something like that could happen. I always wanted a brother or sister because I was so alone growing up. If I'd found out, only after I was an adult, that I had a brother or sister, I don't know that I could have forgiven my parents." She poked her head around the curtain. "Yet you've always seemed very calm about that."

"Because I was."

"But not Eric?"

"He had a lot of resentment, even after he knew the reason our mother walked away. I think being a married man with a family of his own has made it better for him. And I can't even begin to understand what it would be like having a mother who walked away from me. But that's what our mother did."

"And you don't resent her for keeping her secret?"

"What I resent was that Eric's dad put her in the position that forced her to keep secrets from her sons. I don't blame her for what she did, and in time I don't think Eric will either."

"But the good news is you have a brother."

"And the relationship between us is getting better.

Can't say that it's great yet. Especially since we live in two totally different worlds. But it's nice knowing he's out there."

"So, did your mother ever tell you why? Or am I getting too personal?"

"It's personal, but you lived through some of the ups and downs of it, so you have a right to know."

She came around the curtain, with her hair up in a ponytail the ways she'd always put it up at night, but instead of the cute nightwear she used to wear—short shorts, barely there belly shirts—she was wearing knee-length cargo pants, a baggy T-shirt and boots. Still cute, in its own special way.

"She tried legally for partial custody, but Eric's father wanted his legacy and my mother was only the means by which he could get what he wanted. After he had his son, he didn't need her, so he kicked her out. Then after she tried to maintain a place in Eric's life—let's just say that in my own dad's earlier days he wasn't a saint. He smoked some weed, was arrested a couple of times—although he has no convictions.

"But Eric's dad found out and used that to threaten my mother—told her he'd expose her husband, my dad, and by that time she'd had me and he also said he'd expose her as an unfit mother for allowing me to be raised by a man like my dad. Things were different back then. My mother was afraid of losing me, and afraid my dad could lose his medical license, even though there were never any real charges brought against him. Eric's dad had a lot of power and he wasn't afraid to use it. Also, because she'd been so abused by Eric's dad to begin with, she simply didn't have the wherewithal to fight him.

"So, because she feared losing both my dad and me, after she'd already lost Eric, she walked away." He paused, then sighed. It was a sad sigh that resounded loudly through the hut, filling it with the same sadness. "My mother wasn't a fighter, Layla. She was a very quiet, undemanding person. And after all she'd already suffered…"

"I'm so sorry," Layla whispered. "You didn't know this when we were—?"

He shook his head. "My dad only told me the whole story a couple years ago. He kept my mother's secret for a long time, then finally decided it was time I knew everything."

"And you told Eric?"

"He had a right to know. He was settling into his new life and I knew he harbored a lot of resentment for our mother, but because his son was our mother's grandchild, I thought for Riku's sake—that's his name—everybody needed to know the truth. And I did want my nephew to know how amazing his grandmother was. She was part of his heritage and he deserves to know the good about her. Eric didn't want to know, but for the sake of his son I had to tell him."

"I wish I'd known. Wish I could have helped you. Some things are so difficult when you're alone. I really am sorry for that."

"Well, the good news is Eric now has memories of a mother he can be proud of, and Riku has a grandmother who would have loved him more than life itself. He'll understand that when he's old enough. Eric will make sure."

Layla wiped a tear siding down her cheek. "And your father?"

"In Cambodia. Doing well. Running a little clinic in a tourist area."

"And I thought I had it bad because while I had my parents' time, I never really had their love. At least, love in the sense that I think parents should have for their children."

"Maybe they did the best they could, the way my mother did."

"They do," she admitted. "But that understanding comes as an adult, not as a child who was simply lonely. Anyway, I'm going to get some sleep. It's been a long, full day and since Chauncy has vacated my bed now, I think it's time."

This time, Arlo lay awake long after Layla was asleep, thinking back on the day. This morning, he'd known someone was coming. Hadn't known who but wasn't surprised as Ollie would have sent him only the best. And Layla was the best. It concerned him she was here, but he was also looking forward to the next couple of months with her. No deluding himself about anything, though. She was still Layla, and Layla didn't belong here. On top of that, she didn't want to belong here. But over the course of the years there'd been many, many times when he'd wondered what it would be like, having Layla at his side.

Well, for a little while he had that chance, and he was glad about that. What he wasn't glad about were the feelings that would hit him again once she'd gone. He'd been through that and had been nearly crippled by emotions he'd never expected. It wasn't until he'd left her that he'd truly realized how much he'd loved her. This time he was smarter. No hearts involved meant no hearts broken. And she was clear that her heart was in her career and nowhere ese. But his? Where was it?

"Damn," he muttered, as he blew out the kerosene lamp and turned over on his side. Winced because of his back. Then turned again.

"I really do need to look at that," she said from the

other side of the curtain. "Tomorrow. I'll pencil you in as my first appointment of the day."

He smiled. She never gave up. That may have been one of the things he'd loved most about her back then. But now?

"Baby's on the way…"

Layla didn't open her eyes when Arlo's voice wafted over her. It was a dream. They were cozy in their apartment, cuddled up, studying. Maybe some playing mixed in. And he was explaining…

"Contractions just a couple of minutes apart, Layla."

"Dilated?" she asked, her mind still all snuggly on a sofa back in New York.

"Has been since yesterday, when I checked her."

She loved his voice when it was all serious. It was deeper, sexier. "Epidural, I'm assuming," she said.

"We don't do epidural out here."

"Better call anesthesia." He should have already done that. She didn't understand why he hadn't.

"Do you want to come with me, Layla?"

"Where?" she asked, her eyes still closed.

"To deliver a baby."

This time her eyes shot open and she realized where she was. Not in Arlo's arms, studying the basics of childbirth, but in a jungle hut with a patient who was ready to deliver. She bolted upright. "Who's with her?" she asked, sliding off the cot and running over to the door to grab her boots.

"Empty them first," Arlo warned. "I can't handle a delivery and a snakebite at the same time."

Reality. This was her reality for a while. She shook the dream away totally as vigorously as she shook her boots. "How long has she been in labor?"

"Off and on since yesterday. I checked her earlier, when I was making rounds, and contractions were still about ten minutes apart. But it seemed to have sped up."

"How long have I been sleeping?" she asked. The fact was her sleeping was so erratic, she often didn't know.

"About two hours."

"And you've been working…"

"About the same."

Layla grabbed her medical rucksack and rushed out the door. Arlo followed, amused by the way she went from sound asleep to at the ready. She'd always been a little bit difficult to wake, but once he'd succeeded she'd been on the spot, bright-eyed and ready to go. "Her mother's with her. And her grandmother. Also, there's a midwife, and she'll do most of the work."

"So what will we do?" she asked.

"Respect the traditions. I just thought you might want to see how this works, since we've got at least a dozen more pregnant women in the village and you'll no doubt be called to watch but not participate in the birth unless there's a problem."

"I know a lot of places in the world don't welcome outside interference. Is this one of them?"

"No. They love having a hospital. It's the only one around for nearly a hundred miles, so they take pride in having medical services here. But they also have their traditions, which I don't interfere with unless they become a problem." He pointed to a well-apportioned hut, one with a door, at the end of the road. "It's bigger than yours," she said, following him up the path to the front door.

"Because I don't have my parents, grandparents and children living with me. Family is a large part of their tradition."

Which she saw for herself when she and Arlo went

inside. There were women cooking, children playing, men talking. And in the doorway to the area where the bedrooms probably were stood an old woman holding a tiny bundle in her hands. "I see they didn't really need us," Layla said, pushing her way through the crowd to look at the newborn. The old woman, named Hanni, immediately put the baby in Layla's arms then headed off to the area where the food was being prepared. In her medical practice Layla didn't deal with children and, in all honesty, she hadn't even handled one since her rotation through Pediatrics during her residency. And this one—he was so tiny. Red, wrinkled and screaming for all he was worth.

"They named him Arlo," Arlo said, stepping to her side.

"Even though you didn't deliver him?"

"It's a tribute."

"So, how many little Arlos are running around the village?"

"At last count, five. This Arlo makes number six."

"Well, if ever there was a village legacy…" Layla grinned, reaching down to take baby Arlo's tiny fingers. "Suppose you have a son someday and want to call him Arlo? What then?"

"Just accept the fact that he'll be one of the many." He pulled back the blanket to have a better look at the baby. "You look good with a baby. Ever thought that maybe you might…?"

"I haven't changed on that," she said. "I told you back then I didn't want children, and I still don't. I'm the living proof of how badly it can work out when the parents are all about career, and I'd never want that for my child because, in my family, the apple doesn't fall far from the tree, even though the career tree is different." She handed the baby over to him. "Think I'll go look in on the mother to make sure she's getting along OK." And to get away from the cozy feeling of home and family that was coming over her.

"I've got another house call to make after this," he called after her. She heard him but didn't respond as she ducked out of the room and found an empty room down the hall where she could hide long enough to gather her wits. And will her hands to stop shaking. Of everything that was going to be difficult here, this might be the worst. Because she'd had these thoughts before. Although she'd never told Arlo. What was the point when their directions were so vastly different?

It was mid-afternoon when they caught up again. Layla had taken the hospital calls while Arlo had done rounds in the village.

It was nice having her here to help him. While his assistant was good, he wasn't a doctor so his duties were limited. But having two doctors here—the way his parents had been—would be nice. Even after only a day and a half, he was getting spoiled by it.

But not spoiled enough to let himself believe the other doctor would be Layla. Because, as they said, a leopard didn't change its spots. Neither did Layla. One look at the baby and the almost panicked expression on her face had said it all.

"I've got a house call to make. It's out some way, so I thought you'd like to go with me to see some of the countryside. And if you don't, could I borrow your SUV?"

They were both back in the hut, getting tidied up for the rest of the day. When Arlo peeked around the dividing curtain to talk to her, he had to bite his lower lip to keep from laughing. Chauncy had managed to find his way onto Layla's lap, and she was simply sitting cross-legged on the cot, petting him. Normally, he wasn't quite so friendly with strangers, but Layla did have a way about her. Especially considering that Chauncy wouldn't even cuddle up to him that way.

Somehow, seeing a gray, ring-tailed raccoon-looking mongoose-rat creature all cozy with her caused a lump to form in his throat. This was the other side of her, one he'd loved as much as he'd loved her harder side. There'd been times when she'd just snuggle into him for no reason and simply exist in his embrace. No kidding, no anything else. Just touch. Sensation. And he'd enjoyed those moments as they'd felt so caring. So consuming.

"What do we have?" she asked, plucking a quartered mango from a bowl next to her and handing it to Chauncy.

As the juice dribbled down her arm, Arlo could almost imagine himself kissing her arm along its trail. Stopping at her neck. Kissing it…he loved the way she was so ticklish there. As hard as she'd tried to fight it, she couldn't. And the fight…it had always led to more. A little shove back onto the bed, some pillow play, clothes flying everywhere… But these were dangerous thoughts, as he began to experience the stirrings of feelings and emotions he hadn't had in a long, long time. And while they were sexual, they weren't purely sexual the way they had been before. "It's dengue fever. Two members of one household."

"Hemorrhagic?"

Arlo raised his eyebrows in bold appreciation. "I see you know your dengue fever."

"A little. I did some reading on the plane. Not enough, but as much as I could to give me a good start here."

"Well, then—no. It's not hemorrhagic. But it did come on in the typical symptoms: high fever, headache, vomiting, muscle and joint pain, and a characteristic skin rash. We're at the end of it, too. This will probably be my last trip out there, which means the house calls on this one will be yours in the future, because dengue can relapse. So rather than having me do a daily check, you can do one every three or four days for a couple of weeks."

"Your treatment choice?" she asked.

"Supportive, for the most part. It's a mother and her five-year-old daughter. The rest of the family is fine."

"And by supportive you mean force liquids and treat other symptoms as they occur?"

"Exactly. Since it's a virus, that's about all we can do. Kanika and her daughter Achara went home from the hospital yesterday morning. They'd been here the week prior, and now Kanika's mother will be taking care of them until they're fully recovered. People here really opt for short-term stays. Or home care, when they can. So, from here on out it's mostly just rest and proper nutrition. And better mosquito netting."

"Do you see much dengue out here?" Layla asked.

"A fair amount, but not epidemic-sized. There have been efforts by the government to control the mosquitoes, but some of the remote areas such as this don't get a lot of help. I've petitioned for more netting and was allocated some, but not enough."

"Then I'll get some. How many do I need and who do I contact to make arrangements?"

"I've already petitioned for it, Layla. It will get here in due course."

"Could I get it here faster?"

"In the jungle, patience is a virtue. We get what we need, but sometimes we have to wait."

"And in the meantime people are being exposed to

mosquito-borne disease. Why would you want to be patient about that?"

This was the same old Layla. Impatient for results. Impatient to move up. Impatient to get to the next thing on her list. He'd gotten used to it but coming from a place where impatience produced ulcers more than it did results, he'd never been one to indulge. And he worried that she did as it increased the chance that she would continually be dissatisfied in her life.

Impatient people risked feeling overwhelmed. They set themselves up for failure and got down on themselves when it happened. And they burned out easily. Layla was too bright to burn out, but her impatience was leading her straight down that path. He'd warned her over and over when they'd been together. She hadn't listened. Or maybe she'd thought she was somehow impervious to the pitfalls.

He didn't know which, but the Layla standing here with him right now hadn't budged from the Layla of the past. "Because that's the way it is here. We get what we need when it's available and always keep in mind there are twenty-five regions here, and each one has several hospitals just like ours, all needing the same things we need. Everybody gets served, but we have to realize that we're not the only ones in line."

"But what if I can cut that line?"

"I can't stop you. I never could. But be careful that cutting that line doesn't cost you somewhere later in your career. We're not impatient people out here, Layla. And we don't see the stress-related disease brought on by impatience here the way so many doctors see it in the more *civilized* societies. But you already know that."

"So what you're saying is you wouldn't support me trying to use my connections to get you what you need?"

"What I'm saying is we all do what we have to do. If buying netting from a private source is what you must do, then do it."

"And in return I'll get to listen to you complain."

"No. I don't complain about anything anyone donates, Layla. In fact, I'm grateful for it. And if you buy netting, I'll be grateful for that. But you do need to know what you're facing since you'll be working here for a while. It's rewarding and frustrating, in that order. And if you let it, it will tear you up."

"I don't know how you do it, Arlo."

He smiled. "Sometimes I wonder about that myself. But, for the most part, it works out. And I've got five hundred people living in the village and the same number living just outside who support me and help any way they can. And they're not impatient when they have to wait. I'm also not treating one ulcer in my whole practice."

"Point taken. But I still want to support you with some netting."

Ah, yes. The stubborn Layla got the last word. He'd expected it. And back when they'd been together, the making up that had come afterward had almost been worth the disagreement. It had always been more—intense. Arlo smiled, remembering. Almost missing those times. "And let me thank you in advance, because mosquitoes are a huge problem. So, tell me. Does your impatience get in the way of your medical practice? And I'm not trying to start something here. More like curious about an aspect of you I've always known."

"It's part of who I am as a doctor. When I order a test, I don't want to wait days for the results. When I order medications, I want them immediately. My patients expect that from me. So does your grandfather."

"He doesn't mind your impatience?"

"It gets results, so why should he?"

"You're always about the climb, aren't you?"

"That shouldn't come as news. And maybe time has escalated my impatience," she said, smiling. "However it works, it serves my patients well, and that's always the bottom line for me."

"But what about your own personal bottom line, Layla? I know you have an agenda, as most people do, but what happens to you if something derails it? What if you don't get this promotion? You've been working for it the whole time you've been a doctor, so what do you do with yourself when it doesn't happen? Do you take stock of the things you've put aside to get it? Do you regret what you've missed on that climb?"

"I don't know," she said. "For me, my life is designed around forward momentum. If that stopped, if I couldn't get where I wanted to go, I have no idea what I'd do. Maybe try someplace else. Maybe still keep pushing despite the roadblock."

"At what cost, though?"

"Do you really care, Arlo?"

"Surprisingly, yes. I know how you struggle to get ahead. I lived with it until I realized I couldn't compete with it."

"I'm sorry that happened," she said.

"I don't regret what we were, Layla. I walked away from us a better man. But I did worry about your direction. In a lot of ways, it was much more difficult than mine. It still is." And, yes, he still worried. More than he should.

CHAPTER FOUR

THIS WAS CERTAINLY not what she'd expected, but she did like the more mature Arlo, with his dry wit and lack of sophistication. It was easy to see what she'd seen in him first time around, because most of it was still there, but better. Likability had never been a problem. But fundamental differences made up for that. No matter what else, he was a good man. Charitable. Kind. Nearly perfect in more ways than she remembered.

"You drive," Layla said, tossing her SUV keys to Arlo. It was sitting out front of the hospital, all washed and sparkly, thanks to the kindness of several villagers who'd pulled it out of the ditch and brought it to the hospital for her. Then detailed it. "Since you know where you're going and I don't."

They were on their way to visit Kanika, the woman who had had dengue fever.

"You're lucky as most of the way there is on a real road. Dirt. A little rutted. But a road nonetheless."

"And by most of the way you're implying that some of the way is not?"

"I might be," he said, walking around the SUV, looking at every aspect of it. "Nice vehicle."

"A gift from my parents. Rather than telling me they were proud of me, they bought me a car. When I'm gone, you can have it to get you back and forth to those supplies you need and don't always have proper transportation to go and get. And, no, that's not the spoiled little rich girl doing this. It's the practical doctor who wants to help you."

"And the practical doctor in me appreciates your generosity."

"There was a time when you'd have said something cutting about me being a material girl."

"And there was a time when you were. But I was wrong to throw that back at you so much, especially at the end. I knew who you were, Layla, when we got together. You never made any pretense that you weren't. But we were extremely different people going in and our goals couldn't have been more different. We knew that, though, and most of the time we got around it. But when it was time to break up, I needed something to push me in that direction because I was really torn about doing what I'd set out to do or staying with you. So that's what I latched onto. I shouldn't have, and I'm sorry I did."

"You thought about staying?"

"All the time."

"But I drove you away. Isn't that why you left?"

He shook his head. "I always knew what I had to do. In the end, my sense of duty brought me home. You were always upwardly mobile. I was always homeward bound."

She knew that. She'd always known that and while he'd respected her direction, she hadn't respected his. "I wanted someone to love me more than they did their trappings. My parents never did. And you—I expected too much. In retrospect, we probably shouldn't have gotten involved the way we did."

"You regret it?" he asked.

She laughed. "Not a moment of it."

He hopped into the SUV and tossed his medical rucksack into the back seat. Layla did the same, and for the first several minutes of the ride they said nothing. Probably because they were both trying to process what had already been said. At least, that's what Layla was doing. But when Arlo stopped abruptly on the road, jumped out of the SUV and ran across to an old woman hobbling her way just off to the side, Layla called out the window, "Do you need me?"

"No. Waan has severe arthritis and I'm just offering her a ride home. She walks into the village once or twice a week to buy goods from the vendors, but she's really not up to it."

Layla watched him take the woman's packages, then help her over to the SUV. Arlo was such a good man. If she'd thought that once since she'd known him, she'd thought that a million times. He cast her a boyish smile as he helped Waan into the back seat then took his place in the driver's seat, next to Layla. Just looking at him and seeing the pleasure on his face in all the helpful things he did, she thought her heart would melt.

Did he know how drop-dead gorgeous he was? A little unkempt, but it worked for him. Always had. And maybe that was the expectation to beat all expectations. The perfect man for her, if there was such a thing, was more like Arlo, and less like any other man she'd ever met. Or might ever meet. "Is she on any kind of NSAID?" Layla asked, smiling back at the woman, who clearly only had eyes for Arlo.

"I've tried a few, but they bother her stomach. And the better-class drugs, like biological modifiers, aren't practical out here. Too much to monitor, too many lab tests."

"So, what does she take?"

"Nothing," Arlo said, turning off the main road onto

a road that was little more than a path. "She decided she didn't want to worry about the side effects of pretty much anything I could prescribe, and as long as she can get around she's happy. Normally, one of her children will bring her to the village in a truck, but Waan is a proud, independent woman who likes to do it by herself when she can. Kind of like someone else I know."

"Have you researched any of the new drugs on the market? Maybe there's something..."

He shook his head. "She made her decision a couple of years ago, and I respect that. Medicine can cure many things, but for Waan it can't cure the indignities of always being needy. So she isn't." He stopped in front of a pleasant whitewashed cottage, and helped Waan out of the back seat. Then grabbed her packages and extended an arm to help her as they walked together, very slowly, up the path to the door. Once there, he handed her back her packages, bowed in respect to her, then hurried back to the SUV. "She's very traditional," he said. "Won't invite a man into her home unless there's a chaperone."

"Since she doesn't take any medicine, wouldn't she benefit from living in the village rather than isolated, so far outside it?"

"It's her home. She's lived every day of her almost eighty years there. And it was the home of her parents, her grandparents and possibly another generation before that. We might think living in the village would be better for her, but she thinks otherwise, and part of the medicine we practice out here is all tied up with respecting our patients for who they are and how they live, even when we think there might be a better alternative.

"Oh, and she said to tell you that you're welcome any time for tea. She likes having a lady doctor in the hospital." He chuckled. "Which may be code for her allowing you to do a physical on her. She won't let me even approach the subject."

"Maybe I can find a relatively safe histamine blocker or proton-pump inhibitor to take with an every-other-day NSAID. Or even something that combines ibuprofen with famotidine. A dose every other day would certainly be better than nothing. Do you think I could get something like that ordered?"

"You're really up on your pharmacopoeia. I'm impressed."

"I've had to treat too many gastric ulcers surgically, so to prevent the condition I have to be."

"Then I'll see what I can do about getting a trial sample in for Waan. Again, I'm impressed, Layla. I've thought of you in a lot of ways over the years, but never as a practicing surgeon, even though I knew you were one."

She laughed. "I do have my good moments." And one had just happened. This was the first time Arlo had ever complimented on her medical skills in any substantial way. In fact, it was the first time she'd ever had the feeling that he respected her abilities. That meant a lot, as his respect was something she'd always wanted more than almost anything else. And had never felt like she'd achieved.

Settling back into the seat, she closed her eyes, wanting to bask in the moment a little longer, but her basking was short-lived as Arlo swerved to avoid a rut that would have swallowed up a water buffalo, causing the seat belt to lock down on her. So she removed it to reset it and put it back on but, in that instant, when she wasn't belted in, he hit a bump that literally did send her sprawling almost into his lap. He immediately slowed the vehicle, and by the time she'd righted herself they were face to face, gazing into each other's eyes, only inches apart.

"Well, this feels awkward," he teased, stopping the vehicle while she maneuvered back into her seat. "Being close enough that we could have—"

"Kissed," she supplied.

"For starters."

"Maybe once," she said, fastening her belt. "But something tells me a kiss of convenience isn't nearly as good as one of passion. And a bump in the road doesn't really translate into passion."

"You sound more like I did all those years ago. Always overanalyzing everything and drawing conclusions rather than going with the moment."

"Live and learn," she said. "And I had a very good teacher." She'd also graduated at the top of her master-class when it came to knowing how to protect her heart. And, as she was discovering, being near Arlo again made that very difficult. "Also, you may have known where you were going back then," she said, double-checking her safety strap, "but I'm not so sure about now, on this road, which is where your undivided attention should be."

He chuckled. "To think this is one of our better roads."

"No wonder your back aches. I'll bet it has as much to do with the bumps as it does falling through the roof."

"Actually, the road bothers my neck when I'm on the scooter."

"You need a hot tub, like I mentioned before."

"Actually, I'd settle for hot water in a real shower."

"Do you ever get away from here, Arlo? Not to go visit your family, but a day or two away, where you can kick back and do something nice for yourself?"

"Wish I could. But I can't afford it. I do go to a regional hospital a couple hours away from time to time, indulge in a hot shower, surf the internet, spend the night in a comfortable bed if my patient load here permits it. And then, only if the hospital has coverage."

"Well, it's not as nice as a luxury hotel, but I'm glad you have that."

He looked over at her. "You've changed, Layla. You're more accepting of things outside your norm."

She'd changed because she'd believed that if she could have been more for him, things might have ended up differently. So she'd worked on herself, trying hard to cultivate a broader vision. And a more tolerant one. "You grow up in the job. To be a good doctor, you have to. At least, I had to."

Arlo's recognition of her changes was nice. Very nice.

"Heads up," Arlo said, as they made their way up to the front door.

"What?"

"Heads up." He pointed to the snake, in all its green and black checkered glory, in the tree just in front of her, hanging down from a branch. "The element of surprise isn't really a good thing when it drops out of a tree onto your head." He stopped and waited until she caught up, then laid his hand across her back in a protective manner to escort her around the spot where the tree snake was plotting its move.

"It's a golden tree snake, and the bad thing is they conceal themselves pretty well in the trees. Another bad thing is they're very agile, and they bite quickly. Hurts like hell since they usually get you on the neck, face or shoulder. The good thing is they're only mildly venomous—usually just cause a little site reaction—and we do have the antivenin in stock if it turns out you're allergic.

"And just so you'll know, that's the snake you're most likely to find out here. Trees, walls, bushes. Meaning practice keeping your eyes on the ground while looking up at the same time because this little guy does like to have his way with you."

Once she was past the snake, Arlo reached up and pulled him from his branch then carried him off into the bushes to let him go.

"You're even kind to the snakes," she said, as the trail narrowed to a barely passable width, and she was so busy looking for snakes she tripped over a tree root and, for the second time in less than half an hour, almost ended up in his arms. But this time she caught herself before she made the full fall, then jumped back when he attempted to grab hold of her to prevent her from hitting the ground. She slapped him, then laughed. "Thought you were another tree snake."

"Likely story," he said, stepping around her then taking her hand to pull her along. "And I try to be kind. What's the point in anything else?"

How could he just keep saying the right things over and over? How could she protect her heart from that? "So, you really know your herpetology," she said, deliberately avoiding anything that would pull her another step closer emotionally.

"Not as much as I should. Since I've lived here most of my life, you'd think I would have a background. But my up-close-and-personal relationship with snakes starts with me getting bitten and, so far, ending with me surviving. I can usually identify friend or foe, though."

"Sounds like I'll have to rely on you to take care of me. At least as far as the snakes go."

And he would. He had when they'd been together, when she'd been a wide-eyed innocent taking her first real trip into the world, and nothing had changed. She counted on that more than she'd ever wanted to.

"I always tried to, Layla. Even when you didn't want me to."

"I know, and I appreciated it, although I might never have told you." She brushed her hand over his cheek. "I've never *not* trusted you, Arlo. My problem was having that much trust in anyone scared me. Because having that kind of trust can lead to so much pain when it ends."

"How so?"

"Everybody has a personal motive. Brad, my failure of a fiancé, liked having me as a showpiece. Ollie's motive for my promotion brings notice to his surgery since female surgeons comprise less than twenty percent of all surgeons overall, and promoting one to a high position gives his surgery a lot of publicity. Even my own parents, for the sake of their careers, like to present a picture of a perfect family, which we're not."

"And me?"

"You simply came to me first as a friend then as a lover. And there was no pretext or motive to that. So, because of you, I learned to truly trust for the first time. Maybe the only time."

"I don't even know how to respond to that."

"Then don't. Take it for what it is. A simple truth. Something I've learned lately is that not everything needs a response. Some things can stand on their own." She smiled. "But thank you for giving me something to trust the way no one ever had before us, or even after us."

He studied her for a moment. Then finally said, "I think there were a lot of things we should have known about each other before, but didn't."

"Because we jumped in before we were ready. If we'd stood back and really looked at it, I don't think we would have leaped the way we did."

"Common sense isn't part of falling in love. We had

the physical momentum and the friendship. But I think we lacked the common sense. At least I did. Otherwise I wouldn't have fallen so hard."

"But did you fall for me or the idea of what we should be?"

"Both. Not sure in what proportions, though. So…" He pointed to the two faces visible in the doorway. "I think we're being watched. Maybe because they're expecting a sweet."

Before he could pull a handful from his own pocket, Layla reached into her pocket and beat him to it.

He chuckled. "You always were a quick learner."

"And you always were a good teacher."

By the time they'd approached the door, the children had already run out to join them, expecting the candy from Arlo but glad to take it from Layla.

"Friends for life," he said as they stood in the doorway.

"If only it was always that easy."

"Kanika, it's Doc Arlo. May I come in?"

The woman inside poked her head out the door to make sure, then stepped aside to let him in. Arlo spoke to her in Thai as she led them both back to a tiny, curtained-off area where a child lay on a mat on the floor. A beautiful child, with big brown eyes and thick black hair. And a big smile meant for Arlo. "Candy?" she asked in English.

This time he pulled another piece from his pocket and handed it to the girl, who stuffed it into her mouth as quickly as she could. "Achara is still feeling tired," he said to Layla. "She's not eating as well as her mother would like to see. Not drinking as much as she should either. Would you like to examine her while I take care of Kanika?"

"Love to," Layla said, then bent down to the child. "Hello, Achara," she said to the girl. "My name is Layla."

"Doc Layla," Arlo corrected. "The people out here respect the title 'Doc,' so it's always good to let them know you are a doc."

"My name is *Doc* Layla," Layla corrected. "And, while I know you don't understand my words, I promise I won't do anything that will hurt." She looked behind her as Arlo left the room, following Kanika to another part of the hut. "First, I want to do some general vital signs."

Temperature—elevated. Blood pressure—low. Pulse and respirations normal. No bad belly sounds. Lungs clear. But Achara did seem a little listless and, Layla noticed, she was struggling to stay awake. She also had a skin rash on her belly, back and arms.

"Do you hurt anywhere?" she asked the girl, even though Achara didn't understand. "Your tummy?" Layla pointed to Achara's tummy and made a scowling face, hoping the girl would understand her attempt at sign language.

Achara shook her head to indicate no. So Layla did the same things with several of her major joints—arms, hips, knees. Again, Achara shook her head. But when Layla addressed Achara's head, the girl nodded a yes and tears sprang to her eyes. Which meant she had a severe headache. So Layla looked into her eyes then in her nose, only to find signs that the little girl was experiencing nosebleeds.

"Arlo," Layla called out. "I need a second opinion, if you don't mind."

"Right here," he said, entering the curtained-off space. "What's the matter?"

"She has a mild version of the symptoms you'd see in hemorrhagic dengue. What I want is for you to double-check for me, since this is way out of my field of expertise."

"Out here, there will be many times when you don't have someone to double check. I'll do it this time because you haven't even been here very long, but in the future, go with your gut. If you think she's gone hemorrhagic, then proceed accordingly. You're a good doctor. Trust yourself." He pulled his stethoscope from his cargo pants pockets and listened to Achara's chest and belly. Then felt her forehead. Looked at her eyes…

"She's complaining of a headache," Layla said.

Arlo nodded, and kept on with his appraisal by looking up the girl's nose. Then he pressed her belly again and took another listen. "Good catch," he finally said. "But getting Kanika to allow me to take her back to the hospital isn't going to be easy. I was worried about the girl when she took her home but, short of physically forcing her to stay, there was nothing I could do."

"Maybe if you emphasize now that her daughter's in danger, that her condition has gotten worse?"

"Kanika already knows all that. In fact, she told me that Achara wasn't doing as well as she was just a couple of days ago."

"And she still won't let you take her to the hospital?"

Arlo shook his head. "People die there. The villagers know that, and I think it scares Kanika, leaving her daughter alone there. Achara was only there the first time because Kanika was there as well."

"Does she have a husband who might grant us permission?"

"He died in an accident several years ago."

Layla let out a frustrated sigh. "Can we allow Kanika to stay with her daughter? Maybe assume some of her nursing care?"

"We can. If she'll agree to it."

"She'll agree to it, Arlo. She's a mother and her child comes first."

"Since when did you get so…motherly? We never even talked about having children because I believed you'd choose career over having them."

"And I would have. Still would. But that doesn't mean I can't have a few maternal instincts floating around. You know, some maternal instinct. Maybe not for being a mother myself so much but for mothers in general. A good mother will always protect her child. Like yours did."

He thought, for a moment, about the way his mother had protected him, and sacrificed for him, and he could see Layla doing the same. Even though they'd never talked about having a child, he'd known she'd have been a very good mother by the little ways she'd taken care of him. Providing a nice home even when she wasn't domestic, allowing him space when he needed it without asking why, being there when he'd needed her and wouldn't ask. Nursing him through bouts of flu or common colds. "You're always full of surprises, Layla."

"Or maybe you just never noticed the things in me that were always there."

At the time he hadn't and now he was sorry for that. "It was my loss," he said.

"Our loss, Arlo. It was our loss."

As it turned out, Layla's suggestion worked quite well. Kanika was more than happy to work at the hospital, and while she was there she extended her care to a couple of other patients. Basic care. Nothing along the line of anything medical. But delivering meals, changing bed sheets, pouring drinks of water. It was a tremendous help, and he was pleased that Layla had suggested it.

It showed him a different side of her—the side where she took the smaller aspects of patient care into consideration. When he'd thought she was all about the bigger picture, he'd been wrong. She was much more insightful and well-rounded than he'd known.

And now, on the third day of Kanika's duties, she was rearranging the furniture to make it more convenient, recruiting new volunteers to come in and cook, and was in the process of making curtains for bare windows, courtesy of several women who donated fabric…an odd assortment of colors and textures. All this due largely to Layla's simple suggestion. It was all good.

And Layla, with Samron's assistance, was working just as hard, going on the afternoon house calls for him, taking the older woman with her to translate, while he stayed back and kept the hospital open. She also took morning calls at the clinic while he was out in the field. Or sleeping.

Even more good coming about because of something he'd never seen in Layla. Or something he'd totally overlooked. While he'd always known she was a hard worker, he'd always thought of her as someone who didn't join in. But that's all she was doing here. Joining in wherever she could. And seeming to enjoy it.

Sadly, they didn't ever stop to chat, unless it had something to do with a patient, and they didn't even take a meal together. It seemed like the only time they really crossed paths was at night, when they were both getting ready for bed. He could see Layla in silhouette through the curtain as she readied herself for sleep. The first night he'd averted his eyes for the sake of being polite.

But his memories of her perfection, of her beauty, of the pleasures her naked body had given him had taken hold, and those memories were more vivid than anything he could see through the curtain. And more intrusive, penetrating every pore in his body. Trying to work their way into more places than he wanted. She was so beautiful, and curvy, and she had a graceful purpose in every movement.

After that first night of trying not to look, and trying not to remember, he couldn't help but watch the shadowed image of her, the elegant movements, the way she went about things in the same order each night. Layla was all he'd ever wanted in a woman, which had made his only real attempt at relationships after they'd split up impossible. Nobody compared. And it wasn't just in the physical sense. But in her intellect, even her ambition.

Layla was a perfect package and even as he'd walked away from her all those years ago, he'd known he would never find that kind of perfection or determination in anyone else. That had been true then, and still was now. He was a spoiled man—spoiled for something he could not hold onto. Which, little by little, was forcing him to come to terms with the way the rest of his life would be lived.

What would it have been like if he'd chosen another path—one with Layla at the end of it, waiting there for him with open arms?

CHAPTER FIVE

STANDING IN THE doorway of his hut, looking out, Arlo watched the rain for a few minutes. It wasn't the rainy season yet, but it was getting close. Layla was asleep, but his memories and thoughts made him too restless to sleep. And the rain beating down so heavily on the roof, sounding like gunfire, didn't help either.

There was too much of the past swirling around in his head. There were so many good things he'd overlooked or ignored. And now the heavy impact of having her here was something he'd never expected. She was igniting things in him that had died out all those years ago. Giving him hopes to latch onto again, even though he knew he shouldn't. Layla had always made him happy. But he had to be cautious because this was only temporary, just like last time had been.

Without looking back at the curtain, or the now dim image on the other side, Arlo launched into the downpour and bounded across the road to the hospital so quickly it barely raised a blip in his consciousness. Why was he there? He wasn't even sure about that. Probably to occupy space where Layla wasn't distracting him. Where his whole life wasn't distracting him. Where he wasn't questioning his choices and promises.

"Promises," he said aloud. The one he'd made to his

mother to look after his dad after she was gone. The one he'd made his dad to take his mother's place as a doctor after she was gone. The first hadn't worked out since his dad had left shortly after the funeral. Which had left Arlo stuck here in a practice meant for two but now as the only doctor.

And in the early days, when he'd thought about going back to civilization, to Layla, something had always stopped him. A fever outbreak. A critically injured patient who would have died without his help. People who depended on him. People who trusted him to take care of them. That was a lot of responsibility to carry around.

But to toss it aside would be to walk away from someplace where he was needed. And maybe there was a little arrogance mixed in with that—the kind that told him he was the only one who could do this job. That was all about *his* need, though. The need to be needed. Layla had always wanted him, but she'd never needed him. And the distance between those was wider than the universe.

Still, in his more thoughtful moments, when ego wasn't taking over, and the hurt of not being needed by the woman he'd needed went away, he simply saw the need of the village as the binding element. If he left, no one would come to replace him. Like no one had replaced Layla.

Arlo knew these were crazy, mixed-up emotions, but they were all he had. He'd offered Layla his world, she'd turned it down. In retrospect it had been selfish as he'd never stopped to realize how important her world was to her. And had she offered it to him, he would have turned it down, probably with some lame excuse that it wasn't altruistic enough. But in the end, to give yourself over to caring for the sick was altruistic no matter where it happened. That was one of the last things his mother had told him but, by then, it had been too late. Layla had moved on without him. How did he know? In a word—Ollie. Then another three words from Ollie—*"Bad mistake, Arlo."* Then another six—*"How could anyone be so blind?"*

The glum periods didn't get him down too often, though. Not anymore. He hated the feeling, the despair that occasionally took over, because that wasn't him. Couldn't be him, if he wanted to keep doing what he was doing. Which he did. But right now he wasn't on his game. And the last time he'd felt that way had been the evening he'd made the decision that he had to leave her. His mother had been sick, he'd had to go home, he'd asked her to go with him, and she'd refused.

Such a bad time in his life, which had got even worse later when he'd realized how badly he'd wandered through it. But at the time all he could see was that loving Layla wasn't enough for her. She'd needed the one thing he'd never be able to give her—an outlet for her ambition. Anyway, all that was water under the bridge now. He'd made his choices based on the only life he'd known, and she'd made hers based on the very same thing. So, maybe they hadn't been in love the way it's truly defined, but there were too many things yet to explore. So the ending had been left hanging. Not resolved. Simply let go of.

Did he love her? That was the one question he'd never explored too deeply because there was no answer to it. In many ways he had. But in all the ways necessary to make her happy? Obviously not. It was more obvious now than before. But what good did knowledge do when he still had no answers? Well, at least he had his work, and that was a good thing because he loved it here. That was the one thing he didn't doubt, when pretty much everything else right now was shrouded in confusion.

Arlo tiptoed into the ward to look at Achara. She was sleeping peacefully, the way a child should. And Kanika was curled up in the bed next to her.

He looked across the aisle at another patient who'd simply wandered in to sleep. It happened. People simply came when they wanted something and for Niran Metharom, who was sleeping face down on a cot in the corner, it was when he was feeling the effects of having had too much to drink.

Kosum Bunnag, an octogenarian with gastric complaints, came because of gastric upset. Her problem was eating mangos, which didn't agree with her. She knew it and suffered the consequences of gorging herself on her favorite food, and expected Arlo to make it better. If he wasn't there, she simply took a bed and waited. Or slept. Tonight she was sleeping in the corner opposite Niran.

And while nobody here was really sick except Achara, this was his world. It's where he knew himself. Besides, where else would people just admit themselves to a hospital and not even bother to find the doctor?

After taking a quick look at all three of his patients, satisfied they were doing well, Arlo tucked himself into his exam room, ready to peruse a pile of outdated medical journals as sleep simply wasn't in him. But thoughts of Layla were.

"Was there an emergency or something?" she asked him, coming into the exam room, dripping wet from the rain, about fifteen minutes after he'd made himself comfortable.

He looked up, surprised to find her there. Soaked to the bone, with a lab jacket they kept in the hospital more for impression than use pulled over her T-shirt and cargo shorts. She looked so damned adorable he caught himself in a familiar ache. "What?"

"I heard you leave a few minutes ago, and I wondered if you needed help with anything."

"Nope. It's just a restless night. I have them every so often and use the time to catch up on some journal reading. And it's a good thing I did because a couple of people admitted themselves."

"Anything serious?"

He shook his head. "They're fine. Mostly looking for a dry bed and a little reassurance, I think. When they wake up, I'll give them each another a look before I send them on their way."

"So, in the meantime, you read journals."

"Got to keep up some way."

"How do you get them since there's no mail delivery?"

"I print them out at the elephant rescue when I'm there. They have a computer with satellite internet, and a very iffy connection for mobile phones. It's a trade-off. I get to use their conveniences when I need to, in exchange for my half-day at the elephant wash. And that rover I have access to when I need a vehicle."

"Elephant rescue?"

A smile crept to his lips. "I meant to tell you about that. Guess it slipped my mind."

"Tell me what?"

"We donate time at the elephant rescue. We trade our services for the use of the various things they have that we don't."

"And by donate you mean…"

"Whatever's required. Usually we work with the babies. You know, play with them, wash them—simple things."

"A baby elephant wash?"

"Just part of a day, once a week. It works out."

"I'm assuming I'll be expected to—?"

"It's strictly voluntary," Arlo said. "But if you can sleep with a civet cat, I'm pretty sure you can relate to a baby elephant."

"As long as I don't have to sleep with it, too."

Arlo chuckled. "Not usually."

"Then life is good." Layla entered the exam room and hopped up on the exam table, since her only other sitting option was the floor, which was where Arlo was sitting. Cross-legged, barefoot, with his back braced by the wall. "Especially if I can get good phone reception there. Or can log onto my social media page."

"What you learn really fast is that you don't necessarily need the modern conveniences here. Since I grew up here, I didn't have them at my disposal, and I learned how to live life just fine without them. Although I do admit I enjoy surfing the internet every now and then. Or playing an online game."

"Your parents traveled, though, didn't they?"

"Most of the time, yes. A month here, a month there. There are a lot of villages in the area, so they didn't keep a home base the way I do. It was a fun way to grow up, though. Of course, it was all I knew."

"But when you ventured into the outside world…"

"It was a culture shock to some extent. But my parents prepared me for that. So, other than not fitting in too well, it was OK. And my less than sophisticated ways did attract your attention."

"You sat on the floor, cross-legged, when we were attending lectures. There were perfectly good desks but you always chose the floor." She laughed. "And remember that day I caught you staring at the wall? It was like you'd never seen a wall before."

"Hadn't seen that many of them. And I liked the composition of it. It was…sturdy. In the huts where we generally stayed, walls were flimsy, for the most part."

"But it was a wall."

"And it brought me to your attention, didn't it?"

"Speaking of bringing something to your attention, did you see that the shipment of mosquito netting came in? I didn't even know it had been ordered."

He wiggled his phone at her. "After you offered, I went down the road a bit, placed the order—it's in your name, by the way. The bill will be forthcoming."

"So, who delivered it?"

"A friend from the regional hospital. I had it sent there and he dropped it by. He's the nurse who comes out to help when we're desperate. And, yes, he signed for a shipment of drugs and brought them along as well. Paid for courtesy of the government's health program."

"Do you ever get desperate having to rely on so many people?"

"Sometimes. But then I get over it because there are a lot of more serious things to worry about."

"I don't suppose I ever realized how resilient you were. I always knew you were a brilliant surgeon, but I think I tried not to picture this part of you."

"Why?"

"Because I knew it would eventually come between us." She pulled her wet T-shirt away from her skin. "Mind if I put on a dry hospital gown?"

Too bad…he was enjoying the wet look. Enjoyed her with the dry look as well. In fact, there was never a look he didn't like when it came to Layla. And he'd probably seen all of them. "Help yourself."

She returned to the exam room in a thin gown that was a dozen sizes too large for her frame, but this time she sat down on the floor next to him rather than on the table, then cuddled up to him. Something that came so naturally she didn't even realize she was doing it. But he did. Back then, now. And his natural response would have been to put his arms around her and snuggle in even more, which he wasn't going to do.

"I used to enjoy this," she said, leaning her head on his shoulder. "Curling up in front of the fireplace together, even if all we were doing was studying. Too bad we never had much time for it."

"We didn't have much time for anything together, Layla. Too much work, too much study."

She laughed. "The life of a doctor. Coming from a long line of them, I'm sure you knew what to expect. But I didn't. All I saw was the glamorous side—from television and movies. Even from when I fell out of a tree and broke my leg when I was eight and spent a couple of weeks in the hospital, being attended to by the most gorgeous doctor I'd ever seen. At least, gorgeous in the eyes of a child who was totally in love with the image of him, especially the way people looked at him—with so much respect.

"That's why I became a doctor, you know. I always remembered how people looked at him and that's how I wanted them to look at me. Probably also to impress him since I decided, at the tender age of eight, I was going to marry him, despite the fact he was probably forty." She laughed. "Only in the mind of a child, right?"

"A child who set her course when she was eight and never left it. So, would you go back and do it again?" he asked, taking care not to touch her in any way, since he knew their history and remembered what a single touch could start. Not that he was a man who wouldn't want that. But with Layla there were painful aftershocks. Those were what he wanted to avoid as he'd suffered them the first time and had come out unscathed. Well, relatively unscathed. She *had* made him a much more mindful person in that regard. "Medical school to surgeon. Knowing what you know now, would you still make that choice?"

"In a heartbeat. My childhood dream doctor became the basis for a lifelong passion and I never wavered in what I wanted after I was eight. So, what about you when you were eight?"

"When I was eight, I was already a medic of sorts. Fetching supplies my parents needed in the moment, making sure their medical bags were stocked properly. All except for the drugs, of course. Sometimes they'd let me treat minor things like scratches. You know, wash, antiseptic, bandage."

"And you never changed either."

"It's what I knew."

"No regrets you kept it up?"

"My only regret was that I didn't have the opportunity to work with them after I was a real doctor. I wanted that, worked hard to push myself through so I could have it, but it didn't happen."

"I'm sorry," she said, reaching over and taking his hand.

The muscle in his right forearm twitched under her touch, but he didn't pull himself away from her because he liked being where he was. Always had with Layla. "So am I. But what I have now…" He shrugged. "Almost all of it's good."

"Me, too," she said. "I never meant to work for Ollie, given the connection you and I had, but when he made me the offer…"

"He's a great judge of talent. To succeed in his world, you have to be." He smiled. "To my knowledge, he's never been wrong in the doctors he's chosen to work in his surgery. You included."

"I thought for a while it was his way of trying to get us back together."

"Nope. He's not the type to interfere. My guess is that he assumed you'd come back to Thailand with me and was thrilled when you didn't because he'd get his shot at you."

"Well, he's been good to me. And I love working where I do."

He didn't want to let go of her hand, didn't want to get up and walk away. But nothing was stirring at this late hour and they both needed to sleep. She in the relative comfort of the hut and he…someplace where she wasn't. "Look, we're in the rare position of no late-night calls to make and unless something comes in, as Homer said in his *Odyssey*, 'There is a time for many words, and there is also a time for sleep.' So, on that note, Homer and I bid you goodnight."

Unfortunately, what he intended as a dignified exit from the room turned into something much less. As he stood, his back gave out and stopped him halfway to his feet. "So much for the grand departure," he muttered. Then forced himself upright, inch by inch.

Layla laughed. "Off with the shirt, Arlo. This is ridiculous, especially when I can help you." To prove her point, she cracked her knuckles, then patted the exam table. "Face down, get comfortable."

"Don't do this, Layla," he moaned, knowing that so much of her touch would drive him insane.

"Doctor's orders, or I might have to declare you unfit for duty."

"I'm the boss here. Remember?"

"And I'm the one with the magic fingers. Remember?"

He moaned again. "I'll be fine."

"After I'm done with you." She pushed away from him, went to the supply cabinet, pulled out a bottle of jasmine oil, a gift from a patient, and returned to the exam table.

"I'm not going to smell like flowers," he protested.

"What? Not manly enough to be secure in wearing a delicate scent?" She rubbed some on her hands, then bent down and waved them at him. "Tempted?"

"Not yet," he said, enjoying the flirt. He used to enjoy their lighter moments, the teasing, the playfulness. It was one of the things he'd missed most after they'd broken up. "What else have you got?"

She pulled down the neck of his T-shirt just a little and rubbed some of the oil across his chest. "That?"

He chuckled. "How is it that you're the only woman I've ever known who could get away with making me smell like jasmine?"

"Just one of my many charms," she said, patting the exam table again. "So, like I said, shirt off…"

Naturally, he gave in. He always had, because his little pretenses of resistance had never gone very far with her. All she had to do was—

"Let me help you out of your shirt," she said, grabbing hold of the bottom of it and slowly lifting it over his stomach.

Yes, that was always the start of it.

Then her journey went to his chest and it was agonizingly slow. On purpose? Was she taking this so slowly to torture him? Or was he simply primed to be tortured by any intimacy from her? And this was so tactile, so intimate. The chills her fingers were causing attested to that.

"Are you able to get it over your head on your own, or do you need help?"

Another time, he would have taken the help, prolonged

it, begged for more. But not now. So, rather than answering, he tugged his shirt over his head and lay on the exam table as quickly as possible, hoping that the thoughts in his head would turn clinical rather than stirring. "This isn't going to take long, is it?" he asked, trying to dispel the mood sliding down over him.

"As long as it needs to take," she said, taking her place at the side of the table then applying pressure to his lower back.

"In case you were wondering, it's my serratus posterior inferior. It lies…"

Layla laughed. "I showed up to class that day, Arlo. I know where it is." Lower back, and in his case the right side. Which was where she positioned her hands and began a light rub, which elicited an immediate moan. "You're lucky all you did was pull some muscles. Next time you're up on a roof look where you're stepping or you might injure something more important than your serratus posterior inferior."

"Ah, yes, lovely bedside manner. Lecture the patient who's in excruciating pain." He moaned again, and this time sucked in a sharp breath. "Nice hands," he said on exhalation. "I think they've improved with age."

"What? You didn't like my massages back then?"

"Different kind of massages. Those were meant to lead to other things. This one is meant to cure me." It had been so long since he'd experienced a woman's touch in any meaningful way he'd almost forgotten what pure pleasure felt like. But this was it—Layla's touch. Always had been. And as far as he was concerned, this was a massage that could last for hours, or forever, and he wouldn't get tired of it.

"Sounds like the rain's letting up," she said, after he'd been dead silent, except for an occasional moan, for the past five minutes. She hadn't intended this massage to turn into a flirt, but something had grabbed hold of her, and she was fully involved in it long before she realized what she was doing. So many things just seemed to come naturally with Arlo, things she'd taken for granted when they'd been together. And now they were reminders of what she'd let go.

"Then maybe you should go back to the hut and try to get some sleep."

"Are you sure? Because I could keep doing this for a while longer."

"But I can't, Layla. It's—it's making me think things I shouldn't be thinking."

She understood that as she was probably thinking many of the same thoughts. Maybe she was trying to go too far based on something that was no longer there. Or simply getting caught up in the past. Whatever the case, Arlo was right. So she stepped back from the table and picked up a towel to wipe her hands. "Then you'll stay here?" Honestly, she hoped he would because she didn't want to face him for a while. Not until she'd better sorted out her intentions.

"I've got insulin rounds in a couple of hours, and I do want to check my patients here when they wake up, so yes. I'll stay here."

And that was all they said. Layla took the hint to leave and did. Trudged across the muddy road as fast as she could to get away from him, only to find Chauncy, who'd decided not to be a night prowler in the rain, curled up on her cot. "It was a huge mistake," she told the cat as she sat down beside him. "All mine." And one she wouldn't make again.

He'd already checked and released his two late-night admissions and made three house calls by the time Layla wandered into the hospital the next morning. "Sleep well?" he asked, hoping she didn't feel as awkward as he did. And drained because every time he'd tried shutting his eyes her image had been there. Followed by memories, and images of things in the past. Meaning he'd had no sleep whatsoever.

"Well enough. So, how's your back this morning?"

"Much better." That was true. Even just those few minutes under her fingertips had produced more relief than he'd expected. "I think you could have a future as a massage therapist, if that's what you wanted." The air between them was heavy with trepidation and watchfulness. There was no way to get around it other than avoid it. And the best avoidance was work, which he was anxious to get back to. "The patient list is on the desk," he said. "I didn't sleep well so I worked."

"Because of your back?"

He shook his head. "There were too many things rattling around in my brain."

"You used to do that. Get so caught up in your responsibilities you couldn't sleep. Wish I could do something to help. Maybe chamomile tea? Maybe I can order you some when we get to the elephant rescue?"

He nodded and smiled. What was wrong with him wouldn't be fixed by any kind of tea, but he appreciated her gesture. That was always one of Layla's best points—her tenderness. "I'm not used to having anybody take care of me anymore. At least, not the way you used to."

"Sometimes it was the only way we could find time together." She laughed. "You didn't know, but because you were always so busy going one way while I was going another, I actually created a list of things I could do for you—other than the obvious—that would slow you down and allow me some time with you."

He arched surprised eyebrows. "Seriously?"

She nodded. "You couldn't resist homemade chocolate cookies, but when you knew I was baking them, you'd hang around for as long as it took for the first batch to come out of the oven. Most of the time I was very slow getting that first batch done."

"I never knew."

"I had my ways."

"Please tell me that walking up the five flights of stairs to our apartment was for health reasons like you said, and not just a way to have a little more time together. Because you know how I hated those stairs."

"Almost as much as I enjoyed the view walking behind you."

"You little minx," he said, laughing out loud. "I never had a clue."

"You weren't meant to. But it was all fun and games, Arlo. We always knew that's what it was between us. And now?"

"I work. And there's no one here to bake chocolate-chip cookies. Sometimes I wish there was."

"It's got to be a lonely life for you out here. I can't even begin to imagine how you get by."

"One day at a time. Or sometimes hour by hour."

Finally, they were back on track and she liked that. Liked the good things they'd been through together—moments like this one. Wished there'd been more back then. Even wished there could be more now. "After we were done, and after you got here, did you ever wish you'd chosen a different life? Or redesigned the one you had?"

"Not after I got back, but I did have this brief time after we split when I thought I didn't want to come back. A lot of that was tied to you. And Ollie. He'd paid my tuition, as you knew, and he pressured me for about a year to come in with him because he honestly didn't realize that I loved what I was doing here. When he figured it out, that's when he stopped."

"And when he came after me."

"Score one for Ollie. He's always had an eye for pretty girls and an instinct for getting the best doctors. With you, he got both."

"And you got?"

"Everything here. The village. The jungle. The people. Home is home, and this is mine. In the end, it's what I wanted more than anything else."

"Including me."

"Maybe the biggest regret of my life. But it was always a losing cause. This is where I was meant to be."

"Here. In this village. This is what cost me…you. I didn't like it, Arlo, but over time I accepted it. Oh, and how do you pronounce the village's name? Since I lost you to it I should, at least, know how to call it out by name."

He laughed then said something she would never come close to pronouncing. Not unless she was much further along in her Thai language skills, which wouldn't be happening in her two-month stay. "The meaning is village by the big fig tree."

"The tree you see just at the entrance to the village?"

He nodded. "It's a symbol of enlightenment, believed to bring good fortune."

"Well, if you're happy, it's brought you good fortune. So, let me grab that patient list and get started because—" Because almost having him was worse than not having him at all. And sometimes, even now, her heart just hurt. "Because don't we have an afternoon appointment with the elephants?"

* * *

Arlo hid himself in the bushes near the elephant reserve and watched Layla playing with the baby assigned to her care. She looked so happy, playing and splashing. He hadn't often seen her abandon herself this way, and he truly wished she could find more joy in her life. But she went about her life so methodically, like she was laboring under the biggest weight in the world.

Emerging from the bushes after watching her for a while, Arlo waved at Layla as he passed near her, and found himself totally drawn into her smile as she waved back. He'd always enjoyed finding those things that caused her to smile like that or gave her an unexpected thrill or happiness she hadn't expected. She could be like a child on Christmas, excited to open all her presents. And he'd been lucky enough to be part of that occasionally. "Care for a mango?" he called across the compound. "Your baby might love them."

Layla turned to look at him, which was her first mistake. Her second was allowing the hose to point away from the baby. In that split second of distraction the baby grabbed the hose from her hand and started to run off with it, as any toddler, elephant, human or otherwise, might do. And in doing that the baby, named Tika, bumped into Layla, sending her sprawling into the big, orange plastic tub filled with muddy water where Tika had been playing. Seeing that as an opportunity to play, Tika slid into the tub with Layla, pinning Layla to the side at first, then trying to crawl onto her lap as she struggled to pull herself up.

"I see you have a situation," Arlo called out. It was too funny not to laugh, which he and everyone else did, as Layla struggled to get out from under the affectionate ministrations of the two-hundred-plus pounds of Tika, who thought this was the best playtime ever, and wasn't about to let her new playmate out of the water.

"Did I mention that baby elephants love to play?" he said, walking over to the edge of the tub, not to lend Layla a hand but to enjoy a more close-up view of playtime in the elephant compound.

Covered with muddy water, she simply looked up at him. No smile. No frown. No expression whatsoever on her face. "I think she's sprained my ankle," she said, her voice flat. "Could you help me out of here? I want you to have a look at it." With that, she extended her hand to Arlo, who was already feeling terrible about Layla's injury.

"Maybe it's just a twist," he said, as he took hold of her, which was his first mistake. His second was to lean slightly over the tub in case he had to lift her from the water. In that instant, what he never saw coming happened. Layla pulled him down into the tub with Tika and her.

"The twist, Doctor," she said, her face still as serious as it could be, "is that you fell for it." Then she smiled.

"What the—?" he sputtered, still trying to figure out what had just happened when Tika, who was thoroughly enjoying having two playmates now, slid herself over the top of Arlo then splashed around until half the water was out of the tub.

That was the opportunity Layla needed to hop out and grab the hose, then start to refill the tub with water, much to Tika's delight, as she now nuzzled Arlo like a kitten might nuzzle its mother. "I think she loves you," Layla said, turning the hose directly on Arlo. "In a muddy kind of way."

He sputtered as the water hit his face, which, to Tika, was an open invitation to slide across him again, but go on out the opposite side of the tub, leaving Arlo sitting in the middle of a pool of dirty water while Layla continued to hose him down, still trying to keep a straight face.

"You know this isn't funny," he said, attempting to stand—another invitation for Tika to rejoin him in the tub and knock him back into the water.

Layla finally laughed. Smiled, laughed again and wiped at the streams of muddy water dripping from her hair. "When it was me in there, you thought it was."

Arlo managed to slide away from Tika and get himself over to the edge of the tub. When he looked up at Layla, who was still laughing, and who also turned the water back on him, his heart skipped a beat. There was such a vulnerability about her when she let herself go. Not only was she stunningly beautiful underneath all that mud that was caking on her now, her laugh was infectious. It made him laugh along with her.

"When it was you in here, it *was* funny," he said, crawling on his knees then looking over his shoulder to make sure he wasn't going to fall victim to a playful Tika attack again. But she'd found his sack of mangos and was helping herself to a little treat, which gave Arlo a chance to get out of the tub. He held out his hand for the hose, but Layla refused. Instead she turned the water on him again. "You really don't think I'd fall for that old trick, do you?" she asked, taking a couple of steps back from the tub. "You'd have to be pretty naïve to—"

Before she could finish her sentence, Arlo lunged out of the water and grabbed the hose away from her, threatening to turn it on her now. "Mud suits you, so I really should just let you stay as you are," he said, laughing, as she came at him and tried to grab away the hose.

She made another jump at him but again failed to get

the hose. "You know you're just asking for more trouble," she warned him.

"And *you* know I could pick you up and drop you right back in the tub for more Tika play," he said, turning the hose on her.

"If you can catch me." Layla made another lunge at him, this time with the intent of knocking him back into the tub, but he turned the water on her face, and by the time she wiped away enough to see, he'd ducked to the other side of the tub, still hanging onto the hose.

"Oh, I can catch you," she said, edging her way around the other side, hoping to trap him against the fence so she could grab the hose and claim victory.

But he was too fast for her. In fact, as she got so close to him all he could see was the outline of her breasts through her wet T-shirt, he knew he had to get away as the thoughts in his head were suddenly going places he didn't want them to go. So he intended to drop the hose and sprint off to his own baby, Lamon. But before the hose hit the ground, she grabbed it up and hit him with a spray of water as he, too, tried to get across the tub, his intention being to surrender his shirt to cover her up. "Um, Layla," he said, deliberately keeping his eyes above her shoulders, "I think you need to…" As he started to unbutton his shirt, she hopped into the tub with him, knocked him down, then stood over him, aiming the hose over his head with one hand and fist-pumping the air in victory with her other. "Victory is sweet," she said, stepping back and offering Arlo a hand to help him up.

"You really need to cover up," he said, almost in a whisper, struggling now to keep his eyes averted. Being polite wasn't so easy, though, when temptation was so close. "Before someone else sees you."

She looked down at herself, then laughed. "Why, Doctor, you're a bit of a prude, aren't you?" She did try to pluck the stretchy fabric away from her skin, but that was almost impossible.

"Not a prude so much as not wanting everybody here to get a look at you the way I'm seeing you. Especially since you're their doctor."

"Prude," she said, turning the hose on him again.

He was surprised by her lack of modesty, and he was enjoying not only the view but the spontaneity. Was this the real Layla? The one who came out of her shell when she wasn't taking herself so seriously? "Look, let me get up and give you my shirt, OK? And next time wear something more decent." Unfortunately, as she backed away to allow him to rise up to his knees, Tika decided it was time to play again and ran toward the tub. Hopped in. Knocked Arlo back down, as well as Layla, who landed on top of him.

"So, now what?" she asked, still holding onto the hose like it was a trophy.

He smiled, bracing himself for what he knew was about to happen. And it did. Layla turned the hose so the water sprayed down his head, and as he went to grab it out of her hand, she kissed him. It happened so quickly, so innocently, he wasn't even sure it had happened. But the look of total surprise on her face told him it had, and it had surprised her as much as it had him. He didn't react, though. Caution was the better choice here. Wait and see what she did next. All his hopes were pinned on another kiss, but Tika had something else in mind as she slid slightly to the side of him to start a new game, which was much the same as the old one. Water, mud and lots of attempts to sit on their laps.

Certainly, it was safe. But it was also disappointing. And, as he was dwelling on that, Tika lunged, flipping him over, which pinned Layla underneath him. For what seemed like an eternity, he simply stared down at her.

"Mud or not, you're a beautiful woman," he said, lowering his head to capture her lips. But after a brief kiss, which was more a prelude than a real kiss, the way they'd used to kiss, he moved to her eyelids, kissing first the left, then the right. Feeling the slippery mud between their bodies, realizing it heightened the moment rather than taking away from it. Then he kissed her lips again, this time harder, but the sensation ignited him so quickly, he pulled back much sooner than he'd intended.

Layla was surprised judging from the look on her face, possibly by the kiss, possibly by his restraint, and she groped for him, tried to pull him back, but the mud oozed through her fingers, causing her hands to slip away. Yet she reached up and touched his lips. Tickled them the way he remembered, running a single finger from corner to corner. Back and forth, over and over until he could no longer endure it.

Then, without thought, he was kissing her again, slipping his hand underneath her muddy, wet shirt, now transparent enough to see her nipples. And that's when he stopped himself. Pulled back, only farther this time, and simply stared down at her. She felt so good underneath him again. Too good. And, yes, the consequences could be devastating. They had been once, and that was something he never wanted to go through again.

Which was why he rolled off Layla, got himself out of the tub, then removed his shirt and handed it to her. "Put it on," he said, sounding almost grumpy, even to *his* ears. Because, despite what he knew, he still did want to kiss her. And more.

CHAPTER SIX

"EXCUSE ME, DOCTORS," said a tiny old woman, keeping her distance from the very wet, very muddy Arlo and Layla.

She was Sylvie Fontaine, the director of the facility. A volunteer there herself once.

"We have a visitor in need of medical assistance."

Her voice was soft, her accent distinctly French, and the look on her face totally amused, probably because of what she'd just witnessed.

"He's complaining of an upset stomach."

Arlo and Layla looked at each other as Layla buttoned his shirt to be modest while he stood there, bare-chested, looking sexier than any man she'd ever seen in her life. His abs were tight, the proverbial six-pack. His chest bare and broad. His arms strong. Everything about Arlo exuded strength, and she was surprised by her reaction to him. He was beautiful, even if still muddy. Perfect. A man any woman would want. A man she would want if that's why she was here. Which wasn't as that kind of thing, even briefly, was too much of a distraction and she had goals. "How long?" Layla asked, fighting hard to refocus on work.

"He wasn't feeling well last night, and he hasn't gotten out of bed yet today. If one of you could look—" She pulled the remainder of her words, then laughed. "After you've cleaned up."

"Sure," Arlo said, taking the hose from Layla and running it over his head. "Once we're both fit to be seen."

"She seems nice. Very protective of her elephants," Layla commented as Sylvie walked away.

"She is. And she's a good friend."

"Who will, hopefully, let me use her computer to order that chamomile tea. And some chocolate chips. When her assistant showed me in, I noticed they have a proper oven, so maybe she'll let me borrow it to bake cookies." Her eyes lit up. "You do still like them, don't you?"

"That was the one thing you made better than anyone else's." It was obvious the kiss wasn't going to be mentioned and, to be honest, there was no reason to. It had been a spontaneous moment. One that had happened naturally. So, really, what was there to say? They were adults. They didn't have to dwell on what had happened. And the likelihood of it happening again...

"Two days before you left, I baked three dozen. You ate every one of them in a matter of a couple of hours, which was my first clue that something bad was going to happen. You always turned to binge eating when something was about to come down on us. In retrospect, I should have realized that three dozen cookies meant it was going to be really bad."

"Better than taking out my frustrations in a bottle."

"Or we could have talked."

"Not really. By that time, I think we'd said everything that needed to be said. Rehashing what we couldn't have fixed wouldn't have gotten us anywhere." He finished hosing off the mud and handed the hose to Layla, who laid it in Tika's tub. "I mean, we already knew that neither of us would walk away with everything we wanted."

"I suppose toward the end we got into the habit of not talking because to do to that meant the problems didn't exist."

"Again, water under the bridge," he said "Anyway, rather than both of us staying here to take care of one patient, you stay and I'll head back to the clinic."

"I'd rather go," she said. "I scheduled a house call and it's on the way, so—"

Halfway back to the village, fighting to keep her mind on everything but Arlo, Layla noticed a cart up ahead. It was overturned, with a water buffalo standing off to the side of the road, still in its wooden yoke. Her heart jumped to her throat. There was a serious injury up ahead and she didn't have the means to do much more than apply a bandage. "Hello," she called out, wondering where the driver was. Hopefully gone off to get someone to help right his cart. "Does anybody need help? Can anybody hear me?"

She picked up her pace as something raised the hair on the back of her neck. "Is anybody hurt?" she yelled, once she was so close it startled the water buffalo, which scampered away.

Layla's first instinct took her from one side of the cart to the other, looking underneath where she could see something other than the grass, then looking at the corresponding ditch along the road, and even the field beyond that. At first she saw nothing, so she took another look around, approaching from the opposite direction. "Anybody here?" she yelled. "Please, if you can hear me, let me know where you are so I can help."

Stopping, she listened for a moment, then heard it. A faint voice, words she didn't understand. Even so, she recognized the sound of a person in dire trouble. So, once she got herself off the road and climbed waist-high into the ditch at the side of it, she managed to pull herself toward the front of the cart, and that's when she finally saw him. Or rather the small part of him that was exposed from mid-chest up. The grass there was so tall she'd missed him her first time around. Or maybe he'd been asleep or close to unconsciousness and hadn't heard her yell. But he had on her second attempt, and the first thing Layla did was take hold of his hand. Not for an assessment but to reassure him he wasn't alone.

"I'm going to help you," she said, not sure how she was going to do that. "I know you can't understand me but I'm going to do everything I know how to do to get you out of here." Then take him where? Back to the clinic that had nothing to repair the injuries she suspected he had sustained. "My name is *Doc* Layla. Can you tell me your name?"

He didn't answer but he squeezed her hand. "Good," she said. "You just hang in there with me."

Layla ripped some of the tall lemongrass from the ground and managed to clear an empty space for the man's head and shoulder, and she was shocked to see how young he was. Maybe thirty. At first glance he didn't appear to be bleeding. There was no seeming distress registering on his face. More like a look that said he couldn't believe this was happening to him.

"So far, I'm not seeing much," she said, coming up alongside him, then sitting down on the mound of dirt where she'd ripped out the grass. "But I'll keep looking." Because an overturned cart as heavy as this one had to have caused damage. To find it, she needed to be level with him to do an assessment. Underneath him would be dangerous, and there was nothing exposed on either side that would help her.

"Look, I know you've sustained some injuries, so I'm

going to do my best to figure out what they are." Damn, she wished she knew the Thai translation for what she was telling him, but she didn't. "My name is Doc Layla," she said again, then pointed to herself. "Layla."

The young man responded with "Mongkut," which she took to be his name.

"I'm going to examine you, Mongkut," she said, pulling a stethoscope from her rucksack and hoping that he would identify that with doctor. And he did, as a look of relief washed over his scratched face.

What was under the cart, holding him in? Maybe with a little leverage he might be able to crawl out on his own, but until she knew more about what was going on, she couldn't risk it. "I'm afraid I'm going to have to leave you where you are for a little while." If only she had something to give him for the pain. "The first thing I'm going to do is assess your vital signs: your heartbeat, breath sounds, blood pressure. I'm not sure I can see where, exactly, you're injured, but if you're stable enough, I'll run to the village and get some men to come lift the cart off you."

He listened intently, as if he understood every word, then when she finished speaking, he smiled at her and nodded his head in thanks.

Layla's first assessment was his blood pressure. She expected it to be elevated, considering the situation, and her face blanched when she couldn't hear it. Automatically, her hand went to his neck and her fingers to his carotid artery to find a pulse. It was there, but weak. Too weak. So she tried for another blood pressure reading and this time what she came up with was dangerously low, which led her to take a third reading that yielded the same result. That's when her heart started beating faster.

"I think you may have an injury I can't get to," she

told Mongkut, as she removed Arlo's shirt and laid it across her patient's shoulders, like a thin layer of cloth was going to do any good. "So, try not to move while I do the rest of my tests."

Her mind raced with what to do with a crush injury. She knew if Mongkut didn't receive aggressive medical treatment immediately, his chances of survival were very poor. "As I'm examining you, let me tell you what I think is happening," she said, knowing it was more for her own benefit than his. "Now I'm counting your respirations," she said, squeezing her hand inside the cramped space between Mongkut's body and the front rim of the cart to lay her hand on his chest. "Damn," she muttered. He was breathing too fast and too shallowly. "I think we have a bit of a problem here, Mongkut," she said. He roused when she said his name and forced a smile.

"First, there's hypovolemia. That's where you're bleeding internally, and it's nothing that is usually observable on the outside."

She listened to Mongkut's heart and the beat was off. Too slow, too labored, with some kind of arrhythmia she couldn't identify just from listening.

"The next thing that can happen is a cardiac arrhythmia, where the heart isn't beating correctly, and usually not pumping hard enough to distribute oxygen to all the places it needs to go."

She felt his carotid artery again and the pulse there was decidedly slower than it had been only moments earlier. But Mongkut was alert, still showing no outward signs of pain. Yet. Which was often the case when the body was shocked so drastically that the normal reactions weren't felt.

"Finally, we get to renal failure, meaning your kidneys shut down and the waste products start spreading through your body. Sometimes that takes a while, but if you've had a kidney injury, it can happen pretty fast."

She was glad he couldn't understand what she was saying because there was nothing good here. No help, no hospital, no treatment.

"Right now, you're not experiencing symptoms because, as your muscles are breaking down from a lack of oxygen, toxins are building up, getting ready to rush into your bloodstream. But the cart on top of you is acting like a dam, holding those toxins back. Keeping you alive."

Even though Mongkut couldn't understand her, she didn't have the heart to tell him what might happen once the cart came off.

"So, let's hope someone comes along pretty soon to help us." Optimistic words meant for her, not for Mongkut. "Because I'm sure you have a family at home waiting for you."

In her mind she saw a young wife, maybe a couple of young children, perhaps a baby. Sad images. Images she didn't want to have. Images that brought tears to her eyes that she tried hard to sniff back for fear he would see them then begin to sense what was really going on. She didn't want him to know. Not yet. Because if there was life, there was still hope. There had to be hope.

"And I'm not going to leave you, Mongkut," she said, automatically reaching over for the other carotid pulse, knowing the results before her fingers even touched his skin. "So, tell me about yourself," she said, even though that was impossible. But the sound of her voice was comforting to her, so she prayed it would be comforting to him as well. Especially as she struggled to sound upbeat. "Are you from around here?"

He must have guessed that to be a question, because he responded. His voice was weak, but he didn't sound scared, and she was grateful for that. As far as she knew, he was still feeling no pain, which, to almost everybody in his situation, meant nothing was wrong. "I'm originally from California, but my parents moved us to New York when I was young, and I loved our house…"

She looked up the road, hoping to see someone, but no one was coming. So she continued to hold his hand, feel for his pulse and talk—talk about anything. Because the words didn't matter. But being there with him—he needed to know he wasn't alone. Maybe that would ease his fear a little. Because it was beginning to show on his face.

So she talked, describing her house, the journeys she'd taken with her parents, the ups and downs of medical school and, after what seemed like an eternity, she finally heard a sputtering engine, one she recognized as Arlo's scooter. "Sounds like help is on the way," she said, stretching to look over the cart as Arlo came to a stop on the other side.

"Layla?" he cried, running over to her. "Are you hurt?"

She shook her head, fighting for control. "But Mongkut here is."

Arlo jumped down into the shallow ditch next to Layla, then smiled at the young man, who returned the smile. "What do we have?"

Layla swallowed hard before she said the awful words. "Crush injury."

"Are you sure?" Arlo asked, immediately grabbing Layla's stethoscope to listen to Mongkut's chest.

"I've been here fifteen or twenty minutes, and he's shifting down rapidly. Is there anything we can—?"

Arlo pulled the stethoscope off and handed it back to her. "Nothing," he said. "Not a damn thing."

She nodded, too afraid to speak for fear Mongkut

would hear the discouragement in her voice. "So, what happens next?"

"He has a young wife and a baby daughter. His parents also live nearby as well. I think I need to bring them here. He needs them, and they should be with him when he…" He turned his head away. "Can you stay here with him, or do you want me to do that?"

"You know where his family is. You go."

"Are you sure?" Arlo asked, still looking away.

"I think you'd better hurry," she said. "I don't know how long he's been down, but I think it's been a while."

Arlo nodded then turned back to look at her, his eyes brimming with tears. "I'll be back as fast as I can." He pulled her close then hugged her. Then whispered, "I'm so sorry you have to do this."

His touch made her feel better. His kindness, his empathy… "Me, too," she said, wiping back tears. "It's the part about being a doctor I hate. The part I try to pretend doesn't exist until I can't pretend any longer."

With the back of his hand he also wiped away the tears streaming down her face, then kissed her lightly on the forehead. "I wish I could stay here with you, to take care of you and help you through it. You shouldn't have to do this alone."

"Neither should he." She looked down at Mongkut, whose eyes were shut now. "And there's really nothing left to do, is there?" She swallowed hard, as the man's breathing started to go agonal—a sort of gasping that happened just prior to death. "Get his family here, Arlo. Please…"

He nodded, then squeezed her hand, stood up and ran instead of getting on his scooter, which, at its top speed, was painfully slow, leaving Layla alone there, still holding Mongkut's hand. "He's gone to get your family. It shouldn't be long." And it wouldn't be. But she desperately hoped it would be long enough for his family to get here, to help him go on.

Mongkut smiled, then nodded as if he understood, and Layla wondered if somehow he did. "Anyway, let me tell you about the time in medical school when I—" She looked down at Mongkut, who was listening, but she noticed his eyelids starting to flutter. "You can't go to sleep," she said. "Your family's on the way, and you need to stay with me until they get here." She gave his hand a squeeze, but this time he didn't squeeze back. And his eyes finally fluttered shut. "I'm so sorry I couldn't fix it," she said, then stared off down the road, waiting for Arlo to come back. Not letting go of Mongkut's hand, even though he was gone.

An hour later Arlo found Layla sitting in the dark, on the supply-closet floor. Not crying. Barely moving. "What can I do to help you through this?" he asked, sitting down next to her and pulling her into his arms.

"Sitting here like this is good. When I don't see anything around me, I can shut off my mind. Sometimes I have to do that—just shut down."

"What about feeling someone around you? Can you shut yourself off then?"

"I don't know," she said, honestly. She leaned her head into his shoulder. "I don't let myself get this involved, so I really don't know."

"You did everything you could," he said, sliding his arm around her. "His injury was too severe to fix."

"I knew that. But still…" She swatted at tears streaming down her face. "Sometimes there's just so much futility."

"Back when I was a resident, sometimes when I'd

walk away from something I couldn't fix, I'd stand outside in the hall to collect myself before I turned myself loose on the world. Usually, I wanted to punch the wall. I still do, sometimes. Mentally, not physically—hands of a surgeon and all that. So I know what you're going through, Layla."

"You never told me that."

"Because I always wanted you to see me as better than I really was."

"I never saw anything but good in you, Arlo. Even though we had problems, I always thought you were an amazing man and an amazing surgeon."

"Thank you," he said, his voice almost a whisper. "That means a lot to me."

Layla sighed. "What we just did out there—I want to reframe it. I don't want to see it in my mind, but the darkness isn't pushing it away. And I'm not good at forgetting."

"Because you always think there's a way to make things different. Like with Mongkut. His destiny was sealed before you got there, but you helped him. He wasn't alone at the end. You were there, holding his hand. It's a good thing, Layla. Nothing that needs reframing. And I'm so proud of the way you took care of him even when you knew…"

"I'm glad you're here now. You always took good care of me in the bad moments. I liked that. Got spoiled by that."

"I didn't know."

"Because I didn't tell you. What was the point? What was the point in telling you a lot of things? You weren't going to stay. You weren't going to be a real part of my life. I always hoped holding back would keep me from getting hurt in the end."

"Did it?"

"No. I liked us—together. Loved us together. Loved you, Arlo. I loved you."

"But you loved your independence more."

"I needed that independence to survive. Did I love it more? I don't know. Maybe at the time I did because I was struggling so hard to find out who I was. And there was you—the rock-solid man who'd found himself long before we'd met. I wanted to be what you were, Arlo. But I wasn't at a place in my life yet where I could make that happen. All I knew from life was that if it didn't turn out the way I thought it should, it would break my heart. So I really didn't embrace the opportunities I had."

She started to relax against him. "Living large, as they call it. That's what's always frightened me most. I didn't know how to do it because everything I had was handed to me. I'd never had to work hard for anything, and I didn't know how. Which made me hide behind a wall of independence that would have crumbled in a slight breeze had it ever really been tested. It was a façade, Arlo. And I was a fake."

"So even now you hold yourself back. Shut yourself in the dark and pretend the scary things don't exist."

"Sometimes it works."

"And now?" He tilted her face toward his. "Is it working now, Layla?"

Rather than responding, she reached over and ran her hand through his curly hair. Then she kissed him. Thoughtfully, deeply. Urgently. Once, twice, until every pore in his body was filled with longing, and every nerve-ending in his mouth tingled. Harder, deeper, with a need he'd never felt in her before. "Should we stop?" he whispered, pulling back from her, but only slightly. He hoped she would say no, hoped that she would insist on continuing. But this was Layla, and she was not predictable. Not in anything they'd ever had between them.

"Do you want to?" she asked.

He had no will to tell her no, but answered her with his lips pressed to her cheek, causing her to shiver so hard he could feel her body tremble. "I can. Right now…" He brushed the hollow of her temple. "Or now." Next, he brushed kisses to the line of her cheekbone then continued down to her throat, her shoulder, finally nuzzling his way into the top of her breast. "Tell me, Layla. Because I won't stop if you don't."

Again, she said nothing, but she did knot her fists against his chest, then slowly, very slowly splayed them open and pulled him hard against her. Arlo groaned softly, a low growl in his throat almost, then circled his arms, pulling her on top of him. As he slid down to the floor from his sitting position, she slid with him, on top. And they rolled over to let him take the top position, still tangled together, still kissing. Then she reached up, ran her fingers through his hair once again, something she'd always done, something he'd always loved, and she finally spoke. "No, don't stop."

"You're a damn good doctor, Layla. A damned good surgeon. People with your skills don't come along that often, so why give up everything you've worked so hard to accomplish only to become what my grandfather is—a great administrator who's been away from patient care so long he'd be a detriment if he stepped back in. Is that what you really want for yourself? To keep yourself hidden away from your true talent?"

It was evening now, and they were sitting on the front step of the hospital, eating bowls of sticky rice and fruit. What had happened in the closet—they hadn't spoken of it. It had been a brief moment in time, a little bit of history repeating itself, and Layla was afraid to think past that, afraid because she wanted more, but she didn't trust herself enough to believe that she could ever be enough for Arlo. She wanted to be, but her only real confidence was in her ambition and not in what she truly wanted.

Maybe because the one thing she'd always wanted—her parents' respect—had always been refused her. They were excited now that she was finally advancing. Showing more interest in her now than ever before. And in a life where she'd futilely tried to earn their respect, she was afraid to walk away from the sure path. "What if administration is my true talent?"

"What if patient care is?"

"Here, in the jungle, like what you do?"

"Anywhere you want, Layla. You just don't trust yourself enough." Arlo took her bowl and set it down, then took her hand and pulled her up off the step. "I want to show you something."

Rather than heading through the village, they turned away from it and walked, hand in hand, down a moonlit dirt path until they came to a pool of water. In the glow, she could see it was surrounded by massive boulders. And she could hear night sounds: birds and monkeys. Maybe even Chauncy, looking for his lady love. It was a beautiful place, filled with such peace she didn't even think about the snakes or the other things she feared. With Arlo, she was safe.

"See that rock?" he said, pointing to a large round boulder sitting just at the water's edge. "Let me help you up there."

"Why?" she asked, as he pulled her in that direction.

He didn't answer, though. Instead, he bent to give her a foothold, and there she was, sitting atop a boulder and trusting Arlo enough to simply experience the moment without her usual doubt or fear.

"Now stand up," he urged, reaching up to hold her hand as she did so. "And shout, 'I am strong.'"

She hesitated for a moment, not because she didn't want to do as he instructed but because this was a perfect place, a perfect moment and she didn't want that to change.

"Do it, Layla," he urged. "I am strong."

Smiling, she nodded. Then drew in her breath and shouted, "I am strong." And her voice echoed back to her. *Strong...strong...strong...strong.* For an instant the monkey chatter stopped, and the birds went silent, and all she could hear were her words. "I am strong," she whispered. Then she shouted again. "I am strong." *Strong... strong...strong.* And closed her eyes to take in only her voice. *Her voice.* Nobody else's.

"You always have been," Arlo said. "You just never knew that."

She smiled down at him but didn't speak as there were no words to say to the man who'd just given her the world.

CHAPTER SEVEN

"KANYA BANLENGCHIT HAS asked us to take the evening meal with her and her family tonight. She has three small children, so they eat early—if you're interested."

They'd spent the day working, going in different directions, passing each other on the road occasionally, but only long enough to wave or say hello. It was good. He liked the hard work, and watching Layla throw herself into things like he'd never seen her do before made him happy. She was actually smiling each time they met up. Smiling, enjoying her work, anxious to get on to the next patient.

It didn't surprise him that they worked so well together. They shared the same ethic, the same skill. But they'd always been beaten by their different destinations. Not so now. Even though they weren't together, they also weren't apart.

Layla, who was stretched out on her cot with Chauncy, raised herself up to look at him. "Tell her I appreciate the offer, but I'm really exhausted. I don't know when I have ever worked so hard."

"Did you enjoy it?"

She laughed. "If I admit that I did, are you going to tease me about all the times I told you I would hate it?"

His eyes crinkled into a smile. "Probably."

"Have you no pity for the doctor with blisters on her feet?"

"Aloe vera is a good cure for that and, as it happens, several of the ladies here grow it in their gardens."

Layla's response was to moan. "And if I tell you my leg muscles ache, you'll tell me to eat more magnesium-rich foods, then run out and pick me some bananas."

"Thailand does have about a hundred different varieties."

She sat her tea cup aside and dropped back onto her pillows. Chauncy got up from his spot at the end of the cot to investigate what was left in the cup. "Raincheck?"

"Food's been cooking all day. People will be offended."

"So how long before I have to go?"

"Right now," he said, with the most innocent of all smiles she'd ever seen on him crossing his face.

"And when were you supposed to have told me?"

"This morning."

She sat back up, then climbed off the cot. This reminded her of some of their dates. He'd make the reservations then forget to tell her until the last minute. Or he'd accept a party invitation then tell her about it thirty minutes after they were supposed to arrive. Typical Arlo. Actually, she'd gotten used to this and found it almost endearing. Almost. "I'll be ready in twenty. After my shower."

"Dinner's in ten, before your shower."

"You look like you've just stepped out of the shower."

"I did. Ten minutes ago."

She grabbed a towel and some clean clothes from her stack, and brushed past him. "Like I said, twenty minutes. And next time…" She stopped, and mussed his still-wet curly hair. "Give me some warning."

"When I warned you, it took you an hour. Just consider this as my way of saving some time."

"And just consider this as my way of saying thirty minutes now, instead of twenty."

He chuckled as she walked out the door, then threw himself down on the cot. "Don't know about you, Chauncy, but I still can't figure out what women are about."

Kanya put on quite a spread, and Layla savored every bite she took. Unfortunately for her tummy, she took too many of those bites, drank way too much of the various fruit juices and by the end of the meal felt like she wouldn't eat again for days. "Tell her this was amazing," she said to Arlo, who was sitting on a mat across from her. "And that I don't think I've ever eaten so much at any one sitting in my life."

"She'll take that as a compliment. Oh, and there's more. A papaya pudding. It's served a while after the meal to help with digestion."

"Well, I think I'm going to need more help than simple papaya can give me." She watched the children take platters and bowls away from the tables. Dozens of them. "Why so much?" she asked Arlo. "Most of the other meals I've had here are simple. And this…"

"It's a hero's meal. Everyone in the village contributed. That's why there was so much of it—you received what would probably be several days' worth of it for several families. And Kanya was the one to prepare and serve it because Mongkut was her cousin."

"But I'm not a hero. I didn't…" She swallowed hard. "Why would they do this with the way it turned out?"

"It's a traditional way to feed someone important, and what you did yesterday earned you that distinction, even though you probably think you didn't earn it. It's high praise, Layla. It means you're one of them now."

"Even though I couldn't save him?" She waved to a group of women on the front porch who were simply standing there, looking in.

"You stayed with him, Layla. Held his hand. Talked to him. To the people here, that shows great bravery. And compassion. So, like it or not, you're stuck with that reputation."

"I'm…humbled. For all these people to embrace me this way…" Tears welled in her eyes. "Why didn't you say something? Tell me what this was about?"

"Because when you live here, spontaneity is a good thing. I know you've always liked to keep to your rigid schedule, but that's not the way everybody lives their life. And wasn't it fun to just let go and have a good time without overthinking it all day?"

"I do overthink, don't I?"

"Only when you're not sleeping." He smiled, took her hand and kissed the back of it. "You *are* strong, Layla, and you *do* fit in wherever you want to."

She looked at all the people huddling in and outside the hut, talking, laughing, having a good time. "I want to fit in, Arlo. I really do." Somewhere. Anywhere. Here?

It was well into the night when they finally left, after eating leftovers. And Layla was so stuffed and lethargic she was practically hanging onto Arlo, letting him drag her. She'd watched him tonight. Playing with the children. Strumming a guitar and singing. Listening patiently to incessant chatter. Mixing. Mingling. Laughing. Being part of everything. "Is there anything you don't do?" she asked, her admiration overflowing as they entered the hut.

"Besides cooking? Let me think…" He was laughing

as he led her to her side of the curtain then went back around to his own side.

Arlo was one of those men who was too good to be true. The kind a woman would fall for in a heartbeat, provided it was a woman who wanted to share his lifestyle. She could see why he didn't want to change it. This was where he fit. Perfectly. "I'm waiting," she called out, too tired to change into her night clothes.

"And I'm still thinking."

"Maybe start with humility?"

"No. I'm good at being humble."

"Is there such a thing as being too humble to be honestly humble?"

"And you're implying, what?"

"That you're a good man, Arlo. A very good man." Words said as her eyes closed.

On the other side of the curtain, Arlo simply sat cross-legged on his mat, wondering what this was about. They'd had a good evening—maybe one of the best they'd ever had and, for now, that was enough. And what she'd said about him as she'd drifted off left him feeling curious. Good, but curious. Telling him he was a good man was nice. Telling him he was sexy would have been better. Telling him he was the man she'd always wanted would have been the best. But for now he'd settle for good.

"Doc Arlo," someone outside whispered through the mosquito netting. "Dusit—" The woman out there started explaining something even Arlo couldn't comprehend, she was talking so fast. But he knew what this was about. One of his problem patients. Another late-night call because Dusit always seemed to manifest his symptoms in the middle of the night.

As he grabbed up his medical bag and slid into his

sandals, he thought about waking Layla to let her know where he'd be, because these calls to Dusit could run into a couple hours or more. But he hated to disturb her, especially since her sleep patterns were so sporadic to begin with. So he slipped out of the hut and headed off in the direction of the main part of the village, and veered to a side road, hesitating before he approached the house as he really wasn't in the mood for this. Acute patients were one thing. So were chronic patients who worked to take care of themselves. But Dusit was neither. He was a chronic who relied on Arlo too much and did nothing to help himself. And there wasn't much he could do about it.

So, sucking in a deep breath, he proceeded up the front walk until he reached the wooden porch where Dusit Chaichanatham was sitting, eating slices of mango.

"Doc Arlo," the man said, grinning and offering a slice to Arlo.

Dusit was a diabetic with blood sugar so out of control that he was a constant worry for any number of side effects. He was a street vendor in the village who specialized in selling *khanom*—sweets—and he ate too many of his own sweets to be healthy. His weight had ballooned at an alarming rate shortly after he'd turned forty. Plus, he was suffering leg cramps and blurry vision.

"Good evening, Dusit," he said, approaching the front porch. "Are you always hungry this late at night?"

His answer was to down another piece and grin. "Very good," he said.

"How many do you eat before you go to bed?"

He held up fingers to indicate three. Not good. A mango contained considerably more sugar than most fruits. And while they were easy to come by out here, they weren't always the best choice in eating, unless in moderation.

"Do you eat anything else before bed?" he asked, sitting down next to the rotund man on a wooden bench. It creaked under Arlo's added weight, so he decided to stand back up before their combined weight broke it.

"*Khanom chan*," he said, still grinning as mango juice dripped off his chin. A layered coconut dessert.

"Seriously? And is there anything else?" Arlo asked, pretty sure he really didn't want to know.

"*Kao tom mud*," he said. A sweet sticky rice made from black beans, tamarind, bananas and coconut milk. A very sweet dish indeed. "*Itim kati*." An ice cream made entirely of coconut milk because many people in Thailand suffered from lactose intolerance. "*Tuang muan sot*." He patted his belly with that one, which told Arlo the soft, sweet pancake made from coconut and sesame seeds was one of his favorites. "*Sang kaya fug tong*." Essentially, pumpkin custard filled with a sweet cream.

All of it sounded good, and for poor Dusit deadly. "Anything else?" Arlo asked, suddenly realizing that this man's diet consisted mainly of the sweets he sold for a living.

"*Tong yord*."

Arlo moaned with that one as it was an excessively sweet dessert made from egg yolk, sugar, rice flour and jasmine water. Did this man ever eat anything healthy?

"Well, I know you haven't been feeling well, and it may have something to do with your eating habits, like I've told you before." If it didn't, he'd burn his medical credentials and spend the rest of his life washing elephants. "So, what's your complaint tonight?"

"Blurry head. Tingly. Some dizzy."

"Does your lower back hurt?" Arlo asked, indicating the area on both sides of his own back that contained the kidneys.

Dusit shook his head.

"And your feet?"

"Good feet," Dusit said.

"Well, you know what I have to do." He grabbed a blood sugar monitor from his bag. "I know you don't like this, and that you usually refuse, but if you're feeling poorly enough to have your wife come and get me in the middle of the night, I've got to test your sugar level." It was always high, even with insulin shots, which Dusit normally refused as he was deathly afraid of needles. "Let me swab your finger and we'll get this over quickly."

"But no shots," Dusit warned.

"No promises."

"Then no finger." He curled his fingers into a fist.

"No finger, then I have to close your vendor stall down since I am the health officer here, and I believe your sweets are harming you." Over the course of time he'd tried all manners of persuasion, but threatening the man with taking away his livelihood, which he wouldn't do, was the one that worked. And sure enough—one chubby finger popped out of his fist and he stuck it out for Arlo.

The draw was quick, and shortly the meter registered a whopping blood sugar count of five hundred and seventy-five. Normal ranged between eighty and one hundred and twenty.

"It's a problem, Dusit. I can give you a shot to bring it down, but you've got to change the way you eat. And get some exercise."

The man was always either sitting or reclining. He didn't even have to walk to work since his stall was in his front yard. Truth was, Arlo was running out of patience here, as well as fresh out of ideas that might work for Dusit. Maybe Layla could try something different. Fresh eyes on a problem never hurt.

"So tonight it's a pretty big shot. And I'd suggest you quit eating now for the insulin to work."

Dusit huffed out an impatient sigh. "No good letting food waste."

"And no good trying to eat it all because, eventually, that's going to kill you. We've had that talk many times, Dusit. You know what's ahead of you." He filled a syringe with insulin, totally hating how much Dusit required, then indicated for the man to drop his trousers, and when he did so, Arlo jabbed him in the thigh. Dusit's response was to scream so loud and long that the lights from homes all around the area came on. "You may have to have another one in a while," Arlo said, dropping the used syringe into a disposable sharps container he carried in his bag. "I'll be back in a while to check, or I'll be sending my colleague."

"No lady doc," Dusit protested.

"It's not your choice, Dusit. If you cooperate with me, it can become your choice. But until then it's my choice." And he hoped Layla did have something in her bag of medical tricks for Dusit as the man was an eating, breathing stroke waiting to happen.

By the time Arlo was halfway back to the hut, he ran into Layla, who was running in his direction, carrying her medical bag. "Several people reported hearing screaming, so I—"

He waved her off with his hand. "Just an uncooperative patient showing me how uncooperative he can really be."

"Seriously? He woke half the village."

"Man doesn't like needles."

"You had to give him a shot."

"Either that or watch him mango himself to death right before my very eyes." He looked up at the dark sky and blew out a frustrated breath. "He's a serious diabetic. Has vision problems, early onset neuropathy and God only knows what else, since he refuses a physical. He's on my insulin rounds in the morning, but he won't take insulin. And to make matters worse, he's the sweets vendor, and he eats all the leftovers. So—any suggestions?"

"What have you tried?"

"Everything. Talking, educating, reasoning, threatening. Showing him pictures of what his complications can turn into if he's not careful." He reached out and took hold of Layla's hand as they headed back home. "He doesn't respond to anything."

"Some patients won't be helped, Arlo. We both know that."

"He's forty, Layla. Just a few years older than me. And he has young children. They don't deserve to have their daddy die by the time he's forty-five. But I don't know what else to do."

"Would he listen to me?"

"Probably not."

"Could I try?"

"Absolutely. But don't expect much. Dusit's the very definition of stubborn pride."

"And you sound exhausted," she said as they trudged up the wooden steps to their hut.

"I am. Sometimes I wish—"

She laid a finger to his lips to silence him. "Sometimes we all wish we'd made other choices. But you were meant to be here, Arlo, and Dusit's not going to defeat you."

"How did you know that's where I was going?"

"Because I know you, and I know had badly you take it when one of your patients doesn't respond. So…" She stood on tiptoe and kissed him gently on the lips. "Go to sleep and we'll deal with your problem patient in the morning. Oh, and take the cot. Tonight I think you need it more than I do." She brushed his cheek with her thumb, then crossed the room to his mat and lay down there.

For the life of him, there were times when he couldn't figure out why he'd walked away from her. Tonight was one of them.

"He actually came here for his shot," Arlo said, a towel wrapped around his middle and another around his head. "Before I was awake."

He was so distracting, almost naked that way, but she couldn't force her gaze anywhere else. "That's because we had a little talk and I told him if he didn't work harder and make it easier for you to take care of him, we might have to take him to hospital and leave him there for a while until they got his diabetes under control. Mind you, he was eating some pastry when we talked, but he did promise to come for his shot, and I'm glad to hear he did."

"So, where have you been?" He turned his back to her, dropped his towel and pulled on his underpants, then his cargos. No care in the world that he was flashing his bare bum at her. A bare bum she'd always admired.

"Doing your early rounds. You were so exhausted I decided to let you sleep."

He tossed the towel from his head into a hamper with the rest of the towels, then finger-combed his curls. She used to love doing that. Running her fingers through his hair. Massaging around his eyes. Kissing his neck— his neck, maybe the sexiest part of him. She'd loved to nibble his neck.

"I appreciate that. I can't remember the last time I got to sleep in. It was nice. Thank you."

She smiled. "That's what partners are for."

But partners in what sense? Could she mean what he

was thinking about? Nah. While she was committed to doing a good job here, she wasn't focused on anything other than her promotion. So many things had changed about Layla, but so many hadn't. That's something he'd have to come to terms with or else this time, when she walked away, it would be far worse than last time. Because last time his feelings had been practice feelings. He recognized that now. But this time…his feelings were deeper. Much, much deeper. And there was no practice to them as they were the real thing. Last time he'd had wounds. This time, if he let it get away from him, he would have permanent scars.

After a busy morning, Arlo was ready to take a break by midday. Normally he worked straight through, but he'd been thinking about his mother all morning. The work she'd done here. The happiness her life had brought her, and how it had shone on her face. The low moments when she'd thought about Eric. She had been the embodiment of civilized when so much around her hadn't been. Like Layla. Strong, determined and yet gentle in ways she hadn't often shown.

He liked what was coming out in Layla. Nothing was overt. Everything was subtle. But she now carried candy for the children. And she smiled. Maybe that was the best part—her beautiful smile that simply seemed to come more naturally now.

"Care to go get something to eat with me?" he asked as she strolled into their hut only moments after he did. He was seated on the floor, reclining in a pile of pillows. She kept her distance, standing across the dim room. But her arms weren't folded across her chest, the way they were so much of the time. In fact, she looked casual. At ease with herself and her surroundings—something he'd never seen very often in her. It was nice. Dangerous since it gave him crazy ideas that simply had no place between them. But nice all the same.

"I'd sit with you for tea, but half the food vendors in the village were offering me samples today." She patted her belly. "Apparently, I have no will power."

Arlo laughed. "The village does have its charms."

"And calories. Lot and lots of calories."

"Like you have to worry about that." Her body was perfect, and she was one of the lucky ones who could eat everything in sight and not gain an ounce. Back when they'd been together, he had been the one who'd had to watch himself. Now it didn't matter so much as he was so physically active most of the time.

"But it catches up to you. My mother—the svelte, beautiful actress—has been hating life lately because she's put on some pounds."

"If I recall, on the couple times I met her she was very…nice."

"We all change as we get older. For my mom, it's her weight. For my dad, it's his hairline."

"And for you?"

Frowning, Layla thought for a moment. "I'm here. I think that's a huge change."

"But would you be here if there wasn't something substantial in it for you?"

"Probably not. I do like my material world. Maybe not the way I used to. I mean, I don't own fifty pairs of shoes now. But a nice warm shower, a comfortable bed without mosquito netting—my needs are much simpler, but they're still my needs. So, let me ask you what changes you've seen in yourself."

"I think I'm more aware, and tolerant, of people's needs and differences."

"You *were* pretty rigid."

"It was a brave new world out there for me. I was afraid of getting lost in it. I think it's easier to be who you really are when you're where you belong." He pushed himself off the floor, then headed for the door. But before he even got to the shoe rack, someone outside was yelling. "Bleeding bad. Come help."

Layla immediately ran to the door and there, in the street, was a panicked woman who was covered in blood. She was explaining something to Arlo. It took her the length of time it took him to put on his sandals, then he ducked back in the hut. "Bad one," he said. "Grab your bag and follow her. I've got to run over to the hospital and get…" he swallowed. "…my amputation kit."

"What?" Layla sputtered.

"I'm not really sure. But it has something to do with someone caught in a tree, who's bleeding to death. She— his wife—said his leg won't come out."

Layla nodded, her whole body suddenly feeling numb. "Maybe it's not as bad—" She bit back the rest of her words, grabbed her medical kit and ran outside, only to be passed by Arlo, who was on his way to the hospital. They met up, moments later, down the road. "I've never done an amputation," she said. "If that's what this is about."

"Neither have I." Which meant they were going blind into this. But blind together. While it didn't improve the situation, it did make him feel much better that Layla would be the one there to help him.

In the full light of a bright day she could see the drying blood on the woman's clothing. A lot of it. And ahead, where a crowd was gathering, a man tied into a tree. Bleeding. Tied off so he wouldn't fall. *But in a tree.*

"We can't do anything while he's up there," she said to Arlo.

"Unless we can't get him down with his leg intact." He pulled away from Layla, then went to talk to the wife, Naiyana, who was already back under the tree, dropped to her knees and crying, as several women were trying to comfort her. She truly wished she understood the language and vowed that for the rest of her time here she'd work hard on learning more of it. Because, if not for Arlo, she was not sure what she'd do.

"He was cutting a branch of a tree. It was hanging too close to their house, obstructing the light, so he went up to cut it down and somehow—and I don't understand more than the gist of this—it fell back on him, crushing part of his leg, and he can't get loose of it. A couple of the men went up to see what they could do, and decided he needed medical attention, so they tied him into the tree to make sure he wouldn't fall out. Naiyana said there's lots of blood and she thinks he might be dying."

"Is he conscious?" Layla asked, coming up to the ladder still leaning against the tree, then looking up at her patient—who wasn't moving.

"I'm not sure. Possibly fading in and out, according to Naiyana. Apparently, he was delirious earlier. Nothing he said was making sense."

"So…" This wasn't sounding good. And from the look on Arlo's face she knew he felt the same way. Which scared her as she thought of him as almost fearless, able to handle any situation, while she was completely helpless trying to climb a tree. Then getting stuck or, worse, falling out of it. He didn't need two emergencies to deal with, but her hands were shaking. So were her knees. And she was sweating like a genteel lady would never dare to sweat.

"I'll go up first and get myself on that big limb right above him. If I tie myself on, I can reach down and help you. The amputation, if that's what it comes to."

Now her heart was beginning to race, and she feared a panic attack was coming. She was deathly afraid of heights and trees. That one serious fall when she'd been a kid, two surgeries, and three weeks in a hospital and rehab—all that might have been the reason she'd become a doctor. But that wasn't registering right now. The only thing that was registering was climbing a tree and amputating a leg. "Why can't you—?"

"Because I need to be able to help lower him down. In this situation my strength is needed more than my medical skill."

She looked up again, swallowed hard. "I'm not sure I can climb up there, Arlo. You know how I am about—"

"You'll be safe, I promise," he said, putting a steadying arm around her shoulder. "No falling out of the tree like you did when you were eight, and no broken leg for you this time." Pulling her closer, he leaned down and whispered, "I'd never put you in danger, Layla. *Never.*"

"I know that. But still…" She shook her head. "I'm afraid I won't be able to…perform, even if I do manage to get up there." She could almost feel herself falling to the ground. The few seconds of wild fear when her brain wouldn't function, then hitting hard, and a jolt so paralyzing that she couldn't breathe. Then the pain. The excruciating pain and the fear that her parents might not care. Even though it had happened when she'd been only a little girl, she felt like that little girl now. Except this time she had Arlo, and she trusted him with everything inside her. "But I'll try."

"Don't force yourself," he whispered. "I don't want anything happening to you."

She managed a weak smile. "Neither do I." Then melted when he bent to kiss her cheek. "I can do this, Arlo. Remember? I am strong!" Brave words she desperately needed to be true, because too many things in life scared her. Being with Arlo, being without him—she couldn't let the practice of her medicine become one of those fears. "I am strong," she whispered. Then turned to face Arlo. "I am. I really am."

"You are," Arlo agreed, then started up the ladder, leaving her standing underneath her patient, going over the procedure in her mind as her hands began to steady. "Get up there, get myself secured, do my job." She repeated that out loud several times as she walked round and round the tree, surveying the emergency scene from every angle as Arlo got himself secured. "Just do my job." And she could, because Arlo believed in her. For the first time she felt that belief. It was palpable. And it braced her for what she had to do.

"Somewhere in medical school I think they forgot to teach us how to do this," she said as she reached the top of the ladder and slung her leg over the sturdy branch where her patient was dangling, unconscious now, on the far end. "And if I ever open my own medical school…" She began to slide, inch by inch, to the end of the limb.

"Another ambition?" Arlo asked. He was mere feet above her, currently tying himself to the tree trunk.

"Right now, my only ambition is to get this over with and get our patient out of the tree." She inched a little more, then stopped.

"Tie yourself to the trunk, Layla," Arlo said.

"If I do, I won't be able to reach him." She leaned forward, just enough that her fingers could asses the pulse in his neck. "It's pretty weak, Arlo. I don't think we have much time." She moved forward a little more. "What can you see from up there?"

"His leg is stuck in a fork. It's swollen so badly it won't come loose without—"

"And my best position to do that from down here?"

"Another few inches forward, Layla. But be careful."

"Will the branch hold my weight?"

"Virote's weight—that's his name—is pretty evenly dispersed between the limbs, so you'll be good. And since he's basically just flat on his back and not really hanging, that will simplify things for you."

"Nothing's going to simplify things, Arlo. I'm a doctor's who has never done an amputation, and my first is in a tree." She looked up at him, managed a weak smile. "Remember when I was talking about creature comforts? Well, this isn't one of them."

Layla managed to move herself several more inches and that's when she was finally able to get a good look at Virote's leg. The fracture was compound, and bits of bone were shattered and littering his wound. And the bleeding—it was steady. Not profuse but coming hard enough that he would bleed out shortly if they didn't get it stopped. And the only way to do that—

"He already has a partial amp to the leg," she said, applying the tourniquet above the wound to stop the bleeding. "And now…" She shook her head and gritted her teeth. This was the moment when everything she'd ever learned as a doctor would be put to the test.

"Is he secured, in case he comes to?" Arlo asked. He was on his belly now, leaning as far down as he could and still be safe.

"I've just given him a shot, doubled the medication dose, which is the best I can do." Yet, she still feared they could all fall out of the tree if Virote woke up and started to fight.

"Take care of yourself, Layla. And if, for any reason, you get dizzy, or anything puts you at risk, get out of there. I know we've got to treat our patient, but we've also got to keep ourselves from getting hurt. And I don't want anything happening to you. Do you understand?"

Layla nodded as she opened up the amputation kit while Arlo, above her, prepared ropes to lower Virote to the ground once he was free of the tree. "Same goes for you. Keep safe, Arlo. Oh, and about that tea we were going to have—raincheck?"

Her first move to help Virote was to pack as much gauze around the wound as she could without compromising her surgical field. And even out on a tree limb, that's what it was. A surgical field. Then she did a quick assessment of his vital signs. "Blood pressure low," she said, taking the reading off the wrist monitor she'd managed to get on him. "Pulse weak and too rapid," she continued. "Also, he's trying to talk but he's beginning to persever- ate." Repeat the same words over and over. Likewise, he was beginning to trail off some of his words in guttural animal-type sounds. Sure signs of rapid deterioration.

Arlo shouted something to the people below, and sev- eral men turned and ran back to the village. "They're going to get more rope so we can make a sling to lower him when it's done, so—it's time, Layla."

She swallowed hard against the lump that was forming in her throat. Even though Arlo was close. Still, know- ing he was there, looking down at everything she did, made things better. So, first, she took out the scalpel to initiate the procedure, then cleaned the area with alco- hol wipes—not that it made much difference considering how dirty the wound was—then proceeded with cutting through skin, muscle and tendons. But halfway through the procedure the scalpel broke, and Arlo gasped from above. The setback lasted only a couple of seconds as she looked through the kit to see what else she could use. Then she saw them. A pair of trauma shears. And they worked beautifully. Got her through this part of the procedure without a hitch.

"OK," she said to Arlo. "First part's done. Moving on to the second."

"You're doing great," he said.

"And you are so going to owe me a nice dinner in Bangkok before I go home," she retorted, then lurched backward as Virote began to stir. Quickly she drew up another shot of medication and gave it to him—a much bigger dose than she would have liked, but safety was as important up here as the actual procedure. And, luckily, little by little, Virote settled down again. "And if he needs much more to keep him sedated, I'm afraid you're going to have to sing him a lullaby because I've already given him much more than I'm comfortable with."

"Can't sing without my guitar."

"Then you stay here, while I go back to the hut and find it." She checked Virote's eyes and blood pressure. "He's gone again, so let's get this over with. When I get done here, he's going to be all yours to manage because there's nothing I can do to help get him down from this angle. So, are you ready, because I'm going to do this fast." As much for her sake as for Virote's.

"The question is, are *you* ready?"

"I have to be, don't I?" Layla grabbed forceps to clamp the skin and other tissue back from the worst part of the wound and also create a tunnel under the bone, which would allow for better access. Then next use the bone saw.

She wiped the sweat from her face before she started that part of the procedure. Normally, one of her surgical attendants did that, but this was surgery at its rawest, something no doctor could ever anticipate doing, and it was all up to her. Suddenly, all the respect she'd felt she'd never had didn't matter anymore. She had the skill. That's what counted. "I am strong," she whispered, then commenced.

"His vitals are still bad," Layla said to Arlo. He was driving her SUV while she tended her patient. The procedure had gone as well as could be expected, and with the assistance of several villagers Arlo had been able to give Virote a smooth ride to the ground. But the poor man needed more surgery to repair what she'd cut. And they were on their way to the regional hospital where he would be treated for his shock symptoms and stabilized enough to transport him to a public hospital in Bangkok for the next surgery.

"He's lucky to be alive," Arlo said, glancing in the rear-view mirror to see Layla applying another dressing to the still-bleeding wound. "But he's going to need a lot of volume replacement," he commented. Blood transfusion.

"And this is just the beginning of it. After his next surgery, and he's fitted for a prosthesis…"

Arlo interrupted her. "That probably won't happen for quite a while. If ever."

"What? Why not?"

"That's just the way it is. The public hospital will take care of keeping him alive, and even getting him started on some rehab. In other words, living life as an amputee.

But for a prosthesis perseverate the waiting lists are long. Where he should be fitted in six to eight weeks, it'll take twice that long, or more. He'll have good care in the interim, but nothing about it will be speedy."

Layla leaned back against the SUV door and shut her eyes. "Seriously?"

"Like I keep telling you, that's the way it is here, Layla. One of the reasons I stay. Even if I can't provide them the best medical care, given my limitations, I can do something. If we hadn't been here to help him today, the villagers would have attempted something that would have killed him. Or he'd have stayed in that tree until he bled to death. When you live in the jungle, things don't come easy. But there are people like my parents, and me, who do the best we can with what we have. And that's another thing you should address in *your* medical school. The differences in medical care around the world."

"I guess I've been too sheltered, because before I came here, I didn't know… Well, I didn't know pretty much any of this."

"Neither did my parents. A lot of their motivation to come here was to get away from the threats Eric's dad was making. But look at what they did. They became these amazing nomadic doctors who made such a huge difference, which gives me the chance to make a difference as well. They were pioneers in a sense. And it turned into a life they loved with a passion."

She reached across the back of his seat and brushed his cheek. "It's good," she said. "What you do—all good. I'm glad the people here have you." And in so many ways she wished she could have him, too. But could she be the partner he needed? Not in the relationship sense so much as the medical? Could she be to Arlo what his mother had been to his father? Life partners with a common goal?

Arlo knew her as the girl who required fifty pairs of shoes to make her happy and, in so many ways, that's who she had been back when they'd been together and, in a sense, even after she'd come here. Not in the literal sense, of course. But being away from that life made that life she'd lived seem so frivolous. Inconsequential. But could he see past what she'd been, and truly look at what she was becoming? Or was he too stuck in their past to see anything more than what she'd always shown him?

"Well, it's not the prettiest view, but it's the best I could find at a moment's notice." Arlo placed two wrapped sandwiches and a bottle of wine on the stone wall surrounding the garden and reflecting pool, then sat down next to her. "Virote just came out of surgery and he's doing well."

They hadn't left the regional hospital yet. Partly because they wanted to see their emergency through to the end and partly because they were both exhausted. Not fit for the long drive back. "It's been a while since I've heard city sounds," she said, not interested in the food as much as simply sitting here with Arlo, relaxing. "All those horns, and this isn't even a big city."

"Just think what it would be like in Bangkok." He uncorked the wine, which he'd bought at a little market down the street, and poured it into two glasses, not stemware but sturdy hospital glasses.

"I was there for a day before I came out to your hospital. It was…nice. So many things to see and do. But I think I prefer jungle sounds."

He choked, laughing. "Seriously? You're turning into Layla of the jungle?"

"Maybe. I don't know. Probably not."

"Now that's a solid answer, if I ever did hear one."

"I like the people, Arlo. And the challenge of the medicine, even though I've complained about it. It makes me feel alive in a way I've never felt alive before. I think I'll miss it when I go home."

"You're really going back to that?"

"It's who I am. At least, who I know me to be." She took a sip of the wine, then looked up at the stars. Beautiful dots of twinkling diamonds set against a black backdrop. "Do you think I could take some of that with me?"

"I think you can have whatever you want, Layla. Your heart's desire, if your heart is involved." He pulled her to her feet and into his embrace. "Do you remember the nights we'd sit outside on the balcony and just…breathe?"

"Those were nice nights, Arlo. Sometimes after a long, hard day they were the only thing that made sense."

"I still do that. Sit on my wooden step, shut my eyes and just breathe. It puts things into perspective when I think my life is getting too hard, or that I'm just not good enough. And when I'm sitting there, sometimes I can almost feel you sitting there with me. Going through the same struggles, thinking the same thoughts, trying to put things into perspective."

She leaned her head against his chest and listened to the steady rhythm of his heart. Everything about Arlo was steady. She'd always loved that about him, especially as nothing in her life ever seemed steady. "I don't have a balcony now, and my front steps—I live in a brownstone and they open straight onto the sidewalk." And she didn't have him there with her. That, more than anything else, made the difference.

"Does it have a real front door?" he asked.

"It does, with a proper lock."

"I could be jealous, you know."

She leaned her head back and looked up at his face—

his beautiful face. His eyes. His curls. His neck. All with so many memories… "I could send you a proper door when I get home."

"Or give me a proper kiss now," he replied.

Her breath caught in her throat as he took her mouth, the stubble of his beard rough on her skin. But she liked the rugged look of it, the intense feel of it against her, primitive and wild. More sensual and appealing than the clean-shaven face she'd kissed all those years ago.

She wanted to resist him now, knew she should, but nothing in her would acquiesce to that insane notion, and a faint moan recklessly escaping her lips affirmed how very little she could, or would, resist. And all it took was that whisper of a moan to ignite Arlo, causing him to press hard into her, hold her harder, kiss her harder.

Layla's knees went weak with her desire for more of him, and as his mouth roamed without discretion, leaving a trail of heat against the soft curve of her throat then the delicate flesh of her ear, he was the one who groaned, but loud and guttural. For the stars in the heavens to hear.

Layla's arm, where it pressed against Arlo's, burned. But with her free arm she reached up and ran her fingers through his hair, through the curls she'd loved so dearly for so long. Then stood on tiptoe to kiss his neck. Baby-soft kisses, the ones that always gave him goosebumps. That ones that did so even now. "What do we do about this?" she asked, her voice so overcome with want and need it was barely audible. Dear heaven, she wanted the man she'd always wanted, and didn't know how to have.

CHAPTER EIGHT

THE HOTEL ROOM was hot and stuffy, and basic by any definition of the word. But by the time they'd secured the room for the night none of that had mattered. In fact, it hadn't been until just now that Layla had seen the lizard on the wall opposite the bed. Make that lizards—plural. Three of them, simply hanging there and watching.

"They're staring at us," she said to Arlo.

He was sprawled in bed next to her, the bedsheet coming up only to his waist. She, on the other hand, had her part of it pulled up to just below her chin.

"They're just small house geckos," he explained. "*Jing jok*, as they're called here. Harmless. Oh, and they're supposed to bring good luck. So we have three times the luck going for us."

She looked at their clothes piled in a heap on the floor. And two empty bottles of wine on the dresser. They'd stopped for another on their way to the hotel. Regrets? Not at all. In fact, she would have been contented to stay there all day, lounging, making love, spending the day the way they'd occasionally done when they'd both managed to have the same day off with nothing to do.

"Breakfast in bed would be nice," she said, looking at the chip and candy wrappers wadded and tossed at the trash can, but not into it, littering the floor.

"Actually, that would be brunch. And I could go down to the vending machines and grab us more junk food, since this place doesn't have a restaurant."

She shook her head. "I think after the way we indulged last night…"

He chuckled. "We sure did. Three times, if I remember correctly. But all that wine is kind of blurring my thoughts."

She scooted over next to him and laid her head on his bare chest. "I've never been in a hotel like this before." She looked across at the walls. Cement blocks painted yellow. And the furniture—one bed, one rickety chair and a dresser. "Is this where you bring all your women?" she asked, twining her fingers in his soft mat of chest hair.

"What? You're not impressed?"

"I saw the sign informing us we have to pay extra to use the shower."

"But it's in the room. That's better than many of the budget hotels offer. And the room came with a sheet, no extra cost." Arlo rolled slightly to his side and pulled her into his arms. "Unfortunately, all good things must come to an end. We've got a hospital to attend, and the nurse who went down to stay there for us has to leave later this afternoon."

"How did he manage to show up at just the right time?"

"Sylvie called him when she knew we probably wouldn't make it back for quite a while. She was actually in the village, having a pastry from Dusit's stall, when she saw what was happening, so it worked out well for us."

"I was dreading the ride back so late last night. After everything that went on…" She shook her head. "I suppose as good doctors we should check in on Virote before we leave."

"As good doctors I suppose we should conserve water when we shower."

"Hope it's warm," she said.

"Anything's better than a dribbling hose sticking through a window. And it does have a stopcock, so the dribble isn't continuous."

Layla laughed. "You know what? Even the thought of that shower doesn't ruin my mood. After last night…"

"What about last night?" he asked, tucking his index finger under the edge of the sheet and starting to edge it down from her neck. "And do you suppose we should, um, get our money's worth out of this luxurious room before we leave?"

"Depends," she said, sliding down slightly in the bed, then yanking the sheet entirely off him, exposing every bare inch of the most glorious body she'd ever known.

"On what?"

"On if you can put blindfolds on those geckos. Good luck or not, I don't want them watching what I'm about to do."

"Sounds interesting." He rolled totally to his side and propped up his head on his hand. "So, tell me, what would that be?"

She smiled, wrinkling her nose, tossing away the sheet altogether, then also turning on her side to face him. "Let's just say it'll be well worth the effort of blindfolding the geckos."

"Blindfold them, hell. They're going out to the garden."

"Then be glad we rented a room *with* a window, because I'd hate to see you parading down the hall in nothing but a sheet, carrying three geckos." She looked down and grinned. "Especially in *that* condition. On second thought, I think the geckos can wait."

His preference would have been cuddling up with Layla for the rest of the day. It was nice, getting away. Nice not having to worry about so many things. Nice simply feeling human again. No expectations of him. No patients running after him. No nothing. And while he did love his hospital, getting away from it occasionally was necessary.

Unfortunately, that rarely happened. Not because he couldn't get medical coverage for a day or two. He could. But there was nothing that motivated him to go off somewhere alone. And that's where he'd been most of his time here. Somewhere alone. Come to think of it, it had been a long time since he'd shared a bed with anybody for anything other than a few quick moments.

The last person, in fact the only person he'd ever spent an entire night with, was Layla. And that had been so long ago, and they had been in such dire straits by that time, most of the memory was a blur. But he had a new memory or two now. And as he pulled the SUV off to the side of the road, just under the giant fig tree, he laid his head back against the seat, closed his eyes and sighed.

"Something wrong?"

"Just trying to hold on a little longer. Right now, we're still lovers, basking in an afterglow. When I go past the fig tree, we're doctors who will be facing a dozen or more people who missed us when we were gone. I'm just not quite ready to pass the fig tree yet."

"You do know that we're probably going to be up working all night, don't you?"

"You do know that I don't have to care until I'm on the other side of the fig tree, don't you?" He reached over and took hold of her hand. "It was good, Layla. And I'm not just talking about the sex. It was good just being with you, talking, doing nothing, doing everything. Sort of like old times, the way we used to do."

"But you know we're not those two people anymore."

"Life really got in the way, didn't it?"

"I think it does for most people. When you're younger you hope you can capture a single, perfect moment and spend the rest of your life in it. Then add some age, and experience, and you realize that perfect moments are just that—perfect moments. You can't capture them, and you certainly can't spend the rest of your life inside them because reality does finally rear up and show its ugly or even not-so-ugly face."

"And a fig tree is just a fig tree, no matter which side of it you're sitting on. Anyway, I promised a house call sometime later today or this evening," he said, starting the engine again. "And I need to check some stitches I put in one of the children a couple of days ago. And one of us has to go give another pep talk to Dusit…"

What was the point of even thinking about anything personal between them could ever be more than what they'd just had? That one perfect moment or, in their case, night. She had a mission and she wasn't going to stop until she'd completed it. And he was only the means to her carrying out her mission.

He knew that, but it didn't take away the feelings for Layla that were growing. And they were growing fast, which was a huge problem. Because what he was thinking about was something he couldn't have. Just like last time. And what he had was something Layla wouldn't deal with for more than her allotted two months. So, where did that leave them? On a bumpy road back to the village. That's where.

* * *

"You awake?" Layla poked her head into the hut, only to find Arlo stretched out on his mat. They'd spent all of last evening and the whole day today chasing down minor complaints, he going one way through the village and she another.

"Pensri Buajan will be by in a while with food. Apparently, several of the women got together and cooked for us again—actually, they cooked for the whole village, in celebration of saving Virote's life. So we're to be the guests of honor at another celebration." She raised her foot and nudged him in the shoulder, only to have him turn on his side, away from her. "You don't get to sleep through it, Arlo. A lot of people have gone to the trouble of doing this for us, and the least you can do is show up."

"Bad bedside manner, Doctor," he mumbled. "You're never supposed to kick your patient under any circumstances."

"First, you're not my patient. Second, I didn't kick. I nudged."

"Nudge me again like that, and I'll take you to the floor."

Layla laughed. "You're such a faker, Arlo. Being mean-spirited doesn't suit you. You can't even pretend to do a good job of it." For effect, she nudged him with her foot again, only this time he was too quick for her, rolling over before her foot contacted his shoulder, then grabbing it and holding it.

"Put me down," she warned him, balancing herself on one foot. "Or else—"

"Or else what?" He grinned mischievously. "Tell me, Layla. What will you do?"

"This," she said, trying to twist away from him. Only she lost her balance and ended up on top of him.

"Didn't work," he teased, holding onto her as she tried to struggle free. Truth was, he liked her there. Didn't want to let her go.

"I've been pinned down by worse than you, Arlo Benedict."

"Who pinned you?" he asked, his face dangerously close to her.

"His name was James, big brute of a five-year-old. Launched off the exam table and grabbed me around the neck. But I made fast work of that. Took care of him in the blink of an eye."

"How?"

"Bribery. Two lollipops. He was a sucker for a couple of suckers."

"Do you have two lollipops for me?" he asked, still holding on but now more like rubbing her back than latching onto her.

"You had your lollipops yesterday, and the day before. Sort of like paying in advance." She twisted a bit, only managing to find herself deeper in his embrace rather than being free of him.

"And what if I want another one right now?"

"We don't have a door, and I'm not an exhibitionist. I don't like giving you lollipops where everybody can watch us. And because the meal is coming to us—actually, to the hospital—since it's large enough to hold more people than this place is, I think anything we might do would definitely be on exhibition."

"Why do you always have to make so much sense?" he protested, rolling over to his back then sitting up.

"Someone has to." She headed toward the door, then turned back to him. "I'm glad I came here, Arlo. And that's not just about the promotion. It's nice that we're reconnecting, again. I've missed that. And you. I've missed you."

This wasn't what he wanted or needed to hear. He was already soft in the head over this thing, and now with Layla going soft— No, it's not what he needed because, like the first time, they both knew where this would end. Which made everything they were doing a game. They were simply playing games. "Look, I've got to go check on Achara now that she's home again. I'll be back for the party in a while." With that, he pushed himself off the floor, grabbed his medical bag and was on his scooter, putt-putting his way down the road before Layla could say or do something to change his mind. He didn't want to change his mind. This wasn't going to work, and the games were going to stop. Otherwise the rest of her time here was going to stretch out into a miserable eternity he didn't want. Not at all.

The party was long over, and Arlo had never returned. She understood why, and she also understood that her feelings and his were the same. They were going round and round, fighting something they couldn't fight. And it wasn't for the first time. This time they were experienced at it. Knew exactly what it was and where it was going.

And with the better part of two months still stretching out ahead of them—this was a mistake. She'd known, when she'd volunteered for this duty, how it might work out. But there hadn't been a day in the past five years that bits and pieces of Arlo hadn't been in her thoughts. He had always been there in some way. In a surgery she'd known Arlo was particularly skilled at doing, in the twinkle in Ollie's eyes—the one Arlo had inherited from him—in his favorite pillow that she'd tucked back on a closet shelf and couldn't bear to get rid of after he'd left her.

She didn't know if she had it in her to go back to that

place. It had been so bad then, and now that she under-stood him even better—she didn't even want to think about it. So, on her way from the hospital to the hut to which she'd been summoned, she tried putting every-thing out of her thoughts by counting steps. Eyes to the dirt road, counting out loud.

"Well, you aren't what I was expecting." The man, her patient, was older, rugged and very handsome, with silver hair and a short beard with thin, neatly trimmed sides. Silver, like his hair. He was sitting up in the first bed of an otherwise empty hut. Looking flushed, breath-ing hard. But smiling. And he was not a native.

"Who were you expecting?"

"Well, specifically, Arlo. But you're a pleasant sur-prise. It's been a good, long while since I've seen a doc-tor, and seeing how you're a lady doc, more's the better."

He was charming. That much was certain. "Well, Arlo's— Actually, I'm not sure where he is. Probably on a house call somewhere. I'm Layla. Layla Morrison." She held out her hand to shake his. "And I'm assuming you're one of the Dr. Benedicts. Since you're not Arlo, and not Ollie, then you must be—"

"Ward. Does the family resemblance show that much?"

"Trust me, I've been around various Benedict doctors long enough that I can spot them a mile away. So, what's the complaint?"

"A bit of a snakebite, I'm sorry to say. Just above my right boot."

"Arlo wears sandals," she said, as she rolled up Ward's cargo pants to find that the bite mark was above the top of his boot. And also a cross cut mark, where he'd prob-ably tried sucking out the venom himself.

"I've warned him about that, but he never seems to

think his need is greater than someone else's. Last time he had boot money, he spent it on some wood and nails to build a ramp for one of the older women here. She was having difficulty getting up her steps. Time before that, I think it was to help someone start a sugarcane crop. That's what my son does. Puts almost everyone ahead of himself. But you know that, don't you?"

"He's told you about me?"

"Not in so many words. But because he chooses his few words about you carefully, I think you're the one who impacted his life in ways I'd always hoped someone would."

"In ways that wouldn't let us be together. Not in the sense you and your wife were."

"He always said you were ambitious, but ambitions are an odd thing, Layla. Everybody has them, of course. But they can change, and they can certainly be what you want to make of them. Arlo is just as ambitious as you are, and his ambitions are no less important than yours. He told me it was your ambitions that broke you up the first time. But it was about his ambitions as well. He just couldn't see that at the time. I doubt any of us can when we're as involved as the two of you were. And just keep in mind, ambitions are not objective. In fact, they're quite the opposite. Subjective as hell. And that's the end of my fatherly lecture. So, tell me, the bite…" He smiled, even though his face was beginning to bead with sweat. "Bugger was a red-necked keelback. They're usually not aggressive, but I must have done something to make this one angry because it came at me before I had a chance to step away. Went right up to the top of my boot."

"So, since I don't know my snakes, you tell me: Are we in trouble here?"

"Somewhat," Ward admitted.

"How long did this snake have hold of you? Was it less than one second? One to three seconds? Three to five? Ten? Sixty?"

"Probably thirty to forty. It wouldn't let go."

"Which means it had a lot of time to squeeze plenty of venom into your leg. And judging by the second set of marks, it bit you again."

"Well, that little—"

"I don't think getting yourself upset, causing your blood pressure to increase, is going to help you."

"A bottle of whiskey would, though. If you happen to have one handy. Which you probably don't since Arlo prefers wine. Something that came about in his time with you, I believe?"

"Well, now I know I had some kind of good influence on him."

"You had your influence, Layla. Probably more than you know, or more than he'd ever tell you. Anyway, while I've treated snakebites before, this is my first time to be bitten, and as a patient I'm beginning to have some worries over the outcome of this thing. Especially now that a headache and nausea are setting in."

"Well, we have a good stock of antivenin…"

"Not this, you don't. Which may turn this into a sticky situation shortly."

"Are you sure?"

"I know my snakes, and I especially know my antivenins. You don't live most of your seventy years here and not know what's crawling in the grass, and what's available to counteract its poison."

Now she was beginning to panic. Her patient was telling her about his prospects, not the other way around. And she didn't like what she was hearing. There had to be a way—Arlo would know. He always knew. "I think

I'm going to go find Arlo and see what he has to say," she said, trying not to sound as alarmed as she was feeling.

"He'll say the same thing I said. We're in trouble here."

She gave the man's arm a squeeze. "If I can do a field amputation hanging upside down in a tree, this little snakebite should be a breeze." Not that it was, or that she even believed her own words. "I'll be right back." She saw the woman who owned the hut, Naak, standing in the shadows, watching, then pointed to a chair across from Ward. "Can you ask her to stay with you?" Layla asked Ward.

He chuckled weakly. "And to think I only came to let Arlo be the first to know I'm getting married again. Now I'm not so sure."

"Married?"

"If I survive this." He lay back on the bed and shut his eyes. "Don't worry. I'm not going to die in the next few minutes. I just proposed to her a couple of weeks ago and she'll kill me if I die before we marry." He chuckled weakly, then dropped off to sleep.

Layla ran so hard and fast through the village, stopping to inquire after Arlo every few seconds, she didn't even remember arriving at Dusit's home, which was where she was directed. But there she was, standing outside, trying to catch her breath so she could talk to Arlo.

"Layla?" he asked, stepping out, still holding the blood sugar monitor.

"It's your dad," she panted. "Snakebite. Red-necked something-back."

"Damn," he muttered, jamming the monitor into his pocket then dashing back inside to grab his bag. "How long ago?" he asked, running back outside and not even slowing when he passed her.

She ran to catch up with him. "Maybe twenty minutes."

"Any symptoms showing yet?"

"A few. Nausea, headache, sweating. Exhaustion. Arlo, he said we don't have the antivenin."

"Nobody does. It's manufactured in Japan and it's in short supply because a red-necked keelback doesn't usually bite. I've never had that antivenin because I've never had a patient bitten by one of those." He stopped at the entrance to Naak's hut, then shut his eyes. "They're so docile children play with them."

She stepped up to his side. "Well, this one wasn't playing. He bit your dad twice and the envenomation took a long time. I think he's pumped full of the poison. I didn't ask him, but he said it was fatal. Is it?"

Rather than answering, Arlo looked down at Layla. "He might not have enough time left for us to get him what he needs. It's only made in Japan, and you have to have quite a pull with the pharmaceutical company to get it. I'm thinking since Eric lives in Japan, he might have that pull." He sucked in his breath then headed up the stairs. "Go out as far as you can until you get a signal. Then call him. It's a long shot. But it's all we have." He tossed her his phone with Eric's number in it.

"Arlo, your dad tried sucking out his own venom."

"Hopefully, that will prolong his life." Those were his last words before entering the hospital. And seconds later Layla was on her way to find a mobile signal. Wondering what anybody in circumstances like this would do if not for Arlo—and her. For the first time she felt connected. Maybe more connected than she ever had before. She mattered in this. She needed to be here. And it wasn't she who needed the support. It was everybody out here. Everybody. And Arlo. Especially Arlo.

CHAPTER NINE

"How's the snakebite victim?" Arlo asked, as he entered the clinic, fighting to remain calm when nothing inside him was.

"He's seen better days," Ward admitted, as Arlo reached his bedside and bent down to give his old man a hug.

"So, how did you get into this mess, Dad?"

"Wasn't paying attention. Thinking happy thoughts, I suppose."

He peeled back the sheet and looked at his dad's leg. It wasn't necrotic yet, but it wasn't good. There was too much swelling, his dad was diaphoretic and having some trouble breathing. "Tell me, what were those happy thoughts?" he asked, as he hooked up an oxygen mask to the cannister he'd grabbed on his way over. "Anything I should know about before I put this thing on you and tell you not to talk?"

"Well, if I do come out of this somehow, I'm getting married."

Arlo blinked hard at the news. "Seriously? Who? How'd you meet her?"

"She's a nurse who works in the tourist clinic with me near Angkor Wat. I've been working around there quite a while now and— What can I say? She's a great lady and I'm not dead yet—well, that remains to be seen, I suppose."

"This isn't going to kill you, Dad. Maybe make you suffer a bit, but…" He faked a smile as he pulled out a bottle of antiseptic to clean the wound. "Does she make you happy?" he asked, uncapping the bottle and pouring it over his dad's leg.

"Does Layla make you happy?"

"Ah, the question that has no answer." He placed the mask on his dad's face and tightened the elastic straps for a tight fit.

"It has an answer, son. I saw it in her face as clearly as I see it in yours." He reached up to wipe the sweat from his face, but his hands were too shaky. "So, what's the plan here, son? Because if I were the doc in charge, I would be preparing the patient for the inevitable."

"But you're not the doc here, and the plan is Layla getting through to Eric who will ride in on his white horse all the way from Japan with the antivenin." Such a long shot, but it was the only one he had unless someone, someplace else, had some antivenin. Which didn't seem likely given its scarcity. "So, right now, you need to rest. The more active you are, the more the venom spreads."

"Isn't that something I taught you when you were, what? Seven or eight?" Finally, his eyes drooped shut and he took a deep breath that indicated sleep was already overtaking him.

"I was eight, Dad," Arlo said, slapping at the tears streaking down his cheeks. "What you taught me when I was seven was how important the work here is." He took hold of his dad's hand and stayed there, sitting on the edge of the bed, until Layla finally came back almost two hours later. The first thing she did was rush to the bed, look down and sigh a sigh of relief when she discovered that Ward was only sleeping. The second thing she did was pull Arlo into her arms and simply hold him. "We're going to get through this," she whispered. "I promise. We're going to get through this."

He heard the words but had no response to them. All he knew was that he was grateful Layla was the one with him now, whichever way this went. He needed her. Only her.

"Eric's going to grab a supply of the antivenin and fly down here. It's going to be a long flight, Arlo. But he's on his way."

"It may be too late," he said, not even trying to hide the discouragement in his voice.

"How long…?" She didn't finish her question. How could she when what she wanted to know was how long Ward had to live? She didn't know and didn't want to ask. But she had to take charge here and leave Arlo time to simply be his father's son.

"Ten to twelve hours. Maybe up to a day, depending on my dad's sensitivity level."

"Then Eric will get here in time."

"Or it may take only an hour, then all of this is for nothing."

"Not for nothing, Arlo," she said, sitting in a chair opposite him, her hand on his knee while he still held his dad's hand. "For your dad. Or for any patient in the same situation. You don't quit. You never have. And you won't now."

"It's so hard doing this alone. Doing the things I must do. Facing the things I must face. With my parents, they had each other to help them through. I have a civet cat, which says a lot, doesn't it?"

Villagers were beginning to assemble outside, all of

them knowing now that the patient was Doc Arlo's dad. People were bringing food. Various drinks. Women were offering to clean the hospital. Several men were across the street, repairing Arlo's leaking roof. It was an amazing sight, watching everybody come together the way they were. And not just because Arlo was their doctor. They loved him. He was part of them. Part of the heart and soul of everybody here. "Just look at them," she said, as they were going into their third hour of waiting. "You're not alone here, Arlo. Even Dusit is out there, toting a basket of sweets for you."

He chuckled. "Of course, he would. Which means he's going to need another test shortly, and probably a shot."

"You take wonderful care of these people. In turn, they take wonderful care of you. And if you ask me, that's an almost perfect way to run your medical practice, minus the hardships, of course." She stood, then crossed over to the bed to check Ward's vital signs. Currently, he wasn't losing ground, and that's the best they could hope for. "I could sit here, if you want to go grab some sleep."

"I can't sleep," he said, standing, then stretching.

She heard his neck pop. "Can I fix that for you?" she asked, pointing him to her chair rather than the side of the bed.

He didn't answer, but he did sit where she wanted him to, and positioned himself for the neck massage. And the instant she applied pressure with her fingers, he moaned. "Best hands I've ever experienced," he said, relaxing into her touch. "You always knew when I needed it, too, didn't you?"

"We might have been bad at some things, but I never ignored you, Arlo. In fact, there were nights I'd lie awake in bed simply to watch you sleep."

"I knew that."

"Seriously?"

"Seriously. And I liked knowing you were doing it, even though most of the time you weren't sleeping. So, tell me. Why did you watch?"

"I loved the way that your hair would curl down over your forehead. And your neck—did I ever tell you that you have the sexiest neck I've ever seen on anybody? After you'd gone to sleep I loved nuzzling into your neck. Or were you even asleep?"

"Nope," he said, finally fully relaxing. "Not all the time anyway. And I did enjoy the way you'd sort of sneak into me and position yourself so I could feel you pressed to my neck. Sometimes you'd kiss me there. Just a light one. Trying not to wake me up, I suppose."

"So, whatever happened to *that* couple?"

"One went to Thailand, and one didn't. That's the way we started our relationship, and the way we finished it. We both knew what would happen from the beginning, but I think we—or, at least, I—got sidetracked somewhere along the way.

"Did you ever think I might stay with you, Layla?"

"Not think as much as hope."

"But you never asked. Never said a word about it."

"Because we couldn't get past it, Arlo. Not then. And I didn't want to keep on hurting over it so no, I never asked, because I didn't want to be rejected. Especially by the only man I'd ever loved."

"Was I?" he asked.

"You still are. Nothing about that has ever changed." Layla sniffed back tears as she moved her massage more toward the side of his neck. "But nothing about us has ever changed either, has it?"

"You said you loved me before but went right past it, so I didn't know. And this is the first time I really believe that you did…maybe still do. But never when we were together."

"What I couldn't say wasn't what I felt. And I was so afraid of what I felt because the people in my life didn't love me the way I thought they should. I saw my friends get that kind of love. Even just now I saw it between you and your dad. But what I got was always… compromised. There was always another component to it. Another agenda. So I suppose you could say that for me the non-resolution was safer than what I feared the resolution might be."

"Which was why you were so distant so much of the time."

"I was afraid to get closer, Arlo. Because I knew the ending to our story from the very first page."

In the bed, Ward stirred and opened his eyes. Arlo jumped up to be at his side, and Ward gave him a very weak thumbs-up. "Everything's in motion, Dad. Now we're just waiting for the antivenin to arrive. Eric's bringing it, by the way."

Ward attempted a nod and a smile, then went back to sleep.

"So, what is it between you and your brother that you're not close? His money? Do you resent it the way you resented mine?"

"I didn't resent your money, Layla. Money's never been a big thing in my life one way or the other. But when we were together you used your money as a crutch, shutting me out of places where I really belonged. When you had a problem, rather than letting me help you through it, you went on a shopping spree. When you had your infrequent contact with your parents and ended up all depressed, and I'd try to be understanding, you'd push me away and—"

"Go on a shopping spree. It was easier than dealing with the emotions. And it's what I learned growing up. When I had a problem, rather than my parents trying to help me through it, they bought me things. *See this pearl necklace, darling? It'll make you feel better.* When you hear that enough, you start believing it. But what about Eric? If it wasn't about money, then what?"

"We just haven't had our opportunity yet. There was resentment in the past because we shared a mother I knew and he didn't, but we're over that. Or almost over. And as far as his money—or even yours—goes, I don't resent it, but I don't want my life to be about it either."

"And you think mine is?"

"It was. You were the one who supported me, Layla. Took pity on the poor resident, invited him to live with you. Paid for the expensive meals out when you wanted to go out and I was good eating a bowl of cereal at home. You were the one who bought me a watch that cost more than I'd make in two or three years, because you thought it would look good on my arm. And Eric—shortly after he was married, and finally happy, he wanted to come in like a storm trooper and turn my hospital into something that would never work here. For me, when money entered the picture, I got pushed aside. Or what I wanted got pushed aside."

"And what you want is…?"

"What I have. I've never been like other people, Layla. I'm simple. Not in the head, but in the way I want to spend my life. People get too complicated, too cluttered and they lose themselves in all that. Eric did. He was drowning when Michi, his wife, saved him. And you— the kind of ambitions you have—that's way over my head. I'd much rather hike five miles into the jungle to treat a throat infection than sit behind a desk and only come out when protocol dictates I do.

"But people assume that because I'm poor, and will likely spend my life that way, that I'm to be pitied. So they buy me expensive watches and send architects to a jungle to design a state-of-the-art mini-medical center. While their—*your*—intentions may be good, they're not my intentions. But that gets overlooked."

"Wow," she said, stunned. "Have I ever done anything right?"

"You haven't done anything wrong. Neither has Eric. People who care for each other want the best. Only in my case, my best wasn't good enough for the people who cared for me." He glanced at the clock on the wall, then at his dad. "It's getting close," he said, as Ward was beginning to turn a peculiar shade of gray. Layla had put an IV in him hours ago, and the oxygen was helping his breathing a little bit. But he was burning with fever now and shaking so hard the vibration of it traveled through the bed and down to the wooden floor.

"I'll bet Eric will be here within two hours."

"If he holds on that long."

She could feel Arlo's despair. Even though he was fighting hard not to show the fear, she saw it. The distant look in his eyes. The impatient way he ran his hand through his hair. Shifting positions sometimes several times a minute. No looking directly at his dad unless it was in some medical way. "He's in good physical condition overall, Arlo. That's to his benefit."

"Pep talks don't work here," he said, bolting off the bed. "So please—" He stopped, shook his head. "I need some air. Won't be gone long." With that, he strode out the hospital door, pushed his way through all the people out there and headed for a path straight into the jungle.

Layla watched him from the window but didn't go after him. He needed to be alone. With his dad being so sick, and with all the talking they'd been doing, she knew that as well as she knew her own name. Arlo needed space and she wouldn't deprive him of it.

"It's complicated, isn't it?" Sylvie said. She'd come to help and now she was bringing a cup of tea to Layla, who was sitting bedside with Ward, holding his hand. "It turns your world around and there's nothing you can do about it except let it happen and hope you don't perish in it somewhere."

"I didn't mean to fall in love with him the first time I did, and I certainly didn't mean to do it again. And you're right. It's complicated."

"If you want it to be. When I was married, we didn't allow complications. My husband was much older than I and I knew our time together wouldn't be as long as I wanted. So, every day was a gift. And I'm not saying we didn't have problems. Every couple does. But we didn't let them come between us. Which is what I believe is happening to you and Arlo. You're letting the complications keep you apart."

"But how can you get through them?"

"You let the love in. Freely. Fully. Once it's there you'll find that the complications aren't so…complicated."

"So why did you stay here after your husband died? Didn't it hurt to do that?"

"It did, but we loved it here. And that's the thing I can't bear to walk away from. It's still here, and it still keeps me connected to the love of my life." She smiled fondly. "This is my home now. I can't leave it. As they say, home is where the heart is."

And her heart and home were with Arlo. Which proved

Sylvie right. Suddenly her complications weren't as complicated as she knew what she had to do. Finally, after all this time, she knew. Now she only hoped it would be the same for Arlo.

Arriving in the nick of time was just that. Eric had arrived in the nick of time with the antivenin. And now Arlo was watching his brother load his dad onto a helicopter for transport to one of the best hospitals in Bangkok. He'd promised to come back tomorrow to give Arlo a lift there to be with his dad.

And Layla—she was working hard and fast to take all their medical calls. Insulin shots, maternity checks, rashes, everything.

He caught up with her outside Dusit's vendor stall and literally had to take hold of her arm to keep her in place for a moment. "He's going to be OK," he said to her.

She smiled. "That's what the talk on the street is all about."

"Except you don't understand the talk on the street."

"I have my ways, Arlo."

"Like I didn't know that before. So, care to come sit with me for a little while?"

"Will it involve a cup of tea?"

"And a pair of arms around you, if you'd like that."

"Ah, the one offer I can't refuse." She slipped her hand into his. "Are you OK? You look exhausted."

"Probably because I am exhausted. But I'm too wound up to sleep."

"Then think nice, warm soak in a tub."

"I would, except for two things. No warm water. No tub."

She smiled. "That's what you think, Dr. Benedict." She pointed down the road to several men who were hefting an old, galvanized tub of some sort into their hut. "Problem one, solved."

"It's for the water buffalo to drink out of," he said, more frustrated than amused. "Not for people to soak in."

"It can be anything you want it to be, Arlo."

"Then what becomes of the poor water buffalo who's thirsty?" He knew she meant well, but all he wanted to do was talk about their problems rather than try to solve them in some poor water buffalo's trough. Maybe this was a bad idea. Maybe he wasn't ready. Obviously, she wasn't. And right now he simply didn't have it in him to work it out because this was the old Layla, trying to fix matters with her materialist outlook. Expensive watches, a water trough. It was all the same. Something meant to push away the reality of what they needed to talk about.

"Look, let's talk later, OK? Without the trough. Maybe when we can take our situation more seriously." Bad words. He knew that from the look on her face. But it was too late to take them back, and he really didn't want to try and explain. Not now. Maybe not ever since they'd had a variation on this theme before and nothing good had come out of it. "When I'm up to it?"

"Up to it, Arlo? Or do you mean up to dealing with me?"

He held his arms up in surrender. "Look, now's not the time. We might say things we'd regret later on, and I don't want to do that. Not again." And another bad turn of the word. He was sinking here, and didn't know how to save himself. So, for now, he wasn't even going to try. And hopefully, after he'd rested, when they'd come back around to this, and they would, he'd make better sense of it. He wanted to. But in his current condition he wasn't optimistic.

"Just as well," she said, pulling her hand from his. "I

have several more patients to see, plus several hours of charting ahead of me. Need to write up a progress report for Ollie, too. Think I'll take it over to Sylvie's tomorrow, scan it and send it to him right away."

Yep, the same old Layla. Different circumstances, different conditions, same old Layla. And here he was hoping—well, it didn't matter what he hoped, did it? They really hadn't come so very far from where they'd left off last time. One of them wanting to talk, the other putting it off. The beginning of the end of something they both wanted but didn't know how to hold onto.

"Looks like the lady isn't happy with you," Eric said, coming up behind Arlo. "I think she's giving you the cold shoulder." It was early morning, the day after Ward had gone to Bangkok, and Eric was there to fetch his brother.

"To be honest, I'm used to it. That's our history because Layla is ambitious in ways I'm not and, in the end, that's what causes our problems. I can't win over her ambitions and she doesn't see why I can't put aside what I want so she can have what she wants. That's what killed us the first time, and what will kill us again. We can't be together and still go our separate ways which is why I think she is going to have to go back early. This isn't doing either of us any good. We can talk and talk until there are no words left, but there's no resolution. Our destinies are different."

"And you can't compromise?"

"How?" Arlo shook his head. "Look, I know that you're happy now and you want everybody to be as happy as you are. But life doesn't always work out that way."

"I gave up a billion-dollar corporation and moved halfway around the world because I loved Michi more than anything else in my life, and I would have moved heaven and earth to be with her. It was a small sacrifice considering all I've gotten in return. So maybe you just don't love Layla enough. Anyway, we need to fly. I stopped by to see your dad before I came back here and he's up and ready to get out of there. I think we need to fly to Bangkok, grab him, and we can come back. Maybe by that time I'll be able to meet her properly. Or, at the very least, she'll have forgiven you for being so dense about the ways of true love."

"Does it matter? This is history repeating itself."

"It does matter if you're going to patch things up and finally marry her."

"Who said anything about marriage?"

"I did, if you're smart."

"Do you really think I could adjust to living a civilized life? Go back to New York and start to wear real shoes?"

"If Layla means that much to you, you can do anything."

Arlo looked up and down the main road of the village, somewhat pensively at first. Then he smiled. "I do have a brother who owns a fleet of airplanes, so getting back here from time to time wouldn't be a big deal, would it?"

"Any time you want to fly, it's there, waiting for you."

"You do realize that I'm about to become a man of material means, don't you?"

"Then I take it your destiny is in New York?"

"Working for my very ambitious wife, it seems."

Eric chuckled. "Welcome to the road that will lead you to be the happiest man in the world, next to me, of course. Now, on the way to Bangkok, let's discuss how we're going to manage the holidays. Your and Layla's place, or Michi's and mine?"

She wasn't sure what'd she heard, and when she'd realized she was practically eavesdropping, she walked away.

But it sounded like Arlo was getting ready to send her away. Had she heard him saying they were about to go their separate ways?

Angry tears streamed down her face and she didn't even bother to blot them. She'd come to tell him she wanted to stay, wanted to find her happiness in the life that made him so happy. But he had other ideas, and he didn't even have the decency to discuss them with her.

Well, maybe she deserved that. Still, it hurt. Hurt worse this time because she knew so much more. Knew that she loved him and how valuable that love was. Knew she could make sacrifices to be with him. Knew that her true happiness was with Arlo and not in her ambitions and agendas. She'd watched him. Everything he did only made her love him more. And the respect he received—he couldn't walk away from that. She didn't want him to. She'd never had that from anyone. Didn't know what it felt like. But she was so proud of the respect Arlo had earned and, for the first time, knew that was enough for her.

But, in the end, maybe she simply was his holiday. The one he'd get together with every few years, then walk away from when, yet again, he realized their gap was too wide to bridge. Or she realized once more that sometimes love wasn't enough. Well, not now. Not while she had some dignity still intact. Not much, but some. And this time—there was closure.

She'd seen his world, even fancied herself a part of it. Deluded herself into thinking she was fitting in. She was wrong, though. Wrong in so many ways. So she'd go. Go her separate way, like he'd told his brother they would do. But with her head held high, as she'd given it a chance. And failed. Only problem was, even while her head was being held high, her heart was breaking in a way it would never be put together again. Nobody compared to Arlo. She knew that even more now, this second time, than she had the first. Nobody compared, nobody ever would. And in a way, that sealed her destiny.

"It's nothing, Mrs. Anderson. Just a minor infection in your incision. I'll take a culture and call in a prescription. If it doesn't clear up in a week, make another appointment."

All day—consultations, scheduling surgeries, scheduling follow-ups. Not even many surgeries to perform as now her work was all about the administrative side of what she'd rather be doing. But in the jungle. She was assistant chief of surgery now, yet her duties made her restless. Meaning what she'd worked so hard to get wasn't what she wanted after all.

Arlo—she couldn't even begin to count the many times she'd thought of him this past month. Had shed tears. Gotten angry. Shed more tears. More than she'd counted on. More than she'd wanted. But she missed him in ways she'd never known one person could miss another. And working for his grandfather wasn't helping matters because Ollie was always the constant reminder of what she'd almost had.

But that wasn't going to last as she'd accepted the promotion on a temporary basis, then applied for a surgical position, no administration at all, in Texas. This time next week she'd be doing surgical repairs on cowboys.

"Could you pop the chart up on the screen for my next patient?" she asked Jackie Hastings, one of the clerks. "I can't get the computer to do anything, and according to the list I saw printed out earlier, I'm supposed to see somebody named Jeanne Kingston."

"She's on the list, Doctor. But there's another name before hers. It's classified as immediate care."

"By?"

"You," Jackie said. "That's your name on the schedule override."

"Except I didn't override the schedule." Maybe Ollie had, accidentally. Or one of the other three staff doctors. "Well, is the patient male or female?"

Jackie looked perplexed. "There's really no information here except a name I can't read and the diagnosis of heart problems. And it's scrawled on the admit sheet, not logged into the computer."

"So spell the name for me."

Jackie looked at the handwritten admission form and shook her head. "Fig—fig something. Figgy?" She squinted her eyes, then shook her head. "Sorry, I can't make sense of it. I think his name is Mr. Fig?" She squinted again. "Figtree. His name is Mr. Figtree."

Layla gasped, then dropped her note tablet on the desk. "Where is he? What room?"

"Seven," Jackie said. But by the time the word was totally out of her mouth, Layla was running down the hall toward Exam Seven.

"What are you doing here?" Layla choked, fighting hard to keep her composure as she ran into Mr. Figtree's room.

"I needed a doctor."

"For what you're describing as a heart problem."

"A very big heart problem," Arlo said, keeping a straight face.

"Then maybe I should refer you straight to a cardiologist." Dear lord, she wanted to throw herself into his arms. But she didn't know if she should, or if he'd even want it.

"Don't need one," he said.

"Why not?"

"Because I already know the cure."

"Which is?" she asked.

"A secret."

She stood there, scrutinizing him for a moment. He looked so good. But, then, Arlo always looked good. And she'd missed him so badly... "So the cure to your problem is a secret you're keeping from your doctor?"

"It might be. Or I might be ready to get cured." A smile began to curve his lips.

"How does that work?"

Please, please, please let this be what I hope it is.

"By divulging my secret to see what she can do about it."

"Is it a secret or a complication?"

He shrugged. "Remains to be seen. Why did you leave, Layla? You didn't even stay around long enough to say goodbye. When I got back from Bangkok, you were gone. Nothing left behind. And the medic who'd come to take over while I was gone had no idea why you left."

"I left because that's what you wanted me to do." But not what she'd wanted to do.

"I did, occasionally. I'll admit it. But if I'd known you'd actually do it, I would have stopped you."

"Why?"

"Because I love you. Because I want to spend the rest of my life with you. Because I was so damned messed up that I didn't even realize I was pushing away the best thing I'd ever had in my life. I built my life around one thing, Layla, and you plowed through that so easily it scared me. Especially since I didn't want the same things out of life that you did."

"Things change, Arlo. I changed. But not until I realized that what I didn't want was what I wanted most. By then, though, it was too late. You were done with me."

"I wasn't done with you, Layla. I was done with me. At least, the part of me that wouldn't budge enough to let you in."

"Then why did you want me to leave?"

"I was coming with you, Layla. That's what changed. I was coming with you."

She shook her head. "How could you do that, Arlo? This isn't your life."

"Neither is Thailand, without you."

She shut her eyes, so afraid of what she expected to hear yet even more afraid that what she expected, and even wanted, wasn't going to happen. But this was the moment, wasn't it? That one moment when she'd either have everything she wanted or nothing at all. The one where, instead of running away from something, she had to run toward something. The one where she would have everything in her heart rather than trying to save her heart from the pain she always expected.

Arlo crossed over to her and pulled her into his arms. "You know this is where you belong, don't you?"

"I think I've always known that, even though I wouldn't admit it."

"There were two of us in that, Layla. Not just you alone. And suddenly it's not so easy. I've been rehearsing this since the day you left. Wanted to make sure I'd get it right before I came after you. Thought I'd finally got myself to the place where I could go through with it. But what I'm going to say scares me because it can change so many things—for both of us."

"With the way you live, I'd have thought change would be the least of your worries."

"The least, yet the biggest. That day you left… I was

angry at first. Then resigned. Then hurt. I went through just about every emotion you can think of, trying to figure what I needed to do to make it right. Or if I should just let it go. Before I'd gone to Bangkok to get my dad, I'd decided to come back and tell you that I would come back here with you, love you, support you and do whatever it would take to make you happy because you were more important than anything else in my life. Like I told you, everybody always had other plans for me, and I think some of what I was doing was simply to prove that I didn't need to be the object of anybody's pity.

"Where I was—I was poor. You knew that. And that was never going to change. Yet there you were, giving me gifts that cost a fortune, which only pointed out even more vividly just how poor I was. That, in turn, kept me from getting truly involved with you because I was afraid I'd always be seen as the one who wasn't capable of making it on my own. That I'd always need a handout.

"Yet here were these people who looked up to me. They didn't care that I didn't have proper boots or a decent vehicle. They cared for me the way I was. And it felt good, Layla. Damned good."

"I cared for you the way you were, Arlo."

"But always wanted to change me in subtle ways. And some not so subtle ways, too. The first time anyway. Then the second time I could still see it in you—all the questions you asked about why I was doing what I was doing. Every time you asked, it felt like I was letting you down by not being someone different. Yet the villagers loved me for who I am. It's quite a conflict, when you think about it."

"I never meant that," she said.

"I know. But sometimes it's hard to overcome your feelings, no matter how stupid they are."

"Or well founded. I know I gave you reason to think I believed you needed to change. Originally. I thought you did. But that was for my benefit, Arlo. Who you were and who I was—you were so far above me I knew that you'd catch onto it eventually. But if I could keep you tied to me in some way, it would work out. At least, that's what I thought."

"Why did you really come to Thailand?" he asked.

"It was my excuse to see you again. To see if anything was still there. But I also wanted that promotion—wanted it badly enough to work with a former lover under the worst of conditions."

"And?"

"That lasted until the first moment I saw you. Then everything changed, even though I didn't want to admit it."

"Yet you're admitting it now."

"I'm going to Texas next week, Arlo. Took a surgical position. No administration. Just surgery."

"Why?"

"I can't work here. My ambition here is what killed us. And working for Ollie, who's always a reminder..."

"Is your new hospital looking for another surgeon?"

"You'd hate it there. No civet cats."

"Speaking of which, he misses you. Actually, so did I, which is why I'm here. I love you, Layla Morrison. I have almost from the first moment I set eyes on you and I thought by forcing you to leave, I'd get myself back on track. But that track is you, and I want to spend the rest of my life with you, if you'll have me."

Besides her stomach churning, now her heart was beating faster. "I love you, too. For me, I think it was love always. The first time it just wasn't as mature or refined as it needed to be. And the second time, when I looked down and saw those hideous sandals and realized what kind of man practiced medicine in the jungle wearing the worst possible shoes, I knew it was real. I was…am proud of you for who you are, Arlo. For your sacrifices. For the way you've never compromised your beliefs.

"That's all I've ever been about—the compromises I had to make to get where I thought I wanted to be. Then, of all things, discovering it wasn't where I wanted to be at all. I was always scared, Arlo, that you'd get in my way. But what scared me even more was realizing you were my way, and that's exactly where I wanted to be. But I wasn't good enough."

"What do you mean, you're not good enough?"

"The way people respect you—I've never had that. Ollie respects my skills because they advance him, but he doesn't respect me. I know that, and I'm fine with it. And my parents—what they respect is nothing I could ever be about. They try their best, but it's not in them, and there's never been once when they've told me they were proud of me, or that I've done a good job. Then when I saw it, unspoken, between you and your dad…" She shook her head. "I don't fit into that, Arlo. I'm a good surgeon, but that's all I am. You, on the other hand, are so much more and I don't want you giving up everything you've done and earned to move to a place you'll hate, even if you do love me. That will destroy you bit by bit, and I couldn't live with myself knowing I'm the cause. You know where you need to be, and I've always envied that. Embrace it, Arlo. You're a lucky man to have it."

"I'd be a luckier man to have you. Sometimes we don't really know what we want until we've had it and lost it. I lost you once and I'm going to do that again. So, if it's here, fine. Or Texas, that's fine, too."

"Or a little village in Thailand?" she asked.

"You'd do that?"

"When I bought my plane ticket to Texas, I bought another one—to Thailand. I pinned them to my cork board and every time I walked by it, I thought about which one I'd use."

"And?"

"And I'd usually cry."

"Because?"

"Because the one I was most likely to use wasn't the one I wanted to use."

"Well, if you choose to use the one for Texas, I'll buy one, too. And I suppose I could get used to wearing a cowboy hat."

"And cover your beautiful hair? I won't have it. I love your hair. I don't want you covering it up for me."

"Then if not a cowboy hat, what?"

She reached up and ran her fingers through his hair. "I would have you, Arlo. In Thailand, where you belong. And where I want to belong."

"You can't mean that, Layla."

"Yes, I can. And I do. If you'll have me. But only in Thailand, Arlo. Only in our jungle village because where you're happy, that's where I'll be happy."

"And Texas?"

"No civet cats. And I really do need to be someplace with civet cats." She reached up, snaked her hands around his neck and pulled his face to hers. "And you, Arlo. I need to be someplace—anyplace—with you."

Before they kissed, he whispered something in her ear, then leaned back to watch her face for a response.

"A door?" she said, laughing. "You put a door on the hut? Which means we can…"

"We can," he said. "And we will."

For the rest of her life, she would. Love him, work

with him, be his partner in everything. And cherish a life where she was loved above all else. For she loved him above all else, too. Only this time she knew it, and so did he.

EPILOGUE

"IT'S A BEAUTIFUL THING," Arlo said as he handed Mali over to her new parents, Eric and Michi.

She was a child who'd been abandoned at the elephant rescue, and the instant he'd mentioned that to Eric, he and his wife, Michi, had flown in, set to adopt her. They wanted another child and Mali needed a home. It was a perfect match for everybody.

So, after the legalities were attended to, he'd flown to Japan to do the honors, while his dad and his dad's new wife watched the hospital. Arlo was considering this the honeymoon he and Layla hadn't had yet. Of course, now that she was sporting a rather prominent baby bump, the term *honeymoon* took on a whole new meaning. "I'm glad you and Michi have room for Mali in your family."

"Well, if it works out, we'd like a couple more. But having both a son and daughter now makes life better. Which you're about to find out. So, which is it? A boy or a girl?"

Actually, he wasn't going to tell Eric yet that he and Layla were starting their life together with both. Oliver Ward for his dad and grandpa, and Alice Joy for his mother. It was the expanding of a legacy he'd never believed would expand. He still couldn't believe that in another four months he'd be the dad of twins.

"So, where's Layla?" Eric asked, looking over Arlo's shoulder.

"She stopped at a shop down the corridor. Saw some cute baby things in the window and she's all things baby now." Even though her parents weren't. When she'd told them she was expecting, they'd handed her a check and never once congratulated her. It had hurt her. He knew that.

But he had a lifetime of taking care of her ahead of him and somewhere in there he hoped to make up for all the things she'd never had in a family. The things he'd counted on with his parents and the things his children would be able to count on with him. And, yes, in a little village in Thailand. But in a much bigger house, built for them by the villagers. One with doors, running water and real, honest-to-goodness beds.

So, while some might believe it took a village to raise a child, it had taken a village to get him to open his eyes to what he had. And a village to welcome them both home, with open arms. To a place where Layla was loved and where she knew she was respected. To the place she'd always looked for, the place where she fit.

He looked over his shoulder in time to see Layla struggling down the corridor, her arms full of packages. He rushed to help her, feeling almost overwhelmed that so much had happened to him in such a short time. Eight months ago they hadn't even been together and now she was hefting bags full of baby booties, pacifiers and other necessities. All of them ready to be used in a jungle *home*, not hut, where two baby cribs were currently under construction by a grateful man who'd had his life saved in a tree one day. "Want to sit down?" he asked, unloading her of all the bags.

"What I want is to go spend some time with my

nephew, Riku." She pointed to the largest of the bags. "I have a few things for him."

Arlo laughed. "My spoiled little rich girl."

"Not rich, now that my parents have withdrawn my trust fund. But definitely spoiled—by you." She handed him a bag of his own.

"More new shoes?" he said, peeking inside. "I already have ten pairs. Seriously, you can stop now."

"But I found your sandals in the back of the closet, Arlo. Which means instead of tossing them in the trash like I'd hoped you would, you've put them aside just in case."

"Or maybe I have a sentimental attachment to them, seeing how they occupied your thoughts so much of the time. Could be, though, that I'm just keeping them around as a reminder of where we were back then and where we are now." He chuckled. "And for once I don't think you can argue the point."

"Give me time," she said, leaning into him even though his arms were full.

"You've got all the time in the world, Layla. All the time in the world." And she did, because they were both exactly where they needed to be. With each other. Forever.

* * * * *

NEW YORK'S
FINEST REBEL

TRISH WYLIE

To my lovely editor Flo, fellow member of the
'I heart Daniel Brannigan' fanclub.

CHAPTER ONE

'Every girl knows there are days for heels and days for flats. It could be a metaphor for life if you think about it. Let's all make today a heels day, shall we?'

SIREN red and dangerously high, they were the sexiest pair of heels Daniel Brannigan had ever seen. Silently cursing the amount of time it took to haul the cage doors into place, he watched them disappear upstairs.

He *really* wanted to meet the woman in those shoes.

Punching on the button until there was a jerk of upward movement, he tried to play catch-up in the slowest elevator ever invented. After the first of three endlessly monotonous trips, he knew the stairs were going to be his preferred mode of travel in the future. But until he had all of his worldly possessions—few that they were—carted from his truck to the fifth floor, he didn't have a choice.

A flash of red appeared in his peripheral vision.

Target acquired.

Turning in the small space, he assessed each detail as it came into sight. Thin straps circled dainty ankles, the angle of her small feet adding enough shape to her calves to remind him that he was overdue for some R & R. If she lived in the same apartment block he was moving into, it was a complication he could do without. But if the effect her shoes had on his libido was anything to go by, he reckoned it was worth the risk. He hadn't earned the nickname Danger Danny for nothing.

The elevator jarred to an unexpected halt, an elderly woman with a small dog in her arms scowling pointedly at the boxes piled around his feet. 'Going down?'

'Up,' he replied curtly. Rocking forward, he nudged the button with his elbow.

Don't disappear on me, babe.

The adrenalin rush of pursuit had always done it for him, as had the kind of woman it took to wear a skirt so short it made him stifle a groan when it came into view. Flared at mid-smooth-skinned-thigh, the flirty cheerleader number lovingly hugged the curve of her hips before dipping in at a narrow waist. He glanced at the fine-boned hand curled around handles of bags labelled with names that meant nothing to him, mouth curving into a smile at the lack of anything sparkling on her ring finger. On the floor below his, she turned to speak to someone in the hall. To his frustration it meant he couldn't see her face as the elevator creaked by. Instead he was left with an image of tumbling locks of long dark hair and the sound of sparkling feminine laughter.

Fighting with the cage again when the elevator stopped, he did what he had done on his previous trips and nudged a box forward to fill the gap. In the following moment of silence, footsteps sounded on the stairs. A trickle of awareness ran down his spine as he turned, gaze rising until he was looking into large dark eyes. Eyes that narrowed as his smile faded.

'Jorja,' he said dryly.

'Daniel,' she replied in the same tone before she tilted her head and arched a brow. 'Didn't occur to you anyone else might want to use the elevator today?'

'Stairs are good for cardio.'

'That would be a no, then.'

'Offering to help me move in? That's neighbourly of you.' He thrust the box in his arms at her, letting go before she had an opportunity to refuse.

There was a tinkle of breaking glass as it hit the floor between their feet.

'Oops.' She blinked.

Oops, his ass. The fact she'd obviously made interesting changes in wardrobe while he was overseas didn't make her any less irritating than she'd been for the last five and a half years. 'No welcome-home banner?' he asked.

'Wouldn't that suggest I'm happy you're here?'

'You got a problem with me being here, you should have made it known when my application came up in front of the residents committee.'

'What makes you think I didn't?'

'Clue was in the words *unanimous decision*.' He shrugged. 'What can I say? People like when a cop lives in the building. Makes them feel secure.'

She smiled a saccharine-sweet smile. 'The elderly woman you ticked off two floors down is the head of the residents' committee. I give it a week before she starts a petition to have you evicted.'

Daniel took a measured breath. He had never met another woman who had the same effect on his nerves as fingernails down a chalkboard. 'Know your biggest problem, babe?'

'Don't call me babe.'

'You underestimate my ability to be adorable when I set my mind to it. I can have the poodle lady baking cookies for me inside forty-eight hours.'

'Bichon.'

'What?'

'The dog. It's a Bichon frise.'

'It got a name?'

'Gershwin.' She rolled her eyes when she realized what

she was doing. 'And I'm afraid that's my quota for helpful-
ness all used up for the day.'

Bending over, he lifted the box at their feet, held it to
his ear and gave it a brisk shake. 'You owe me a half-dozen
glasses.'

'Sue me,' she said as she turned on her heel.

As he followed her down the hall Daniel's errant gaze lowered to watch the sway of her hips before he reminded himself who he was looking at. He had done some dumb things
in his time but checking out Jorja Dawson was stupid on a
whole new level. If she were the last woman left in the state
of New York, he would take a vow of celibacy before getting involved with her. He even had a list of reasons why.

Casually tossing long locks of shining hair over her shoulder, she reached into her purse and turned to face him at the
door to her apartment. 'I don't suppose you're considering
showing your face at Sunday lunch once you've unpacked?
Your mother would appreciate it.'

Number six on his list: *Family involvement*.

He looked into her eyes. 'Will you be there?'

'Never miss it.'

'Tell them I said hi.'

'Are you saying you don't go because I'm there?'

'Don't flatter yourself.' He moved the box in his arms to
dig into a pocket for his key. 'If I rearranged my life around
you I wouldn't be moving into an apartment across the hall
from you. But just so you know—' he leaned closer and lowered his voice '—you'll move before I do.'

'You've never stayed anywhere longer than six months,'
she stated categorically. 'And even then it was because the
army sent you there.'

'Navy,' he corrected without missing a beat. 'And if there's
one thing you should keep in mind about the Marines, it's
that we don't give up ground.'

'I've lived here for more than four years. I'm not going anywhere.'

'Then I guess we'll be seeing a lot of each other.'

Something he could have done without, frankly. Not that he was likely to tell her, but she was the main reason he'd debated taking the apartment. She was a spy who could report back to the rest of the Brannigan clan in weekly discussions over a roast and cheesecake from Junior's. But as far as Daniel was concerned, if his family wanted to know how he was doing they could ask. When they did, he'd give them the same answer he had for the last eight years. With a few more recent additions to throw them off the trail.

He was fine, thanks. Sure it was good to be home. No, he hadn't had any problems settling back into his unit. Yes, if the Reserves called him up again he would go.

They didn't need to know more than that.

'You know *your* problem, Daniel?' She angled her head to the irritating angle she did best. 'You think your being here bugs me when to be honest I couldn't care less where you are, what you're doing or who you're doing it with.'

'Is that so?'

'Mmm-hmm.' She nodded. 'I'm not one of those women you can turn into a gibbering idiot with a smile. I just hope your ego can handle that.'

'Careful, Jo, I might take that as a challenge.'

There was a low burst of the same sparkling laughter he heard on the stairwell, making him wonder why it was he hadn't recognized it before. Most likely it was because she didn't laugh much when he was around. The second it looked as if she would, he'd say something to ruin her mood. He'd been good at that long before he'd started to put any effort into it.

'I had no idea you had a sense of humour,' she said with enough derogatory amusement to tempt him to rise to the bait.

Before he could, she opened the door to her apartment

and stepped over the threshold. She turned, her gaze sliding over his body from head to toe and back up again; her laughter louder as she swung the door shut.

Daniel shook his head. *Damn, she bugged him.*

Damn, he bugged her.

Leaning back against the door, Jo took a long breath and frowned at the fact her heart rate was running a little faster than usual. If taking the stairs in heels had that much of an effect, she might have to consider taking a gym membership.

Granted, a small part of it could probably be chalked up to frustration at her inability to hold a conversation with him without it turning into a verbal sparring match. But she hadn't been sparring alone. To say they brought out the worst in each other would be the understatement of the century.

Heading across the open-plan living area to her bedroom, she resisted the urge to hunt out fluffy slippers and a pair of pyjamas. If he drove her into ice-cream-eating attire on his first day there wasn't a hope she could survive the next three months. When her cell phone rang an hour later, she checked the name on the screen before answering.

'I still can't believe you've done this to me.'

A smile sounded in Olivia's voice. 'Which part? Moving out, putting you in a bridesmaid dress or telling Danny about the apartment next door?'

'I think you know what I mean,' Jo smirked sarcastically. 'I need a new BFF; my ideal man could have moved into that apartment if you hadn't mentioned it to Mr Personality.'

'Since when have you been looking for an ideal man? And anyway, he won't be there long. Short lease, remember?'

'If he renews I'm making a little doll and sticking dozens of pins in it.' Leaving the mirror where she had been staging a personal fashion show in front of hyper-critical eyes, she headed for the kitchen. 'But just so you know, he's determined I'll move first.'

Since everyone who had ever lived in Manhattan knew what their apartment meant to a New Yorker, she didn't have to explain how ridiculous it was for Daniel to think she was going anywhere. The apartment she'd shared with Olivia—and from time to time still did with Jess—was a few hundred square feet of space she could call her own.

She hadn't worked her butt off to end up back in a place she'd sworn she would never find herself again.

'You saw him already? Is there blood in the hall?'

'Not yet. But give it a few weeks and only one of us is leaving this building intact.' Lifting the empty coffeepot, she sighed at the heavy beat coming from across the hall. 'Can you hear that?'

She held the phone out at arm's length for a moment.

'My brother and classic rock go together like—'

'Satan and eternal torture?' Jo enquired.

'Probably not the best time to mention he's agreed to be in the wedding party, is it?'

'I am *not* walking up the aisle with him.'

'You can have Tyler.'

Good call. She loved Tyler Brannigan. *He* was fun to be around. 'I thought he was determined he wasn't wearing a monkey suit. How did you talk him into it?'

'Danny? The same way we got him to his niece's birthday party last month. Only this time Blake helped…'

Meaning he'd lost a bet. Jo smiled a small smile at the idea of Liv's new fiancé tag-teaming with the rest of the Brannigan brothers against one of their own on poker night. She spooned coffee granules into the percolator. *Go Blake.*

'How did he look to you?'

The question made Jo blink, her voice threaded with suspicion. 'Same as he always looks. Why?'

'I take it you haven't watched the news today.'

'No.' She stepped into the living room and pointed the remote at the TV screen. 'What did I miss?'

'Wait for it…'

The report appeared almost instantaneously on the local news channel. Unable to hear what was said without racking the volume up to competitive levels, she read the feed across the bottom of the screen. It mentioned a yet-to-be-named Emergency Services Officer who might or might not have unhooked his safety harness to rescue a man on the Williamsburg Bridge. If it was who she thought it was Jo could have told them the answer. The camera attempted to focus on a speck of arm-waving humanity among the suspension cables at the exact moment another speck closed in on him. For a second they came dangerously close to falling; a collective gasp coming from the crowd of gawkers on the ground. At the last minute several more specks surrounded them and hauled them to safety.

A round of applause sounded on the screen as Jo shook her head. 'You got to be kidding me.'

'I know.' Olivia sighed. 'Mom is climbing the walls. It was tough enough for her when he was overseas…'

'Did you call him?'

'He's not picking up.'

Jo glared at the door. 'I'll call you back.'

In the hall, she banged her fist several times against wood before the music lowered and the door opened.

'Call your mother,' she demanded as she thrust her cell phone at him.

'What's wrong?'

Ignoring what could have almost been mistaken for concern in his deep voice, she turned her hand around, hit speed-dial and lifted the phone to her ear.

'You're an inconsiderate asshat,' she muttered.

The second his mother picked up she thrust the phone at him again, snatching her hand back when warm fingers brushed against hers.

'No, it's me. I'm fine. Someone would have called you if

I wasn't. You know that.' He took a step back and closed the door in Jo's face.

Back in her apartment, she froze and swore under her breath at the fact he had her cell phone. Her life was in that little rectangle of technology. Hadn't stopped to think that one through, had she? Marching back to the kitchen, she lifted the apartment phone, checked the Post-it note on the crowded refrigerator door and dialled his sister's new number.

'He's talking to your mother now.'

'What did you do?' Liv asked.

'Told him exactly what I thought of him.'

'To his face?'

Picking up where she'd left off, Jo hit the switch on the percolator. 'I've never had a problem saying what I think to his face. You *know* that.'

There was a firm knock against wood.

'Hang on.' When she opened the door and her gaze met narrowed blue eyes, she took the phone from him, replacing it with the one in her hand. 'Your sister.'

Lifting the receiver to his ear, he stepped across the threshold. 'Hey, sis, what's up?'

Jo blinked. How had he ended up in her apartment? Swinging the door shut, she turned and went back to the kitchen. If he thought it was becoming a regular occurrence, he could forget it. She wanted to spend time with him as much as she loved the idea of having her fingernails pulled out. Glancing briefly at the room that seemed smaller with him in it, she frowned when he looked at her from the corner of his eye.

His gaze swept over her body, lingering for longer than necessary on her feet. What was *that*?

Jo resisted the urge to look down at what she was wearing. There was nothing wrong with her outfit. If anything, it covered more than the one she was wearing last time he saw her. Personally she loved how the high-waist black pants made her legs seem longer, especially when accompanied by a pair of deep purple, skyscraper-heeled Louboutins. Five feet six inches didn't exactly make her small. But considering the number of models towering over her like Amazons on regular occasions during working hours, she appreciated every additional illusionary inch of height. She shook her head a minute amount. Why should she care what he thought? What he knew about fashion wouldn't fill a thimble. His jeans were a prime example.

Judging by the way they were worn at the knees and around the pockets on his—

She sharply averted her gaze. If he caught her looking at his rear she would never hear the end of it.

The man already had an ego the size of Texas.

'It's my job,' he said with a note of impatience as he paced around the room. 'The line didn't reach… There wasn't time… I knew they had my back. You done, 'cos I'm pretty sure your friend has three more calls to make…'

Unrepentant, Jo grabbed her favourite mug and set it on the counter. She hoped Liv gave him hell, especially when he had just confirmed his stupidity. What kind of idiot unhooked his safety harness that high up? Hadn't he heard of a little thing called gravity?

Turning as the coffee bubbled, she leaned her hip against the counter and folded her arms, studying him while he paced. His jaw tensed, broad chest lifting and lowering beneath a faded Giants T-Shirt. He looked…weary? No, weary wasn't the right word. Tired, maybe—as if he hadn't slept much lately. Not that she cared about that either, but since Liv asked how he looked, apparently she felt the need to study him more closely than usual and once she'd gotten started…

Okay, so if injected with a truth serum she supposed she would admit there were understandable reasons women tended to trip over their feet when he smiled. Vivid blue eyes, shortly cropped dark blond hair, the hint of shadow on his strong jaw... Add them to the ease with which his long, lean, muscular frame covered the ground and there wasn't a single gal in Manhattan who wouldn't volunteer their phone number.

Not that they'd hold his interest for long.

'Well, you can stop. I'm fine. Don't you have a wedding to plan? Said I would, didn't I?' His gaze slid across the room. 'She'll call you back.'

Before he hung up, Jo was across the apartment and had swung the door open with a smile. But instead of his taking the hint, a large hand closed it, his palm flattening on the wood by her head. His body loomed over hers. If they'd been outside he would have blocked out the sun.

'We obviously need to talk,' he said flatly.

No, they didn't. Jo gritted her teeth together, rapidly losing what was left of her patience. She was contemplating grinding a stiletto heel into one of his boots when he took a short breath and added, 'Butting your pretty little nose into other people's business might be okay with other folks. It's not with me.'

'Try answering your phone and I won't have to.' She arched a brow. 'Is the fact your family might think you have a death wish so very difficult for you to grasp?'

'I don't have a death wish.'

'Unhooking your harness is standard procedure, is it?'

'Go stand on the chair.'

She faltered. 'What?'

'You heard me.'

When she didn't move, he circled her wrist with a thumb and forefinger. The jolt of heat that travelled swiftly up her arm made her drop her chin and frown as he led her across the room. Now he was *touching* her? He never touched her. If anything it had always felt as if there were a quarantine zone around her.

'What do you think you're doing?' she asked.

'Staging a demonstration…'

Her eyes widened when he released her wrist, set his hands on her waist and hoisted her onto an overstuffed chair. 'Where do you get off—? Don't stand on my furniture!'

Feet spread shoulder-width apart on the deep cushions of the sofa, he tested the springs with a couple of small bounces before jerking his chin at her. 'Jump.'

'What?'

'Jump.'

That was it, she'd had enough. She wasn't the remotest bit interested in playing games. What was he—*five*?

But when she attempted to get down off the chair, a long arm snapped around her waist and she was launched into mid-air. The next thing she knew, she was slammed into what felt like a wall of heat, a sharp gasp hauled through her parted lips. She jerked her chin up and stared into his eyes, the tips of their noses almost touching. What. The. Hell?

'You see…' he said in a mesmerizing rumble '…it's all about balance…'

Surreally, his intense gaze examined her face in a way that suggested he'd never looked at her before. But what was more disconcerting was how it felt as if there weren't anywhere they weren't touching. The sensation of her breasts crushed against his chest made it difficult to breathe, the contact sending an erotic jolt through her abdomen. How could she be attracted to him when she disliked him so much?

When she was lowered—unbearably slowly—along the length of his large body, Jo had no choice but to grasp wide shoulders until her feet hit the cushions. She swayed as she let go. For a moment she even felt light-headed.

'I knew what I was doing.' Stepping down, he lifted her onto the floor as if she weighed nothing.

Taking an immediate step back, Jo dropped her arms to her sides. Her gaze lowered to his chest. She should be angry, ticked off beyond belief he had the gall to touch her and—worse still—have an effect on her body. She liked her world right-side-up, *thank you very much*, and if he knew what he had done to her...

Folding her arms over heavy breasts, she lifted her chin again. 'The giant footprints you've left on my sofa make us even for the half-dozen glasses.'

'If you've got nothing better to do with your time than talk about me to my family, try taking up a hobby.'

A small cough of disbelief left her lips. 'I have plenty of things to fill my time.'

'Dating obviously isn't one of them,' he said dryly.

'Meaning *what*, exactly?'

'Meaning I may have forgotten why it is you've stayed single for so long, but after an hour it's starting to come back to me.' He folded his arms in a mirror of her stance. 'Ever consider being nice from time to time might improve the odds of getting laid?'

'Since when has my sex life been remotely in the region of any of your business?'

'If I had to guess, I'd say around about the same time my relationship with my family became yours.'

Reaching for the kind of strength that had gotten her through worse things than an argument in the past, Jo smiled sweetly. 'Try not to let the door hit your ass on the way out.'

'That's the best you've got?' he asked with a lift of his brows. 'You're obviously out of practice.' He nodded firmly. 'Don't worry, we'll soon get you combat-ready again.'

Jo sighed heavily and headed for the door. She didn't look at him as he crossed the room. But for some completely unknown reason, just before he left, she heard herself ask, 'Don't you ever get tired of this?'

Where had *that* come from?

Daniel stopped, turned his head and studied her with an intense gaze. 'Quitting on me, babe?'

She frowned when the softly spoken question did something weird to her chest. 'Don't call me babe.'

When he didn't move, the air seemed to thicken in the space between them. Stupid hormones—even if she was in the market for a relationship he was the last man—

'You want to negotiate a truce?'

She didn't know what had possessed her to ask the question in the first place and now he was asking if she wanted them to be *friends*? She stifled a burst of laughter. 'Did I give the impression I was waving a white flag? I'm talking about you, not me. You look tired, Daniel.' She pouted. 'Is the energy required pretending to be a nice guy to everyone else finally wearing you down?'

His eyes darkened. 'Questioning my stamina, babe?'

The 'babe' thing was really starting to get to her.

Taking a step closer, he leaned his face close enough for her to feel the warmth of his breath on her cheeks.

'Bad idea,' he warned.

Ignoring the flutter of her pulse, Jo stiffened her spine. Since childhood she'd had a code she lived by; one she still found hard to break, even for the tiny handful of people she allowed to occupy an equally tiny corner of her heart. Show any sign of weakness and it was the beginning of the end. The masks she wore were the reason she had survived a time in her life when she was invisible. At the beginning of her career they gave the impression professional criticism never stung. So while her heart thudded erratically, she donned a mask of Zen-like calm. 'Am I supposed to be intimidated by that?'

He smiled dangerously in reply. 'Keep challenging me and this is going to get real interesting, real quick.'

'Seriously, you're hilarious. I never knew that about you.' Raising a hand, she patted him in the centre of his broad chest. 'Now be a good boy and treat yourself to an early night. Can't have those good looks fading, now, can we?'

She flattened her palm and pushed him back to make enough room to open the door. 'What would we use to fool members of the opposite sex into thinking we're a catch if we had to rely on our personality?'

'You tell me.'

Moving her hand from his chest, she wrapped her fingers around a muscled upper arm and encouraged him to step through the door with another push. When he was standing in the hall and looking at her with a hint of a smile on his face, she leaned her shoulder against the door frame and angled her chin. Her eyes narrowed. It felt as if he knew something she didn't.

She *hated* when he did that.

'Admit it: you missed this.'

Lifting her gaze upwards, she studied the air and took a deep breath. 'Nope, can't say I did.'

'Without me around there's no one to set you straight when you need it.'

'You say that as if you know me well enough to know what I need.' She shook her head. 'You don't know me, Daniel. You're afraid to get to know me.'

'Really,' he said dryly.

'Yes, really, because if you did you might have to admit you were wrong about me and we both know you don't like to admit you're wrong about anything.' She glanced up and down the hall as if searching for eavesdroppers before lowering her voice. 'Worse still, you might discover you *like* me. And we can't have that, can we?'

Rocking forward, he lowered his voice to the same level. 'I don't think there's any danger of that.'

Jo searched his too-blue eyes, suddenly questioning if he even remembered how the war between them began. Looking back, she realized she didn't; what was it that made him so much more difficult to get along with than every other member of his family? Everyone got to a point where they started to try and make sense of their life. She was at peace with a lot of the things she couldn't change. But since Daniel was the only person she'd ever been immature around in her entire life, she couldn't help but wonder why. Apparently he wasn't the only one in need of a good night's rest.

She rolled her eyes at the momentary weakness. 'Whatever you tell yourself to help you sleep at night.'

'I sleep just fine,' he said tightly. 'You don't need to worry about me.'

'I wasn't—'

'Just do us both a favour and stay out of my business. If you don't, I might start poking my nose into yours.'

'I have nothing to hide,' she lied. 'Do you?'

'Don't push me, babe.'

She managed to stop the words *or what?* leaving her lips, but it wasn't solely the need to strive for maturity. There was something else going on; she could *feel* it. It was more than the chill in his gaze, more than the rigid set of his shoulders or the unmistakable edge of warning in his deep voice. What *was* it?

As if he could read the question in her eyes, Daniel frowned and turned his profile to her. A muscle tensed on his jaw, suggesting he was grinding his teeth together. But even if she had the right to ask what was wrong, before she had the chance, he turned away. When she ended up staring at his door again, she blinked and shook her head.

Well, Day One had been great.

She couldn't *wait* for Day Two.

CHAPTER TWO

'Is it just me or does coffee taste better when they make those little love hearts in the foam? It's funny the things that can make a difference in how we feel.'

JORJA DAWSON had breasts. Considering he was a man and she was a woman, part of Daniel's brain had to have always known that. Fortunately, in the past, they had never been pressed against his chest in a way that made them difficult to ignore.

It was the kind of intel he could have done without.

Judging by the way the tips of those breasts were beaded against the material of her tight-fitting top before she hid them beneath folded arms, the spark of sexual awareness had been mutual. She should just be thankful he had an honourable streak. If she ever found out he'd been as aware of her as she was of him, she would have a brand-new weapon at her disposal. One that, were she foolish enough to use it, would leave him no choice but to launch a counterattack with heavy artillery until she offered her unconditional surrender.

In terms of fallout, it would be similar to pulling the pin on a grenade he couldn't toss to a safe distance.

Number two on his list: *sister's best friend.*

Since every guy on the planet who didn't have long-term plans knew to avoid that minefield, it wouldn't matter if she wore nothing but lacy underwear to go with the shoes he would have been happy for her to wear to bed. She could have pole-danced for him and he would still resist the urge to kiss her.

'Whatever you tell yourself to help you sleep at night.'

When the echoed words led directly to the memory of the unspoken questions in her eyes, he pushed his body harder in the last block of a five mile run. She'd hit a nerve but there was no way she could know he wasn't sleeping. Or that he was sick of waking up bathed in a cold sweat, his throat raw from yelling. It had to stop before he did something stupid in work again or was forced to look for another apartment. He would damn well *make* it stop.

But distracting himself from the problem with thoughts of Jorja Dawson's breasts wasn't the way to go about it.

Slowing his pace to a walk, he shouldered his way into a busy coffee shop and pushed back the hood on his sweat-shirt. After placing his order, he looked around while he waited for it to arrive, his gaze discovering a woman sitting alone by the windows. It was exactly what he needed: *another woman*.

Questioning if he was forming a fetish, he started his assessment with her shoes—a pair of simple black patent heels with open toes—before he moved up the legs crossed elegantly beneath the table to a fitted skirt that hugged her like a second skin. *Nice.* Continuing upwards, he was rewarded with a glimpse of curved breast between the lapels of a crisp white blouse as she turned in her seat. Then his gaze took in the smooth twist of dark hair at the nape of her neck in the kind of up-do that begged to be unpinned so she could shake her hair loose. She was even wearing a pair of small, rectangular-framed reading glasses to complete the fantasy.

But when she turned again, he shook his head. Used to be a time he was better at sensing the presence of the enemy.

She looked up at him when he stopped for a paper napkin at the condiment station beside her. 'Are you kidding me?'

'I can't buy a cup of coffee now?'

'You can buy it somewhere else.'

'This is the closest coffee shop.'

'You can have the one two blocks down. This one is mine.' She returned her attention to her computer screen. 'It's my work space every Monday, Wednesday and Friday morning.'

'I must have missed the notice on the door,' Daniel said as he pulled out the chair facing her and sat down. He smirked when she scowled at him. 'Good morning.'

After an attempt to continue what she was doing while he looked through the window at the steady build of people headed to their offices, she sighed. 'You're going to be here every Monday, Wednesday and Friday, aren't you?'

'Not a morning person, I take it.'

'This is your plan?' She arched a brow when he looked at her. 'You're going to be there every time I turn around until you wear me down and I move? Wow…that's…'

'Effective?'

'I was going to say adolescent. I can't tell you how reassuring it is to know the city is in the hands of such a mature example of the New York Police Department.'

When her fingers began to move across the keyboard again, Daniel realized he didn't have the faintest idea what she did for a living. He wondered why. Hadn't needed to know was the simple answer. Though it did kind of beg the question of why it was he needed to know *now*.

Know your enemy and know yourself and you could fight a hundred battles, as the saying went. With that in mind he took a short breath. 'So what is it you do anyway?'

She didn't look up from the screen. 'It's the first time you've been tempted to ask that question?'

'I don't have a newspaper to pass the time.'

'They're on a stand by the door.'

'It's an internet thing, isn't it?'

Long lashes lifted behind her glasses. 'Meaning?'

'You're one of those people who reports their every move every five minutes so the universe can know how much time they spend doing laundry.'

'Yes, that's the only thing people use the internet for these days.' She reached for her coffee. 'It's because working on-line isn't a physical job, right? Anyone who isn't lifting heavy objects or doing something with their hands instantly earns a low ranking on your Neanderthal scale of the survival of the fittest.'

'You might want to slow down on the caffeine intake. I think you're close to the legal limit already.'

Setting the cup down, she breathed deep and went back to work. 'I write a blog.'

'You can earn a living doing that?'

'Among other things,' she replied.

'What's it about?'

'Don't you have somewhere you need to be?'

'Nope.'

'Fine, then. I can play the "get to know me better" game until you get bored and leave. It shouldn't take long with your attention span.' Lifting her coffee again, she leaned back in her chair and looked him straight in the eye. 'I work for a fashion magazine and as part of my job I write a daily blog on the latest trends and the kind of things twenty-something women might find interesting.'

'You're as deep as a shallow puddle, aren't you?'

'Not everything is about the meaning of life. Sometimes it's more about living it. For some people that means finding joy in the little things.'

'Like spending money on the kind of clothes that will put them in debt?'

'Like wearing things that make them feel good.' She

shrugged a narrow shoulder. 'I assume it's how someone like you feels when they wear their uniform of choice.'

'I don't wear a uniform as a fashion statement.'

'You're saying you don't feel good when you wear it?'

'It's a matter of pride in what I do.'

'And doesn't that make you feel good about yourself?'

She was smart, but *that* he'd known. Trouble was she wasn't entirely right. 'It's not as simple as that.'

When her head tilted at an obviously curious angle, he lounged back in his chair. Since she'd given him the opening with the topic of conversation, he openly checked her out. 'I take it the librarian look is in vogue now.'

'It's better than the mugger ensemble you're wearing.'

Lowering his chin, he ran a large palm over the faded U.S.M.C. lettering on his chest. 'I've had this since basic training. It has sentimental value.'

'Wouldn't that suggest you have a heart?'

'Bit difficult to walk around without one.'

'As difficult as it is to survive without sleep?'

Daniel stared at her without blinking.

'Thin walls…' she said in a soft tone that smacked too much of sympathy for his liking before she shrugged. 'Try falling asleep without the television on, you might get more benefit from the traditional eight hours—especially if you're watching something with that much yelling in it. What was it—horror flick of the week?'

'You're worried about me again? That's sweet.' Feeling sick to his stomach at how close he'd been to humiliation, he got to his feet. 'Now I know you spend your nights with a glass pressed to the wall I'll try and find something on the nature channel with whale song in it.' When his trip to the door was halted by the brush of cool fingers against his hand, he looked down at her. 'What?'

Dropping her arm, she avoided his gaze and shook her head. 'Forget it.'

'You got something to say, spit it out.' He checked his watch. 'I have an appointment with my boss in an hour.'

The statement lifted her chin again. 'Because of what happened yesterday?'

'Hardly the first time I've had my ass hauled across the coals for breaking the rules.'

'You saved a man's life.' She shrugged her shoulders and looked away. 'I'm sure that counts for something.'

She was reassuring him?

'Not that you don't deserve it for doing something so asinine,' she added. 'You could have placed other members of your team in danger.'

That was more like it. It was also pretty much exactly what he expected to have yelled at him in an hour. 'We all do what we gotta do when the situation calls for it.' He lowered his voice. 'You should know that better than most.'

She looked up at him from the corner of her eye. 'And there you go thinking you know me again.'

'Did it ever occur to you that you don't make it easy for people to do that?'

'People who want to make an effort.'

'And how many tests do they have to pass before you talk to them like they have an IQ higher than a rock?'

'Stupid is as stupid does,' she replied with a smile.

'I take it back. If you're quoting *Forrest Gump* at me you obviously need more caffeine.' He placed an apologetic look on his face. 'I'd get you some before I leave but I'm not allowed to buy coffee here.'

'You're the most irritating person I've ever met.'

'See you later, babe.'

'Not if I see you first.'

'Still rusty.' He shook his head. 'Keep practising.'

* * *

'How's the challenge coming along?'

'Hmm?' Jo blinked at her erstwhile roomie, a second night of interrupted sleep catching up with her.

He must have moved his bed after the conversation in the coffee shop. The yelling had been further away but, like the first time, when it came it was torture. She doubted anyone could hear a human being in that much pain and not feel the effect of it emotionally.

'The challenge the magazine gave you?' Jess prompted. 'The one where you wear outfits from the centre pages to discover if different images change how people see you? I'm assuming that's why you look like a French onion seller today. Not that the beret doesn't work for you.'

Yes, she liked the beret. It was the kind of thing she'd have chosen herself, especially when it had a little touch of France to it. But since she wasn't supposed to wear anything the magazine hadn't chosen for her...

Lowering her chin, she idly rearranged the crumbs on her plate with the prongs of her fork. Wasn't as if he would tell her what had caused the nightmare if she asked him, was it? That part of not pushing the subject she got. Where it began to get weird started with the fact she hadn't felt the need to talk it through with his sister. His family cared about him. If he was struggling with something that happened when he was overseas they would want to help in any way possible. Not that he would make it easy. Trouble was she couldn't forget how the colour drained from his face when he'd thought she knew.

It felt as if the man she had known and disliked so much hadn't come home and someone new had taken his place. Someone she could empathize with and wanted to get to know better.

It was just plain *weird*.

'Earth to Jo...'

'It's going fine,' she replied as she speared another piece

of cake with her fork and popped it into her mouth. 'Mmm, this one…'

When she risked a brief glance across the table at the only person who knew when she was hiding something, Jo was relieved to find amusement sparkling in Liv's eyes.

'You said that about the last two.'

Jo angled her head. 'Remind me again why we're doing this with you instead of Blake?'

'Because he's more interested in the honeymoon than the cake we have at our reception.'

Fair enough. She reached for a second sample of chocolate cake. 'I lied, it's still this one.'

'You know chocolate is a substitute for sex,' Jess commented. 'It's an endorphins thing.'

'It's more than that,' Jo replied. 'You never have to worry if chocolate will call…it never stands you up…and it doesn't mind keeping you company during a rom-com on a Friday night.' She sighed contentedly as she reached for another sample. 'Chocolate is *better* than sex.'

Jess snorted. 'The hell it is.'

'She's young.' Liv nodded sagely. 'She'll learn.'

'If she tried having it occasionally she'd learn a lot quicker.'

'She scares them off.'

Jo waggled her fork in the air. *'Still in the room…'*

It wasn't her fault guys found her intimidating. With the kind of life experience that went beyond her twenty-four years, she was self-sufficient and hard-working with her focus fixed firmly on her career. If there was overtime available, she took it. Holidays people with family commitments didn't want to work, she volunteered. But regardless of her career, she was also very open about the fact she wasn't interested in getting involved, even if she wasn't prepared to explain why. Put everything together it was difficult for guys to envisage her needing them for more than one thing.

Though in fairness there were plenty of them who wouldn't see that as a problem.

There was a short debate on the merits of vanilla cream before Jess asked, 'How's our new neighbour?'

'In order to be "our" new neighbour wouldn't you need to be there more than once a week?' Jo smiled sweetly.

'You need reinforcements, you just have to yell.'

'You *like* Daniel.'

'Everyone but you likes Danny.' Jess shrugged. 'He is what he is and doesn't make any excuses for it. There's a lot to be said for that.'

'There's nothing hidden with him,' Liv agreed. 'When we were kids his bluntness got him into trouble, but honestly? We all kind of relied on it.'

Jo was beginning to wonder if anyone knew Daniel as well as they thought they did but she didn't say so out loud. She couldn't. Not without telling them there were *some* things he kept hidden.

'You could try taking the high road,' Jess suggested.

'I get nosebleeds.' Jo frowned.

The chocolate cake was gone and how had they got from the subject of her sex life to Daniel in the space of two minutes anyway? Apart from spending time with the friends it felt as if she hadn't seen much of lately, part of the appeal of the cake tasting had been the opportunity to take a break from him.

'You make a decision on the cake yet?' she asked.

'I'm swaying towards different layers of these three.' Liv pointed her fork at the emptiest plates.

'What's next on the list?'

'Flowers.'

The conversation swayed back towards wedding plans as they left the bakery and made their way past the public library to the nearest subway station. Jess glanced at the steps in front of the large Grecian columns where several men in helmets and bulletproof vests were gathered around one of the stone lions.

'Isn't that Danny?'

Oh, *come on.*

Reluctantly—as Olivia and Jess headed towards him and she lagged a step behind—Jo had to admit the uniform was sexy in a badass/mess-with-me-and-die kind of way. But then she'd always known Daniel had an edge to him. While he could attract women with a smile, he could make grown men cower with just a look. She had seen that look once. When was it? Tyler's thirtieth, which his younger brother deigned to make an appearance at? Yes, she thought that was it. A giant with a brain the size of a pea was foolish enough to manhandle his girlfriend within Daniel's line of sight. All it had taken was that *look* and a quietly spoken *'show the lady some respect'* and he'd backed down with a string of mumbled apologies. When it was over Daniel had simply continued what he was doing as if nothing had happened.

Jo wondered why it had taken seeing him in uniform for her to remember she'd been impressed by that.

'Ladies.' He nodded once in greeting.

Gathering herself together, she stepped forward and gave the answer everyone expected. 'Officer Moron.'

'Really?' he questioned with a deadpan expression. 'When I'm holding a gun?'

'What can I say?' She shrugged. 'Guess I must like living on the edge.'

While she cocked her head in challenge, he shot a brief downward glance at what she was wearing. It lasted less than a heartbeat, was immediately followed by a cursory blink and then his intense gaze locked with hers, leaving her feeling suddenly…exposed. Whether it was because she'd never noticed him looking at her before or because she was more aware of when he did, she didn't know. But neither option sat well with her. Particularly when she suspected the momentary sense of vulnerability she'd experienced stemmed from the sensation he knew she was remembering things she'd chosen to forget.

Jess chuckled at the interaction. 'Hey, Danny.'

He turned on the charm with the flick of an invisible switch. 'Hey, gorgeous.'

Jo inwardly rolled her eyes at her friend's reaction to his infamous smile before allowing her gaze to roam over the crowd. If she focused on something else, with any luck, she could try and pretend he wasn't there. All she needed was something to take her mind off—

Her stomach dropped to the soles of her strappy heels. 'I've got to go.'

'I thought we were going to look at flowers?'

Looking into Liv's eyes, she used the tone that translated into a hidden message. 'I'll call you later.'

'Okay.'

She didn't look at Daniel as she left, but Jo could sense his gaze on her as she merged into the crowd. How it made her feel helped explain the secret she kept from his sister. Only someone with a shadowy secret of their own could understand what it meant to bring it into the cold light of day. Gaze fixed on the figure she could see moving into the park, she shut down emotionally in preparation.

It was the only way she could deal with it.

The dream began a handful of hours before dawn. New faces—a different scenario—but the outcome was always the same. As he jerked back into reality, pulse racing and heart pounding, Daniel wondered why he was surprised at the latest additions. There was nothing the damn thing loved more than new material.

At times he swore he could hear scaly little demon hands being rubbed together with glee.

Grabbing the sweatpants on the end of his rack, he hauled

them on and swore when he stubbed his toe on a box on his way to the kitchen. As he reached for a light switch he froze. The second he yanked open the door to the hall she jumped and dropped her keys.

'Damn it, Daniel!' Jo exclaimed.

Leaning a shoulder against the door frame, he folded his arms across his chest. 'Late night or early start?'

It was a question that didn't require an answer; the outfit she had been wearing outside the library said it all. With considerable effort, he dragged his gaze away from the perfect rear poured into tight black trousers that ended halfway down her calves.

'Who made you the hall monitor?' Keys in hand, she stood up tall and turned to face him.

'I'm a light sleeper.'

A brief frown crossed her face before her gaze landed squarely in the centre of his naked chest. The former should have bugged him more than the latter, especially when it was dangerously close to the kind of look that had forced him to move apartments over the years. Instead he was more bothered by the jolt of electricity travelling through his body from the point of impact. The fact she continued staring didn't help. If anything it aided the flow of blood that rushed to his groin in response.

'Isn't it usually the guy who sneaks home after the deed is done?' he asked as if bringing up the subject of her sex life again would distract his misbehaving body. When her gaze lifted sharply, he changed the subject. 'Didn't occur to you that having a cop for a neighbour might involve him greeting you with his service weapon if he hears you creeping around in the dark?'

'The lights are on,' she argued.

'It's the middle of the night.'

'I don't have to answer to you.'

'Do you have any idea how much paperwork I'll have to fill out if I accidentally shoot you?'

She arched a brow. *'Accidentally?'*

'That's what I'll call it.'

A lump appeared in her cheek as her gaze searched the air. 'That's twice in twenty-four hours you've threatened to shoot me. I wonder if that's enough for a restraining order. Remind me to ask your sister.'

'He tossed you out of his apartment, didn't he?'

'What is it with this sudden obsession with my sex life?' She looked into his eyes. 'If I didn't know any better I might think it's been a while for you.'

Longer than he cared to admit, but it wasn't as if he could share a bed with a woman for long. He could guarantee his complete and undivided attention while he was there; took a great deal of pride in that fact. But when it came to leaving them satisfied, there was just as much emphasis on the word *leaving*. Preferably before he was dumb enough to fall asleep and risk making a fool of himself.

'Worried I might be lonely, babe?'

She scowled. 'Don't call me babe.'

'If the shoe fits…'

'You know by saying that you're saying you think—?'

'You don't have to like someone to think they're hot.'

'I… You…' When her mouth formed words that didn't appear she clamped it shut, took a short breath through her nose and snapped, 'What are you doing?'

Damned if he knew but the fact it had flustered her worked for him. 'Isn't he a little old for you?'

Something unreadable crossed her eyes before she blinked and lifted her chin. 'Who are we talking about?'

'The guy you were with in Bryant Park.'

'What guy?'

Nice try, but Daniel had never been known to give up that

easily. 'The one you argued with before you dragged him into the subway station.'

'You were spying on me?'

'You think when I'm dressed like that I'm supposed to ignore what's happening around me?'

She sighed heavily and turned away. 'I don't have the energy for this.'

'It's Wednesday. We'll pick it up in the coffee shop.'

'No, we won't.'

As her door opened he saw her shoulders slump as if she'd been putting considerable effort into disguising how exhausted she was and the proximity to home allowed her to relax. Most folks were the same at the end of a long day but Daniel knew it was more than that. If he hadn't, he would have got it when she glanced over her shoulder.

Long lashes lifted and for a split second what he could see in her eyes made him frown. He recognized it because he'd seen it in the eyes of men in combat and guys who'd been on the job as a cop for too long. Given no other choice he might have admitted he had been avoiding looking for it in his own eyes in the mirror of late.

If a person's eyes were really the windows to the soul, part of hers was close to giving up the fight.

He took a step forward before he realized he was doing it, compelled by the need to say something, but unable to find the words. With the men he had worked with they were never needed. There was a silent understanding, an empathy born from shared experiences. A nod of acknowledgement could say as much as a hundred words. Cracking jokes or discussing something inane was more welcome. But someone as full of life as Jo shouldn't—

When her door closed with a low click, Daniel made a snap decision. It wasn't as if he had much choice. If she was in trouble and his family knew he hadn't done something, they would make the roasting he got from his captain look like a weekend barbecue. Taking a long breath, he stepped back and closed the door. In order to prepare for battle he was going to need a few more hours of—hopefully uninterrupted—sleep.

Come daylight he was venturing into enemy territory.

CHAPTER THREE

'We all know a new outfit can lift our spirits. But how often do we look at the person wearing one and wonder if it's a hint of something bigger happening inside?'

'COME on, Jack, pick up.'

Jo rubbed her fingertips across her forehead to ease the first indications of a massive headache. Touching the screen to turn the phone off, she set it down on the table beside her computer. She was going to have to go over there. It was the only way she could be certain where he was.

Sighing heavily, she reached for her coffee cup only to frown at how light it was. If she was going to get a day's work done in half the time she was going to need a constant supply of caffeine.

'That his name, is it?'

The sound of a familiar deep voice snapped her gaze to another coffee cup being held out towards her. She blinked at the large hand holding it. 'Eavesdrop much?'

'Let's call it an occupational hazard.' Daniel rocked his hand a little. 'You want this or not?'

Her gaze lifted, lingering for a moment on his chest when she remembered what it had looked like naked: taut tanned skin over muscle and a six-pack to make a girl drool. Frowning at the memory, she moved further up until she was looking into too-blue eyes and asked, 'Why are you buying me coffee?'

'You looked like you could do with it,' he replied.

'You don't even know how I take it.'

'Since you're a regular, I surmised the guy behind the counter would. Turns out I was right.'

Jo's gaze lowered to the temptation as she weighed up the risk involved with accepting it. Not that he would wait for an invitation to join her, but apart from the fact she wasn't in the mood to get into a verbal sparring match with him—

'Your loss.' He shrugged. Setting it down on the opposite side of the table, he pulled out the empty chair and sat down.

'There are other tables in here, you know.'

Daniel didn't say anything, his steady gaze fixed on hers as he took the lid off his cup.

'We're not picking up where we left off last night, if that's what you're thinking,' she said.

'Technically it was this morning.'

'I've stayed out of your business.'

'Glad to hear it.'

'How about you return the favour and stay out of mine?' She smiled sweetly, determined not to look at the abandoned coffee on the table in front of him.

Daniel brought his cup to his face and took a deep breath. 'Nothing quite like a cup of Joe to kick-start the morning...'

While her eyes narrowed at the innuendo, he lifted his other arm and tapped the lid of the abandoned coffee cup with a long forefinger. 'Sure you don't want this? Seems a shame for it to go to waste...'

'What do you want?'

'Suspicious, aren't we?'

'I've met you.'

'And still not a morning person.' He inclined his head towards the cup. 'Another shot of caffeine might help.'

Jo fought the need to growl. She wanted that coffee so

badly she could taste it on her tongue. Despite her strong-willed determination to stop it happening, her gaze lowered to watch the tip of his forefinger trace an almost absent-minded circle around the edge of the plastic lid. It was one of the most sensual things she had ever seen, adding a new dimension to the temptation, which had nothing to do with caffeine. For a moment her imagination even wondered what the movement would feel like against her skin…

Reaching out, she waggled her fingers. 'Give.'

His hand moved, fingers curling around the cup to draw it back towards him. 'How much trouble are you in?'

Her gaze snapped up again. 'What?'

'Answer the question.'

'Why would you even care if I was in trouble?' She arched a brow. 'I'd have thought the idea of my body lying in an alley somewhere would have made your day.'

'Is there a chance that might happen?'

'Not like it would be the first time.'

'That's not funny.'

'No, but I have dozens of jokes from that period of my life if you need them.' Angling her chin, she pulled one at random from the air. 'You know the best part about dating a homeless chick? You can drop her off wherever you want.'

Daniel didn't laugh. 'Do you owe him money?'

'Owe who money?'

'Jack.'

'No.'

'Then what's going on?'

A short burst of laughter left her lips. 'I'm supposed to confide in you because you bought me a cup of coffee?'

'If you're in some kind of trouble, tell me now and—'

'You'll help?' The words came out more sharply than she intended and, when they did, she felt a need to soften them by adding, 'You can't, and even if you could you'd be the last person I'd go to for help.'

Great, now he was never going to leave it alone.

She might as well have dangled a scented cloth under the nose of a bloodhound.

'I'm aware of that,' he said flatly.

'Then why are you doing this?'

When she thought about it, she realized it was simply what he did. All she was to him was another citizen of the city of New York. One he probably felt pressured to help because of her connection to his family. She shook her head. She didn't need this, least of all from him.

'Tell me what's going on.'

The tone of his deep voice inflicted more damage than anything he'd said or done in five and a half years to get to her and she hated him for it. Mostly because the rough rumble was accompanied by a softening of the blue in his eyes, which made it feel as if he understood. As always when there was the slightest danger someone might see through one of her masks, Jo fought fire with fire. 'I'll tell you what's going on when you tell me why it is you can't sleep.'

To his credit he disguised his reaction better than he had before. But the second the softer hue of his eyes became an ice-cold blue, Jo regretted what she'd said. She shouldn't have thrown it in his face. Not to get at him. It was *low*.

'What makes you think I'm not sleeping?'

Jo wavered on an indecisive tightrope between familiar ground and freefalling into the unknown. 'You were awake in the middle of the night. And you still look tired.'

'I work shifts. And it's not always easy to adjust,' he replied without missing a beat. Stretching a long arm across the table, he set the coffee beside her computer. *'Your turn.'*

It would have been if he'd told her the truth.

'You've been a cop for, what, eight years now?'

'More or less.' He nodded. 'And can have your every move reported back to me if I have to. Your point?'

'How long does it take to adjust?'

'I was overseas seven months. I've been back one.'

'What happened when you were over there?'

'We got shot at.' Lifting his cup to his mouth, he took a drink without breaking eye contact. 'Avoid the subject all you want, but we both know if I want to find out what you're hiding I can do it without your co-operation. I'll start with Liv.'

It was an empty threat. Jo reached for the coffee he had given her. 'Your sister won't tell you anything.'

'Meaning she knows what it is.'

'Meaning she wouldn't betray a confidence.'

A corner of his mouth tugged upwards. 'You know my family. They'll organize an intervention if they think something is wrong. If you've never been on the receiving end of one I can tell you they're a barrel of laughs. Nothing beats a little quality family time when it's five against one. And I did say I'd *start* with Liv…'

'What makes you think you're not the only one who doesn't know?' she asked.

'If I am you've just made it easier for me.'

The message blood was thicker than water was clear. But she wasn't so far removed they wouldn't rally to her aid if she needed help. Jo had known that for years. They were all cut from a cloth threaded with loyalty, honour, integrity and at least a dozen other positive attributes she'd had absolutely no experience of in a family until she met the Brannigans. To Jo, they were everything a family should be. It was part of the reason she'd never understood why Daniel didn't appreciate them more. But the comment he made about family interventions explained a lot. It was an insight into why he was fighting his demons alone.

She lifted the coffee cup to her lips. 'When you speak to them you should mention the problems you're having adjusting to shift patterns. Your brothers might be able to offer some words of advice.'

'Maybe you should just tell me what's going on before this starts to get ugly,' he smirked in reply.

'We could do this all day.'

'Next round's on you. I take mine black.'

She sighed. 'You're not going to back down, are you?'

'Not my thing.'

'Which brings us back to why you need to know. Correct me if I'm wrong, but I don't think you've answered that yet.'

When he didn't reply, she set her coffee down and went back to work, answering some of the comments on her blog while he reached across to the next table and lifted an abandoned newspaper. They sat in silence for a while until Jo could feel a tingle along the back of her neck. Without lifting her chin, she looked up from beneath her fringe to discover him studying her intently. 'What?'

'Were the glasses a fashion accessory?'

She focused on the screen again. 'I get headaches if I work at the computer for too long.'

'So where are they?'

'I left them in the apartment.'

'Other things on your mind…' he surmised.

'I can make the print bigger on the screen if you're so concerned about my eyesight.'

There was another moment of silence, then 'Just out of curiosity, what look is it you're aiming for today?'

'It's called Gothic chic.'

At least that was what the magazine had called it. Of all the outfits she had worn during the challenge it was the most outlandish. But since she'd awoken with a need to face the world with a little more bravado and it was the kind of outfit that required confidence to carry it off…

'Might want to remember vampires aren't supposed to walk in direct sunlight before you step outside,' he said.

'Are you going to tell me to avoid holy water, garlic and crosses too?'

He nodded. 'And teenage cheerleaders with wooden stakes...'

Turning in her chair, Jo stretched her legs and pouted. 'You don't like the boots?' she asked as she looked at him. 'They're my favourite part.'

Daniel leaned to the side to examine them, a small frown appearing between his brows. 'You can walk in those things?'

'Women don't wear boots like these for comfort.'

Bending forward, she reached down and ran her hands over the shining leather, tucking her thumbs under the edge at her thigh and tugging as she lifted her foot off the ground. Her hair fell over her shoulder as she turned her head and smiled the kind of small, meaningful smile she'd never aimed at him before. 'Didn't we talk about how people wear things because of the way they make them feel?'

The glint of danger in his eyes was obviously intended to make her stop what she was doing before she was any deeper in trouble. *Foolish man.* He really didn't know her at all.

Daniel gritted his teeth together as she repeated the motion with her hands on her other leg and tossed her hair over her shoulder as she sat up. When she smiled across the room, his gaze followed her line of vision to the barista who was smiling back at her.

The one who had known how she took her coffee.

The second his gaze shifted, Daniel glared at him. But the guy who immediately went scurrying back to his coffee beans wasn't the source of his annoyance. Neither was the fact his plan to purposefully avoid looking at her feet as he approached the table had backfired on him, though, with hindsight, forewarned might have been forearmed. What got to him was how well her diversionary tactic had worked.

There wasn't a male cell in his body that hadn't reacted to those boots and the strip of bare skin below another sinful short skirt. He had spent every moment since he'd sat down with her consciously stopping himself from looking at the straining buttons on her black blouse and once again she'd got him with footwear. But if she thought it would distract him from his target for long, she was mistaken.

He was a Marine, for crying out loud; the phrase 'courage under fire' was as good as tattooed on his ass.

Watching with hooded eyes, he saw her slide her computer to one side before resting her elbow on the table. Setting her chin in her palm, she leaned forward, feigned innocence with a flutter of long lashes and asked, 'Something wrong?'

'You done?' he questioned dryly.

'Done with what?' Amusement danced in her eyes. 'You might need to elaborate.'

If he didn't know what she was doing, he might have been tempted to play along. But if he did, Daniel knew what would happen. He would play to win.

'Tell me what's going on.'

When she rolled her eyes, he set his forearms on the table and leaned closer, his gaze locked on hers while he waited. Up close she did have pretty spectacular eyes. A little large for her face maybe, but they were so deep a brown it was difficult to tell where the irises began.

He'd never noticed that before.

After studying him for a long moment, she lowered her voice. 'What if I told you it was private?'

'I'd tell you I won't share it with anyone else,' he replied in the same low tone.

'Why should I believe you?'

'A man is nothing without his word.'

'Tell me why you need to know.'

He wondered when she thought he'd handed over control of the negotiation. Dragging his gaze from mesmerizing eyes, he considered what to tell her. She was right; they could do this all day. Until one of them bent a little nothing would ever change. Of course knowing that meant he had to ask himself if he *wanted* their relationship to change. But since it felt as if it already was…

'I recognized what I saw in your eyes before you closed the door this morning.' He looked into them again as he spoke. 'I've seen it before.'

'What did you see?' she asked in a whisper, forcing him to lean closer to hear her.

'Resignation.'

She stared at him and then blinked as if trying to bring him into focus. 'If you knew me as well as you like to think you do, you'd know…'

'I'd know?' he prompted as she frowned.

'Why I don't want to talk about it.' Dropping her palm from her chin, she leaned back and swiped a strand of hair behind her ear. 'People keep secrets for a reason.'

When she reached for her computer, Daniel felt the lost opportunity as keenly as he sensed she wasn't just talking about herself. But if she knew the reason he wasn't sleeping, why hadn't she pushed the advantage? Lifting his coffee cup, he looked out of the window and questioned what he would have done if their places had been switched. The exact same thing was the honest answer. It was what he was doing already. He knew there was something wrong and was giving her an opportunity to tell him. In turn, she was refusing to open up.

Number four on his list: *nothing in common.*

So much for that one…

'You want another coffee?' she asked.

He looked at her cup from the corner of his eye. 'What did you do, inhale it?'

'Figured if you were planning on digging in, I may as well top up on supplies.'

Since sitting still for any amount of time inevitably led to reminders of his sleep deprivation, Daniel shook his head.

'Think I'll head down to the station and look through mug-shots for Jack before my shift starts.'

Jo sighed heavily as he stood up. 'Dig all you want. I'm telling you now there's only one way you'll find out and that avenue isn't and never will be open to you.'

'And there you go challenging me again…'

Taking a step forward, he set his coffee cup hand on the table by her computer and the other on the back of her chair. As her chin lifted he leaned down, smiling the same kind of small, meaningful smile she'd aimed at him when she'd pulled her little stunt with the boots.

'When I want something, nothing gets in my way,' he told her in a deliberately low, intimate tone. 'Make it difficult for me, I'll want it more and work twice as hard to get it. So feel free to keep doing what you're doing, but don't say you weren't warned.'

When her eyes widened he leaned back, lifted his hands and turned away. She could interpret his words any way she liked. If she came to the conclusion he was talking about more than the secret she was keeping, he wasn't certain she'd be wrong.

Gothic chic was either going to be the death of her or get her arrested. For starters, her feet were killing her, but if she'd known she would end up walking the length and breadth of her old neighbourhood looking for Jack she would have changed. When it came to getting arrested, she might be grateful. Even if the charge was related to standing still for too long on a street corner as she tried to get her bearings, she could take comfort from the knowledge she was safe in the back of a squad car. When she looked over her shoulder and thought she could see someone moving in the shadows, her pace quickened.

If Daniel saw where she was, she could imagine the lecture she'd get on personal safety. There hadn't been a single set of flashing lights she hadn't looked at twice or an echoing siren that hadn't turned her head. Every time it happened she would find herself thinking of him and what he'd said before he left the coffee shop.

He couldn't possibly have meant what she thought he meant. But what was worse was her reaction. Instead of being outraged or angry or laughing in his face, she had been turned on, *big time*. Her breath had caught, her pulse had skipped, and her breasts had ached. She'd even had to press her thighs together. No man had ever had such an immediate erotic effect on her.

That it was *him*?

A shiver ran down her spine, forcing her to look over her shoulder again. Ridiculously she wished he were there, but in her defence she was starting to get seriously creeped out. The presence of a six-foot-two police officer could have made her feel better, even if they argued every step of the way.

Taking a breath, she shook off her paranoia. She could take care of herself. Harsh truth was, until Liv, the only person she had ever been able to depend on was herself.

Tugging the edges of her long black coat together in an attempt to hide what she was wearing, she stopped and looked up at the neon sign before opening the door. If Jack wasn't in there she swore he was on his own this time.

'Well, *hello, gorgeous*! You want to come over here and—'

Jo glared at the man who stepped in front of her. 'I have pepper spray and I'm not afraid to use it.'

She didn't, but he didn't know that.

'Mikey, leave the lady alone,' a voice called from behind the long wooden bar. 'She's *way* out of your league.'

She smiled when she got there. 'Hey, Ben.'

'Hey, Jo,' he beamed in reply. 'How's my best girl?'

'She's good. He here?'

Ben nodded. 'Back room.'

'He run up a tab?'

'Made a deal with you, didn't we?'

'Thanks, Ben.'

Jo made her way through the crowd, regretting how much time it had taken to get through her work so she could begin the search. If she'd got away earlier, not only would it not be dark outside, it wouldn't have got to the point where she had to attempt to carry Jack home. She sighed heavily.

Ahead of her was the inevitable debate about whether or not it was time to leave. She knew exactly what he would say, the excuses he would make, how many random strangers she would have to be polite to while she gritted her teeth. It was a scenario she'd experienced countless times.

No matter how far she managed to get from her past, she could always rely on Jack to remind her of her roots.

The thought of Daniel being able to do the same thing…

She rolled her eyes. *Enough with the thinking about him, already!* It was getting to the point where it felt as if he were with her wherever she went.

Daniel leaned back against the wall and frowned. Any guilt he might have felt about tailing her had disappeared within five minutes of arriving at her destination.

What the hell had she got herself into?

Judging by the number of times she did a double take at passing police vehicles or lifted her chin when she heard a siren, it wasn't anything good. He waited to see if she spent the same two minutes in the eighth bar as she had in the other seven. When she hadn't reappeared after twenty minutes he was contemplating crossing the street. Then the doors opened.

The man staggered back a step as she helped him get his arm into the sleeve of his coat. He had obviously been in the bar for a lot longer than she had. Placing his arm across her shoulders, she wrapped one of hers around his waist before steering him along the sidewalk.

What was she doing with a guy like that? Apart from the fact he was twice her age, she shouldn't be with someone she had to go searching for in bars. Daniel was disproportionately disappointed in her considering their relationship. He might have made several digs about her sex life, but a woman who looked as she did, who was as smart as she was and could turn a guy on the way she'd—

Grinding his teeth together hard enough to crack the enamel, he thought about finding the nearest subway station. Why should he care what she was doing when she plainly didn't? But before he could leave the man staggered sideways, slammed Jo into a wall, and something inside Daniel snapped.

Reaching a hand beneath the neck of his sweater to pull out the badge hanging on a chain around his neck, he checked for traffic and jogged across the street. Once he'd caught up to them, he set a firm hand on the man's shoulder and pushed him back a couple of steps. 'NYPD—you, over there.' He pointed a finger at Jo. 'And *you* stay right where you are.'

Her eyes widened in disbelief as he turned towards her. 'You're following me now?'

'Cop, remember? What did you think I was gonna do?'

'You're *unbelievable*!'

'And you're damn lucky you had a bodyguard for the last couple of hours considering where you are. What the hell did you think you were doing coming out here alone? Do you have any idea the number of shots-fired reports we get from this neighbourhood?' When her companion staggered forward, Daniel glared at him from the corner of his eye. 'I wouldn't if I were you, buddy. I'll tell you when you can move.'

The man lowered his chin, his words slurred. 'You can't talk to my—'

'Shut up, Jack,' Jo continued, frowning at Daniel. *'How dare you—?'*

'Oh, I dare,' he replied. 'What's more, you're going to tell me exactly what's going on and you can do it here or you can do it at the nearest precinct. *Your call.*'

'You can't *arrest me.*'

'Wanna bet?'

'I haven't *done* anything!'

Daniel nodded. 'Okay, then, I'll arrest him. Seems to me he could do with a night in a cell to sober up.'

When he turned, a hand gripped his arm.

'Don't.' The dark pools of her eyes sparkled as she let go of his arm, gathered control and lowered her voice. 'I just need to get him home.'

Going to the nearest precinct felt like the better option to Daniel, but something stopped him. She was still angry—he could feel it radiating from her in waves—but he had been in enough situations to know when there was more to the story. It made him wish for better light so he could search for a clue. If he'd had a flashlight he would have aimed it at her eyes.

Taking a long, measured breath, he gave *good old Jack* the once-over while making his decision. 'How far?'

'Four blocks.'

'And you were planning on carrying him there?'

'Daniel—'

'You lead the way, I'll bring him, and when we get there we're having a long talk.'

'You *think*?'

Crossing his jaw as he watched her turn and walk away, Daniel reached out a hand and grabbed hold of a sleeve before the man next to him fell over. 'Throw up on me and I'm still arresting you.'

The journey took twice as long as it would if all three of them had been able to walk in a straight line. Most of which an impatient Daniel spent shutting the guy down every time he tried to start a conversation. Once they got there Jo ushered the older man into the bathroom of a sparsely furnished one-bed apartment. Daniel paced the small living room while he waited. Then something caught his eye.

Stopping in front of a set of bookshelves, he reached out and picked up a framed certificate that had been presented to Jorja Elizabeth Dawson for perfect attendance in the sixth grade. Lifting his chin, he then discovered a photograph propped against a pile of books further in. It was a younger Jack standing in front of what looked like a Ferris wheel, his arms around a skinny kid with long, dark pigtails and a huge grin that revealed two missing front teeth.

Daniel realized his mistake in an instant and the second he did felt like the biggest jackass on the face of the earth. Glancing at the hall from the corner of his eye he found Jo watching him in silence.

'He's your father,' he said with certainty.

'Yes,' she replied.

'You should have told me.'

'If I'd wanted you to know, I would.'

After placing the certificate back on the shelf, he turned towards her and shoved his hands into the pockets of his jeans. 'How long has he been drinking?'

'It would be quicker to tell you when he wasn't.' She shrugged a shoulder and damped her lips with the tip of her tongue as she avoided his gaze. 'It's worse one month than the other eleven. This just happens to be that one month.'

When she looked at him, Daniel experienced a sensation he'd never felt before. Inwardly squirming didn't quite cover it. Not when it felt as if his internal organs were trying to crawl away and find a place to hide.

He took a deep breath. 'Jo—'

The door behind her opened and Jack appeared, taking an uneven path from wall to wall until he stopped and swayed on his feet. As Jo turned towards him Daniel stepped forward and freed his hands.

'I owe you an apology for the misunderstanding.' He held out an arm and shook her father's hand. 'Daniel Brannigan. I'm a friend of your daughter.'

There was a soft derisive snort from his right. 'Bit of an exaggeration, don't you think?'

'I was worried about her.'

'Since when?'

Considering he deserved whatever she tossed at him, Daniel sucked it up and looked her straight in the eye as he added, 'I thought she was in some kind of trouble.'

'Not my Jo,' Jack slurred. 'She's a good girl.' He dropped his chin and squinted. 'You're a cop?'

'Yes.' Swearing inwardly, Daniel reached for his badge to tuck it away. 'Emergency Services Unit.'

'People need help they call 911.' Jack grinned. 'Cops need help they call the ESU.'

'That's us.' Daniel nodded.

'You want a drink?'

'Good luck finding one,' Jo interjected. 'I cleaned you out last night.'

Daniel shook his head. 'No, thank you. I'm just gonna see your daughter home safely if that's okay with you.'

'That won't be necessary,' she said tightly.

He looked into her eyes again, his tone firm. 'It's the least I can do.'

'Okay.' She smiled sweetly. 'We can have that talk you wanted on the way back. While I get Jack settled, how about you have a *good long think* about the things you want to say to me?' Scrunching her nose in mocking delight, she placed an arm around her father's waist. 'Come on, Jack, let's go.'

As they left Daniel dropped his head back, stared at the ceiling and took a deep breath.

It was going to be the longest subway ride of his life.

CHAPTER FOUR

'Don't you love it when you find something you forgot you bought in the sales? It's true what people say: look closely and you might be surprised what you find.'

'You know what this reminds me of?'

Daniel's gaze shifted to tangle with hers from across the compartment. 'We're talking now, are we?'

'No. I'm talking. You don't get to speak yet.'

As the train slowed he glanced out of the window behind her. Jo had a sneaking suspicion he was counting down stations in the same way an imprisoned man might mark off the days of his sentence on a wall. But if he thought she'd forgive him because he'd had the sense to keep his mouth shut since they left Jack's place…

'It reminds me of the number of times I've heard my best friend complain about her brothers running background checks on every guy they ever saw her with.' She angled her head in thought. 'I used to think it was funny, now not so much…'

'We were looking out for her,' he said flatly.

'Why can I hear you?'

When he breathed deep and exhaled in a way that suggested he was running out of patience, she folded her arms.

'Beats me why you didn't put one of those tracking anklets on her.'

'If you mean a tether, we considered it.'

It was exactly the kind of opening he should have known not to give her. 'What gives you the right to interfere in other people's lives?'

'It's called concern.'

'It's called harassment.'

'I'm not going to apologize for following you.'

Her brows lifted. *'Excuse me?'*

'While you were giving me the silent treatment, I had time to think it over.' Stretching long legs, he spread his feet a little wider and shrugged. 'Considering where you ended up I'm not sorry I followed you. From now on, if you have to go there at night, I'll be going with you.'

Oh, no, he wouldn't. 'I'm not your sister.'

'I'm more than aware of that,' he replied tightly.

'You can't tell me what to do.'

'No. But I can tell you how it is.' Briefly glancing at the other passenger in the compartment, he brought his legs back towards him. Leaning forward, he rested his elbows on his knees and lowered his voice. 'Something happens to you I won't have it on my conscience. It's crowded enough already.'

When she frowned he leaned back, his profile turned to her and the muscle working in his jawline. Jo wanted to stay mad at him, still hadn't forgiven him and refused point-blank to be told what she could and couldn't do. But at the same time—much as she'd prefer if it didn't—the insight softened her a little, especially when telling her had obviously cost him something. It was his way of making amends, wasn't it?

Drumming her fingers on her arm, she tried to decide if she felt like being reasonable. On the one hand, she'd been conscious of the fact she was alone at night in an area where she was likely to get mugged, or worse. On the other, she'd grown up in that neighbourhood, could take care of herself and wouldn't have been so creeped out if she hadn't been *followed*.

It wasn't that she didn't appreciate the concern for her safety—as unexpected as it was coming from *him*—or that he'd apologized to Jack and shown respect to a man many people would at best have pitied. It was just, if she was honest, it stung that he knew.

Everyone had things they weren't comfortable with other people knowing. As he'd been when he told her something he had to know would leave her more curious than before…

Darn it, she really didn't want to be reasonable.

But he wasn't *forgiven*.

As the train rocked along the tracks she thought about the last time she had to deal with someone who'd learnt about Jack. Difference was with Liv she had been in control what she chose to divulge. Liv hadn't pushed. Liv would never have followed her. But even after six years and with a traumatic experience to bond them together, Jo knew she held things back. It was what she'd done for the vast majority of her life. She didn't think she would ever change.

As he looked out of the window behind her Daniel stood up. 'We change here.'

Jo grimaced when she got to her feet. Determined not to reveal she was suffering in the name of fashion, she grabbed hold of one of the vertical metal bars while they waited for the train to stop and the doors to slide open. Walking with an enviable ease to the other side of the platform, Daniel looked over his shoulder and stilled.

'What's wrong?'

'Nothing,' she answered through gritted teeth.

Turning, he studied her feet while she focused on the bench in the middle of the platform. 'Would kill you to ask for help, wouldn't it?'

'They're blisters, not broken legs.'

As she sat down he turned to check the tunnel for signs of an oncoming train before pushing his hands into the pockets of his jeans. Since he took a good long look at her boots when he turned around, Jo leaned back on the bench and allowed her coat to fall open. Resting her palms on the plastic beams, she crossed her legs. When his gaze shifted sharply to the extra inches of thigh the move revealed, she stifled a satisfied smile. Knowing she could get to him had always helped, even if the rash impulse to discover just how much she affected him in *that way* probably wasn't the best idea she'd ever had.

With a single blink, his gaze snapped to attention and locked with hers. She jerked her brows in reply.

It earned an almost imperceptible shake of his head. 'I'd heard women don't wear boots like that for comfort.'

Goosebumps erupted on her skin when she heard his voice. Deeper, rougher, it conjured up the kind of thoughts her self-preservation was forced to stamp with 'CENSORED' before her imagination provided the images to go with them.

'These boots definitely weren't made for walking,' she mused as she rocked her crossed leg.

'Begs the question of why you didn't think to change.'

Jo angled her chin. 'You have a real problem with what I'm wearing, don't you? Don't tell me you prefer your women in crinolines. Carrying a parasol maybe? Someone who will drop her handkerchief and swoon as you pass by…who'd be *eternally grateful* when you come to her rescue…'

'You really gonna go there?'

It would seem so. She shrugged a shoulder. 'It's half your problem with me. Neanderthal man meets modern-day, independent woman and he doesn't know what to do with her.'

The smile was slow, deliciously dangerous and steeped in heady sensuality. 'You have a lot to learn about a man like me, babe. When you're ready to find out, let me know.'

She would have called him on the 'babe' thing again if the

invitation hadn't felt like six-foot-two of blue-eyed Death by Chocolate. But there was no way she was letting what he'd said slide. 'Is that supposed to scare me?'

'What makes you think that's what I was aiming for?'

'You think I can't take you on and win, Danny?'

He smiled again. 'I'm Danny now, am I?'

An answering smile formed on her lips before she realized it was happening. When it came, his smile grew.

Thought he had the upper hand, did he? Well, in that case, she might have to give in to the impulse to find out how much of an effect she had on him. Rationalizing it as the need to know what she had to work with, she lifted her chin, stretched her arms out to her sides and arched her back. Purposefully pushing her breasts forward in a way she knew would strain the buttons on her blouse to the breaking point, she parted her lips and took a deep breath. To top it off, she shook her hair off her shoulders, caught her lower lip between her teeth and let it slowly slide free. When she was done she looked at him.

A burning gaze travelled the length of her body and back up. It lingered on her breasts for a moment, making them swell against the decadent lace of the bra she'd forgotten she had until she went digging in a drawer for the kind of underwear befitting her outfit.

When his gaze found hers, he nodded. 'You do like living on the edge.'

There it was again: that deeper, rougher voice…

It was beyond tempting to ask what he planned to do about it. But before she could weigh up the risk the opportunity was lost to the sound of an oncoming train.

Stepping over to the bench, he held out a large palm and jerked his chin. 'Up.'

Jo stared at his hand as brakes squealed and a rush of air whispered strands of hair against her cheeks. But she couldn't back down, not after her show of sexual bravado. Sliding her palm across his, she felt the same jolt of heat travel up her arm she had experienced the first time he touched her. By the time long fingers closed around hers and he tugged her to her feet, it was spreading over her entire body. Drawing a long breath, she avoided his gaze by looking over a wide shoulder at the train. As it stopped she took a tentative step forward and grimaced when her ankle turned.

The grip on her hand tightened. 'You got it?'

The question raised a small smile. 'You tell me.'

Threading his fingers through hers, he stepped forward to push the release button on the train doors. Holding them open with his arm to allow her to step inside, he leaned closer to inform her, 'I know what you're doing.'

'Do you?' she questioned over her shoulder as the doors slid shut behind them.

'Mmm-hmm,' he replied with a firm nod, his too-blue eyes darkening as she turned and looked up at him.

When the train jerked into motion, she rocked forward, a low gasp hauled through her lips when her breasts made contact with his chest. If it felt as good as it did with layers of clothing between them the thought of skin-to-skin was enough to form a moan in the base of her throat. She tried to take a step back, but a long arm wrapped around her waist, holding her in place as he lowered his head and spoke into the hair above her ear.

'How close do you want to get to that edge?'

Jo's heart kicked against the wall of her chest, her blood transformed into liquid fire.

Turning his hand against hers, he made enough room to rub his thumb against her palm, the long fingers of his other hand splayed possessively over her hip. 'If you're curious what's on the other side, I can take you there.'

His low, rough voice made the words *take you* sound like a promise of ecstasy. A distant whispered *yes* echoed inside her and made her slide her lower body across his. When

Daniel tensed in response and the fingers on her hip pressed tighter, a surge of feminine empowerment washed over Jo.

Turning her head, she lifted her chin and spoke in an equally low tone into his ear. 'This would be working a lot better if you *stopped talking.*'

'Someone who makes a living with words should know what they can do.' The hand at her hip slid dangerously close to the curve of her rear. 'Only takes a few and our minds fill in the rest.'

Jo took a breath of clean, masculine scent and resisted the urge to rub her cheek against his jaw. 'It takes the *right* words.' She smiled languidly. 'And I think you'll find I have the advantage there…'

'Lay a few on me and we'll see.'

What they were doing should have felt weird but didn't. If anything it felt like an adult version of the 'fun' she needed to draw her back from the past. She glanced at what she could see of his face. Instead of fighting her attraction to him the way she knew she should, she decided to enjoy the ride. Just for a little while. She'd never had a male playmate before but it was an exhilarating experience. Especially with a Marine-turned-cop she could go toe-to-toe with on equal terms…

The movement of the train rocked their bodies while his thumb traced circles in her palm. His head moved a fraction, the millimetres of space between her cheek and his jawline tingled with static. 'Chickening out on me, babe?'

As if. Lowering her voice to an even more intimate level, Jo carefully enunciated each word. 'Anticipation…longing… *desire*…' Lifting her hand, she set her palm on his upper arm, curling her fingers around the dark material of his jacket and the tight muscles underneath. 'Heighten…intensify… quicken…' She sighed breathily as her hand moved up his arm and across a shoulder to the rigid column of his neck. 'Tighten, strain, grasp, reach—' She gasped, held her breath for a second and exhaled on a blissful sigh. 'Release.'

'*Jorja.*'

The growled warning made her lean back so she could see his face. What she'd done might have ended up doing more for *her* than she'd planned, but it was obvious it had done just as much for him. His eyes were as dark as storm-filled skies. Waves of the kind of tension that could only be eased with physical satisfaction rolled off his large body, seeped into hers, and made her ache for the satisfaction to be mutual. When his gaze lowered to her mouth, it elicited an unintentional swipe of her tongue in preparation.

She wondered what kissing him would feel like…

Okay, that was enough. She really needed to snap out of it. She couldn't hand him a victory like that when he would never let her forget it. Daniel equalled arch nemesis. Any *other* guy who had the same effect on her equalled candidate for the kind of sex she obviously needed more than she'd realized.

Dropping her chin, she looked up at him from beneath heavy lashes. 'I have another word for you…'

'Trouble?'

'*Disappointment.* I'd learn to live with it if I were you.' Adding a sweet smile, she dropped her hand from his neck to his chest and pushed as she looked over a shoulder. 'Look at that, it's our stop. Doesn't time fly when you're having fun?'

Stepping onto the platform ahead of him, Jo held her arm out to her side to regain her balance before she let go of his hand. Without warning he yanked her back towards him. As she stumbled a large hand wrapped around the back of her neck and the world as she'd known it came swiftly to an end.

Firm lips crushed hers in a bruising kiss that rocked her back on her heels. She squeaked in surprise, blinked wide eyes and grasped hold of his shoulder to stay upright. But when he canted his head, she closed her eyes. As it always had in every other aspect of their relationship, her competitive streak kicked in. He couldn't light up her body like a roman candle on the fourth of July without repercussions.

Absorbing the intensity of the kiss, she bundled it into a fist in her chest and tossed it back at him. Her lips parted. His tongue pushed inside, duelling with hers. It was angry and messy and uncoordinated and without a doubt the hottest kiss she'd ever experienced and Jo *hated him* for that. She didn't want to spend the rest of her life comparing every kiss to one and have the rest fall short. Not when it was obviously meant to punish her for what she'd done to him on the train. He just couldn't back down and let her win one, could he?

He didn't know *how*.

When the kiss ended as suddenly as it began, Jo's eyes snapped open, the sound of ragged breathing making her realize the train had left. She stared up at him. To her surprise he didn't look at all victorious. If anything he looked as angry as she felt. Without saying anything, he released her, turned and headed straight for the exit. She gritted her teeth and followed him to give him a piece of her mind, frowning with frustration when her feet wouldn't allow her to match his long stride. As he reached the turnstiles Daniel glanced over his shoulder. When he turned and marched right back towards her, Jo froze. What was he—?

She was swept off her feet before she had time to figure out what he intended. 'Put me down!'

'We go at your pace we'll be lucky to get back before Thanksgiving,' he said tightly.

'I can still *walk*.'

'The expression on your face that suggests it's over broken glass says otherwise. Stop squirming.'

Lifting her higher, he turned sideways and pushed his leg against the turnstile. His gaze was fixed firmly ahead, his jaw set with determination; she knew there wasn't a hope in hell he would put her down any time soon. *Fine, then*, he wanted to carry her for two blocks, he could go right ahead. She hoped he strained something while doing it. Sighing heavily, she placed an arm around his neck. When they hit the sidewalk and a passer-by smiled, she pointed at her feet.

'Blisters,' she explained before the woman got the idea what she was seeing was anywhere in the region of romantic.

'Ah,' the woman said in reply.

Having started, Jo found the prospect of talking to random strangers infinitely preferable to talking to *him*.

'Lovely evening.'

'Yes, it is.'

She swung her legs a little and tried to ignore the fact a large hand was wrapped around her knee. 'Enjoying the city?'

A couple wearing the obligatory 'I heart New York' T-shirts lifted their gazes from the map they were poring over. 'Yes, thank you. It is wonderful.'

'Wait. Go back,' she demanded before craning her neck to look at the tourists. 'Are you lost?'

Daniel sighed impatiently before turning, remaining silent while the couple held the map out. Jo offered directions and tips for places to visit. Smiling brightly, she then enquired where they were from and said she hoped they enjoyed the rest of their trip. She even got to try out some conversational—if a little on the rusty side—French. They were a lovely couple.

'You going to do this the whole way back?' Daniel asked as he started walking again.

Jo ignored him and looked around. 'Hi, how are you?'

'I'm good, how are you?'

'I have blisters.' She pouted.

When he finally shouldered his way into the foyer of their apartment building, he headed for the stairs.

'If we'd taken the elevator you wouldn't have to carry me any more,' she pointed out after the second flight.

'We rescued two people stuck in an elevator yesterday. It occurred to me at the time if I ever got stuck in that ancient contraption the guys would never let me hear the end of it.'

'Two people stuck in an elevator.' She pondered. 'I wonder what they did to pass the time...'

'Two *men* stuck in an elevator.'

'I wonder what they did to pass the time...'

He glanced at her. 'Forgiven me for following you yet?'

It didn't escape Jo's attention he hadn't mentioned any forgiveness for kissing her. But either way her answer was the same. 'No.'

Eight flights later and—to her great irritation—without Daniel so much as breaking a sweat, they were at her door.

'Key,' he ordered.

'You can put me down now.'

'Key.'

Tugging on the strap across her breasts, she removed her arm from around his neck to unzip the small bag at the end of it and dig for her keychain. Lifting it in front of his face, she jangled it for effect. 'Happy now?'

'I will be when you put it in the door.'

'And how exactly am I supposed to do that from way up here?' When he simply leaned forward, she muttered under her breath, 'Planning on tucking me into bed too?'

'That an invitation?'

'I can't believe you just said that out loud.' Swiping her hair behind her ear, she focused on getting the key into the lock and turning it.

Daniel carried her inside, waited for her to hit the light and then kicked the door shut. Unceremoniously dumping her on the cushions of the sofa, he sat down on the chest she used as a coffee table and raised a palm. 'Give me your foot.'

Jo wriggled up the cushions, swiping her hair out of her eyes. 'You're kidding me, right?'

'I'm not leaving till I see how much damage you've done. Give me your foot.'

'Sure you're not trying to sneak a feel of the boots? You know you can get therapy for that, right?'

'It's amazing to me you've lived this long without someone strangling you.' He waggled long fingers. 'The sooner you give me your foot, the sooner you can get rid of me.'

'Well, when you put it *that* way…' Raising her foot, she set it on his knee, her pulse thrumming while she waited for the opening she needed to slap him.

Daniel ran his palms along her boot. When he got to the top Jo pressed her lips together at his expression. He didn't deserve a smile for the hesitation.

'Problem?' she asked.

'No.'

'The zip is at the back.'

'I know.'

'Do you also know in order to take it off you're going to have to touch me?' Seemed to Jo it hadn't been an issue before he dumped her on the sofa.

His gaze lifted and locked with hers as a heated palm set against the back of her thigh drew a gasp through her lips.

'It doesn't go any higher than that,' she warned.

A low rasp sounded as he opened the zipper. Slipping long fingers under the edge, he pushed the leather down her leg and lifted her foot with his other hand. As the boot descended his hand smoothed over her skin, distracting her from the sharp sting at her ankle with an excruciatingly gentle caress.

Despite how mad she was at him for kissing her, there wasn't an inch of her body that didn't ache for that touch. But since it was Daniel, she still couldn't wrap her head around it. Her heart hammered erratically. Had he changed or had she? Heat seeped into her skin and travelled back up her leg. When had it happened? *How* had it happened? Her pulse sang with intense pleasure. Who cared when it felt so good?

Setting the boot aside, he lowered his gaze and ran his palm up her calf. Jo swallowed in an attempt to dampen her dry mouth, caught her lower lip between her teeth to stop another moan from escaping. She really should put a stop to what he was doing. In a little minute, she vowed she would.

Leaning to the side as one hand smoothed over the top of her foot, he used the long fingers curled around the back of her calf to lift her leg so he could look at her ankle. 'Is the other one as bad as this one?'

That deep, rough voice again…

Jo silently cleared her throat. 'Probably.'

Oh, good, now *her voice* sounded different.

'Let me see,' he demanded.

One. More. Minute.

Setting her foot on the floor, she raised her other leg and held her breath while he repeated each slow move. With a second opportunity to take everything in, the way his hands touched the leather felt reverent, the way they smoothed over her skin more decadent. She should have been prepared for the effect it had on her knowing what he could do with a kiss, but she wasn't. Jo doubted anything could have prepared her for what felt like tenderness, especially from a man like him. If he added tenderness to a kiss, would it still be as hot? She should *not* want to know the answer to that question as badly as she did.

'You have a first-aid kit?' he asked.

'Mmm-hmm.'

His gaze lifted, a smile forming in too-blue eyes when she didn't say anything else. 'Want to tell me where it is?'

'Bathroom.'

'I'll find it. You stay here.'

Once he stood and walked away, Jo hauled a breath into

her aching chest and exhaled it with puffed cheeks. Time seemed to be slipping from her grasp along with her sanity. That minute was bound to be up. Her eyes widened when she remembered what the first-aid kit was sitting beside in her bathroom cabinet. He'd better not think *that* was an invitation.

But when he reappeared, Daniel simply set the first-aid kit on the chest, sat down and reached for her foot again.

'I can do that,' Jo said when she found her voice.

Selecting what he needed, he ripped open a small white package and curled a hand under her calf. 'As appreciative as I am of your footwear, you should consider flats from time to time. This might sting.'

'Ouch!'

A corner of his mouth lifted as he reached for a Band-Aid. 'They're blisters, not broken legs.'

'And now he's funny again.' She frowned as he swapped one foot for another. 'Could you get a move on?'

'Almost done.'

She gritted her teeth. After he smoothed a second Band-Aid in place, she snatched her foot back.

''Night, Daniel,' she hinted heavily.

He pushed upright, but instead of standing straight he leaned over her, his gaze locked with hers. Jo's eyes widened when he laid his hands on the cushions at either side of her hips. What was he doing? Her stupid, errant tongue damped her lips in preparation as his face angled over hers.

He couldn't seriously… She shouldn't want… She lifted her chin an unconscious inch. But instead of kissing her, Daniel stilled and a devastatingly sexy smile formed on his mouth.

''Night, babe,' he said in *that* voice.

Jo blinked as he crossed the room and she heard the door

close. Now he knew what he did to her, he would use it every opportunity he got. Reaching to her side for a throw cushion, she pressed it tight to her face and screamed in frustration.

CHAPTER FIVE

*'Much as I adore summer, I love the rich colours of the
fall. Breathe deep right now and even in the city you can
sense the approach of something spectacular.'*

SHE started it. Hardly the most mature response, but, since
he had spent every waking hour replaying the hottest kiss of
his life over and over in his mind, Daniel didn't care.

Even the fact she was who she was didn't make a difference any more, particularly when he took into consideration
how he'd reacted to the box that had greeted him directly at
eye level as he opened her bathroom cabinet. It wasn't that
he didn't think it was sensible to have them there. It wasn't
as if she'd been unfaithful to him or he'd been a saint since
the day they met either. But for a split second it had been
hard to resist the urge to bring the box back with him, toss
it in her lap and demand she told him who she'd used them
with.

As it was, he had slammed the cabinet shut and swore
there was only one man she would be using them with in the
not-too-distant future. She might have unwittingly caught
his interest with a pair of red stilettos, but she knew exactly
what she'd been doing on the train. Just as he knew exactly
what would happen if she discovered he was attracted to her
and used it against him.

Unfortunately, when he'd rolled out the heavy artillery, he'd discovered he was dealing with guerilla warfare. She'd hit him hard and fast, disappeared behind the woman who'd bugged him with very little effort, then hit him again when he attempted a temporary ceasefire by doing something *nice*.

Those boots had a lot to answer for.

He liked to think he'd launched an effective counterattack before he'd left her apartment. She was angry he had kissed her. Most likely wasn't any happier she'd kissed him back. But she had made it obvious she was open to it happening again. The way Daniel saw it, considering there hadn't been a whole heap of finesse involved in their first kiss, his next step was to right that wrong.

Taking a stealth approach, he entered the coffee shop by the door furthest from her table. While waiting for his order he did a little reconnaissance. She wouldn't catch him out the same way twice. Starting with her hair—since it was as far as he could get from the danger zones—he discovered a sleek ponytail. His gaze moved lower to discover a white dress and what looked like a low scooped neckline—needed to be ready for that one, then. Lower still and he frowned as he wondered if there was a worldwide shortage of skirt material. When he remembered how soft her skin was at the back of her thighs he tore his gaze away. He wasn't convinced he could handle what was on her feet. Not when his body was primed for a lot more than a kiss.

'Figured it was too good to last,' she muttered as he set a coffee cup beside her computer and sat down.

'Miss me?'

'How about you disappear for more than thirty-two hours and we'll see if it helps any? A decade might do it.'

Easing the lid off his cup, Daniel stared at her and waited to see how long it would take for her to crack under pressure. To her credit she lasted longer than he expected. In the end it took a yawn she covered with the back of her hand to break the silence.

'Did you go see Jack again last night?' he asked. Since she didn't reply, he took it to mean 'yes'. 'I thought we'd agreed you wouldn't go there alone.'

'Don't remember agreeing to that.'

He reached out a hand. 'Give me your cell phone.'

The demand lifted her gaze. 'Am I grounded, too?'

'No,' he replied. 'But you're about five seconds away from a curfew. *Phone.*'

'What do you want it for?'

'I'm going to put my number in it. The next time you have to go there at night, you'll call me.'

'No, I won't.'

Daniel rested his elbow on the table while he took a drink of coffee.

'You can hold your hand there till you get cramp. I'm not giving you my cell phone.' She focused on her screen again. 'I don't need a bodyguard and you work shifts. Not like you can drop everything and come running to my aid if you're working at night, is it?'

'If I'm on duty, Tyler will go with you.'

'Again, don't need a bodyguard—but if I did I have Tyler's number on speed-dial.'

Daniel frowned when his mind decided to make a connection between his brother and the box in her bathroom cabinet. 'I'm not kidding around here, Jo. Give me the damn cell phone.'

The sharp tone lifted her gaze again. Whatever it was she discovered when she searched his eyes softened her voice. 'I can take care of myself.'

'Humour me,' he replied with more control.

'Not something I'm usually prone to do…'

'Make an exception this time.' He used a beckoning motion with his fingers. 'If it helps tell yourself just because the number is there doesn't mean you'll use it. We can argue that one later.'

Angling her chin, she pouted and thought it over. 'I don't suppose you'll consider going away once the number is there?'

'Not till I drink my coffee.'

She brightened. 'Can you drink it faster?'

'Any particular reason you're uncomfortable with me being here?' he enquired.

Avoiding his gaze, she shrugged. 'No more than usual.'

Daniel smiled. Now he knew what to look for, she sucked at lying. 'If you don't give me your cell phone I can make this cup last all day.' He purposefully lowered his voice. 'There's a lot to be said for taking things slowly…'

Frowning, she lifted a pile of papers, produced her cell phone and reached out to drop it in his hand. Wasn't prepared to risk touching him, was she?

His smile grew. 'See now, was that so difficult?'

'Pushing your luck,' she said as she looked at her screen and lifted her fingers to the keyboard.

Daniel entered his number, sending a text to his phone so he had hers. When he was done, he held his hand up, her phone dead centre in his palm.

She glanced at it. 'You can put it on the table.'

'You want it, come get it.'

'With lines like that I can see how you're the equivalent of catnip to the ladies…'

With a small sigh, she reached out. When her nails scraped against his skin, every muscle in his body jerked in response. His fingers closed around hers. Full lips parted, her breasts rising on a sharp inward breath as she looked into his eyes.

'Tell me you'll call me,' he said.

'You said we'd argue about that later.'

'That was a couple of minutes ago.' When she tugged on her hand he tightened his hold. 'Say it.'

'Daniel—'

'Why did I follow you, Jo?'

She arched a brow. 'You know if you keep reminding me what you did it's not going to help me forgive you any quicker.'

'Why do you think I did it?'

'You told me why.'

'That I wouldn't have it on my conscience if anything happened to you—still true—but I told you that *after* I saw where you were.' Relaxing his hold a little, he brushed his thumb over the soft skin on the back of her hand as he lowered his arm to the table. 'Now ask yourself why I followed you in the first place.'

'It's what you do.' Her gaze was drawn to the movement of his thumb.

'Not with everyone. Not enough hours in the day…'

'Not what I meant. You're a cop and a Marine, your whole life is based on a sense of duty towards others. You figured you had to get to the bottom of it because of my relationship with your family.'

Daniel nodded. 'That's what I told myself.'

She slipped her hand free and lifted her chin. 'It's not that I don't appreciate your concern—'

'Concern would be part of it,' he allowed as he set her cell phone down. 'Same kind of concern you felt for my safety when I unhooked my harness on the bridge that day.'

'That wasn't concern for your safety.' She scowled. 'It was incredulity at your stupidity and anger at your lack of consideration for the people who care about you.'

'You'd have been fine if I fell.'

'Wasn't the fall that would have done the damage, it was hitting the water that would have got you killed.'

Daniel kept pushing. 'You'd have been okay with that?'

'Of course I wouldn't have been okay with it. You *know* what it would have done to your family.'

'But you'd have been fine.'

'I'm not having this conversation any more.' Grabbing her cell phone, she slammed it down on the pile of papers before flicking her ponytail over her shoulder and aiming the scowl at her screen. *'Go away.'*

Daniel took a breath. 'We may have been arguing since the day we met, but we've known each other for almost six years. It's difficult *not* to care about someone who's been there that long. Something happens, you notice the gap left behind. Might take a decade for you to miss me, but I like to think you'd get round to it if you knew I wasn't coming back.'

Fine-boned fingers stilled on the keyboard as her gaze focused on an invisible point in the air a couple of inches above the screen. During the following silence Daniel tried to figure out if he regretted what he'd said. He probably should, if for no other reason than the fact it explained her second appearance in his nightmare.

'Why are you telling me this?'

The question was asked in so low a voice he almost missed it in the ambient noise of the coffee shop. While he reached for the lid of his cup, he considered the answer.

Getting them to the point where they both accepted the inevitable conclusion of their volatile attraction was one explanation. It was certainly the one at the forefront of his mind. But the fact he wasn't firing on all six cylinders might have had something to do with it. If he hadn't been driven by the need to pick up where they'd left off, he could have tried grabbing some sleep before he went looking for her.

Too late now…

It was bound to happen at some point. Focus was the first thing to go, swiftly followed by hand-to-eye coordination; the latter of which probably explained the reason he was having so much damn difficulty putting the lid back on his cup.

He frowned at it in annoyance.

Resisting the need to yawn when she yawned had been more than a natural reflex. It was a reminder his body could only run for so long on adrenalin alone. His work provided regular top-ups. As did spending time with Jo with the electricity of their attraction constantly crackling in the air between them. But strip those things away and Daniel was bone-tired, off his game and a shadow of his former self.

'You asked if I ever got tired of this…' It was as close as he could get to the heart of the problem without giving too much away. 'Maybe you were right.' When he managed to slot the lid into place, he stood up. 'On that note, since I covered half of someone's shift this morning and I'm back in at four, I better get some sleep.'

He was at the door when she stopped him.

'Danny?' She turned in her seat to look at him.

'Yes?'

'If I need help, I'll call.' The concession was followed by a lift of her brows to indicate it was his turn.

'You won't go there alone at night.'

She shook her head. 'I can't make that promise.'

'You'll change before you go and you'll be *careful*.'

'I'm always careful.'

'Flat shoes, loose clothes.' He waved a hand up and down. 'The kind that cover you from head to toe…'

The smile in her eyes wavered on her lips. 'Should I put a bag over my head?'

'A ski-mask would probably help you blend in more easily in that neighbourhood.' When she rolled her eyes, he fought a smile of his own. 'First sign of trouble, you call.' He nodded his head at her cell phone. 'My number's under *H*.'

'I've said I…' She blinked. 'Why is it under *H*?'

Cutting the smile loose, he reached for the door. She was checking her phone as he passed the window, what looked like a burst of laughter leaving her lips before she shook her head.

He might have ended up saying more than he'd intended, but he was definitely gaining ground.

Of course she would notice if he were gone for ever. Did he really think she was so detached from her fellow human beings?

She would probably have got mad at him if he hadn't caught her off guard. It was his voice to begin with—the words laced with sincerity. But what got to her was the slight tremor to his hand when he put the lid back on his cup. While he frowned at it, she studied him: the lines of tension at the corner of his eye, a slight hint of grey beneath his tan. Added to the secret she kept for him, they lent a deeper meaning to the question she'd asked the night he moved in. Jo would dare anyone not to stop and think about how they felt after that. Even if they weren't convinced they wanted to know the answer.

Closer to the top of the well of memories she'd chosen to forget, she remembered how he looked the last time she saw him before he went overseas. It was one of the rare occasions he'd made an appearance at Sunday lunch and the last time he sat in his place opposite her at the table. She remembered how laid-back he'd been while an underlying note of tension in the room had said everything about his family's concern for his safety.

Had she taken the time then to think about what it would be like if he hadn't come home? If the chair opposite hers had remained empty for as long as his father's before the family moved around the table? She would like to think she had. But she couldn't remember worrying beyond keeping an eye on the news reports, wondering where he was if anything happened to a Marine. It was the same thing anyone would have done if they knew someone in a war zone. But when it came down to it she'd assumed how she would feel if something happened to him would be attached to his family. If they were hurting, she'd hurt for them. Grieving, she would feel grief for their loss. Part of the trouble was she'd never been able to remove his family from the equation. She still didn't.

But for the first time she thought about how she'd feel if it was just Danny and Jo and then Danny wasn't there any more...

She *would* miss him. Who would she argue with the way she argued with him? But it couldn't be anything more. Jo knew all about the gap a person could leave behind and what it did to people who loved them. She could never allow herself to care about someone so much she disappeared into that hole.

Not after she'd watched it happen to someone else.

Having spent a good portion of her time in the coffee shop staring into space, she returned to the apartment. An entire day at home during the week was a rare luxury when more often than not she was running all over Manhattan by mid-afternoon. So after checking in with the office to discuss images for her assignment and catch up on the gossip, she settled down with some freelance work. The first time she thought she'd heard something, her gaze lifted from the computer. Shaking her head when she found nothing but the usual city soundtrack running in the background, she went back to work.

There it was again.

Pushing back her chair, she walked to her bedroom door where it was muffled, but louder. When it stopped, she held her breath and waited, heart twisting the second it started again. It was no less torturous during daylight hours than it was at night. Did he *ever* sleep? She glanced across the room at the large clock on the kitchen wall. It was almost three. Hadn't he said he had to be in work at four? The dilemma made her waver on her feet. He would *hate* that she knew.

A text to her 'Hot Neighbour' wouldn't be any better than

turning up at his door. Either way there had to be a reason she knew he was there and might be late for his shift. She could say she hadn't heard his door close but then he might think she was listening for his movements. Up until, well, a few hours ago, if she was honest, she'd rather have poked red-hot needles in her eyes than allow him to think that.

The second hand on the clock sounded a 'Don't. Let. Him. Be. Late.' with each tick in the silence broken by an agonized cry from beyond the wall.

Okay, that was it. She was going over there.

When the door yanked open, the sight of a naked muscled chest made her breath catch—forcing her gaze sharply upwards. What she found didn't have any less of an effect, albeit in a different, more worrisome way. His eyes were red, his jaw was tense and he frowned as he blinked her into focus.

It did something to her heart she had to ignore.

Lifting an arm, he rested a large hand on the edge of the door by his head. 'What?'

'You said you had to go to work at four.' She held out a mug. 'You're going to be late.'

A brief glance at his wristwatch was swiftly followed by a low expletive before he lifted his gaze and his eyes narrowed. 'How did you know I was still here?'

'I didn't,' she lied with a shrug. 'Thought I'd check…'

His frown darkened. 'You shouldn't do that when you're not any good at it.'

When she didn't say anything, his gaze searched the hall. Suddenly slicing through the air, it slammed into her, driving the air from her lungs.

'Since the first night?' he asked grimly.

Jo nodded.

A shadow crossed his eyes, revealing something she never expected to see. Coming back at him had always been easy when he was cocky and in control; tossing jibes the equivalent of bouncing pebbles off an armoured tank. He knew who he was, what he was capable of, was calm under pressure and unwavering when it came to what he wanted. She supposed there had always been something she found sexy about that, even when they argued.

But the tiny crack in his control, the mere hint of a vulnerability that made it feel as if he desperately needed something he hadn't found? It echoed deep inside Jo where she kept her own vulnerability hidden. Unlikely as it would have once been, she wanted to be the one to give him that missing something. She just wished it didn't feel as if the one thing he needed was the one thing she could never give him.

'Thanks for the coffee.' He reached out and took the mug from her hand. 'And the wake-up call.'

Jo took a step forward when he stepped back. 'Danny—'

'Don't.' A large hand nodded once in a 'calm down' move she suspected wasn't solely for her benefit. He took a deep breath, crossed his jaw, looked anywhere but at her, and then used his forefinger to emphasize each word. 'Just…*don't*…'

When the door swung shut in her face, Jo stared at it for a long time without moving. Whatever headway they had made in the coffee shop disappeared like early morning mist. Crossing the hall had been a mistake. Why couldn't she have left it alone?

The answer was simple: She *did* care.

Probably more than she should.

'Damn it!' Daniel threw his gloves at the truck.

'We can't save them all,' his partner said flatly.

'Two inches, Jim.' He demonstrated the distance with a gap between his thumb and forefinger. 'All I needed was *two inches* and I could have put pressure on the artery.'

'And once we'd freed his leg he could have gone into shock and died anyway. You know that. Let it go.'

Except he couldn't let it go, could he? Not so far away there were scaly little hands rubbing together in glee. Didn't take a genius to work out what he would see in his nightmare the next time he closed his eyes, did it? Daniel's gaze sliced through flashes of red and blue neon reflected on rain-soaked surfaces to the collapsed wall several ESU squads had been working on. The man who had died had gone out for a carton of milk, walked past an abandoned building at the wrong time and that was that. Game over.

When they had arrived at the scene Daniel had volunteered to crawl inside a narrow space deemed unsafe for a paramedic. He'd been there for three hours as he talked to the guy to try and keep him conscious while they dug him out. Mike Krakowski, forty-three, wife, two kids, somewhat ironically—possibly because the universe had a sick sense of humour—a construction worker. Mike had lost consciousness a half-hour ago and when his pulse stopped beating there hadn't been a damn thing Daniel could do about it.

His partner slapped his shoulder. 'Walk it off, brother.'

Pacing around the emergency vehicles, he tried to roll the tension out of his shoulders and neck. He *hated* that Jo knew. The thought she knew because she had heard him yelling made it worse. There was only one thing he wanted to see in her eyes and sympathy wasn't it. So much for gaining ground…

He wondered how the residents' committee felt about subletting on a short-term lease. Moving from hotel to hotel the way he had after he landed stateside wasn't an option Daniel favoured, having tried it. Wasn't as if he could spend a night on someone's sofa either and he sure as hell couldn't go home. A handful of hours in the room he shared with Tyler growing up and keeping his distance from his family would have been a complete waste of effort.

Not for the first time, he missed the respite of being overseas. Turned out the scaly-handed little sucker hadn't liked the background noise of bullets firing and exploding shells. Frightened of losing its plaything, Daniel assumed, since a lack of sleep could have led to a fatal error a lot faster out there. So while many of the men he shared sleeping quarters with would toss and turn on their racks, he'd slept like a baby. He'd been paying for it with interest ever since.

Heading back to the truck to help pack away the equipment, he decided avoiding Jo for a few days was the only option open to him. Much as beating a retreat went against every instinct the Marine in him possessed, he didn't have a choice.

The next time he faced her, if there was so much as a *hint* of sympathy in her eyes…

Remind him of how much less a man he felt compared to the way he used to be and he'd be honour-bound to prove her wrong. Strong as she was, he doubted she was ready for the full force of that, especially when it had been held inside him for so long. The thought of what was involved got his juices flowing and reminded him how primed he was for more than a kiss, but she was still *Jo*. He wouldn't do that to her. The very fact he reacted the way he did to her knowledge was dangerous enough.

Let her get any closer…

Bending down, he picked up his gloves and tucked them in his back pocket. *Game over.*

CHAPTER SIX

'There's nothing quite like rearranging a closet to make a girl feel she's in control. The smallest of moves can have a domino effect on our lives.'

WHAT did he think he was going to do—assume a new identity and move to another state? It was something he might want to consider, because by Monday—when he hadn't shown up in the coffee shop—Jo was good and mad at him.

It felt as if her body were tuned in to him; didn't matter what time of night it was or how quiet he was on his way into the apartment. Once her subconscious assumed he was restless, she got restless. Before she knew it, she was blinking into the darkness, waiting. When the yelling came, as it inevitably would, for Jo it felt worse than before.

Each night he was shredding a jagged little slither off her heart and his answer to the fact she'd kept her mouth shut to protect his secret was to *avoid her*?

She was going to kick his ass.

Halfway up the second flight of stairs in their apartment block, she heard a familiar deep rumble. Picking up the pace, she arrived—a little breathless and ready to spit nails—at the top of the sixth flight. Rounding the corner she discovered he was talking to the head of the residents' committee.

Heart thudding erratically and unable to blame it *entirely* on the stairs, she gave him the once over. As usual he was in the prerequisite jeans, presently matched with a dark round-necked sweatshirt and a charcoal sports jacket. She had seen him in similar clothes a hundred times, so what was it that suddenly made him more of a feast for the eyes than before? No one had the right to look that good when they hadn't slept in as long as he hadn't so her singing pulse could just *shut up*.

She glanced at the bag in his hand. 'Are those cookies?'

'Freshly baked…' Daniel smiled his infamous smile at their neighbour who behaved liked a giddy schoolgirl in response.

'Danny confessed to a sweet tooth,' she explained. 'Have to look after our boys in uniform when they're away from home, don't we?'

'Yes.' Jo nodded. 'It's a long way to Staten Island.'

Daniel leaned forward and turned on the charm. 'Still too far away from home baking, right, Agatha?'

She patted his arm. 'Let me know when you run out.'

'You're too good to me.'

'Yes, she is.' Reaching out to ruffle woolly white ears, Jo crooned, 'Isn't she, Gershwin?'

When her hand dropped Daniel replaced it with his.

'Bye, little guy. Look after your mom.' As their neighbour left, he tilted closer to her and lowered his voice. 'Did I mention this is the second batch she's baked for me?'

Jo didn't say anything as they waved goodbye but as soon as the door down the hall closed, she swung on him. Aiming a brief glance over a wide shoulder, she grabbed a fistful of dark sweater and backed him into the elevator.

'*Stay*,' she ordered before turning to close the cage door.

Just once was it so much to ask the stupid thing to close without having an argument first?

'Need a hand with that?' a deep voice enquired.

'Don't make me hurt you.' It took several angry attempts

to achieve her goal before she pressed the button and turned on him again.

Leaning against the back of the cage, he reached into the bag before tilting it towards her. 'Fresh-baked cookie?'

'I hope you choke on them.' She folded her arms over her breasts. 'How long are you planning on avoiding me?'

'That's what I'm doing, is it?' Taking a bite of toffee pecan, he leaned his head back and frowned as he studied the creaking mechanism above their heads.

Jo was too mad at him to play games. 'You think you're the only one losing sleep since you moved in across the hall? But did I say anything? No. What I did was make sure you weren't late for work. Thanks for that, Jo. No problem, Daniel. That's all it would have taken. We could have gone on pretending I didn't know. Instead you asked, I answered and now you've decided to punish me for not lying when *apparently* I wasn't any good at it to begin with.'

When his gaze locked with hers, a warning sparkled in his too-blue eyes.

She sighed. 'Our apartments wrap round the building. We share a wall. How long did you think you could hide it?'

Daniel tossed what was left in his hand back into the bag. When his gaze lifted to the appearance of their floor—despite the speed of the elevator—Jo could sense she was running out of time. What would it take to get through to him?

'Why do you think I didn't say anything, Danny?'

It was a question she would prefer not to answer, but even the softening of her voice wasn't enough. His shoulders lifted a very visible inch and the knuckles of the hand holding the bag went white. Ridiculously, it felt as if she was losing him.

As the elevator shuddered to a halt he stepped forward and looked her straight in the eye.

She lifted her chin. 'I'm not moving.'

Setting his hands on either side of her waist, he simply

lifted her out of the way and set her down at the back of the elevator. When he did Jo dropped her arms and lost it.

'You can't avoid me *for ever*!'

As if it knew not to mess with him, the cage door moved with one sharp tug. The second he stepped into the hall, he turned and yanked it shut again.

Her eyes widened. 'What are you—?'

Reaching through the cage, he hit the button to send her back to the ground floor.

Forget kicking his ass. She was going to *kill him*.

If he'd been in a better mood the expression on her face as the elevator descended would have made him laugh out loud. Instead he turned and walked away.

He didn't get far before her voice sounded.

'Go ahead and avoid me for the next fifty years. Up until a few days ago you could have gift-wrapped that for me and it would have been the best present I've ever been given!' There was a pause he presumed was to allow her to take a breath. But when she spoke again he could hear something new threaded in her voice. 'I'm not angry you don't want to talk about it. I get that part. Probably better than you think. But they'll be selling ice cream in hell before I try talking to you again.'

Daniel stilled and took a long, calming breath. It wasn't what she said, what got to him was the note in her voice that almost sounded…*hurt*.

Shaking his head, he headed for his apartment. He'd been tossing pointed verbal spears at her for years without leaving a mark but a silent response had hit the target?

How did *that* work?

He'd braced himself for several things when he laid eyes on her again. With hindsight the stand-to-attention greeting from his body should have been higher up the list. But when it came to the things he knew he would struggle with most like sympathy, pity—hell, even being *nice* to him would have done it—there hadn't been one. Instead he got the kind of response he should have known to expect from her. Not only had she called him on what he was doing and set him straight, she kicked him to the kerb for punishing her for something that wasn't her fault. It was the note of hurt in her voice and his answering guilt for causing it that said the most about the change in their evolving relationship.

Stepping out of the hall, he closed the door and found his gaze drawn across the room to the item on the kitchen counter.

By the time she made it to the top of the stairs he was leaning on his door frame, ankles crossed and a hand held out in front of him. Gauntlet casually swinging on his forefinger, he watched from the corner of his eye as she glared at him before pointedly focusing on her destination. When she came to a halt in front of him she pressed her lips together, took a breath and looked at his finger.

'Is that my mug?'

He let it swing a little harder. 'Yes.'

'I hate you.'

'I know.'

Snatching the mug, she fitted her key in the lock, stepped inside her apartment and slammed the door. Daniel stayed where he was and waited. *Four, three, two...*

The door swung open again.

'You know what I hate most?' she snapped.

'That you didn't think of the elevator trick first?'

'I *hate* that you can make me this mad.'

He nodded. 'It's a talent.'

'I'm normally pretty Zen about the universe, despite everything it's thrown at me. But you—*you* bug the hell out of me.' She waved a hand at his face with attitude. 'That whole "nothing gets to me" façade you got going on bugs me more than anything. Especially now I know it's a big fat lie.' Her eyes widened when a slow smile began to form on his face. '*Really*, you're doing that *now*? When I've just told you I can see right through you?'

'I doubt that.'

If she could see right through him she would know he was thinking how beautiful she was when she was angry. He'd always thought it was a cliché but with Jo it was true. She flashed fire from her eyes; the full force of a passionate nature he'd only got glimpses of in the past made it difficult not to cross the hall. It didn't matter if she unleashed all of her inner fire on him, erupted in an inferno and left him in a pile of sated ashes. If anything it made him want her more.

'Don't do that,' she warned.

His smile grew. 'What am I doing?'

'You know what you're doing.'

'Thinking about coming over there so we can make up?'

'We don't have that kind of relationship.'

'Didn't use to,' he allowed.

'Just because we made an attempt at trying to be friends doesn't mean—'

'That's what you're calling this?' He raised his brows in disbelief. There was no way she could be that naïve.

'I—'

'You're telling me you haven't thought about it.'

She opened her mouth, closed it and then opened it again. 'What are we talking about?'

'I think you know what we're talking about.'

'You mean sex.' She frowned at his chest. 'With you…'

'I was talking about the kiss in the subway station, but if you want go there…'

'I haven't thought about it,' she lied.

Daniel shook his head. 'We've already established you shouldn't do that when you're not any good at it.'

'You're telling me you *have* thought about it?'

'If you mean sex…with you…'

Her eyes narrowed.

'I'm a guy, of course I've thought about it.'

She lifted her chin. *'And?'*

Daniel shrugged in a way he hoped didn't give away the fact just talking about it was turning him on. 'I think two people who spark off each the way we do could have pretty spectacular sex. You don't?'

'I meant the… Yes… *No*… I mean I don't know much about—'

'Spectacular sex?' The fact he had flustered her again brought a knowing smile to his mouth. 'You should try it. There's a lot to recommend it.'

'Wasn't where I was going.' She frowned.

'No?'

'Would you quit that?'

'What am I doing now?'

'Looking at me like a man looks at a woman.'

'Bit difficult to avoid…' His gaze travelled the length of her body, lingering on her breasts.

'That's second-date territory you're in right now.'

'We've had coffee three times.'

She gasped in outrage. 'Those weren't *dates*.'

Unable to resist any longer, Daniel nudged his door frame and stepped forward. 'When it comes to the kiss in the subway station, I think we can do better.'

'Danny, stop.' Her tone was suddenly more of a plea than a warning. She took a step back. 'You and me? *Huge mistake*.'

Reaching out, he took her hand and brought her back to her door frame. 'Who are you trying to convince?'

Before she could reply, he released her hand and framed her face. The tip of her tongue swiped her lips, moistening them in preparation as her gaze lowered to his mouth. When she looked up, doubt flashed across her eyes. He would have used every lesson he'd learnt from the seduction handbook to remove that uncertainty. But as his head lowered her chin lifted and their mouths met before he was ready.

A jolt of electricity zipped through his body. At first he froze, determined to ignore muscles that jerked in response so he could carry out his plan to demonstrate more finesse. He wanted to savour her, spend hours kissing her.

Starting with her mouth…

Capturing her lower lip first, then the upper, he drew from the experience of a lifetime of kisses that paled in comparison. If he'd known kissing her could feel so good, they'd have been doing it a lot sooner. When a breathy sigh escaped her lips, he breathed it in; the first brush of his tongue against hers met with a low hum of approval at the back of her throat. While she simply stood with her spine against the door frame and allowed him to explore, it was easier to control the pace and the demands of his body. The second her hands flattened on his stomach and she started doing a little exploring of her own, his control was tested as it had never been tested before.

The need to thrust against her was excruciating, but he forced himself to settle for pinning her to the door frame with his body. The desire to palm one of her perfect breasts was agonizing, but he forced himself to settle for a hand on her ribcage. Minutes dissolved into nothing but nipping, licking, and the kind of restless hand exploration that skirted them close to the point of no return. In the end it was the woman who was supposed to be lost in the moment *with him* who broke the kiss to point out a different kind of danger.

'Danny…' she mumbled. 'Elevator…'

Listening for long enough to hear someone fighting with the cage door, he leaned back in. Knowing that door they had at least another couple of minutes.

But Jo ducked out of the way, her voice thickened by the drugging effect of desire. 'We're not the only people who live on this floor.'

'They live at the opposite end of the hall,' he replied in a rough voice, which said just as much about the effect desire was having on him. 'But if it's doing it for you go ahead and think about getting caught…'

'You're *bad*,' she whispered.

'I haven't even got started yet,' he whispered back.

To prove his point he allowed his hand to slide up her ribcage so the tip of his thumb could brush the underside of her breast. Her kiss-swollen lips immediately parted on an inward, stuttered breath, head turning as she attempted to look down the hall.

'They can't see what I'm doing,' he reassured her.

She looked into his eyes again. 'Didn't I say where you're headed right now is second-date territory?'

Leaning forward, Daniel nudged his nose against the hair at her temple, breathing in lavender-scented shampoo. 'So when do you want to go out?'

There was a heavy sigh as her hands smoothed across his chest. 'We can't go on a date. We can barely manage a civil cup of coffee.'

'We just need to learn how to communicate better.'

Seemed to Daniel they were making some real headway in that department. He moved his nose to the other side of her temple and took another breath. The lavender wasn't having a calming effect on his body but the fact she was finding him hard to resist certainly seemed to be doing something to his sense of well-being.

She shook her head. 'We can't.'

'Making an effort not to bite each other's heads off might be a good place to start.'

'I meant *this*.'

'You don't mean that,' he said with conviction.

'Yes, I do.'

'No, you don't.'

'Yes, I do.' As he lifted his head she looked up at him from underneath her fringe. 'Could you stop acting like you know me better than I know myself?'

Considering she was no more able to keep her hands off him than he was to keep his off her, Daniel refused to back down. 'Would you have crossed the hall and kissed me?'

'No.'

'Do you regret that I crossed the hall to kiss you?' When she avoided his gaze and focused a small frown on his chest, he added, 'Remember, you suck at lying.'

'No,' she confessed reluctantly. 'I don't regret it.'

A step in the right direction…

She sighed again. 'But I should.'

And a step back…

Lifting the hand at her waist, he smoothed a strand of hair off her cheek. 'Tell me why.'

'There are at least a dozen reasons why we shouldn't be doing this.'

'I had ten on my list.'

She shot him a brief look of frustration. 'The very fact you even *have a list* should tell you I'm right.'

'I've been narrowing it down some.'

When she frowned, he brushed his thumb against her breast and felt her body respond to his touch.

'Danny, stop.'

He leaned in to nuzzle his nose into the hair above her ear. 'Do I need to remind you what I said about making things difficult for me when I want something?'

'There's no room in my life for involvement.'

'You forget you're talking to the guy who never stays in one place long enough for it to get complicated.' He brushed her hair off her shoulder to access her neck.

'I can't think when you're doing that.'

The breathless honesty made his mouth curve into a smile against her skin. *'Good.'*

'But we need to be sensible for a minute.' Her hands flattened against his chest and pushed.

Lifting his head so he could look into her eyes, Daniel discovered the kind of steely determination that suggested he wasn't the only one she was resisting.

'Give me some space, Daniel. I mean it.'

The use of his full name made him frown.

'Please.'

A flash of vulnerability combined with the word she had never used around him before made him step back, but only as far as the opposite side of the door frame. Dropping his arms, he pushed his hands into the pockets of his jeans.

'I'm listening.'

'Don't do that,' she warned with a brief glare. 'If you want us to communicate better it has to start somewhere.'

'We were communicating fine until you started overthinking it.'

'We can't just jump into bed,' she protested.

'No?'

'No. Because to categorize it as friends with benefits we'd need to be friends in the first place and we're *not.*' When he opened his mouth she shook her head. 'I'm not done. Even if we were friends, we both know this is complicated.'

Number nine on his list, as it happened. Or was it eight? If it was eight, what was nine? While he tried to remember Jo continued listing the reasons they shouldn't get involved.

'Your sister is my best friend and your family—'

'What happens between us is no one's business but ours,' he replied in a tone that wouldn't accept any argument on the subject. 'We're consenting adults.'

'You're saying we sneak around and have secret sex?'

'There's a lot to recommend that one too.'

'I can't *lie* to your sister.'

'I didn't ask you to,' he said. 'I'm saying we see where this takes us before we complicate it with outside opinions.'

'We both know exactly where it will take us.'

'Sometimes these things are just a flash in the pan—burn hot, fizzle out fast.' But as the words left his mouth Daniel knew he didn't believe them. Once wouldn't be enough with her, just as one kiss hadn't been enough. After a second kiss he was ready for a third, a fourth and a fifth; preferably within the next few minutes. He wasn't looking for a commitment any more than she was. It wasn't something he could even begin to contemplate until he kicked his subconscious into line. But spending what was left of his short lease with Jo suddenly felt like pretty good therapy to him.

Ignoring the warning in her eyes, he took a step forward. 'Can't hurt if we manage to communicate better, can it? If we follow this through to its natural conclusion, it'll be our decision. I'm not about to send out a mass email so people who know us can add their two cents. If you choose to tell Liv, that's up to you. Won't be you my family will come down on when we're done. It'll be me and I can handle that.'

'I won't be made out to be the victim of seduction.' She frowned. 'I'm a big girl. If something happens, it'll be on equal terms.'

'Wouldn't have it any other way.' He flashed a smile. 'All I'm doing is laying it out for you.'

She wavered. 'So we just try to communicate better and see what happens…'

'Exactly.'

'Knowing neither of us want to get involved…'

'You want no strings, I'm your man.' That she was getting closer to seeing things his way brought his hands out of his pockets. But as he lifted his arms she glanced down.

'What happened to your hand?' Frowning, she took it in one of hers to study the damage more closely.

Daniel looked at the red scratches across the joints of his fingers and knuckles as if he'd forgotten they were there. He forgot a lot of things when he was kissing her.

'Scraped it on a wall,' he replied.

'Does it hurt?'

'No.' Not in the way she meant.

'Looks like it hurts,' she said in a low voice. 'Don't you wear gloves when you're working?'

'They got in the way.' It was as much as he was prepared to say on the subject. Turning his wrist, he threaded their fingers together, his free hand sliding under the hem of her blouse to touch the baby soft skin on her flank.

She trembled in response, long lashes growing heavy and another stuttered inward breath hauled through parted lips.

'I don't know what changed between us or why, but—'

'It's changed,' she finished. 'I know.'

'May as well explore it now it's here…'

Jo searched his eyes in the same way she had when she woke him up. It made him feel equally exposed, like standing in open ground without cover. Remaining still, he forced himself to endure the onslaught with more courage than last time. Her decision might ultimately rest on whether she found what she was looking for but he couldn't do much about that.

It was either there or it wasn't.

'You know I'm going to ask at some point.' She lowered her gaze to watch her palm flatten on his chest. She nodded. 'Just so you're ready for it next time…'

Daniel doubted he would ever be ready and was about to tell her it was a no-go area when she took a breath and confessed, 'I can't believe I'm even contemplating this…'

'It's not going anywhere,' he replied roughly.

'Hmm…' She pushed out her lower lip. 'Not till your lease is up.'

'Not till my lease is up.'

'Well, then,' she said softly as her fingers flexed against his sweater. 'If you're going to convince me to go against my better judgment you best get started.' The hand on his chest slid up around his neck, her gaze focused on his mouth. 'For the record, it could take a *lot* of persuasion.'

Daniel's head lowered. 'I can do persuasion.'

'We'll see…'

CHAPTER SEVEN

'I always thought creamy vanilla was the ice cream for me, but recently someone persuaded me to try some wild cherry. Oh, my, what have I been missing all these years?'

'CHEESE slice and a diet soda, please,' Jo said with a smile before she turned towards Daniel. 'Stubborn. Now you think of one word to describe me. And *be nice*.'

He reached a long arm across the heated glass cabinets to pay for their order. 'Because calling me stubborn was supposed to be a compliment?'

'You're saying you aren't?'

'I prefer to call it determination.'

'Admit when you're wrong a little more often, it *could* be called determination,' she allowed, adding an innocent flutter of her lashes when he glanced at her.

'I can admit when I'm wrong.'

'Can you do it out loud?'

When he took a long breath, Jo bit her lip to stifle a chuckle. While the back-and-forth between them hadn't changed all that much, it was less sharp than it had been before. Both of them putting more effort into it helped, as did Daniel's newfound ability to know when she was teasing him instead of taunting him. But there were times she still wondered how long it could last.

'Your turn,' she prompted. It was met with a long enough moment of consideration to merit a sigh. 'Can't think of a word that isn't an insult, can you?'

'I can think of several words that aren't insults after the last few days.' A smile hovered at the corners of his mouth. 'Move closer and I'll whisper them to you.'

'Do I have to remind you why we're in a public place?' She waved an encouraging hand between them. 'Work with me here.'

If all it took to remove any remaining doubts from her mind were the constant reminders of why they were trying to communicate better, they'd have been eating in. Knowing what she did of his wicked streak, quite possibly off each other's bodies. But since the night they had their elevator argument, Jo had been ignoring the small voice inside her head: the one that still thought where they were headed was a huge mistake. When he wasn't there it was louder. Then she would lie in the darkness, hear him on the other side of the wall, and the only thing she could think about when she saw him again was making him feel better. Granted, it made *her* feel better too, but it still hadn't silenced the voice.

'Fearless.'

She blinked. 'What?'

'You wanted a word I'd use to describe you.' Taking their order with a nod of thanks, he turned towards the door. 'There you go.'

'That's how you see me?'

'What's wrong with it?'

Apart from the fact he couldn't be more wrong? 'It's a compliment,' she replied.

'Underestimating me again?' Holding the door open, Daniel lowered his voice as she walked past him. 'Being bad isn't the only thing I'm good at.'

Jo ignored the hum of delight whispering over her body when she thought about how very good he was at being bad.

She could hold a conversation with him without thinking about sex every five minutes. She darn well could!

'No one's fearless,' she announced. 'Everyone's afraid of something; by overcoming it they earn the word *brave*.'

He adjusted his longer stride to hers when they hit the sidewalk. 'What are you afraid of?'

'Oh, no,' she laughed. 'I'm not falling for that one. I say spiders, you'll start a collection.'

'Might consider one of those big hairy guys you keep in a glass case. I heard they're a low-maintenance pet.' He smiled when she shuddered. 'One word wasn't enough to begin with. If I had two I'd have said *fearless* and *wary*.'

'Isn't that an oxymoron?'

'You think I don't know what that means.'

'Word-of-the-day calendars can be very educational.'

'I have another one: manicured and mischievous.'

'Careful, Danny.' She smiled. 'It's starting to sound like you've put some thought into this before today.'

'Tornado in high heels, that's another one…'

Despite the fact she liked everything he'd come up with so far, Jo tutted. 'Little too far over the word-count now.'

'Your turn again. And after you laid stubborn on me, try harder. I might bruise easier than you think.'

When they stopped at a crossing she took her time picking another word. Had to be careful his ego didn't engulf Texas and try to take over the world, didn't she? Mentally crossing out everything pre-communicate-better-days too— *which might take a while*—she gently swayed the skirt that lent itself to the motion. Theme of the day was vintage and the black and white striped fifties dress was the most 'her' she had felt since she started the challenge. It was a much-needed reminder of what her life had been like before everything changed so fast it felt as if her feet had barely touched the ground.

'Can't stop doing that, can you?' he asked.

'Doing what?'

'The thing you're doing with your skirt.'

Rocking her hips a little more, she brightened. 'Is it bothering you?'

'No. Just wondered if you knew you were doing it.'

She shrugged. 'It's a fun dress.'

'And now I'm wondering if you still leave out cookies and a glass of milk for the jolly fat guy in red.'

Despite the obvious amusement in his eyes, Jo felt the need to defend what for her was an ethos for life. 'If you don't make time for fun every now and again the big, bad things can be harder to take.'

'Are you saying I don't know how to have fun?'

From the well of memories she had chosen to forget she sought one that associated Daniel with the kind of fun things she attached to his three brothers. She had dozens of memories of them tossing a football and joshing around but Daniel, not so much. What did he do with his time apart from work, a daily run and utilizing every tool in the seduction toolbox to turn her into a boneless heap of wanton woman?

'Define your idea of "fun" for me,' she demanded as they entered Washington Square Park and she looked up at the iconic arch modelled after the Arc de Triomphe in Paris.

If he asked she would tell him eating lunch close to its shadow was one of her favorite fun things to do, especially on a day like the one they were experiencing. Spiffed up to its former glory, with a backdrop of clear blue sky. She'd stare up at it and imagine she was sitting by the original.

She made the same vow every time she saw it: *Soon*.

Since she was moving up the magazine's shortlist each year, she felt closer than ever to fulfilling the promise.

When she looked at Daniel and found innuendo glinting in his eyes, she felt the usual response skim through her veins and tighten her abdomen. But that wasn't what she'd meant.

'I mean outside of adult fun. What do you do to relax when you're not working?'

'Run, train, gym time; long hours dedicated to maintaining the level of fitness you finally got round to noticing...'

He cut loose his infamous smile, *on her*.

Wow. That thing really did pack a punch up close.

She had forgotten that. But since the memory of the last time he unleashed it on her was buried so deep there must have been a very good reason for forgetting it, Jo decided not to go digging. 'Toss a football in the park, play practical jokes on the guys in your unit or meet up with friends for a beer...' She lifted her brows. 'When's the last time you did anything like that?'

'We tossed a football in camp when I was overseas. Not much else to do when we weren't being shot at.'

She didn't get how he could be so blasé about his time there when it was obvious whatever happened still tortured him. The subject of his nightmares was one they'd avoided but maybe...in the bright light of day...while they were getting along better...

'Not like my inbox was overflowing with emails, was it?' he asked before she could find a place to start.

Jo shook her head. 'You didn't want to hear from me.'

'You'd be surprised the difference an email can make to a Marine in a war zone. I saw guys go for days on the smile they got hearing from folks they barely knew in high school.' His gaze swept the surrounding area for a place to sit before he laid a large palm against the small of her back to guide her. 'It's a reminder of home. Some guys needed that.'

'Did you?'

'My problem was never remembering.' He frowned.

The unspoken *'it's trying to forget'* made Jo's voice soften in response. 'You're not a machine, Danny.'

'There are times it would be a lot easier if I was.'

'You say the stupidest things sometimes.' But as they approached an available bench she wondered what she'd have done if she'd thought an email made a difference to him back then. Even if it was from someone he hadn't liked. 'If I'd known I'd have written.' She smiled up at him. 'You'd have got *War & Peace* on everyday life in Manhattan.'

'With daily tips for the fashion-conscious Marine…?'

'I heard it's all about the camouflage this season.'

'I'll think about letting you write next time I go.'

'You're going again?'

'Not likely to happen soon,' he said in a tone that suggested he was disappointed. 'There's three months left on my papers before I decide whether to re-up.'

'You've already decided, haven't you?'

'Once a Marine, always a Marine.'

Jo frowned at how little she liked the idea of him being overseas again. She might not have lost sleep over it last time, but she knew she would now. 'You're a cop too. Doesn't that mean anything?'

'I've been both for a long time.'

'I know, but it's like you're married to the Marines and fooling around with the NYPD on the side.'

'I don't fool around,' he said seriously.

If he thought it was something she needed to hear, it wasn't necessary. Any relationship she'd heard he had might not have lasted long, but she couldn't remember there ever being a suggestion he was fooling around. He wasn't the kind of guy who cheated on a woman. It was part of the Brannigan loyalty and honour code.

'Kinda feels like you're more faithful to one than the other,' she pointed out in relation to his work. 'Semper Fi, that's the motto, right?'

'*Ooh-rah*,' he replied in a low rumble, smiling when she rolled her eyes. 'The Marines are my first love. You never forget that. Being a cop is different. It's a marriage that was arranged for me before I was born.'

'You didn't want to be a cop?'

'Let's just say it took a while to find my niche.'

Since she'd always assumed all of the Brannigans had the same calling, Jo was surprised. But if he'd loved it so much, 'Why did you leave the Marines?'

'I didn't.'

'You switched to the Reserves and came home.'

'Things change.'

'Do you regret it?' she asked as she sat down.

'Not on the good days,' he replied.

It seemed a tad ironic to Jo she had accused him of not knowing her when she was discovering so many things she hadn't known about him. Usually she liked to think she swayed towards giving people the benefit of the doubt. But with Daniel there had always been a wall of distrust; one they built higher and wider every time their paths crossed. She was still wary of him but that was understandable. Trust wasn't built overnight.

As he turned to hand over the pizza box, she looked into his eyes and saw a hint of shadow. Experiencing an immediate pang of regret, she tried to lighten the mood. 'I've decided I'm giving you a relaxation make-over.'

'If it involves bubble baths and scented candles you can forget it.'

Curling her fingers, she punched him in the upper arm to even up the score for the sucker punch of his infamous smile. 'Don't mock what you haven't tried.'

Daniel glanced at his arm as she shook her hand. 'Been wanting to do that for years, haven't you?'

'You have *no idea*.' Unfortunately, now she knew who would come out of it worse, it wasn't an option any more.

Reaching out, he captured her hand and ran his thumb over the rise and fall of her knuckles. As he repeated the caress heat rushed up her arm in waves. That part she'd almost gotten used to. What she found harder to handle was the message she could read in his eyes as he did it. At first she'd thought it was her imagination. Then, as it was with everything between them of late, she chalked it up to one of the numerous sexual messages he silently transmitted to her. It had been easier to think of it that way. But in the sun-light—the vivid blue of his eyes bright enough to put the sky to shame—it felt like something more.

I'll take care of you, it said.

Jo didn't like it. She didn't need him to take care of her. She could take care of herself.

Holding her gaze hostage, he did something unexpected and bowed his head to place a kiss on the skin he'd caressed. Jo watched, mesmerized, as his chin lifted and he smiled.

Seriously, where had *this* Danny been hiding for the last five and a half years?

'Let me know if you need anywhere else kissed better…'

'Well, that's a shame.' She sighed and reached into the box for her slice of pizza. 'Opportunities to be gallant are rare in this day and age. And you just blew yours.'

When there was a chuckle of deep laughter, she turned her head to study the effect it had on his face. Mocking amusement she was used to; the glint in his eyes that hinted he knew something she didn't and his enjoyment was at her expense, she knew all too well. But the way it relaxed some of the tension around his eyes, suggesting he'd experienced a moment of the kind of fun he obviously needed thanks to *her*?

Well, as it happened, it felt pretty darn good.

She was smiling back at him when her phone rang. Digging in one of the pockets of her skirt to retrieve it, she checked the number and frowned. *Darn it.* Not now.

'Hi, Stu… No, I appreciate it.' She glanced at Daniel from the corner of her eye. 'Can you try and keep him there for me? Thanks.' Pushing the phone back in her pocket, she dropped the pizza into the box and wiped her hand with the napkin. 'I have to go.'

'I'm coming with you.'

Yes, she'd thought he might say that. While he could catch her off guard with some things, in others he was as predictable as queues for the Empire State Building. She shook her head, 'It's your day off. You're going to do something fun.'

'It took two days and a late night for you to free up time in your schedule,' he pointed out. 'Your idea of what we did with it may have differed from mine, but the general idea was to spend it together.'

'I know,' Jo replied with another pang of regret.

He had been remarkably patient in regard to her schedule versus his shift pattern. Discussing it made her realize the number of times he would have to sacrifice much-needed sleep to see her. For a second it made her resent the intrusion of the present by the past a little more than usual. But he had been right about what he could see in her eyes the night he surprised her in the hall. For one month out of every twelve, she was resigned to doing what she had to do.

Leaning forward, she placed a quick kiss on a clean-shaven cheek before standing up. 'I promise to make it up to you when I get back.'

'Nice try.' He stood up with her. 'I'll drive you there. It'll be quicker.'

Not in Manhattan traffic, it wouldn't. 'I know what you're doing and it's not that I—'

Taking a step forward, he laid a hand on the wide red belt at her waist, his voice low. 'Are we headed for an argument?'

'I don't want us to be,' Jo confessed.

Avoiding his gaze, she brushed an invisible piece of lint off his jersey with the backs of her fingers. No matter how addictive it had become, she liked being able to touch him. She liked the heat she could feel through his clothes, the solidness of his presence. But since she couldn't get used to him being there, she lowered her arm.

'Sooner we go, sooner we can be back,' he said firmly.

When he took her hand and turned them around, Jo tried to find a way to get out of it. The idea of him taking a deeper step into her old world than he already had sent a chill down her spine. Jack was the key to a door she didn't want to open.

Behind it was the old Jo, the invisible girl who had been lonely and lost. Despite the need she had for it, Jo knew the risk associated with accepting help. She had watched the effect it had on some of her peers; how well-meaning people with good intentions could begin to make decisions for them until they didn't have control over their lives any more. With hindsight the new Jo supposed it wasn't *that* dissimilar to the battle for independence teenagers fought everywhere. But in the present it felt like a much-needed reminder not to lean on a man like Daniel, even for a moment.

Huge mistake, the little voice repeated.

Something dangerously close to panic crossed her chest as his truck came into sight. Glancing down the street, she saw the sign for the subway station. Looking at his truck again, she frowned at the idea of an argument. The phrase 'rock and a hard place' jumped into her head.

'Danny...' When they stopped to cross the street, she tried to reclaim her hand. 'I—'

'I know you don't want me to go with you.' Tightening his fingers, he turned to face her. 'But if you want me to bend a little from time to time, you have to do a little bending of your own. You know that, don't you?'

Oh, he was *good*. Negotiation 101 obviously hadn't been lost on him during the NYPD training. He knew exactly the tone of deep, rough rumble to use on her, had enough sincerity in his eyes to make her feel she was letting him down if she didn't make an effort. She frowned at his chest again. If it was something other than Jack she could try to bend, but—

'Look at me, Jo.'

With a blink, she obeyed.

'We're good right now, aren't we?'

She nodded. They were. It was another part of the reason she didn't want to take him with her.

'So we go in, you do whatever you need to do, and then we get to enjoy the rest of our day.'

It sounded so simple when he put it like that.

Nudging the tip of his nose against hers, he angled his head and placed a kiss on the corner of her mouth. 'I can think of at least a half-dozen fun things we can do when we get back…'

Eyelids growing heavy, Jo smiled as he placed another kiss on the other corner of her mouth. She knew what he was doing but while the rest of the world disappeared around them she could feel her resistance melting away.

'You have a one-track mind,' she mumbled as he changed the angle of his head.

'There's a reason for that.'

Slanting his mouth over hers, he spent several minutes persuading her to go against her better judgment. She might have issued the challenge after their elevator argument but if she knew how well he could do it…

He lifted his head, long fingers flexed around hers, his alert gaze sweeping over the traffic while she stared at him.

If she could just figure out what it was that hadn't been there before. What made her see him differently and want him so much the memories of all the times they argued faded into the distance…

'Let's go, babe.'

CHAPTER EIGHT

'The jacket you never wore? The jeans you swore you'd get back into one day? Sometimes you have to be firm about the things you keep and the things you let go.'

JO LEANED across the wooden bar to greet the man in front of the optics with a kiss above his greying beard.

'Well, aren't you a picture?' he said with a smile.

Taking a step back, she placed her hands on either side of her waist and struck a pose. 'You like?'

'I do.'

The sound of laughter pulled her gaze to the other side of the room as her hands dropped. 'How far are we in?'

Daniel noticed the change in her voice; as if it was a question she had asked a hundred times but already knew the answer. He stored the information away with her reaction to the phone call. The change in her then had been immediate too. One minute he was sitting next to bright, full-of-life, sassy, sexy Jo and the next it was like sitting next to a shell. At the time it had felt as if something were stolen from him.

Daniel had resented the hell out of that.

'Coming up on three hours,' the man replied.

Jo glanced to her side. 'Sorry.' She waved a hand, 'Daniel, meet Stu. Stu, meet Daniel.'

They shook hands across the bar.

'First time she's brought anyone with her in ten years,' Stu said with a smile. 'Can I get you anything?'

Daniel shook his head. 'Designated driver.'

'Better order something if you're staying.' Jo looked across the room again. 'This could take a while.'

As she walked away, Stu explained, 'It's in the timing. She takes him home too early, he finds his way back. If not here, it's somewhere else.'

Nodding as if he'd already known, he watched her father greet her with an arm around tight, narrow shoulders before making introductions. Immediately Daniel wanted to scoop her up and take her back to where they were before the call came. But he had to treat it as a recon mission. With that in mind he'd let her handle Jack her way, *for now.*

'You could try barring him,' he said dryly.

When he looked at Stu again, he discovered he was being studied with caution. 'Jo said she'd prefer to get a phone call than spend time searching for him.'

'It's good to know she has people who will do that,' he replied with sincerity.

The older man visibly relaxed. 'Used to be more of us, but bars change hands over the years.'

When Jo returned, she lifted her chin a very visible inch before looking Daniel in the eye. 'Is there any point telling you to go home?'

'No,' he replied.

'Figures.' She flashed another smile at Stu. 'I'll take one of your famous coffees if there's a pot on the go.'

'Is the designated driver sure he doesn't want one?'

'He takes his black.'

'I'll bring them over.'

They were sitting in a corner booth when Daniel broached the subject with, 'How many bar owners have your phone number?'

'Danny—'

'It's just a question.'

'No, it's not.' She sighed heavily. 'It's an opening to an argument. Don't make me regret bringing you here.'

Stu arrived with their coffees. As he watched him return to the bar Daniel lowered his voice. 'I'm not going to argue with you.'

'I'm glad to hear it.'

'But I'm not going to stay silent.'

'If what you have to say involves a lecture on how to handle Jack you can forget it. I've been doing this for a long time. I don't need your help.' She reached for her coffee and took a sip.

When she glanced across the bar as she set her cup down, Daniel lifted his hand. Sliding it beneath a curtain of silky hair, he wrapped his fingers around her neck, soothing tense muscles with a firm, circular movement. It took a minute, but eventually her head became heavy against his forefinger.

'*Mmm*, that feels good.'

Ignoring the reaction from his body to the low moan, he smiled. 'Magic fingers…'

'And I didn't even have to put coins in the slot.'

'You can pay me later.'

The brief smile his comment earned faded as she glanced across the bar again. 'It's not that there aren't some things I'm fine talking about…'

'So start there.'

'…but before I do I want your word you won't interfere.' With a blink of long lashes, her gaze tangled with his. 'I mean it, Danny. No advice, no leaflets for places I can get help and when we leave here we don't talk about it again.'

'I'm not the first person you've said that to.'

'You're not the first *Brannigan* I've said it to.' She shrugged a shoulder. 'Liv tried to get involved once.'

If she hadn't, they would have had words. Considering she only tried *once*, it was still tempting. But if he opened his mouth in Jo's defence his sister would know something was up. She could be intuitive that way.

He took a short breath. 'I can't give you my word—'

'Then we're not talking about it.'

'I'm not done.' He moved his fingers to ease the returning tension in her neck. 'Learning to communicate better after so many years of arguing was never going to be easy. If blunt is what it takes from time to time then—'

She arched a brow. 'You know I'm going to remind you of this when it's your turn, don't you?'

The fingers on her neck stilled. She didn't know he had no intention of talking to her about his nightmares. If he hadn't been likely to talk about them before, spending time with her had made him twice as determined. He didn't want the darkness of his subconscious to intrude on what was rapidly becoming a haven. He dropped his arm to his side.

'I shouldn't have said that,' she said with regret. 'I knew this would happen. I should have listened to the voice that told me—'

'What we're doing is still a huge mistake?'

A hint of astonishment mixed with a sparkle of anger in her eyes. 'Not what I was going to say.'

'Tell me I'm wrong.'

'What's happening between us has nothing to do with this,' she argued.

Putting together what she said with his thoughts on the subject of discussing his nightmares, Daniel realized, 'You don't let your old life cross over into the new one and vice versa, right?'

'Not if I can help it,' she admitted.

'How's that working out for you?'

'Was going pretty well…'

'Until me…'

Her expression softened. 'Until you…'

Reaching out, his fingers sought the knots of tension at

the base of her neck again. 'Start with something simple. Tell me how you met Stu.'

Louder laughter pulled her gaze across the room while she considered what to tell him. Judging by the brief frown on her face, it wasn't that simple.

'I was fourteen,' she said in a low voice. 'Figured if I couldn't stop him drinking, I'd make it more difficult. I went to all the bars within an eight-block radius to see where he'd run up tabs. Deal was, they'd stop giving him credit and I'd pay them off a few dollars a week. The ones who gave me most trouble, I paid first. The patient ones—guys like Stu—would take less on weeks I found it tough.' She took a breath. 'Took two part-time jobs and a few years, but I got there. Even made a few friends along the way…'

Earning their respect as she did it, Daniel surmised. He would have liked to have met her back then. But while fourteen-year-old Jo had been surviving the Urban Jungle, a twenty-year-old Daniel was in theatre with the Marines. He could imagine what she would have thought of him if she'd met him before he'd signed up at eighteen. He was a loose gun then; the kind of guy who was more trouble than he was worth. Looking back, he knew he would have had more respect for her than he had for himself.

'Did it slow him down?' he asked.

'No.' She shook her head. 'It forced him outside the eight-block radius. That's when he started disappearing.'

Daniel's fingers stilled again. 'He's the reason you were homeless when Liv met you.'

She shrugged as if it didn't matter. 'I couldn't make the rent. He disappeared when we were already on shaky ground with the landlord. When I knew I couldn't hold out I scouted around for some place dry close to school, packed what I could carry and left. The rest you know.'

Anger flared inside him. 'Why didn't you ask for help? There are people out there who—'

'I was eighteen,' she said with a glare of warning. 'I could take care of myself. All I needed was a few weeks to finish high school and get my diploma.'

Fingers moving, his gaze slid across the bar to acquire a new target. What kind of man did that to his kid? Why was she still taking care of him?

'Where was your mother?' he asked.

Her neck stiffened. 'She died.'

'When?'

'Accident when I was eight.'

'What happened?'

'Hit and run on her way back from the local store.'

He remembered her saying something about Jack being worse one month out of twelve. 'The anniversary of her death is this month, isn't it?'

'Yes.' Leaning forward to reach for her cup, Jo dislodged his hand with a subtle shrug of her shoulders. 'And we're done talking about this now.'

Daniel's gaze slid back to his target. He knew exactly who he was talking to next. Five minutes should do it. But before he went looking for a window of opportunity he had to ask the question he didn't want to ask.

'Was he ever violent with you?'

'Don't—'

'I need to know.'

The rough tone of his voice turned her head, her gaze searching his eyes before her expression softened. 'He's not that kind of drunk. Jack gets happy. That's half the problem. People buy him drinks 'cos he's such a fun guy to be around.' When laughter sounded she smiled ruefully. 'See what I mean?'

'You were lucky,' Daniel replied, when what he really meant was *Jack* was lucky.

'Yes,' Jo said dryly. 'I spent every waking moment of my

adolescence being eternally grateful for the fact my father is an alcoholic.'

Despite thinking it was the most honest thing she'd said on the subject, Daniel shook his head. 'Not what I meant.'

The unexpected touch of a fine-boned hand on his thigh drew a sharp hiss of breath through his lips. His thoughts stuttered to a standstill. As always every muscle in his body jerked in response, searing heat seeping into his veins and thickening his blood.

'I know what you meant,' she said in an intimate voice. 'But you don't have to worry about me.'

Daniel disagreed. Way he saw it, while they were together she was *his* to take care of and *his* to protect.

'He would never hurt me,' she reassured him.

'Would he know if he knocked you over or if you injured yourself carrying him upstairs?' He clamped her hand to his thigh when she tried to remove it. 'How about when you have to clean up after him or when you're losing sleep worrying where he is? Not every bruise is visible.'

'If you don't stop that I'm going to make you leave.'

She could *try*.

'I'm not going to pretend I don't care.'

'Did I ask you to?' She frowned. 'But what you have to remember is this isn't because it's me, Danny. You're *that guy*: the one who feels he has to make a difference.'

'Don't make me out to be a hero.' If she knew him better she would know how woefully short he fell of the definition.

'Then stop trying to be one.' When a second attempt at freeing her hand didn't get her anywhere, she shook her head. 'I don't need you to rescue me. I need you to trust I know what I'm doing and believe I have my reasons for doing it.'

'Tell me what they are.'

As she tore her gaze from his a pained expression crossed her face. 'I don't want to have a fight with you. But if you keep doing this I won't be able to stop it happening.'

'You give me one good reason why you keep doing this and I'll back off.'

'Why do you need to know?' She jerked her brows. 'And don't say it's part of the whole communicating-better thing because this has nothing to do with us.'

'This is a prime example of you not making it easy for people to get to know you,' Daniel replied flatly.

'Getting to know me better isn't high on your list of priorities when you're trying to get me into bed.'

'If it wasn't we'd already have shared a bed.'

'You say that like I don't have a choice.'

'Tell me you don't want me.' When something close to a growl sounded in the back of her throat, he leaned closer. 'I can tell you how much I want you. You're never out of my head. I've spent dozens of hours thinking about the places I want to kiss you and the things I want to do to you. I want to explore every inch of your body, discover all the hidden places you never even knew you had. I want to drive you so crazy that if I don't take you, we'll both go insane. I want—'

'*Stop,*' she breathed.

'Tell me you don't want me.'

Her eyes darkened. 'You know I do.'

'If I get to know you better, the experience will be better for both of us. You have my word on that.'

She blinked. 'You're very good at this.'

The statement lifted the corners of his mouth. 'Only when I think it's worth the effort.'

'I won't fall for you,' she said firmly.

Daniel shook his head. 'I don't want you to.'

With another blink, she lifted her chin. 'No falling for me either.'

His smile grew. 'Okay.'

'One reason I keep doing this…'

'Just one.' He nodded, silently adding another *for now.*

'Coney Island.'

Daniel wondered if there would ever be a time she didn't surprise him. 'Am I supposed to know what that means?'

'No,' she replied. 'But I can explain it.' She stared into the air beside his head and took a short breath. 'I was ten or eleven. Jack quit drinking for long enough to remember he had a kid and we went to Coney Island for a day.' Her mouth curled into a wistful smile. 'We went on every ride, ate cotton candy and corn dogs until I felt sick and it was one of the best days of my life.'

When her gaze met his, he caught a glimpse of sweet and vulnerable woman at odds with her usual sass and confidence. Something he didn't recognize expanded in his chest, filling the cavity and making it difficult to breathe.

'That's one of the reasons I keep doing this,' she said with a shrug of a shoulder. 'Because I still remember Coney Island and the day I got my dad back.'

As she avoided his gaze Daniel wrapped his arms around her and pulled her close. She nestled her head in the curve between his neck and shoulder. When he felt the warmth of her breath against his skin a wave of protectiveness washed over him, tightening his hold. In response she relaxed with a sigh, which gave him the impression what he had done held more value than anything he could have said. But when she looked up at him and smiled tremulously, the something he hadn't recognized shifted inside his chest again and Daniel sensed trouble. He brushed her hair back from her cheek, focusing on the movement as he bought time to seek out the source of the danger.

Trouble was, she might think she liked living on the edge, but she didn't know how sharp it could be if a person stood on it for long enough. The question had never been *when* he would fall, it was always *where*: one side heaven, the other hell. He had visited the latter too often over the years. It shouldn't have been a surprise he wanted to reach out and grab a taste of the alternative, even if it was just for a while.

But hold on to it for too long and there was a chance he might haul her into the abyss with him, clinging desperately to whatever light he could find in the darkness. It was why he could never ask for something from her that he couldn't return. Risking his life was easier than emotional involvement. When the stakes were at their highest he felt more alive, stronger; free of the things that weighed him down. It was how he felt when he kissed her.

Oh, yeah, he was in trouble all right.

To make matters worse, she angled her chin, her expression suggesting she knew something was wrong.

Daniel took a short breath, 'How much longer do you think we'll be here?'

She glanced across the bar. 'An hour, maybe two…' She looked at him again. 'If you want to go—'

'No,' he said firmly. 'I was just thinking we skipped lunch and you should eat. If Stu can't rustle up a sandwich, I'll go get us something.'

Releasing her, he slid around the booth and walked away. While there were certain things he couldn't give her, he liked to think he could make up for it in other ways. He wanted to take care of her. Not out of a sense of duty attached to his job or the responsibility that stemmed from her connection to his family. Strangely enough it wasn't entirely because she meant something to him, though there was no denying she did. When he thought it over, it kept coming back to one thing. The same thing that had made him retreat when he thought he might hurt her and try to make amends when it felt as if he had.

She was *Jo*.

It was as simple and as complicated as that.

CHAPTER NINE

*'There's a lot of truth in the sayings on a fridge magnet.
For example: How many roads must a man walk down before he'll admit he's lost?'*

HE WAS driving her just the tiniest bit crazy.

'Could you quit doing that?' She slapped his hand.

'Isn't clearing up after dinner usually one of the things a guy gets brownie points for doing?'

'I could be a closet neat freak for all you know.'

Glancing around her apartment, he had the gall to look amused. 'Can't be easy in Aladdin's cave…'

Considering every eclectic knick-knack, photo frame and somewhat haphazard arrangement of soft furnishings was a much-loved memento of the life he had turned upside down, Jo took offence. 'People who live in an apartment for longer than a handful of months have been known to make it look like home.'

Daniel leaned back against the counter. 'Apparently they also make friends with everyone inside two blocks. You should be more careful when you live alone. Think about varying your routine. The guy in the Chinese place knew your name and where you lived from your order.'

'Traditionally that's how food gets delivered,' Jo said dryly as she folded down the edges of the cartons.

'Not when an order is being collected.'

'Do you see potential serial killers everywhere you look?' She frowned at how snippy she sounded. 'I trust in my initial impression of people. There tends to be truth in it until our heads get in the way. You should try it some time.'

'You know I'm going to ask the obvious now, right?'

'Not going there.'

'I can take it.'

'Not my main concern.'

'It's because it opens us up to my initial impression of you, isn't it?' He opened the refrigerator door. 'You telling me you're not curious?'

Placing the cartons on a shelf, she turned to take their glasses to the sink. 'It's got nothing to do with curiosity. I doubt you even remember when it was.'

'I have a long memory.'

She sighed. 'Revisiting the things that started us arguing in the first place probably isn't wise at this point.'

'Can't be any worse than the mood you've been in since I got here. When you're ready to tell me what the problem is let me know.' Closing the door, he pushed his large hands into the pockets of his jeans and continued the conversation as if he hadn't made her feel like a petulant three-year-old. 'We met the fourth of July weekend Liv brought you home.'

No, they didn't. If she was in a better mood than the one she'd been in since *before* he got there, she could have told him exactly when they met. It was—

Lifting her chin, she blinked as the memory made its way up from the deepest recesses of the well where she stored the things she'd chosen to forget. Suddenly she could remember the first time he sucker-punched her with his infamous smile. She could see what he was wearing, how gorgeous he looked, most of all she remembered how she'd *felt*. It didn't take a genius to work out the events between their first and second meeting had an effect too. But it certainly shed a different light on her reaction to him when he foolishly opened his mouth that fourth of July weekend.

'You were quieter then,' he said.

'Bit difficult to get a word in edgeways when your family is gathered en masse.' Setting the glass on the drainer with a shaking hand, she took several calming breaths.

'Roomful of cops is normally enough for most people.'

She nodded. 'There was that too.'

'Shouldn't be a problem unless you feel guilty…'

Grimacing, Jo reminded herself he couldn't possibly know what she currently felt guilty about. Instead she thought back to her feelings that day. 'Bit hard to avoid guilt when you're somewhere you know you don't belong.'

'That's how you felt?'

'I didn't belong anywhere back then.'

'What about now?'

'I like to think I've claimed my own little corner of the world. You should try that some time too.'

'You think I haven't?' he asked as she turned to face him.

Jo avoided his too-blue gaze when it felt as if he could see right through her mask of calm. 'The big pile of unpacked boxes in your apartment would suggest otherwise.'

'Short lease, remember?'

That big ticking clock she could hear? The one telling her how little time she had to repair the damage inflicted by the war *she'd* started? Oh, yes, she remembered. Since it sped up the countdown, it added to the regret she felt for taking the assignment she was offered that afternoon.

Daniel had started texting her when she was in the office preparing for an editorial meeting. Initially a continuation of the word game they'd played—one she didn't intend to play while they were *working*—she ended up grinning like an idiot by the time they were swapping comments chock-a-block with sexual innuendo. He really was *bad*. An hour later the girls sitting at the desks next to her demanded to know who 'he' was because it had to be a man to put a smile like *that* on her face. They asked for details and it was tempting to share them, if for no other reason than she hadn't been able to with anyone else.

She was dangerously close to blushing—and she had *never* blushed—when her editor appeared, sent everyone scurrying back to work and asked if she could have a moment. To make matters worse the epitome of unabashedly single, career-driven woman felt the need to enquire about her 'availability' for a big assignment before offering it to her. As a result the words 'yes' and 'absolutely' left Jo's lips before she had time to consider exactly what it meant.

When looking around her apartment led to thoughts of how much she would miss it when she was gone, she frowned. 'Don't you want a place you can call home?'

'New York is home, doesn't matter where I live in it.'

Jo disagreed. She had lived in the city her entire life, but since four weeks of that time had involved sleeping beneath an underpass she knew the difference between living somewhere and having a place to call home. She looked into his eyes again. 'What is it about here you like best?'

He thought about it for a moment. 'You work in New York, you see people face to face. It's not like California where you spend half your life in a car or overseas when you fight an enemy without ever looking into their eyes.'

It was the kind of insight that would have made her like him a lot earlier if she'd given him half a chance. 'When were you in California?'

'I was stationed in San Diego with the Marines.'

Another thing she hadn't known. 'You said work in New York. What is it you like about living here?'

'Same answer.'

'Nothing else?'

'You could try telling me what you're looking for,' he replied with a hint of a smile.

A lump appeared in her throat, forcing her to take a moment and swallow it so she could control her voice. She didn't deserve a smile. Not when she'd been the way she was with him since he landed at her door. It wasn't his fault her head was a mess. Not *entirely*. 'I don't get how you can see here as home without looking for a few hundred square feet to call your own. Aren't you sick of living out of boxes?'

'You forget up until not so long ago those boxes were in storage. Everything I needed I carried on my back.'

'Everything a *Marine* needed,' she clarified. 'You're home now, so why not make one? You can't tell me after the number of times you've moved apartments there haven't been places you liked enough to stay.'

'There were.'

'Then why do you...?' Her voice trailed off as some of the pieces slotted together. 'You move because of the nightmares, don't you? The minute someone hears you or you *think* they've heard you...' She knew instinctively she was right but it didn't make sense. He'd been moving from place to place for as long as she'd known him. She took a short breath. 'I'm just gonna jump right in here...'

'Do you have another speed?'

'Did something happen when you were overseas?'

'It's not the first time you've asked that question.' His eyes narrowed. 'What makes you so sure something happened?'

'If it didn't where do the nightmares come from?'

'How about we try to forget I have them?'

'Go back to pretending I don't know?' Her eyes widened in disbelief. 'Can you even *do* that?'

'Works better if you don't bring it up.'

'How long have you had them?'

The desire she felt to give him what he'd been searching for returned with the shadows in his eyes. There was no point denying it. Since the first night she heard him yelling beyond the wall, it had felt as if he were calling out to her.

Now, if she could take his pain and give him even one night of peace, she would do it for him. Any secrets he wanted to stay hidden she would keep safe, tucked away with one she already carried for him. But when it came to anything more, she couldn't see past a sudden crippling fear of falling for him.

Using every trick she had learnt in the past to hide how she really felt, she lifted her chin. 'What happened to trying to communicate better?'

'The theory behind that was we wouldn't argue as much.' He smirked. 'In case you hadn't got it by now, pushing me on this will have the opposite effect.'

'If having an argument is what it takes to get you to talk to me then we're about to have one.'

'We both know you've been itching to pick a fight with me since I got here.'

The sensation he was backing off again wasn't helping. She *hated* when he did that. Frustration bubbled inside her. 'How long, Daniel?'

'And now I'm Daniel again.' Taking his hands out of his pockets, he pushed off the counter and headed for the chair where he'd tossed his jacket. 'How about I go back into the hall and we try starting tonight over again?'

Jo followed him. 'Whether you like it or not we've been in these nightmares together since you moved in.'

'Now you're using guilt to get me to talk to you?' His fingers closed around his jacket. 'Keep this up and we'll go from communicating better to name, rank and serial number.'

'Do you have any idea how difficult it is to hear you in that much pain?' She frowned as the truth left her lips. 'I spend half the night waiting for it to start and when it does it's *hell*.'

When he clammed up in a way that suggested he had never intended to talk about it, Jo wanted to slap him. Knowing she would have equal difficulty discussing certain things didn't seem to make a difference. She just wanted to help or offer comfort or simply listen while he talked it through. Not to feel so cut off from him when they suddenly had so little time left.

'Yesterday you wanted one reason why I still help Jack. Now I'm asking you for an answer.' Taking a breath, Jo vowed it was the last time she would bend unless he bent a little in return. It was uncomfortable, not to mention a little scary, being out on a limb alone. *'How long?'*

She didn't think she could get into an argument without other things spilling out in the heat of the moment. Things she wasn't ready to talk about yet, if ever. Avoiding his icy gaze, she pointed across the room. 'I'll be over there on the sofa while you decide whether to stay or go.'

It was as much leeway as she could give him. His refusal to talk to her about the nightmares after she'd talked to him about her past felt like a rejection. What was worse, it *hurt*. She should have kept her mouth shut, had no idea why she had confided in him in the first place, and if the first time she shared things with someone ended with her feeling like a fool…

Suffice to say she wouldn't be in a hurry to do it again.

Daniel wavered in a manner that would get him killed on the front line of a battlefield. As she sat down, switched on the television and started jumping between channels he ground his teeth together. But what difference did it make how long he had nightmares? Wasn't as if she could figure out the rest without help, even if she'd worked out why he moved apartments a tad too quick for his liking. Drawing a breath, he decided he could give her the one thing she wanted to know. But it was a case of give a little to get a little. Once he had answered, she was telling him what had been bothering her.

Tossing his jacket back on the chair as she settled on a channel, he walked around the sofa and sat down beside her.

'Eight years.' He eased the remote from her hand. 'And we're not watching a chick-flick.'

'We're not watching something with explosions and a high body count either,' she retorted.

'Car chases.'

'No.'

He continued scrolling through the options at the bottom of the screen. 'Alien invasion: that one's good.'

'Nerd.'

'Bank robbery it is, then.'

She sighed heavily. 'You're going to criticize the police procedure the whole way through this, aren't you?'

'Yup.' Tossing the remote out of her reach, he leaned back and stretched his arms over his head, casually dropping one of them on her shoulders on the way back down.

Her head turned, brows lifted as she looked into his eyes. 'Seriously?'

'What?'

'That move went out with drive-ins.'

'I heard they were making a comeback.' Setting his feet on the chest she used as a coffee table, he pulled her closer to his side.

It took another five minutes for her to take her shoes off. Tossing cushions out of the way, she leaned into him and curled her legs beside her body. Finally she took a breath and looked up at him, her voice low and soft. 'You can't have gone that long without sleep. You wouldn't be upright.'

'Eventually your body says enough's enough. I'm due an eight-hour coma soon.' He reached out and tucked a strand of hair behind her ear. 'With any luck it'll get here at night so I don't wake you up.'

She grimaced. 'Despite what you think I didn't say that to make you feel guilty.'

'I know.' But since he'd already given her more than he planned, it was his turn. 'Tell me what's been bothering you since I got here.'

Turning her head, she dropped it back against his arm, closed her eyes and scrunched up her face. There was a low, strangled sound from the base of her throat before her eyes popped open. Then she turned towards him, tucking her legs underneath her. 'Can we talk about the whole thoughtful and protective combo you've been using on me first?'

'*Okay,*' he replied with suspicion.

'Could you stop doing it?'

He stifled a smile. 'Taking the independence thing a tad too far, don't you think?'

'See?' She scowled. 'You're doing it again. It's the tone you use.'

'I only have the one voice.'

'No, you don't. It changes.' Lifting a hand, she counted them off on her unfurling fingers. 'There's your considerate voice, your seductive voice, your "I'm in trouble if I don't shut up soon" voice—'

He captured her hand. 'Let's go back to the problem you have with thoughtful and protective.'

'I don't like it.'

Yes, he got that from the number of times she'd resisted it. 'Protect is what I do,' he reasoned. 'Along with the word serve it's written in big letters along the sides of vehicles with big flashing lights on top. You may have noticed them in the city.' A corner of his mouth tugged wryly as he admitted, 'Thoughtful I have to work on from time to time.'

'No,' she said with a small pout. 'You're pretty good at that one too.'

He took a breath. 'Let me get this straight. You want me to not care what happens to you and be more inconsiderate.'

Jo opened her mouth, closed it and rolled her eyes. 'It sounds stupid when you put it like that.'

'Little bit.' He nodded.

She jumped from one subject to another. 'You can't text me when I'm in work.'

'If you were busy you wouldn't have answered.'

'That's not the point. Some of those messages were…' She rocked her head from side to side while seeking a word in the air beside his head.

'I could point out it takes two people to have text sex.'

'We weren't having text sex.'

'Text foreplay,' he corrected. 'Still takes two people.'

She changed subject again. 'What happened yesterday?'

'Might need you to narrow that one down…'

'You backed off,' she said with a note of accusation.

'Said I would, didn't I?'

'Not to the point where finding food was as urgent as someone lying across the bar with a gunshot wound.'

The second he realized he'd stepped into an ambush Daniel swore viciously inside his head. He'd been right to think she knew there was something wrong. On the way home he'd put her uncharacteristic silence down to exhaustion. But she'd been thinking about it the whole time, hadn't she?

'And there's that look again.' She aimed a brief glare at him. 'I swear you're turning me into a harridan.'

'A what?'

'Never mind.'

Without warning she changed position, freeing her fingers so she could brace her hands on his shoulders as she straddled his lap. When she wriggled her hips Daniel clamped his hands on her waist to hold her still before their bodies aligned. It was difficult enough to stay one step ahead of her without the kind of moves he'd pictured them doing naked.

'Talk to me,' she demanded.

'You know I can move you off me if I want to end this conversation.' He set his feet on the floor in preparation.

'Still sitting here, aren't you?' She arched a brow. 'Did you feel bad about trying to play me?'

What the—? Daniel frowned. 'When did I do *that*?'

'All those thoughtful things you claim you have to work at—they're part of your campaign to get me into bed.'

'Considering my many skills in the art of seduction, I'm a little insulted by that.' He shook his head. 'Guy can't make the effort to be nice to you, can he?'

'Being nice isn't supposed to take effort.'

'That's the thing with resistance. It makes everything more difficult.'

'So stop resisting and tell me what happened yesterday.'

Daniel sought a safe route through the minefield they were entering and—since it seemed pointless trying—dumped pretence in favour of a little dose of honesty. 'Think you'll find it any easier to talk to me about why you still have doubts than I'm finding this?'

'No,' she admitted in a thicker voice. 'But while we're on the subject, why don't you have doubts?'

'When it comes to sleeping with you, I thought I'd made it clear where I stand.' One of his hands slipped from her waist to her hip. 'I can run through it again if you like…'

Her eyes darkened. 'Not necessary.'

'Well, then…' Sliding his hand further down her leg, he edged his fingertips beneath the hem of her skirt. Gaze fixed on her face, he watched her reaction as he touched the soft skin on the outside of her thigh.

Full lips parted as she sucked in a low breath. Her long lashes lowered as she focused on his mouth. Distracting them from the topic of conversation wouldn't take much, but while Daniel knew he could get lost in her, he sensed a small corner of her mind wouldn't be there. Selfishly he wanted it to be; for her to share with him the moments when everything became sharper, clearer, there was one common goal and nothing else mattered. No yesterday, no tomorrow, no half an hour ago or two hours from then. He wanted her to see the side of him few people did outside his working environment—before the mistakes were made or the self-recrimination could set in.

'Do you think about when this is over?' she asked in a smaller voice as if she stepped inside his thoughts. 'About the mess we could leave behind?'

'Yes,' he said roughly.

'Me too,' she whispered before distracting him with a swipe of her tongue across her lips. 'Best-case scenario, we end up in a better place than we were before. Worst case—'

'We end up saying things to each other we can never take back,' he finished.

'Yes.'

When Daniel looked into her eyes again he found enough vulnerability to punch a hole in his chest. She didn't just have doubts, she was genuinely terrified…of *him*? What had he done to frighten fearless Jo? When the thought entered his mind, he dismissed it as swiftly as it arrived. A woman didn't kiss as she did, move as she did or look at a man the way she did when she wanted him if she didn't have an intimate knowledge of sex. So what else could it be?

He thought out loud. 'Maybe the problem we have right now is trust…'

Her gaze lowered to the hands that had moved from his shoulders to his chest. 'You're saying you don't trust me.'

'No, babe, that's not what I'm saying.' He took a long breath and chose his words carefully. 'I can't promise you this won't be a mess when it's over…'

'I know.' She smiled the same tremulous smile that had sent up a warning flare for him in the first place.

'Do you know I would never willingly do anything to hurt you?' It floored him how much he needed her to know that. But even as he said the words he knew he had to amend them. 'If anything I said or did in the past—'

'Don't.' She pressed a forefinger to his mouth for a second. 'I get it. You think *I* don't trust *you.*'

'Why would you? I haven't done anything to earn it.'

She thought it over for a second. 'It's not that I *don't* trust you. I'm just—'

'Wary,' he supplied, feeling the something he still didn't recognize expand inside his chest when her eyes warmed at the understanding.

'Yes.'

'I'm not sure you should trust me, Jo,' he heard his voice say. 'When I'm around you, *I* don't trust me.'

'Why not?' She used the hand on his jaw to turn his head when he broke eye contact. 'No, I need to look into your eyes when you tell me so I can see if they're there.'

'See if what's there?'

'The blue goes cloudy. You have shadows.' Her fingertips whispered over his jaw. 'They're how I know there's something you're not telling me.'

Daniel felt as if something heavy were pressing down on his chest, each breath requiring considerably more effort.

As if she could sense it, Jo angled her head and looked deeper into his eyes, her hand turning so the backs of lightly bent fingers could skim the side of his neck. 'Tell me why you don't trust yourself around me.'

'I carry a lot of baggage. I'm not willing to offload it on you.' He frowned, both at the confession and the roughness of his voice. So much for the techniques the Marines taught in the event of capture and interrogation. She might as well hand him a pen and paper so he could save them both time by mapping out the weaknesses in his lines of defence.

'You think you're the only one with baggage?'

'No.'

Hand turning, she ran her fingertips under the curved neckline of his sweater, her gaze lowering to watch what she was doing. 'Shall I tell you a secret?' she whispered as her gaze tangled with his again.

Daniel nodded, mesmerized by her eyes and hypnotized by her touch.

'I want you more than I've ever wanted anyone.' When she smiled, it was steeped in sensuality. 'I fantasize about you, what we'll be like together and how it will feel. Right now, when we're like this, I doubt my doubts.'

If she was saying what he thought she was saying…

Leaning in, she pressed her lips to the throbbing pulse on his neck. A jolt of heat seared through his body, settling hot and heavy in his groin. Moving his hands to the curve of her spine, he slid her forward on his lap, aligning their bodies the way nature intended. She took a shuddering breath when she discovered what she was doing to him, moved her hips in a way that made him stifle a groan. He wanted her with a desperation he'd never experienced before. It suddenly felt as if she were a lifeline and if he didn't grab hold of it and hold on tight—

When she whispered in his ear, her warm breath caressed his skin. 'What scares me is how I feel when I can hear you on the other side of the wall and I can't get to you. The times when you're so far away from me it feels like I can't reach out and touch you…'

Daniel had experienced similar scenarios, so he knew how it felt from her point of view. But he had never been on the other side.

She took another shuddering breath. 'I need to know that you're with me and we're in this together…'

For the first time in his life he knew what it felt like to be trapped and helpless. The kind of faith it took to hand over control. He didn't consider himself a hero when he went to work. He was just a guy doing his job, failing more often than he would prefer. The real heroes were people who trusted completely and laid their lives in another person's hands.

'I'm right here, Danny. Let go…'

The words were so low they were almost lost in the storm he could feel raging inside him. It was possible she might not have said them, the need coming more from him than from her. But even if he hadn't imagined them he couldn't let go. If he did a mountain of torn and bleeding emotions would collapse and he would be crushed under their weight. He was too worn down, too exhausted from fighting the demons who took him to hell night after night. If she knew how inadequate he was, the number of times he'd failed someone who reached out to him…

'Jo—' He choked on her name.

'Shh…' Pressing soft lips to his mouth, she fed him kiss after desperately needed kiss.

At first there was only the taste of her, her heat and a sense of glory he had never known could be found in surrender. Then she rocked her hips, grinding her heat against the tight fit of his jeans and lust exploded inside his body with the force of a percussive blast.

With the equivalent of a dying breath, Daniel dragged his mouth from hers to rasp, 'Tell me to go.'

'No.' Full lips curved into a decadent smile against his mouth. 'Make love to me, Danny. *Take me to bed.*'

It was the sweetest command he'd ever been given.

CHAPTER TEN

'Mix and match can have a disastrous outcome if you get it wrong. But step outside your comfort zone and you might discover something unique.'

DENSE lashes fluttered as he started to wake up, the movement absurdly delicate against the masculinity of his face.

Jo smiled when she was looking into vivid blue eyes. 'Good morning, sleepyhead.'

''Morning,' his deep voice replied, the mattress dipping as he rolled towards her. 'What time is it?'

'Saturday o'clock and I believe your shift doesn't start until midnight.' Moving closer to the edge of the pillow, she rested her cheek on her palm. 'I've been thinking…'

'Uh-oh…'

'You know what I've never done?'

'Spent the night waking someone up so you can sleep?'

It was the kind of opening she could have used to get him to talk to her. But considering the major step forward they'd taken in intimacy she found herself wary of taking an equally giant step back. 'I've never spent the day in bed with a sexy naked guy,' she confessed with a dramatic sigh. 'Don't suppose you know where I could find one?'

'I prefer not to start my day with hitting someone.'

'Guess I'll have to settle for you, then.'

He smiled lazily. 'How come?'

'Because you're the only naked guy here?'

'I meant how come you've never spent a day in bed with a sexy naked guy before?'

'Workaholic.' She rolled her eyes. 'Sad, I know.'

'No,' he said in a lower voice. 'Just surprising…'

'There's a little more to my job than sitting in a coffee shop three times a week.'

'After seeing your work schedule I don't doubt that.' He stretched his large body, claiming even more of the bed. 'What I find tough to believe is some other guy hasn't *tried*.'

Jo stifled another smile. 'Correct me if I'm wrong, but until recently weren't you convinced men were throwing me out of their apartments in the middle of the night?'

'That was before I knew you better.'

'And you think you know me better now?'

'I'd like to hope so.' He took a long breath. 'But it's more a case of show than tell.'

Heat flared through her body when he slanted his mouth over hers. Her skin was hyper-sensitive, as if everywhere he'd kissed and caressed while he undressed her had been branded by his touch. If there had been any question her body was tuned into his there was no doubt now. His need magnified hers. His desire for her made her want him more. For years they had been unable to hold a conversation but in one night it felt as if they'd learnt to communicate without words. He dragged his mouth from her lips to blaze a heated trail down her neck, his magic fingers skimming her body from hip to waist. A purr of sinful pleasure ran through her body in response; the combination of strong male and gentle touch unbelievably carnal. But when he moved his hand higher and got to her ribs, she squirmed.

'Mmm,' he hummed in a low, vibrating rumble into her ear. 'That I didn't know.'

'Don't,' she warned unconvincingly.

He did it again.

Amid squeaks of protest and bursts of laughter, naked limbs tangled with sheets. Deeper chuckles of laughter joined hers, filling her with a sudden burst of undiluted joy. When they rolled off the edge of the bed and she landed on top of him, Jo leaned back and blew a strand of hair out of her eyes. She still didn't know why their relationship had changed, but as she smiled down at his grinning face it didn't matter.

All that mattered was he looked as happy as she felt.

Beyond happiness she could feel an irresistible, heart-warming tenderness. Whether it came from him or from her, she didn't know. She ran her fingertips over early morning shadow and warm skin, her gaze studying the different shades of blue in his amazing eyes. How he had looked at her as their bodies joined together was something she would never forget. It felt as if he had given her something she never had to give back. To deny she had given him something in return was pointless.

For the first time, instead of allowing someone to occupy a tiny corner of her heart, she'd given part of it away.

Without warning emotion clogged her throat. Leaving him would be one of the most difficult things she'd ever had to do. How was she supposed to tell him she was leaving when she couldn't cushion it with the confession she didn't want to go? She would miss him. But she'd been alone before. She could do it again. She didn't have a choice. Not if giving up the dream within her grasp meant replacing it with one she could never—

'What is it?' he asked in a deeper, rougher voice.

Unwilling to take a chance he would know she was lying—even if it was just with a shake of her head—she leaned down and pressed her mouth to his. The one more minute she'd once wanted had become one more day. She didn't want what they had to be over yet. She wasn't ready to let go.

In the absence of honesty, she sought the lightness she'd been aiming for when he awoke.

'Know what else I figured out when I was thinking?' she mumbled against his lips. 'A woman must have taught you some of those moves you used on me last night.'

'Not going there,' he mumbled back.

'I'm thinking older woman, younger Danny…'

His mouth curled into a smile. 'Jealous?'

'Since I'm reaping the benefits I was thinking more along the lines of a thank-you card…'

'What makes you think I'm not a natural or inspired?'

'Inspired is good. I'd roll with that if I were you.'

He did, reaching a hand above them for a pillow when Jo was pinned beneath him. Tucking it beneath her head, he smiled a predatory smile. 'This whole day in bed—does it have to be *in* the bed to count?'

She batted her lashes. 'What did you have in mind?'

'Again,' he said in a rumble so soft it was more like a vibration in his chest. 'More a case of show than tell…'

The 'interrupt the interrupted sleep' ploy was clever; he had to give her that. He was feeling better than he had in…

Yeah, it had been a while.

The first real test of how well they were doing appeared on their third night together. When he jolted into reality she was staring at him with wide, fear-filled eyes. But it hadn't been fear for herself, it was fear for *him*. Daniel felt the whispered caress of her touch soothing him. But when he looked at his hands and saw how tight he was holding her upper arms, he was filled with horror. What the hell was he doing? A wave of nausea rolled over him at the thought of leaving a bruise on her skin and he knew he had to get away from her. *Fast.*

She hadn't tried to stop him when he said he was going to run it out of his system. But before he left, her soft voice asked, 'What did it mean?'

He froze in the doorway. 'What did what mean?'

'You kept saying you needed two more; two of what?'

He walked away without answering. But despite the vow he made to place some distance between them, after a quiet shift filled with thoughts of her he was back at her door. Seeing her robbed him of his ability to speak. Determined to show her how much he needed her when unable to say it aloud, he kissed her welcoming smile and took her straight back to bed. One eight hour coma later and he was able to demonstrate what a damn fine specimen of manhood he could be when firing on all six cylinders. Unfortunately, it also meant something else.

But if he was being forced to leave her bed again he was determined to give her an afternoon to remember.

Leaning against a tree at the edge of the photo-shoot in Central Park, his gaze took in the details of a world he knew next to nothing about. Judging from what he had observed he wouldn't have the patience, whereas Jo seemed to thrive on it. She was animated, lively and enthusiastic; sparkling as if she inhabited some kind of secret magical kingdom. She obviously loved what she did. It glowed from her eyes.

For a second he found himself curious what it would feel like to have her look at *him* that way. But since it made the something he didn't want to identify ache in his chest…

'And that's a wrap, boys and girls!'

While models and assistants breathed a visible sigh of relief, the photographer held out a hand to Jo and waggled his fingers. 'Hand it over, my sweet. Have to be careful what awful images of me you place in the public domain…'

'With someone as photogenic as you?' Jo scoffed as she gave him a small digital camera.

Head bowed, he scrolled through the images. 'Not that one. *Definitely* not that one, and when I've deleted everything which doesn't meet my approval we can discuss your new friend.'

'What new friend?'

'The guy who has been watching your every move for the last fifteen minutes.' Waving a hand at a security guard with a silent *let him through* as Jo's gaze found Daniel, he made the comment, 'Obviously doesn't work in fashion…'

'No,' she replied. 'He's a—'

'Don't tell me. It's much more fun to fantasize.'

Daniel stepped over the line to claim his place beside her. 'Hey, babe.'

'Hello, handsome.' The photographer grinned.

Jo bit her lip and stifled a chuckle. '*Behave.* Christophe Devereaux, Daniel Brannigan. Danny, this is Chris.'

'Explains a lot about the smile you've been wearing this morning,' the man remarked as he looked Daniel over. 'How long have you been dating? Because seriously, honey, those clothes?'

'Kinda work for him, don't you think?'

'I suppose, in a blue collar kind of way. But picture him in Armani or Gucci or maybe a little—'

'Not gonna happen,' Daniel said dryly when he got tired of being talked about as if he weren't there. Being objectified was both uncomfortable and unfamiliar and since he'd been dressing himself from the age of two, he didn't need any help.

'Not a fan of labels,' Jo felt the need to explain.

It wasn't necessary in Daniel's opinion. He didn't have to answer to anyone, least of all a guy who obviously spent too much time in front of a mirror.

Christophe blinked. 'Well, *that* must be refreshing…'

Judging by the soft, almost affectionate smile she gave him, Daniel assumed it was a good thing. Somewhat pathetically it forced him to resist the urge to smirk at her friend. Five minutes in her magical kingdom and he suspected he wouldn't be viewed as much of a prince.

'You done for the day?' he asked.

'Yes. But you already knew that or you wouldn't be here. *Someone* obviously sneaked a look at my planner this morning...' Leaning forward, she placed the air kisses Daniel had always hated above each of her friend's cheeks. 'I owe you one for today. Thanks for letting me sit in.'

'We'll call it even for the support you gave me when I was a virtual unknown; nothing quite like a mention on that blog of yours to raise one's profile.' He aimed a haughty, almost territorial look at Daniel. 'Take care of her or you'll have me to deal with.'

Somehow managing to keep a straight face, Daniel gave him a nod in reply. It wasn't much of a threat. What was the guy going to do, fluff him to death? Eager to leave, he took Jo's hand. 'Let's go.'

'Just out of curiosity,' she said as they walked through the park, 'what would you have done if I'd met Liv today the way I was supposed to?'

'Still bugging you, isn't it?'

'That I'm keeping something from my best friend?'

'Even when we come out there will be certain things you can't discuss with her, you know that, right?'

Her eyes widened. '*When* we come out?'

Oh, no, she didn't. 'We're not arguing today. I have plans for what's left of it.'

'Where are we going?'

'Wait and see.'

'Is it a surprise?' She brightened. 'For *me*?'

He smiled when it literally put a skip in her step. 'Do I need to explain the concept of wait and see?'

'Are we there yet?'

'No.'

Several repetitions of the same Q&A later, he stopped in the middle of a path and her brows lifted in anticipation.

'You have two choices. Zoo—' he jerked a thumb over his shoulder '—or that...'

Leaning to the side to look around him, she stilled and for a moment Daniel thought he'd got it wrong. Then her face lit up. 'Are you kidding me?' She threw herself at him. 'I *love* this!' After a tight hug, she stepped back and grasped hold of his hands. 'You're coming on all the rides, right?'

'I'm not sitting on the little wooden horses.'

'Ever kiss a girl on a carousel?'

'Wouldn't that be kissing and telling?'

As they stepped through the gates she turned towards him. 'I refuse to participate in my surprise until you agree to do everything with me.' She focused on his mouth, looked into his eyes and smiled meaningfully. 'But I promise to make it worth your while if you do…'

'Attempting to bribe a police officer?' Daniel assumed a deadpan expression. 'You know I can arrest you for that.'

'Silly.' She rolled her eyes. 'If you put me in a cell for the night how will you collect your reward?'

If he was getting to spend the night with her it would be a good point. 'You want pink fluffy stuff on a stick or do you want to eat something sensible?'

'Pink and fluffy.' She tugged on his hand. 'We can take it on the carousel with us.'

Leaning against a ridiculous-looking wooden horse was as much of a compromise as he was prepared to make. While the platform began to move he watched her suck her fingers before peeling off another lump of fluffy candy. She'd been driving him crazy with that move while they stood in line; the glint in her eyes telling him she knew exactly what she was doing. Reaching out, he curled his hand around the back of her neck and pressed his mouth to hers. Intended as punishment for her actions, it instead led to the first sugar rush of his life. When he lifted his head she stayed where she was, eyes closed and a blissful smile on her face.

She sighed. 'Carousels officially rock my world.'

Daniel smiled. Not as much as she rocked his.

Several rides later, he was hooked on her enjoyment and feeling pretty damn proud of himself for satisfying her need for fun. It was another thing he could add to his new list, having scrapped the one he made before they got involved. Now she was his to take care of, his to protect and her needs were his to satisfy; the mantra of *his, his, his* going a long way towards pacifying his inner Neanderthal every time one of the guys running a ride was foolish enough to flirt with her.

They took a break to grab a couple of soft pretzels with mustard. Jo shared her pretzel with a horde of cocky, well-fed pigeons while Daniel managed to share a dollop of mustard with his jeans. Biting down on a corner of her lower lip when he did it, she helpfully tried to remove the stain with a paper napkin until he was forced to remind her they were in a public place. Where there were *children* present. After a leisurely kiss to promise she could do whatever she wanted to him when they got home he watched as she looked over the crowd and smiled. Following her line of vision he discovered one of the children he'd mentioned with what was either a mother or a nanny; lightning-fast fingers fixing a braid in dark hair.

'Do you remember her?' he asked.

'My mom?'

When her smile faded a little, Daniel sought out a hint of regret for asking but couldn't find it. Hypocritical as it was, he wanted to know everything about her while remaining unable to give her the same in return.

He nodded. 'Yeah.'

Jo took a short breath and thought about what to tell him the way she always did when they discussed a subject she found difficult. It was how he knew when she was sharing things with him she hadn't told anyone else, the knowledge both humbling and adding to his guilt for being unable to do the same.

'Little things,' she replied as she fed the last of her pretzel to the pigeons. 'I can remember how she brushed my hair. She used to follow the brush with her hand.' A hint of wistful smile appeared. 'I still do that.'

'I know.' It was part of her morning routine. Watching her dress was almost as fascinating to him as taking her clothes off. When she looked at him in a way that suggested she knew what he was thinking he added another prompt. 'Keep going.'

There was another moment of thought as she selected a gift for him from a cache of precious memories. 'She used to hum when she was doing housework. My dad would say one of the reasons he loved her was because she had a song in her heart. He used to wink at me before he sneaked up behind her to dance with her. It drove her crazy if she was in the middle of doing something but she always laughed.' Jo nodded and smiled again. 'She had a great laugh.'

'What did she look like?'

'On rare occasions Jack will tell me how much I look like her.' She shrugged, the smile disappearing as she hid the hint of pain in her eyes with a blink of long lashes. 'I think it made it difficult for him to look at me when she was gone.'

Despite the matter-of-fact tone to her voice it was the first time he'd felt any empathy for her father. Daniel didn't want to imagine a world without Jo in it but he knew it would be a darker place. 'When did you start calling him Jack?'

'When he stopped being my dad.' She looked into his eyes and angled her chin. 'What was your dad like?'

Swift change of subject noted, Daniel shook his head and avoided her gaze. 'You already know the answer to that.'

'I know what everyone else in your family remembers.'

'You'd be better sticking with their impression. They argued with him less.'

'What did you argue about?'

'His disappointment in me was a favourite topic.'

Disbelief sounded in her voice. 'He *said* that?'

'With due cause.' He glanced at her from the corner of his eye, unwilling to go into detail beyond, 'None of the others ever mention how close I was to being the first Brannigan on the wrong side of the law?'

Her eyes widened. *'Shut up.'*

Pushing to his feet, Daniel turned and held out a hand, drawing her upright when her palm slipped into his. 'What do you want to do next?'

She smiled brightly. 'Finish talking about this comes to mind. I want to know what kind of trouble you got into.'

'And take a chance you might look at me differently?' A frown crossed his face as they walked towards a line of stalls. It was closer to the truth than he cared to admit. But since he wasn't convinced he wanted to know why, he left it alone.

'Well, *that* deserves a suitable punishment,' she retorted. When he glanced at her again, she was looking around. Her eyes lit up. 'Marines can hit targets, right?'

An hour later, he was trying to figure out how he'd ended up being the one carrying a three foot stuffed rabbit through the park. If making him feel like an idiot had been her goal he wasn't the only one who could hit a target. He held it up by long ears and gazed at it in disgust. 'It's cross-eyed.'

'Our imperfections make us unique,' her voice replied from above his head. 'Didn't anyone ever tell you that?'

Daniel looked at the pond. 'I wonder if it floats.'

'You *wouldn't.*'

'You can go get it when you fall off those rocks.'

'You see…' She turned and cocked a hip. 'I heard from a reliable source it's all about balance…'

He shook his head when she had to hold her arms out to her sides to stay upright. 'I'm not wading in after you.'

'You've got a lot to learn about when a girl wants to be

rescued and when she doesn't.' She turned her back to him and held her arms above her head. *'Catch.'*

Taking an immediate step forward when he realized what she was doing, he caught her in his arms as she fell.

'And you didn't drop the bunny either.' She grinned after checking. *'My hero.'*

Daniel nodded. 'You can use it as a life-preserver.'

Stepping closer to the edge of the water and swinging her back and forth, he smiled when she protested between bouts of lyrical laughter. Stilling, he looked down at her, his gaze roving over her face as he found himself wondering why it had taken so long to open his eyes and see what was right in front of him. Would it have made a difference if they'd got together earlier? Would his life go back to the way it was before when they were done? Maybe he should try to talk to her about—

'That one's new,' she murmured.

'What is?'

'The look in your eyes…'

Before he could scramble his way out of it or distract her with a kiss there was the sound of tinkling music.

She sighed heavily. 'That's my cell phone.'

'Don't answer it.'

'I have to.' She wriggled in his arms until he set her on her feet. Predictably the call resulted in the disappearance of Jo and the reappearance of dull, emotionless Jo.

Before she could say the usual words at the end of the phone call, he took a breath and held out his arm. 'I'm not carrying this thing on the subway.'

'A gentleman would,' she pointed out.

'Pity you're dating me, then, isn't it?'

She didn't try to stop him coming with her. But she would if she knew what he was planning to do. He'd had enough.

First opportunity he got—and he would damn well *make one*—Daniel was having that talk with Jack. Way he saw it, it was overdue.

CHAPTER ELEVEN

'When shopping it's important to keep an open mind. You can't always get what you want but be patient and you might discover exactly what you need.'

'I BETTER make him something to eat,' she said when they got Jack to his apartment a little after dark.

Daniel nodded. 'What else?'

'Check he has groceries.'

'You get what he needs from the store across the street. I'll make him something to eat.' When she wavered he added a firm, '*Go*. I've got this.'

Ignoring the voice in her head, Jo reached for her purse. If she was totally honest, breaking the habit of a lifetime to accept help probably stemmed from the need for a little space. As much as she had loved their afternoon together and felt bad for once again having to interrupt it, the one day she wanted kept turning into another and another. But she couldn't keep stealing memories, threading them together like glowing beads on a precious necklace. She had to tell him, especially when hiding it was slowly killing her. Trouble was she still didn't know why it was so darn difficult to find the words.

Seemed to Jo she'd been spilling her guts on pretty much every other subject, including things she'd never shared with anyone else. He was almost as good at getting her to do that as he was at avoiding sharing anything with her that did more than scratch the surface of his life.

Yes, that was bugging her too.

Halfway to the store she realized she hadn't checked the refrigerator to see what was there. But when she returned to the apartment she heard Daniel's voice say, 'I think it's time we had a talk.'

Jo froze inside the doorway. What was he doing?

'I'm only gonna say this once. You might not care what effect your actions have on your daughter, but I do. Cause her any heartache I'll be in your face 24/7. We clear?'

She was about to take a step forward when Jack replied, 'I love my Jo.'

'Did you love her when she ended up living on the streets because of you?' Daniel asked bluntly. 'She could have died. Someone she knew did—she tell you that?'

'No.'

'Course she didn't. Jo deals with things on her own; kills her to ask for help even with small stuff. If she knew I was talking to you right now she would kick my ass.'

True. Or at least be angry with him for interfering. But instead she remained frozen to the spot, unable to breathe.

'She's like her mom,' Jack said.

'Losing her that way can't have been easy.'

'It wasn't.'

'I'm sorry, Jack,' Daniel said with sincerity. 'I genuinely am. But do you think your wife would be happy Jo lost both her parents that day?'

Jo's eyes widened. How did he know that?

'If you want to honour her memory, this isn't the way to do it.' Daniel's voice took on the rough edge that always got to her. 'One day your beautiful daughter will meet someone, get married and have kids of her own. You want to miss out on your grandkids too? Wouldn't your wife want you to look for a piece of both of you in their eyes?'

Jack cleared his throat and answered, 'She would.'

The pain in his voice made Jo regret all the times they hadn't talked about her mom. They should have. But at eight she had found grief hard to handle and in later years she'd had too many other things to deal with. Then it was too late. Or so she'd thought. Hadn't been when she talked to Daniel, had it? Memories of her mom had flowed off her tongue as if they'd needed to be said. There had to be trust between them for her to have done that. The same trust that allowed her to stand silently by a door and let Daniel handle Jack his way.

She'd never let anyone do that before.

'You're going to have to shape up,' Daniel said. 'If I was the father of those kids I don't think I could trust you with them. But I'd want them to get to know you in the same way I'd want them to know about their grandmother. It would be nice if they could hear it from the man who loved her.'

Jo looked down and realized she had set a palm on her stomach. There was no question of her being pregnant but she had never thought about the kind of man she would want to be the father of her children. Frankly she'd never thought about *having* children. After all, she was twenty-four, wasn't like there was a rush. But with his mile-wide protective streak she knew Daniel would be an amazing dad. The thought of smaller versions of him another woman had given him...

Wow. Jo really didn't like that image *at all*.

'Still love her,' Jack said in a low voice.

'You ever think about getting grief counselling? I know someone who runs a group. It won't stop you drinking—you're the only one who can do that—but it might do you good to talk about her.' There was a brief pause before Daniel said, 'Lock stuff away, it can be harder to deal with. Trust me, I *know*.'

'You're a good man,' Jack said. 'Glad my girl has you in her life.'

So was she. There were dozens of things she would never forget about her time with him. But suddenly it didn't feel like enough any more.

'I'll drop the card by next week,' Daniel's voice said. 'Now let's see what we can get done before Jo comes back.'

As they moved she slipped back through the door, quietly closing it behind her. At the bottom of the stairs she swiped her cheeks and stared at the moisture she found on her hands. Crying was right up there with blushing on the list of things she never did. What was happening to her?

Pushing through the door, she walked across the street in a daze. She felt as if she was in shock. Not the least little bit as she'd thought she would feel if she fell in love. Surely feeling so numb meant she *wasn't* in love? Inside the store she picked up a basket and wandered aimlessly along the aisle. If she hadn't known there was a chance she was *falling* in love then what had she been so afraid of? Why was it so difficult to tell him she was leaving? Would she have reacted the way she did to the image of kids she hadn't given him?

Was she having a teensy little bit of a meltdown?

If it hadn't felt that way she might have reacted quicker when she rounded the corner. But by the time she realized what was happening it was too late.

Where was she?

With everything squared away and Jack sound asleep on the covers of his rack, Daniel drummed his fingers on the kitchen counter. He checked his wristwatch. She should have been back already. Restless, he decided to go look for her.

Jogging down the stairs and across the street, he opened

the door to the convenience store and checked the aisles. No Jo. Walking to where he assumed the checkout was he rounded a corner. There she was. An unwarranted sense of relief washed over him, but when her gaze darted to him and a brief look of agony crossed her face, he knew something was wrong.

Stilling, he looked to his left. *Son of a—*

'Don't move!'

Swiftly identifying the weapon pointed at the man behind the counter, Daniel made eye contact with the perp holding it. 'Take it easy. No one needs to get hurt.'

'Anyone come in with you?'

'No.' He took an instinctive step closer to Jo to shield her body with his. 'But you might want to think about locking the doors.'

'I said *don't move*!'

An unfamiliar buzz of fear swarmed over him, immediately replaced by a gathering rage he had to beat off with a mental stick. Since going Marine on the guy who'd placed his woman in danger wasn't going to help anyone but him, Daniel reined in his emotions and replaced them with rigid control. 'I'm just gonna lock that one.'

Without looking at her, he pointed a finger at the door a couple of feet past Jo. From what he could tell it was one of only two points of entry for a tactical team. While placing her within snatch and grab territory, it also put her directly in the line of fire. Daniel would take a bullet before he let anything happen to her. It was as simple as that.

'Why are you helping me?' The perp's gaze shifted between each of his hostages before he came to the conclusion Daniel was the greater threat.

Good call.

'I'd prefer not to get shot.' When a low gasp came from over his shoulder as the gun swung towards him, Daniel shrugged his shoulders and sent her a hidden message. 'I've got a hot date with a fiery redhead tonight.'

She was smart enough not to mention he was a cop, but he didn't want her to identify him by name. If an association was made between them, she could be used for leverage.

'Give him the money,' he told the man behind the counter.

'I don't want money. I want *my kid*,' yelled gun guy.

Couldn't walk into a simple hold-up, could she?

'I already said she's not here,' said the man behind the counter, drawing the perp's focus.

'Then you call her and get her to bring him down here.' The gun turned sideways, prodding the air. 'Do it *now*!'

Daniel moved his arm back and pointed his finger at the ground to indicate Jo should get behind him. In his peripheral vision he saw the slight shake of her head. She had chosen the wrong time to defy him. If he didn't have a job to do they'd be having the argument of a lifetime.

Sirens sounded in the distance.

'You called the cops?' the guy yelled.

Since he doubted the convenience store had a silent alarm, Daniel assumed a witness called 911. 'Still time to get out…'

The gun shifted direction again. 'Did *you* call them?'

'With my record?'

'What did you do?'

'Dealing.' He patted a pocket of his jacket to gauge the level of interest. 'Get us out of here before the cops arrive, I'll give you a sample.'

'I want my kid.'

So much for that idea. 'You do what you gotta do but I can't be here. They find me carrying, I violate my parole.'

'No one's going anywhere till I get my kid.'

'You've got hostages. They'll send in a SWAT team.' Daniel suppressed a threatening smile in case it fed into his deep-seated need to go feral. 'I heard those guys shoot first, ask questions later.' When his words garnered a glance towards the back of the store, he took a step forward. 'Let's go.'

'They'll catch us.'

Another step. 'Not if we move now.'

'I need time to think.'

Another step. 'I'm not going back inside.'

'Shut up and let me think!'

When there was a low clicking that indicated a round had been chambered, Daniel knew he was out of time.

'Get down!'

Launching forward, he grasped the gun arm, pushing it back and up. Tins scattered as he slammed it against a metal shelf. Once, twice and there was a cry of pain before the gun hit the ground. He kicked it out of reach, stepped forward, hooked an ankle and toppled the guy back onto the floor. Dropping to his knee, he flipped the body over, twisting the arm he held as he reached for the other one. From the moment he moved until the guy was restrained took less than ten seconds.

Once it was done, his gaze immediately sliced through the air to Jo. 'You okay?'

She nodded.

It didn't slow his heart rate. If anything, the fact she was standing on her feet added to the flood of rage he'd been suppressing. Which part of *'get down'* hadn't she got?

'I'm okay,' another voice announced, making Daniel swear viciously inside his head. There had been two hostages, Officer Brannigan, count them; one, *two*.

'Both of you get out of here. *Now.*' As he fought the red haze rapidly forming around the edge of his vision, he turned his head and saw her take a step towards him. 'I mean it, Jo,' he warned. 'You walk out that door, you go straight to the nearest squad car and you damn well stay there.'

It was the first time since his pre-Marine days he'd been

angry enough to yell his damn head off. He'd let her leave
the apartment alone. Better still, he'd *sent her* to the store.
If he hadn't gone looking for her, if he hadn't been there, if
a loose round had gone off…

Grinding his teeth together, he focused on deep, measured
breaths. His initial reaction was they'd gone beyond a promise she'd never go to the neighbourhood alone at night. If he
had his way she'd be lucky to ever see daylight again. His
second thought was every day of a life they shared would be
a battle between her independence and his need to protect
her. Fact was she didn't belong in his world any more than
he did in hers.

'Who *are* you?' asked a muffled voice from the floor.

'You don't stay still, I'll be your ticket to the nearest emergency room.' Adjusting his position, he reached into the back
pocket of his jeans. When he heard footsteps, he held his
badge over his head.

'Yeah, we know. Still got a bit of a problem with taking
time off, don't you?'

He glanced upwards. 'Hey, Dom.'

'Hey, Danny.' Dom grinned.

As the perp was cuffed and taken from him, Daniel got to
his feet and headed for the door. He'd known the payback for
his eight-hour coma was going to be a bitch, been prepared
to pay the price when he knew there was time with Jo as a
reward for holding on to his sanity. But to have one of the
scenarios associated with his nightmares become *reality*…

As he crossed the street his gaze cut through flashing
lights to locate her. Adrenalin still pumping, every tense
muscle in his body strained with the need to get to her, haul
her into his arms and never let go. But as she started to turn
towards him, he stopped dead in his tracks.

For a second everything simply went silent.

Then it hit him.

How could he not have known? How in hell had he not

seen it coming? He'd stood on the edge of bridges, rappelled out of choppers, faced gunfire, crawled into narrow spaces where he could be crushed like a bug and had never once been as fearful as he was in that store. And now he knew why.

Turning away before she looked at him, Daniel dug out his cell phone. The call he made for back-up would most likely add to the fallout but he needed time to regroup and he couldn't do that when she was there.

Unable to tear her gaze from him for long, Jo watched as he paced the street while talking on the phone. She wanted to be strong. As calm and collected as he was. But in comparison to the numbness she felt walking into the store, her emotions were all over the place. If he'd been shot…if she'd *lost* him while he tried to protect her…

'You're Danger Danny's girl?'

Nodding, she dragged her gaze from him to look at the uniformed officer. 'I'm Jo.'

'Dom Molloy—I worked with Danny out of the ninth before he moved to the ESU. It's nice to meet you, Jo.' The dark-haired man smiled in greeting. 'I need to ask some questions and take a statement. You feel up to that?'

She nodded again. 'Yes.'

'We'll go over here where it's quieter.'

'Okay.' Jo looked over her shoulder at Daniel while they left. She didn't want to be somewhere she couldn't see him, but she wasn't going to let him down. She would answer all of the questions clearly and concisely and make sure everyone knew how amazing he had been. The need to step into his arms and stay there until some of his warmth and strength seeped into her shaking body would have to wait.

In comparison to the event itself, which had happened in slow motion, the wrap-up seemed to fly by. Next thing she knew a voice called her name and she was blinking in surprise.

Liv folded her in a brief, tight hug before studying her face with concern. 'Are you okay?'

'I'm fine.' Her gaze moved from Liv to Blake and then back to Liv again. 'What are you doing here?'

'Danny called.'

'She was too wound up to drive,' Blake explained.

'What he means is I was worried sick about you.'

Jo opened her mouth to say there was no need when a deep voice sounded behind her and her breath caught.

'She's given a statement. She can go now.'

Spinning on her heels, she looked up at Daniel and drank in the sight of him. Her gaze lowered briefly to his chest to take inventory while she curled her fingers into fists at her sides. He was okay, she reassured her pounding heart. He was *right there*. She could stand and look at him without feeling the need to cling to him like a drowning woman. She *could*!

'What happened?' Liv asked.

'Suspected EDP; she walked into a 10-52.'

Jo had no idea what that meant but she was too busy trying to keep her head above an unexpected wave of pain to ask. The image was too close to her earliest memory of him—the ache to have him acknowledge her existence as desperate as it had been back then. If Mr Cool-Calm-And-Collected didn't look at her soon she was going to—

'Why are you in street clothes?' Liv inevitably asked.

'I'm off duty,' her brother replied.

'Then why are you here?'

'None of your business,' he said in his don't-mess-with-me voice. 'And if you cross-examine her on the way home there'll be one less monkey-suited brother at your wedding.'

'Like Mom will let that happen.'

Daniel crossed his jaw. 'Get her out of here, Liv.'

'Wait a minute.' When he walked away, Jo followed him. 'I don't even merit a "see you later"?'

He kept walking.

'Come back here.' She scowled at his broad back. *'Danny!'*

He turned and looked her straight in the eye. 'If I come back over there I'm going to yell at you.'

Even hidden behind a mask of restraint, the force of his anger knocked her back on her heels. She was wrong. He wasn't the least little bit cool and calm. Judging by the set of his shoulders he was barely collected. It might not have been the reaction she'd hoped for but it was better than nothing.

'What were you doing in there?' she asked in a far from steady voice.

'My job.'

'Is part of your job to see how many times you can almost get yourself killed before you get it right?'

'If it costs our life to get someone out, that's the price we pay.' He waved an arm at his side. 'Ask any of these guys in a uniform and they'll tell you the same thing.'

She gaped at him. 'You have no idea why I'm upset right now, do you?'

'I *warned you* about the danger in this neighbourhood,' he replied through gritted teeth.

'You're *blaming me* for this?' She could hear her voice rising. 'Do you think I went looking for a speeding bullet so you could jump in front of it and prove me wrong about needing to be rescued? I *know* the risks you take for other people, Danny. I just don't want you to take them *for me.*'

'I'm supposed to stand there and let you get shot?'

The thread she was hanging from snapped. 'Do you think I wanted you in there? I spent every second after I walked into that mess *praying* you wouldn't come find me! I knew what you would do but knowing and seeing it happen are two different things. Danger is *your* addiction, Danny, not mine. I know it doesn't matter to you who it is you're trying to save—'

'It doesn't matter who—?' He clamped his mouth shut, then nodded firmly. 'That's it. You're leaving now.'

'I'm not—' When he stepped forward, Jo took a step back. *'Don't you dare!'* He bent at the knee and tossed her over his shoulder, marching forward while she struggled. 'Put me down, Danny! I *hate* when you do this.'

'Where's your car?' he barked at his sister.

'End of the street,' she replied on what sounded like a note of amusement.

'Don't *help* him.' Jo lifted her hands, attempting to get her hair out of her eyes so she could glare at his sister. 'I want you to file for a restraining order. If you don't I'm reporting your unmitigated jackass of a brother for assault.'

He tossed her higher up his shoulder and kept walking.

Not caring if she was dropped on her rear, Jo continued fighting. 'You might have fooled me for a while, you great ape, but now I remember everything that bugged me most about you.'

He stopped and swung her from side to side before asking, 'Jeep on the corner?'

'Yes,' Blake said.

Was no one on *her* side?

'Don't for a single second think we're kissing and making up after this either,' she said without thinking as he started walking again. 'There isn't anything you can say or do that—'

'Did she just say kissing?' Liv asked.

'Yup,' Blake replied.

Daniel dropped her onto her feet by the Jeep and aimed a filthy look her way. *'Well done.'*

'Like they hadn't figured it out already,' Jo bit back before glancing at Liv. 'Thanks for jumping to my defence.'

'After you kept this little secret?'

'Leave her alone,' Daniel warned.

A burst of laughter left his sister's lips. 'Oh, I haven't even got started on you yet. If you think I'm not going to ask what your intentions are towards my best friend—'

'This is where I tend to leave them to it,' Blake told Jo in a low voice.

'Tempting,' she replied. 'But give me a minute.' Placing a thumb and forefinger between her lips, she whistled loudly.

When the siblings looked at her, she drew on her rapidly waning strength and looked at Daniel first. 'You're in enough trouble already. If you weren't such an idiot you would know what I needed to avoid this meltdown when you walked out of the store. In case you hadn't got it already, protecting me from your sister *wasn't it.*' She turned her attention to Liv. 'And if you can think of a way I could have told you I was using one of your brothers to test the chocolate theory, feel free to let me know.' She glared at each of them in turn and lifted her chin. 'Anything else anyone wants to say?'

'I'm good.' Liv nodded before looking at Daniel. 'You?'

He glanced down at her from the corner of his eye. 'I ever thank you for bringing her home with you?'

'You're welcome.'

When he looked at her, Jo could feel some of his anger had dissipated, but not by much. She really didn't think she could take much more. For sixteen years she had stood on her own two feet, faced everything life threw at her and *nothing* had ever got to her the way he did. She should hate him for that, but she didn't. That was the problem. She felt so many things at once she couldn't untangle them to make sense of it all.

'Finished yelling at me now?' he asked in a gruff voice.

Oh, that was *so* unfair. He'd even managed to say it in a way that made it feel as if she weren't the only one struggling. The girl who had always considered herself a fighter had never felt the need to run away more keenly.

'You want me to leave? Congratulations, Danny, *you win.*' The secret she'd kept tripped off the tip of her tongue. 'I'm booked on a flight to Paris in six days.'

Daniel looked stunned. 'What?'

'You heard me. No big deal, right? Just moves our schedule up a little.' Unable to continue looking at him and with her throat closing over, Jo turned away. When she reached for a handle to open the Jeep, her shoulders slumped. 'Can someone open the door, please?' There was a high-pitched blip and a click of locks. 'Thank you.'

The trip home was long and interminably silent, but Jo didn't want to talk. Instead she turned her head and watched the blur of colours and lights and people as the city went by. It wasn't how she'd wanted to tell him, but it was done now and there was nothing she could do to take it back.

'Where are we going?' she asked when something outside the windows didn't seem quite right.

'Our place,' Liv replied.

Jo shook her head. 'No, Liv, I want to go home.'

They conceded without too much fuss, which Jo appreciated in her exhaustive state. But after insisting she would see her all the way into the apartment, Liv turned to her with concern in her eyes. 'You're not okay, are you?'

Jo shook her head.

'Brannigan men can be a little thick-skulled. But Danny—'

'Liv—' Jo grimaced '—please don't.'

'Just this one thing and then I'll stop.' She took a short breath. 'Back when Danny was a kid he could make his body and his hands do whatever he wanted them to do. I heard he could toss a perfect spiral with a football at two—throw a killer curve with a baseball at three. Dad thought it made him cocky; felt he had to bring him down a peg or two by pushing him till he learnt he had limits. All it did in the end was make Danny twice as determined, ten times harder on himself, and half as communicative. Dad never broke him, not on the surface. But it doesn't mean he doesn't have feelings or can't be hurt…'

'I know,' Jo said on a harsh whisper.

'Try telling him what Paris means to you and he might—'

Emotion clogged her throat again. *'Liv—'*

'I'm stopping now.' She folded Jo into another hug. 'You had a rough night. Go get some sleep. I'll check in on you in the morning.'

Jo stood in the centre of the room for a long time after her best friend left, feeling more alone than she'd ever been. Paris had been her dream for a long time. But with it far off in the distance she'd never spared a moment to think about the things she would leave behind. She had worked long and hard, fought for a sense of security and been blessed with more than she dared hope for in the days when it all seemed so far away. But to leave the city she loved, her home, her friends...

To leave the man she loved...

It might have taken a while for her to admit it, but it was there: solid and fixed and unshakable. She loved him.

But there was no point pretending he felt the same way. If he wanted to share his life he would want to share it all: the good and the bad. By holding back he was saying she wasn't the one for him. If he could share everything with her the way she had started to with him... If she knew he loved her as much as she loved him...

She shook her head and held back the tears she desperately wanted to shed. In six days she would go to Paris.

End of story.

CHAPTER TWELVE

'New shoes, desserts, nights out; what do they have in common? When there's more than one option available there's nothing worse than having to make a choice.'

THE scenario of the nightmare was no surprise after the events in the convenience store. But the outcome was different.

A shot rang out.

Daniel looked at her. He knew she could see the agony on his face but fought to hide it from her. She staggered forward as he turned, reached for him as he dropped to his knees. Then she was sobbing, their fingers trying to stem the flow of red.

'It's okay,' he said gruffly.

'Don't leave,' she choked.

The pain flayed her soul. As Jo woke up she curled into a ball, hot tears rolling down her cheeks, soaking the pillow. It was the first nightmare she'd ever experienced. How he had got through so many of them…how strong he had to be not to lose his mind… He was so very brave…

She stilled and held her breath, blinking in the darkness, listening to the sounds coming through the wall. The impetus came as a large chunk was torn off her heart. She had to go to him. She didn't have a choice.

Not when he was calling her name.

* * *

When Daniel opened the door large watery eyes looked up at him. After tossing tangled tresses of hair over her shoulder, her hands tugged on the belt of a dressing gown. She made a quick study of his face, scowled briefly at his naked chest, then caught her soft lower lip in her teeth and took a breath.

'I can't do this any more,' she confessed in a crackly voice as she shouldered past him. 'We need to talk.'

Talking was the last thing he wanted to do, particularly if it involved sitting still. When something happened Daniel couldn't control, his reaction had always been the same. He had to keep busy. Keep moving. Keep pushing his body until his mind had time to work through it. Lying down sure as hell hadn't helped. Not when he'd been subjected to eight years' worth of failings in one session.

It was tough to believe he could love someone enough to deserve them when he was filled with self-loathing. He frowned as he closed the door. 'You're supposed to be with Liv.'

'I wanted to sleep in my own bed.' Realization crossed her eyes. 'What was the plan if we didn't walk into a stick-up? A night in one of the hotels you stayed in after you got back?'

He scrubbed a palm over his face. 'Jo—'

'Make me coffee.'

'I'm not making you coffee.' He glanced briefly at his watch. 'It's four in the morning.'

'We're talking about this.'

'No, we're not.'

'Yes, we are,' she insisted. 'If you don't talk about it then everything stays locked up in your head and no matter what you do it won't go away. I think you know that.'

He did. He'd said something similar to Jack. But pushing him when she already had him on the run wasn't the right move.

Daniel looked anywhere but into her eyes. Way he saw

it, she was right to get as far away from him as possible. It wouldn't take long for a smart woman like her to work out how much more he needed her in his life than she needed him. Since he didn't plan on sticking around for that revelation, he should thank her for beating him to the punch.

'Do you know you were calling my name tonight?' she asked.

He nodded.

'You remember every detail of them when you wake up?'

He nodded again.

After a brief silence, she sighed. 'Go put on a T-shirt. I'll make my own coffee.'

Daniel used it to buy time, splashing water on his face and blinking at the bathroom sink before he dug out a T-shirt. He had to let her say her piece. The break had to be clean. If it wasn't it would take longer to heal. When he returned, she was sitting at the breakfast bar, her gaze fixed on his chest as he walked across the room. He lifted a fist to rub the ache it created, a cavalry charge of sensation thundering across his senses. Coupled with the need to do something physical, his body leapt to attention—cocked, primed and ready for action. But no matter how tempting it was when she looked ruffled and soft and sexy, he couldn't get lost in her any more.

Waiting for him to sit opposite her, she slid a mug across the counter. 'You should drink decaf.'

'Bit pointless drinking coffee if it's not got caffeine.'

She flashed a brief smile. 'I feel the same way. But you should consider it.'

'It won't make a difference.'

'Are the nightmares always worse after your eight-hour coma?'

'Payback.'

Inky lashes swept downward, her gaze studying her mug

as she turned it in her hands. 'Did you have the nightmares when you were overseas?'

'Slept like a baby.'

'Explains why you're happy to go back.'

'It's part of it,' he allowed.

'What happened to me in this one?' she asked.

Daniel pressed his mouth into a thin line. Even while she was sitting in front of him, the images remained sickeningly clear in his mind. He honestly didn't know how he could look at her every day, feel the way he did and resist the urge to smother her in the protectiveness she didn't want from him. She would try to soothe and reassure with a whispering touch and softly spoken words but even that wouldn't help.

A man like him should take care of the people he loved. It wasn't supposed to be the other way round.

'We're not talking about it,' he said firmly. 'I know you want me to but I can't.'

Her gaze lifted, her voice soft. 'Yes, you can.'

'No.' He amended the statement, 'I *won't*.'

'Not to me…'

'Not to you…' Looking into her eyes was costing him, but he forced himself to do it without wavering.

She stiffened. 'You were never going to talk to me about this, were you?'

'No.'

The sense of betrayal was palpable. While she'd trusted him with her body and some of her closely guarded memories, he had let go in the bedroom the way she wanted him to but never with anything else.

When her gaze lowered again, Daniel's roved over her hair, long lashes, lush lips and everything in between as if he felt he had to memorize her before she disappeared. She was so damn beautiful, so fragile in body but so strong in spirit. If she needed him as much as he needed her…if she loved him even half as much as he loved her, then maybe—

She cleared her throat. 'About Paris…'

'What about it?' he said flatly.

'I didn't plan on telling you the way I did.'

'Good to know.'

She shrugged. 'It's been my dream for a long time. I've wanted to go there since I went to work at the magazine and heard about the shortlist they have for the position.' She swiped a strand of tangled hair behind her ear. 'Career-wise it's a golden opportunity.'

Daniel quietly exhaled the breath he hadn't realized he was holding. *Her dream* and he would let her give it up for a *maybe*? He was a selfish son of a—

'I wasn't supposed to go this year,' she continued. 'The girl who was broke her leg and if I'd known—'

'When did you know?' he heard his voice ask.

'Since the day you started texting me.'

'The night you had sex with me for the first time…'

'The night we *made love* for the first time…' Jo corrected. 'And I swear if you try to make me regret a single—'

'That's what was bothering you.' It made sense to him now. By ambushing him and pushing him on things he didn't want to talk about, she found a way to avoid telling him. Did she know then how much he needed her? How desperate he was to have her?

'Among other things.' She nodded as if confirming his thoughts. 'I wanted to tell you…tried…I just couldn't…'

Do that to him? In case he begged her to stay?

'Before you got on a plane would have been nice,' he said dryly before lifting the mug to his mouth. Since drinking the coffee had the same effect as swallowing acid, he set it back down. 'What else didn't you tell me?'

'Don't do that,' she warned as her gaze lifted. 'I could have left you a Dear Danny letter. Instead I'm here trying to do what you won't: *talk*.'

'If you want to leave, leave.'

'You say that like I think I need your permission.'

A corner of his mouth tugged wryly. 'It's just as well you don't. Didn't hesitate when it came to accepting the offer, did you?' He leaned forward, lowering his voice conspiratorially. 'I'd heard when couples get involved in more than spectacular sex they talk over a decision like that.'

Averting her gaze, she blinked with bewilderment into the middle distance. 'Why do I suddenly feel like this is my fault and nothing to do with you? How did that happen?' She arched a brow at him. 'If you're done playing the jilted lover, maybe you should take a look at the facts and be honest with me. We both said we weren't looking for anything serious. We agreed to see where it took us and that we wouldn't fall in love. Did any of that change for you?'

'Did it change for you?'

'I asked first.' When she realized what she'd said she rolled her eyes. A huff of laughter left her lips, but when she spoke there was a crack in her voice. 'You think this is easy for me? You think I found what happened last night easy? I'm going to Paris. That's not going to change. But if there's something you want to say to me before I go—'

Drawing on every second of training he'd ever been given, Daniel looked her straight in the eye and lied. 'There isn't.'

Time stretched like taffy while she decided whether to believe him. Daniel's protesting heart thundered in his chest while he maintained rigid control over the crippling weakness of his emotions. She'd never know how staggeringly unprepared he had been to fall in love or how far out of his weight he'd been punching when he got involved with her.

'That's that, then.' She stared at him for another moment. For a second he thought he could see her eyes glistening but when she spoke again her voice was flat. 'I've got to go.'

He might have had the strength to leave it at that if she hadn't glanced at him as she stood up. She did it as if she couldn't help herself, a brief frown indicating her annoyance.

But that one brief glance into her eyes revealed enough raw vulnerability to tear through Daniel like a knife. It twisted sharply in his chest as he realized what he'd done, or rather *hadn't* done when he should. At the one time she'd needed him anywhere close to as much as he needed her, he'd let her down. With a blinding flash of clarity he realized what she'd wanted from him outside the convenience store. The one simple act it would have taken to avoid what she referred to as a meltdown.

The knowledge broke him so hard and so comprehensively the walls of his resistance collapsed into dust. While he couldn't get down on his knees and beg her to stay or ask her to give up her dream for a maybe, there was one thing he could do.

Across the room in a heartbeat, he flattened his palm on the wood, his voice gravelly. 'I can't leave you like this.'

'You're not the one doing the leaving, remember?' She yanked on the door handle. 'Let me go, Danny.'

'Not till you let it out.' He reached out to draw her to him. 'Come here.'

'No.'

When she took a step back, he took a step forward. She slapped his arms with the backs of her hands, tried to twist free and then pushed him hard in the chest with her palms.

'That's it,' Daniel encouraged. 'Go ahead and hit me if that's what you need to do. I can take it.'

'Why are you doing this?' she choked as she shoved his chest again. 'Why can't you just leave me alone? I *hate* you.'

'I know.'

Her small hands curled into fists against his shoulders. Leaning on them, she lowered her head and pushed her full body weight against him. 'And I *never* cry!'

'Delayed shock,' he reasoned as he circled her body with his arms.

'Let me go,' she pleaded.

'I can't, babe. Not till you let it out.'

Somewhere in the middle of mumbled protests and calling him names, her fists gripped handfuls of his T-shirt. Then she wasn't pushing him away any more. She was holding on tight and leaning on him. It was so close to what he wanted her to do for the rest of their lives Daniel came dangerously close to confessing how he felt, the words forming in his chest instead of his mind.

'I've got you,' he said gruffly.

The first racking sob ripped his heart out. He tightened his arms in response, holding her close as pain reverberated through his body. All she needed was a moment to get it out and then she would be fine. She would rediscover the joy she found in life, light up from inside the way he loved best and at least while she was in France, living her dream, Daniel would know she was happy.

So he held her while an eight-year-old mourned her mother and a fourteen-year-old showed how scared she had been every time a difficult bar owner got in her face. He smoothed silky hair while the eighteen-year-old faced her first night without a roof over her head and watched a boy she knew bleed to death in the arms of a female cop who would become her best friend.

He remained silent and solid; standing guard over her so the world would never know she had a moment of weakness after a lifetime of being strong. It was their secret. One he would keep for her until the day he died.

'Tell me to stay,' she whispered in a voice so low and muffled he had to strain to hear it.

'I can't do that,' he whispered back.

If she wanted to stay he wouldn't have to tell her. Part of the reason he loved her so much was because she was a born fighter. She might not believe it in her weakened state but his Jo was fearless in the face of adversity. She reached out and grabbed what she wanted with both hands. It was the final confirmation Daniel needed that he wasn't it. Not for her.

Gradually she regained control. 'I'm okay now,' she said against his chest. Leaning back, she swiped her cheeks. 'Might need a tissue, but apart from that…'

'You can use my T-shirt,' Daniel volunteered roughly.

She smiled tremulously. 'Shut up.'

When she looked up at him, as hard as it was to take, he knew she was going to be fine without him. A long enough break from him to catch up on her sleep, the first glimpse she got of her dream and she would bounce right back—probably a lot faster than he would. Unable to resist, he lowered his head for a soft, slow kiss; one intended to show her how he felt when he still couldn't say the words.

He loved her—he always would—and if she ever needed a chest to cry on all she had to do was come find him and he'd be there.

As their lips parted her fingertips whispered over his jaw, head leaning into the palm that framed her face.

He looked into her eyes. 'Go grab your dream, babe.'

'You try and get rid of a few,' she replied with a small, wavering smile as she lowered her hand to his chest.

'I will,' he promised.

When she dropped her arm and stepped around him, Daniel stayed where he was, unable to watch her leave.

CHAPTER THIRTEEN

'The mark of a best friend is someone who will tell you yes, your ass does look big in those jeans. It may be tough to admit but sometimes we all need an intervention.'

ATTENDING Sunday lunch with the Brannigans might not have been the best idea she ever had. Not when pretending she was fine and looking forward to Paris was wearing her mask thin.

Surrounded by people who looked like Danny in a house filled with pictures of him didn't help any more than the work she'd used to fill the days before she left. But at least now she knew why he had been so easy to avoid. According to his siblings he had an EMT cert due for renewal; one that required he immediately jump on an empty spot in an available course.

Jo knew she should be grateful when there was a very good chance seeing him again would have resulted in the same plea she'd made last time. But she ached for another glimpse of him in the same way her chest ached if she held her breath for too long. She missed him so much the pain was debilitating.

She missed the little leap of anticipation her pulse made when her phone said she had a text or there was a knock on her door. She missed the kiss that suggested the time he'd spent away from her was filled with thoughts of getting her naked again. She missed the calmness on his face when he slept in bed beside her; how it smoothed out the creases at the corners of his eyes. She missed his clean masculine scent, the heat of his touch, the punch of his infamous smile, the rumble of his voice and the sound of his laughter... She even missed arguing with him at the times he bugged her most. She just missed him.

'Who's for cheesecake?' his mother asked.

Since the traditional gathering for Sunday lunch had been turned into a 'Bon Voyage' party, Jo pinned yet another false smile into place. 'Me, please.'

Turning to hand over the pile of dessert plates to Liv in the seat beside her, she saw her friend still. 'You okay?'

'Forgive me,' she whispered as she looked into Jo's eyes and took the plates.

'What for?'

The sound of a door slam was followed by a familiar deep voice. 'I know I'm late. Not my fault. Took half of Ed Marks' shift when his wife went into labour and at the end of it some idiot flipped over a car avoiding a cat.'

Jo's breath caught. Oh, she was *so* not ready for this. She couldn't sit there, *opposite him*, and pretend she was fine.

'Your plate is in the oven,' his mother called. 'It's hot, so use a cloth.'

Frozen in place, gaze glued to the table in front of her, Jo wondered if she looked as shocked as she felt. Her cheeks felt as if they were on fire.

'How do you flip over a car avoiding a cat?' Tyler asked from further down the table.

'Beats me,' Daniel's voice said as he got closer.

By the time Jo saw his waist appear she was pretty sure she was having a panic attack. She checked for the symptoms. Racing pulse, lack of oxygen, light head, shaking hands... She stifled a burst of semi-hysterical laughter.

Just as well there was a fully re-certified EMT in the room, wasn't it?

'Can't blame the driver for a series of freak events.' He dropped the plate into his place and shook his hand.

'I said the plate was hot,' his mother said as he kissed her cheek. 'Boy or girl?'

'Don't know yet.' He pulled out his chair. 'Said I'd be happy with a Danielle or a Daniel… So what's the big family emergency I had to…?'

As his voice trailed off if felt as if the whole room went silent. Jo continued staring at the table, her heart beating so loud she was surprised no one could hear it. This was *not happening* and she was not going to cry even if it felt as if she'd sprung a damn leak over the last few days.

As he sat down opposite her she thought about looking at him and knew she couldn't do it. It had been difficult enough leaving him last time without telling him how she felt. She didn't think she could do it twice.

'Jo?'

Her gaze jumped sharply to the left where a cheesecake was waiting on a serving dish. She couldn't eat that. She'd choke.

'I don't think… I'm not…' Pressing her lips together, she sucked in a breath through her nose and swallowed hard before looking at Daniel's mother. 'Packing still…blog to write…' She flashed a smile as she jerked a thumb over her shoulder. 'I should…' She nodded. Pushing her chair back, she stood up and ducked down to kiss a cheek. 'Thanks for lunch.'

Practically running into the hall, she yanked her coat from the rack and left. It was official: she would have to live in France for the rest of her days.

As she stormed down the path and argued with the latch on the gate, she started to get angry at him for the first time since he'd let her walk away. Why couldn't he have left things the way they were when she hated him? She'd been *comfortable* hating him. He had no business making her fall in love with him, and what the hell was with the whole tenderness thing when her heart had been breaking? She swung open the gate. Of all the inconsiderate, unforgivable, inconceivably hurtful things he could possibly have done—

'Why aren't you in Paris?'

She swung around when she heard the deep rumble of his voice, anger giving her the strength she needed to face him. 'Did you know I'd be here?'

'Did it *look* like I knew?'

'I don't know. I couldn't look at you!'

He frowned at her, looking every bit as angry as she felt. 'Somewhat ironic considering I couldn't keep my eyes off you.'

Jo glanced at the house, realization dawning when she saw a twitching curtain at a window. 'Were we just ambushed?'

'I thought you'd met my family,' he said dryly. 'Didn't I mention how much they love to stage an intervention?'

'Staging an intervention suggests this is a problem which can be fixed,' she snapped at him. 'Since you made it obvious it can't you can go back in there and explain why.'

Daniel's eyes narrowed. 'What happened to equal terms and not being made out to be a victim of seduction?'

'You want to tell them I seduced you, go right ahead, but if you think for a single second I'm going to let them look at me like some poor broken-hearted sap who was foolish enough to fall in—' She slapped a hand over her mouth, her eyes widening with horror.

Angling his head, Daniel looked at her from the corner of his eye and took an ominous step forward, his voice low. 'You want to finish that sentence for me?'

Jo dropped her arm to her side and glared at him. 'How about you hold your breath while you wait? And don't think I haven't figured out another of your lies, Daniel Brannigan.

I *knew* you had a problem with me being here on a Sunday. The second you thought I was gone you were back in that chair.'

He stilled and rocked back on his heels. His gaze searched the air for a moment as he crossed his jaw and then he looked her straight in the eye. 'I got to give it to my family—their timing is excellent. Having carried this around for a week I'm ready to offload and it's not like either of us was going to make the first move this time, was it?' He took a short breath. 'You want to know the problem? For five and a half years you were a giant pain in my ass. There were times I used to wish you would get hit by a cab or a piano would fall on you.'

'That's so sweet.' She smirked.

He took a measured step forward, the predatory gleam in his eyes making her feel as if he were a hunter and she were the prey. 'Then you start dressing like every guy's ideal cross between a librarian and a stripper.'

She gasped. 'I have *never* dressed like a stripper!'

'One word: *boots*. And did it sound like a complaint?' He took another measured step forward. 'You make me crazier than any woman I've ever known. You're so confident and independent you make it virtually impossible for a guy to figure out where he's supposed to fit into your life.'

She popped her fists onto her hips and angled her chin. 'He could try not letting me leave. It's a lot easier to fit into someone's life if they're on the same continent.'

'You said it was your dream.'

'Dreams *change*.'

'I know.'

She faltered. 'Are you telling me they're gone?'

He stilled a couple of feet away from her. 'Oh, I'm sure they'll be back. But it turns out they're less frequent when I have a bigger problem to deal with.'

'Feel free to not talk about that either.'

'I'm over here trying to tell you I'm in love with you and you'd still prefer to fight with me? Okay.' He shook his head and folded his arms. 'What do you want to know? Should I start at the beginning? First nightmare was my dad having his heart attack. I couldn't resuscitate him.'

'You weren't here when he died.' Jo frowned. 'Liv said he was on his own.'

'He was.' Daniel nodded. 'He died a couple of hours after I left. I came home on leave to tell him I was staying in the Marines, he reminded me he'd agreed to give his consent on the proviso I would come back and join the family business. Didn't mention he wanted me here 'cos he was sick, but after an hour of yelling at me about loyalty, duty, responsibility and not reacting particularly well to the fact Uncle Sam had taught me not to flinch under fire, I thanked him for his support over the years and walked out.'

The information made her frown. 'How does that make his death your fault?'

Pressing his mouth into a thin line, his shoulders dropped in a very visible hint of the weight he'd carried for so long. 'You need more, here goes. Next up was Liv—I was standing in the station the night she walked in covered in blood. At the time I thought it was hers—she wouldn't let me near her, said she was evidence. Brannigans watch over each other: my dad did it for Johnnie, Johnnie did it for Reid and so on till it was my turn with Liv. I figured she was tough, she knew what she was getting into—she didn't need my help. I was *wrong*.'

Since Jo knew more about the events of that night than he did, she had to clear her throat before she could speak. 'That wasn't your fault any more than Aiden's death was Liv's.'

He ignored her. 'The two more I was yelling about that night? Inches of space I needed to put pressure on an artery. Guy was trapped under a wall. He died.'

Her gaze immediately lowered to the hand he had scraped

on a wall, the pieces falling into place. 'They're all the people you've lost or came close to losing. You torture yourself even though you know it wasn't your fault.'

'It's my job to save lives—to be there when people need me. No matter how I try I keep messing that up.'

When her gaze lifted, for the first time Jo could see through the shadows in his eyes to the pain; the starkness of it almost breaking her in two. 'You were there for me,' she told him in a voice thick with emotion. 'Doesn't that count?'

'Except I wasn't, was I?' His deep voice was rougher than she'd ever heard it before. 'The one time you needed me to be there I let you down.'

Jo searched his eyes, frowning with confusion. 'You threw yourself in front of a gun for me. I've never been as scared as I was when you did that. I tried to find the words to tell you but I couldn't. If you'd died saving me, if I'd *lost you*…'

When he looked at her with enough yearning to take her breath away, she blinked. 'Wait a minute…what did you say?'

He pushed his hands into the pockets of his jeans. 'The one time you needed—'

'No.' She made a jumping motion with her forefinger. 'Go back further…' A sudden flare of hope made her heart falter and skip a beat. 'Did you say you're in love with me?'

The warmth in his eyes seemed to smooth the grimness from his face, making him look younger and unbelievably vulnerable. 'Was beginning to wonder if you'd noticed…'

Jo's faltering heart leapt, did handsprings and swelled to proportions that made it feel as if it couldn't be contained in her chest. 'If you're in love with me, then why did you let me leave, you idiot?' Realization dawned. 'You were scared…*of me?*' She took a step closer and looked deeper into his eyes, searching for answers, her voice filled with wonder when she found them. 'No, not of me—of how you felt about me… But I asked if you wanted to tell me anything and—'

He shifted his weight from one foot to the other in a move

she found impossibly endearing. 'I'm not the kind of guy who's gonna read you poetry or wear his heart on his sleeve. I think you know that by now. When it comes to how I feel the only way I can show it is by—'

'Protecting the people you love and looking after them.'

'Yes.'

'The things I told you I didn't want from you...'

His mouth tugged wryly. 'Yes.'

'So you were afraid to tell me you needed me because you didn't think I felt the same way?'

He let out a long breath. 'I'm always going to need you more than you need me.'

'You are *so* competitive.' Jo shook her head, the move immediately contradicted by the smile blossoming on her lips. She shrugged a shoulder a little self-consciously. 'I know I may have given the impression I don't need you but I thought you knew me better by now. I don't need you to protect me from every bump in life. But that doesn't mean there aren't times... I've needed you for longer than... I guess I was so focused on other things... Maybe I never knew...but I do now...'

Daniel released a small smile. 'You know you've been doing that a lot this last while.'

'Losing the ability to speak?' She puffed a soft burst of laughter. 'Yeah, I'd noticed that. I blame you.'

'Nothing new there, then.'

'Oh, there's something new,' she whispered.

As if some kind of shutter had been lowered, her feelings showed clearly in her eyes for the first time. Daniel's hunger for her entwined with a depth of tenderness that shook him to the very foundation of who he'd thought he was. The connection he felt to her in response to her need was a visceral tug. It drew him forward and pulled him in. He took his hands out of his pockets as he stepped forward.

She took a stuttered breath when he was close enough to

drag a knuckle along the skin of her cheek, her hand shaking as it flattened on his chest, directly above his pounding heart. Her throat convulsed before she spoke. 'You're wrong to think I don't need you, Danny. I needed you the day we met but I was too scared to admit it. What we have now was a dream too far out of my reach then, so I told myself I didn't want it.'

He threaded his fingers into silky hair as he framed her face. 'Your dream involved a guy who could feed you one of the worst lines you'd ever heard?'

Jo shook her head. 'That's not when we met.'

'What?'

'You think we met that fourth of July weekend. We didn't. We met two months before that.'

Daniel frowned. 'I'd have remembered.'

'Would you?' She lifted her brows and smiled tremulously. 'I was no one then.'

'You've never been no one,' he said firmly.

'I was invisible to most of the world; though in fairness that was partly my fault.' She blinked and took a deep breath. 'Make yourself invisible and you can fall between the cracks in the system. That worked for me for a long time. But you wouldn't believe how badly you want to be seen when you're homeless. The number of people who will walk past you without ever looking you in the eye…' When her voice wavered she took another short breath. 'Liv was the first. Then one day she was there with her partner talking to me when another squad car pulled up across the street and you got out.'

Daniel frantically searched his normally reliable memory as inky lashes lowered and she focused on the hand resting on his chest.

'You started talking to Liv, exchanged a few jokes with her partner—'

'Tell me I looked at you,' he rasped.

Her gaze lifted, shimmering with deeply felt emotion. 'Oh, you did something much worse. You looked straight into my eyes and smiled at me.' She blinked back tears. 'It was…the sun coming out from behind a cloud or… *stardust*. I'd never seen anything like it before. When you took it away…when you left…' She cleared her throat and shrugged. 'For a second you had turned a graduate of the school of hard knocks into some starry-eyed, weak-at-the-knees daydreamer and I *hated you* for that. Because when you were gone and I wasn't blinded by that infamous smile of yours I had to open my eyes again.'

Daniel hadn't known it was possible to love someone the way he loved her. He wished he had been ready for her back then, that it hadn't taken so long to see what was right in front of him. Most of all he wished he'd been brave enough to take a chance on what he could have missed if the people who loved them hadn't banged their stubborn heads together. But if she'd fallen in love with him, unworthy as he was, he couldn't be too far beyond redemption to turn things around.

'Starry-eyed dreamers didn't survive in the world I lived in then,' she explained in her softest voice. 'So I toughened up, got twice as hard and the next time you saw me you didn't stand a chance.'

When the memory came to him, Daniel closed his eyes for a second. 'Did you have a really dumb hat?'

She blinked at him. 'What?'

The image was still foggy. 'It had ears.'

'Floppy dog ears.' She nodded as if he were insane to think anything else. 'I had three but it was my favourite. They were winter ski-hats a store donated to charity.'

Daniel smiled indulgently as he tucked a strand of hair behind her ear. 'It was *May*.'

'A person loses something like seventy per cent of their body heat through their head so I figured at night…' She bit down on her lower lip. 'You remember.'

'I asked Liv about you.' He wrapped an arm around her waist and drew her to him. 'Thought you were under age... You looked about sixteen with those braids in.'

'Nope, eighteen. I can't believe you remember.'

Lowering his head, he breathed in lavender shampoo, a deep-seated sense of contentment washing over him. 'You didn't look like that next time I saw you...'

'Liv took me for my first girly make-over.'

Nudging the tip of his nose into her fringe, he pressed a light kiss to her temple, his mouth moving against her skin as he confessed, 'You deserved better than that line. You were right to cut me down the way you did.'

'It was a really bad line,' she agreed as she hooked a thumb into one of the belt loops of his jeans. 'But you didn't deserve my response, Danny. I started a five-and-a-half-year war between us when we could have been doing this...'

'No,' he disagreed. 'You were eighteen. I was twenty-four. Six years made a bigger difference then. But even if it hadn't we weren't ready for this. While you were stepping out into the world and claiming a corner of it, I'd already started to retreat.' Leaning back, he used a thumb beneath her chin to lift it and looked into her mesmerizing eyes. 'I'm not gonna find talking about the nightmares easy, babe. But I'm willing to try. You'll have to work with me on that and a couple of other things. Being less protective won't be easy either and I know we'll argue about that. I can be—'

'Oh, I *know*. But so can I...' She silenced him with a soft, all-too-brief kiss. 'Still fell in love, didn't we?'

'You better be sure about that,' he warned. ''Cos once you say you're mine, that's it. We're gonna have to work at this every day but—'

'We will.' Love glowed from her eyes, lighting her up like a beacon. 'I love you, Danny. Even when I wanted to I couldn't make it go away. I don't want it to now. So if you need me to say it—yes, I'm yours.' She sighed, her gaze lowering. 'I can't get out of Paris…'

'I don't want you to, babe.' Daniel shook his head, his palm smoothing over her hair. 'The last few days I've run over dozens of different ways we could have made this work if you loved me the way I love you. How long will you be gone?'

'Three months.' She grimaced.

'Half a tour of duty…' He smiled when she looked at him. 'Way I see it, you going overseas is no different. You'd wait for me, right?'

She nodded. 'Yes.'

'Well, then, look at it this way—we get more opportunities for phone sex and conjugal visits…'

'I do fly home for Liv's wedding next month,' she pouted.

'I reckon I can book some time off either side of that for a couple of long weekends in Paris.' He lowered his head. 'How hot do you think I can make you for me before I get there?'

'Pretty hot.' She smiled as her chin lifted. 'If you pick the right words…'

'I'll buy a dictionary.'

'Did I mention the reason I'm still here is because of an air traffic controller thing? Or ground crew… I forget now…' she mumbled against his mouth.

'Tell them I said thanks.' He angled his head. 'How long have we got?'

'Two days…'

Her lips parted when he kissed her; the sweet taste of her breath caught on his tongue. His fingers slid deeper into her hair, palm cupping the back of her head as he deepened the kiss and the arm around her waist brought her closer. Perfect breasts crushed against his chest, fine-boned hands gripped a shoulder and the back of his neck. They could pack a lot into two days. It was sure as hell a challenge he was willing to accept. But before he did…

He leaned back and looked down at heavy-lidded eyes and kiss-swollen lips. 'They're at the window, aren't they?'

Jo glanced sideways and chuckled. 'Yes.'

'Want to see how fast I can make them move?' He grinned. 'You stay here. I'll be right back. Watch the window.'

As he turned and jogged towards the house, Jo looked at the window and laughed. Biting down on her lip, she gently swung her skirt while she waited for him to come back. She'd never been so happy. Danny loved her. He. Loved. Her. How could she have been so afraid of something so wonderful? Everything was so clear to her now, as if a veil of fear had been removed from her eyes. She should have viewed love the same way she viewed life and the moments of fun she was so addicted to. Grabbing hold of the good things and holding on tight made the tough stuff easier to take. Together they could face anything, even if it was the weaknesses within themselves. Her pulse sang loudly with a mixture of love, lust and joyous laughter when he returned and finally Jo could hear what it was saying. It had been singing to him all along. Two words, repeated over and over again in elated recognition.

It's you: he was her guy.

'Miss me?'

'Yes,' she answered without hesitation.

'Just so you know. If I ever thought I'd be doing this, I didn't picture it with an audience.' He took a deep, satisfied breath and smiled. 'But since one of them brought you into my life and the rest of them kept you here until I was ready for you, it seems kinda appropriate.'

Jo smiled back at him. 'What are you talking about?'

'This.'

She gasped as he lowered to one knee. 'Danny, you don't have to do that.'

His brows lifted. 'You think I'm letting you go to Paris without everyone knowing you're mine?'

'I'm coming back.'

'And when you do we plan on spending the rest of our lives together, right?'

'Yes.'

He waved the small box in his hand. 'That's usually what one of these says to the world.'

'You bought a ring?' Her eyes widened.

'Do you think you could shut up for a minute?'

She pressed her lips together. 'Mmm-hmm.'

When he spoke again his deep rough voice was laced with heartfelt sincerity. 'Jorja Elizabeth Dawson. You've been an adopted member of this family for a long time. I want to make it official by giving you my name. I love you, Jo. Will you…' he smiled his infamous smile '…marry me?'

Jo tried loosening her throat to speak.

'This is traditionally where you give me an answer,' he hinted heavily.

When she nodded frantically in reply, it shook the word loose. 'Yes.' She framed his gorgeous face with her hands and leaned down to kiss him. 'Yes, yes, yes.'

Large hands lifted to her waist, squeezing tight as he pushed to his feet and her arms moved to circle his neck. It felt as if they couldn't hold on to each other tight enough, even when he crushed her to him and lifted her off her feet. After swinging her feet from side to side, he set her down and opened the box. 'For the record, I did look at rings when I was running through ways of making this work. Did it while wearing tactical gear, so didn't take *any* flack from the rest of the team. Then I remembered this.' He took the ring out and reached for her hand. 'You can thank Grandma Brannigan and the fact I was her favourite grandson after I rescued her cat from a tree when I was seven. Might need to get it resized but...' He stared at her finger as it slipped into place. *'Maybe not...'*

Jo smiled at the winking sapphire, the same blue as his eyes when they darkened and she knew he wanted her. 'It fits.'

'Guess you were meant to have it, then, weren't you?'

She beamed when he looked at her.

'You ready to go back in? Sooner we finish lunch, the more time we can spend in bed before you leave.'

'I'm a course ahead of you,' she pointed out smugly as their fingers threaded together. 'Eat fast.'

A suspicious silence met them in the hall as Danny took her coat and hung it on the rack. It was just as quiet in the dining room when they stepped into it hand in hand. When Danny looked down at her from the corner of his eye she grinned. Who did their family think they were kidding? It was only as they approached the table emotion started to get the better of her. When he reached for her chair, his mother broke the silence.

'Everyone move round. Give Jo her place beside Danny.'

Long fingers squeezed hers as everyone moved and he led her around the table. She'd watched it happen with Johnnie's wife and when Liv brought Blake home, but Jo had never thought one day the gesture would be made for her. It was almost too much. Suddenly she belonged in a way she never had anywhere else. Sitting by the man she was going to spend the rest of her life with, she looked at the faces of the people she loved as they acted as if nothing unusual had happened.

She held up pretty well until she got to Liv, but when she did there was no stopping the tears. *Thank you*, she mouthed.

Liv's eyes shimmered, a hand waving in front of her body until Blake placed a napkin in it.

When Jo looked at Danny, he shook his head and glared at his sister. 'Stop making my fiancée cry.'

It was all it took to fill the room with sound.

'Missed your chance, Ty.'

'Not over till the pretty lady says, "I do."'

'I'm not wearing a monkey suit twice in one year.'

'You'll do as you're told, Reid Brannigan.'

Danny leaned in for a quick kiss before fending off his mother's offer to reheat his food, leaving Jo to sigh happily as she was handed a slice of cheesecake. Turned out the ideal guy *had* moved in across the hall from her.

Who knew?

* * * * *

MILLS & BOON

THE HEART OF ROMANCE

A ROMANCE FOR EVERY READER

ODERN

Prepare to be swept off your feet by sophisticated, sexy and seductive heroes, in some of the world's most glamourous and romantic locations, where power and passion collide.

STORICAL

Escape with historical heroes from time gone by. Whether your passion is for wicked Regency Rakes, muscled Vikings or rugged Highlanders, awaken the romance of the past.

EDICAL

Set your pulse racing with dedicated, delectable doctors in the high-pressure world of medicine, where emotions run high and passion, comfort and love are the best medicine.

ue Love

Celebrate true love with tender stories of heartfelt romance, from the rush of falling in love to the joy a new baby can bring, and a focus on the emotional heart of a relationship.

Desire

Indulge in secrets and scandal, intense drama and plenty of sizzling hot action with powerful and passionate heroes who have it all: wealth, status, good looks…everything but the right woman.

EROES

Experience all the excitement of a gripping thriller, with an intense romance at its heart. Resourceful, true-to-life women and strong, fearless men face danger and desire - a killer combination!

To see which titles are coming soon, please visit

millsandboon.co.uk/nextmonth

JOIN US ON SOCIAL MEDIA!

Stay up to date with our latest releases, author news and gossip, special offers and discounts, and all the behind-the-scenes action from Mills & Boon...

 @millsandboon

 @millsandboonuk

 facebook.com/millsandboon

 @millsandboonuk

It might just be true love...

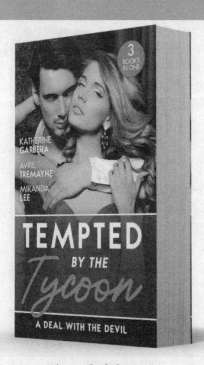

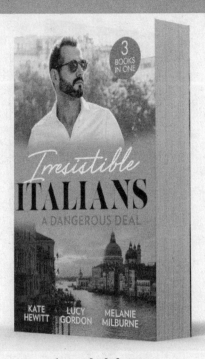